A SILENT
WAY TO
DIE

A SILENT WAY TO DIE

A KEMBER & HAYES MYSTERY

N.R. DAWS

 THOMAS & MERCER

Published by Thomas & Mercer, Seattle

www.apub.com

Amazon, the Amazon logo, and Thomas & Mercer are trademarks of Amazon.com, Inc., or its affiliates.

ISBN-13: 9781542031059
ISBN-10: 1542031052

Cover design by Ghost Design

Printed in the United States of America

*For my wonderful wife, Jane, and our beautiful
daughters, Laura and Holly.*

PROLOGUE

She wielded her shepherd's crook with elegant sweeps as she coaxed the recalcitrant ewes along the cold-hardened track. Her thick smock buttoned high around her neck against December's bite, she felt the burn of icy air in her lungs from the harsh morning frost. Reaching a break in the hedgerow, she leant against a five-bar gate to rest. Maybe half an hour to get the stray ewes back to the flock, then she would have her breakfast.

She caught her breath and stopped as a match scraped into life nearby. It flared briefly in a bloom of smoke and the end of a cigarette caught and glowed. The smoker exhaled a white cloud.

'You startled me,' she said, her heart racing as an officer in a long coat and peaked cap stepped from the shadows, putting himself between her and the purple-pink glow of sunrise.

'Sorry about that.' A young man's voice. He picked a piece of tobacco from his tongue and smiled. 'I was watching, fascinated by how you manipulate your crook to keep your sheep on the straight and narrow.'

She squinted, trying to see the face still concealed by partial shadow, the rising sun behind him giving the fields a sheen of ever-changing hues.

'You're not from the countryside?' She thought everyone was familiar with shepherding.

The man gave a short, staccato laugh. 'Not at all. Born and bred in the smoke of Manchester but I move about a lot. The war.' He shrugged and sucked on his cigarette.

'Ah, you're—?'

'Out for a stroll.' Sunrise-tinged smoke drifted away. 'Couldn't sleep. You know how it is?'

Something about his polite, open manner and almost musical voice put her at ease. 'Not much hustle and bustle in my line of work,' she said. 'Unless these girls kick up a fuss, of course.'

'Do you enjoy it? Tending sheep, I mean.'

She shrugged. 'It's all right. I'd rather work in a shop, perhaps one of those fancy department stores in London, but my brothers have joined up and Dad needs me on the farm.'

The man smiled gently. 'All the men gone off to war, to have all the adventures.'

She nodded. That one sentence contained all the truth about her life at that moment and she had a sense that this man knew exactly what she was feeling. The disappointment and frustration of being thought of as 'just a girl' weighed heavily.

'Look.' The man tapped a packet of Craven A cigarettes. 'I know you've work to do but would you like a crafty one before you go? I'm enjoying talking to you.'

She hesitated, looking at the proffered packet. 'I don't. My dad . . .' But she was mesmerised by the protruding white stick.

'You ever try one?'

She looked around with a pang of guilt, feeling suddenly stupid at the thought that her father might be within earshot.

He smiled and held the packet higher, conspiratorially, encouraging her to take one. She put the end between her lips with shaking fingers, felt her pulse quicken and her breath become a notch shallower.

'When I light the match, put the end of the cigarette to the flame, and suck with your mouth but don't breathe in until your mouth is full of smoke.'

She watched intently, bending forward, awaiting the striking of the match. With the ewes becoming restless, baaing and bumping, the match still unlit, she became distracted, enough to be spun around and gripped across the throat by a strong forearm.

A hand covered her mouth, stifling any cry, the smell and taste of raw tobacco in her nose and mouth as the unlit cigarette crushed into her face.

She kicked her legs as the grip tightened. The hand didn't move, holding her breath in its power. She tried to kick harder, but she could feel her strength already beginning to ebb away, her fight already gone. She felt herself deflate like a punctured barrage balloon and crumpled to a soft bundle on the rough ground, still held in the suffocating embrace. A pulsing roar filled her ears but was gone as quickly as it had come. She thought she knew what was happening but didn't understand why. What had she done to deserve this? *I'm sorry Dad*, she said in her head.

As her lungs burned for want of oxygen rather than because of frosty air, orange tones coloured the sky but her eyes, full of shadows, found it increasingly difficult to focus. Her mind fogged but no longer cared as she caught the last words she would ever hear.

'Sorry, but you really are so beautiful.'

CHAPTER ONE

Detective Inspector Jonathan Kember of the Kent County Constabulary put down his bone-handled knife and fork and looked up with enquiring eyes.

The merest smearing remained on the plate after his meal of sardine fritters, meant as a lunch but much delayed by his chasing of ever-elusive black-marketeers. On his day off too. Never mind it being nearly the shortest day of the year, it had been his shortest day off of the year.

Alice Brannan, joint licensee of the Castle pub in Scotney village with her brother Leslie, a pinafore tied around her slim waist and tight, blonde curls contained beneath a scarf tied in a turban, reached forward to take his plate. 'Would you like some pudding, duck?'

Kember smiled up at Alice's expectant face, her cheeks ruddy and eyes bright.

'It's stewed rhubarb,' she said. 'The Taplow sisters had a bumper crop this year so we bought and bottled some to tide us over the cold months.'

'That would be lovely,' Kember said, struggling to keep his smile fixed in place and not wishing to seem ungrateful. Stewed fruit had never been his dessert of choice but rationing had rather reduced everyone's choices. Except for the rich, of course.

'I'll fetch you some,' Alice said, leaving Kember alone in the empty saloon bar. He could just see through to where Les Brannan was locking the door of the public bar as the last customer left on the stroke of the two o'clock closing time.

At the mention of their names, Kember's thoughts had turned to Elsie and Annie Taplow, who ran a bed and breakfast establishment at the northern end of Scotney village. They had experienced the horror five months before of renting one of their rooms to a woman pilot from the Air Transport Auxiliary who had become the first victim of the Scotney Ripper, as he had been named. That had been the day his serial-adulterer wife had thrown him unceremoniously and humiliatingly out of his own house in Tonbridge in order to install her latest lover. He had stayed at the Castle during the murder investigation before enduring a few weeks in Pembury Hospital, recovering from an injury to his leg from an exploding grenade as the killer had tried, but failed, to flee from justice. The doctors had removed all the shrapnel but he often fancied he could feel something still in there.

Kember felt bitter about being suspended over his handling of the investigation, a decision he had brooded over in hospital, giving his doctor the erroneous impression that he was suffering from mild depression. A shortage of policemen at Tonbridge, combined with his status as a seconded Scotland Yard detective, meant his discharge from hospital had coincided conveniently with his reinstatement. Kember had almost laughed at the absurdity. Almost. With no home left in Tonbridge, he had taken up the Brannans' offer of a reduced rental for one of their rooms. He'd offered the full rate but they'd insisted, stating the gratitude of the villagers for his work in making Scotney safe again.

But it hadn't all been down to him.

Alice returned with the warm dessert and spooned a dollop of mock clotted cream over the rhubarb, which immediately started to separate as the margarine melted.

Even though Alice was a couple of years younger than him, Kember felt like he'd returned home to his parents. She fussed, clucked and smothered, and he let her, enjoying being looked after at the end of increasingly difficult days working out of Tonbridge Police Station. For an extra fee, she washed and ironed his clothes and had proven a dab hand as a barber, offering to give him the occasional trim, for another fee. He'd have to get another place of his own, sooner rather than later, but the arrangement suited him, for now.

She was still apologising for the lack of real cream when someone rapped on the door of the saloon bar.

A chill draught sliced into the pub like a shard of ice as Alice answered the door.

'Good afternoon, Alice. Is the inspector at home?'

Kember recognised the voice of the village policeman, Sergeant Dennis Wright, and was already standing when Alice brought him through.

'Sorry to disturb you, sir,' Wright said, his large frame and neatly trimmed beard appearing around a glazed partition. He held his helmet under one arm. 'You're needed at the station.'

Kember sighed. *And there goes my afternoon,* he thought. Many believed their time off should be sacrosanct but his chosen career, and especially the war, had taught him that crimes and criminals followed no rules. 'Is it something you can deal with? Can't it wait until Monday?'

'The duty sergeant at Tonbridge asked me to pass on a message.' Wright raised his chin to stretch his neck muscles and flicked a glance at Alice. 'I'm afraid not, sir.'

Kember's left eyebrow raised questioningly and he reached for his grey raincoat. 'All right, Sergeant. Let's go.'

'You want to put some Brylcreem on that before you go,' Alice said.

Kember looked back and saw Alice touching the back of her head. He ran his hand over his own head, trying to smooth down the hairs of his double crown that sprouted like weeds.

'I hate the stuff, I'm afraid,' Kember said, donning his dark-grey, short-brimmed fedora. 'Sorry Alice, duty calls.'

As soon as they were outside and striding towards the police station, Wright said, 'Chief Inspector Hartson has requested your attention regarding two incidents, sir.'

'Incidents?' Kember said.

'I've been making enquiries about a local Scotney man, a labourer aged fifty-five who disappeared last night, and a respectable young lady aged twenty-one, from Tonbridge, who failed to return home from Paddock Wood last night.'

'Please tell me there's a simple explanation. Caught in last night's air raid, perhaps?'

'A few stray bombs did fall south of the railway line but the main raid wasn't in our neck of the woods, sir.' Wright continued to stare ahead. 'Jettisoned on the way home, I'd say.'

'Any indication of eloping? It isn't uncommon when there's a significant age gap or when one party is from a class different to the other, as your descriptions implied.'

'There's no suggestion that they knew each other. They had different reasons for being out and about, and they disappeared at different times in different places. Not so simple, I'd say.'

Kember pinched the bridge of his nose with forefinger and thumb. With crime figures up all over the country, even in Tonbridge and its environs, and last year's multiple killings in Scotney still fresh in their minds, the last thing they needed was another murderer. Chief Inspector Hartson would be particularly thrilled when he realised New Scotland Yard would be swarming all over his patch again. The Yard had sent a team earlier in the year to investigate a triple murder at nearby Brenchley which was why Kember had found himself leading the Scotney Ripper investigation. It had all been a matter of resources.

'Are Tonbridge sending anyone down?'

'I did have a quick word with the duty sergeant, but at this time on a Friday afternoon, I was whistling in the wind. And the chief did ask for you to look into both cases personally.'

Kember groaned inwardly. Force Headquarters at Maidstone would be equally uninterested in dispatching anyone at this time and at least twenty-four hours would elapse before New Scotland Yard came sniffing. Being just before the start of the weekend, especially the last one before Christmas, Kember knew he had no hope of any assistance until well into Monday morning at the earliest. In truth, he suspected help during Christmas week would be as rare as sightings of Santa and might not arrive until the new year. All the initial legwork and paperwork would fall to him, the interesting work to Maidstone and glory to the Yard.

As the highest-ranking police officer nearest to the incident of the missing man, Kember understood it made sense for him to respond. But he wasn't the duty detective inspector so didn't understand the reasoning behind giving him the Paddock Wood case as well. It did not make his already disrupted day off any more joyous.

'There's one more thing, sir,' Wright said, with a sideways glance at Kember.

Kember steeled himself. 'Go on.'

'The missing young lady . . . is the chief inspector's niece.'

Lizzie Hayes, wearing the wings of the Air Transport Auxiliary on her Sidcot flight suit, hands steady on the control column, urged the twin-engine Avro Anson into a long, sweeping curve.

She had her lips pursed, not under any pressure from flying, because she revelled in being a pilot, but with the effort of crafting a civil response to a recently posed, stupid question from the RAF Scotney control tower.

'Thank you *so* much for your concern, Cuckoo.' Lizzie spoke into the radio's mouthpiece, almost spitting out the air station's call-sign. 'Apart from being a highly trained pilot perfectly capable of landing this aircraft on my own, I've probably been flying for longer than you've been out of short trousers. Lost Child out.'

Lizzie grimaced at the patronising call-sign of the ATA that they were forced to use and glanced at her co-pilot sitting to her left listening to the exchange on her headphones. Felicity 'Fizz' Mitchell, a Scot whose default was to not suffer fools gladly no matter who they were, glanced back, her eyes narrowed to slits amid a thunderous expression. Lizzie shook her head in warning for Fizz to not respond and returned her attention to bringing the Anson back to level flight, all the while searching the sky for any sign of bandits.

Taking her turn as pilot of the Number Thirteen Ferry Pool's air taxi, Lizzie's objective right at that moment was to land safely at RAF Scotney in Kent. They had first called this place home a few months ago at the start of what was to become the Battle of Britain. Then the Luftwaffe had changed its strategy to the relentless day and night Blitz of London at the start of September, eventually concentrating mainly on the night bombing of Britain's cities. That was not to say daylight hours were safe from fast raiding parties and Lizzie was mindful of the need to get her aircraft down in one piece. After receiving devastating news earlier in the day about the death of a friend at Duxford, what she didn't need was some bloke, probably a spotty kid straight from school, sitting in the comfort of the control tower, warning how dangerous things were and telling her how to fly.

The Anson pulled into a tighter bank as Lizzie dropped the port wing even further and it seemed to her that the whole of southeast England lay below. The day was cold but mostly clear and the main street of Scotney village, with its Norman church marking the northern end and the railway station crossing to the south, cut a swathe through the monochrome, wintery patchwork of fields and woodland. The silver thread of the River Glassen meandered to the east while a mile north of the village sprawled the extensive manorial estate of Scotney, with its white, stuccoed manor house, requisitioned and turned into an air station by the RAF.

While Fizz began cranking the landing-gear handle, Lizzie glanced over her shoulder at the shriek of laughter slicing through the engine noise. The Anson's current payload consisted of the two pilots and their five passengers. Three of them, including Fizz, were women from the original ATA detachment posted with Lizzie over five months earlier, just as hostilities had escalated in July. They had spent today ferrying warplanes around the country for the RAF. Another two women, new recruits, sat smiling at something the only male passenger on board had said. The laughter had sounded a little forced, perhaps slightly too hearty. With her main attention on flying, Lizzie couldn't tell who had laughed but suspected it hadn't been one of her friends.

The old guard had good reason to be wary of men. The ATA detachment at RAF Scotney had been stalked, terrorised and murdered by the Scotney Ripper. These two new ATA pilots sitting in the cabin were a reminder of the terror and loss.

A frosty radio call from the Scotney control tower grabbed Lizzie's full attention.

'Hello Cuckoo, this is Lost Child,' she replied. 'Request permission to land, over.'

Lizzie pulled on the controls of the Anson to maintain height as a cold air pocket tried to drop the aircraft lower.

'Lost Child, Cuckoo here. Permission granted,' came the tinny, humourless voice over the radio.

Lizzie's feet danced on the rudder pedals, urging the Anson to fight against a vicious crosswind.

'Making final approach, over.'

She throttled back and turned her head to speak over her shoulder.

'Not long now,' she shouted to her passengers, above the engine and wind noise. 'Buckle up tight, it's going to get a bit hairy.'

'Hairy?' said a voice from the back. 'I've already grown a beard back here.'

'Well, you've always had a moustache problem,' said another.

'You speak for yourself.'

The laughter drowned beneath engine noise as the Anson dropped through a cloud, and Lizzie increased power to counteract another deep plunge through a pocket of freezing air. Wind noise increasing as the undercarriage slowly descended from the engine nacelles, Fizz cranked the lever through the last of its 140 turns and the Anson juddered along its entire length as the undercarriage locked into position. With more drag, the speed dropped rapidly and the wings waggled, testing whether to pull the Anson off course. Lizzie tightened her grip on the control column, steering to port and pushing hard with her left foot to bring the aircraft back level and pointing towards the runway.

'Steady on,' the man shouted, 'there's a G and T with my name on it and I'd like to live long enough to drink it.'

More laughter from behind but Lizzie's concentration denied her a smile. She lowered the flaps and the speed dropped further. 'If we get down in one piece the first round is on me.'

A chorus of approval from her passengers was cut off as a series of gusts buffeted the Anson, threatening to dump it in the fields short of the air station. Another wing dip, level off, a drop-rise-drop, left stomachs queasy.

'Stand by,' Lizzie shouted as she eased the throttles back on both engines.

The Anson levelled out, decreased in speed and descended until the large, rubber tyres touched wet grass, turning the aircraft from a relatively graceful bird into an ungainly, speeding animal. Now out of its natural environment, ground turbulence threatened to spin the heavy Anson or tip it on its nose. Lizzie, a veteran of thousands of flying hours in many aircraft, was having none of it and tamed the beast, steering it towards a waiting ground crew sheltering from the biting wind inside a hangar.

CHAPTER TWO

Flight Lieutenant Ben Vickers, officer in charge of the RAF Police responsible for the safety and security of RAF Scotney, stood to the left of Flight Captain Geraldine Ellenden-Pitt, officer in charge of Number Thirteen Ferry Pool. To her right, Wing Commander John Matfield, second-in-command of RAF Scotney, wearing his usual pristine uniform, squinted up at the sky. Vickers saw Matfield sneer as an Anson came into view, and they watched as the aircraft swept around in a wide arc, passed through low cloud and made its final approach to land.

Matfield's sneer slowly transformed into a scowl and Vickers noted Geraldine's look of satisfaction as the twin-engine aircraft settled gracefully onto the grass strip, decelerated and trundled to a stop over by its dispersal pen near to where they stood. They both knew the smooth landing would have irked Matfield, who disliked women being on the air station, especially as pilots.

Ground crew immediately swarmed over the Anson as the engines spluttered to a halt and the door was flung open. A fuel bowser grumbled its way towards the aircraft and engineers wedged chocks around the tyres. As soon as everyone had left the aircraft it would be checked over, refuelled and made ready for action.

Lizzie and the three other established pilots familiar to Vickers descended the ladder and saluted before climbing into the open back of a waiting Bedford lorry. One of the newcomers stepped lightly from the Anson, her brown hair flicking in the wind, followed by the other who fought to keep her blonde waves in check. Both saluted and hauled their kitbags into the back of the lorry, joining the others to await their flight captain.

Geraldine began to turn away when a man in an army-style greatcoat clunked down the ladder. Placing a cap on his head, the man looked across and strode over. Standing before them, Vickers could see the man was about Geraldine's height, aged maybe fifty with short, grey hair. His uniform displayed ENSA insignia.

'Martin Onslow,' the newcomer announced brightly. 'Director of the ENSA concert party entertaining you this week.'

Vickers caught Matfield's look of distaste at the man's accent.

'You must be Group Captain Dallington, sir.' Onslow saluted.

Matfield's eyes flicked to Onslow's cap badge before giving him a cold stare. 'Civilians have no need to salute, Mr Onslow.'

Vickers exchanged a wide-eyed look of astonishment with Geraldine. Dallington, the commanding officer of RAF Scotney, had always required the civilians of the ATA to salute RAF officers.

'Ah, but I'm in the Entertainments *National Service* Association,' Onslow replied. 'That makes me a serving officer.'

Matfield's lip curled with contempt. 'But you're American.'

'Born in Canada, actually. Moved to England when I was twenty. Is that a problem?'

Matfield ignored the question. 'I'm afraid the group captain is indisposed so he sent me.' Vickers caught a hint of *and I'd rather be anywhere else* in his tone. 'I am Wing Commander Matfield. This is Flight Lieutenant Vickers, head of the RAF Police on the station. He'll be looking after you.'

The two men shook hands.

Onslow turned to Geraldine and smiled. 'And this is?'

'Flight Captain Ellenden-Pitt, head of the ATA detachment here,' Geraldine said with a smile.

'She's also' – Matfield raised his chin to stretch his neck muscles – 'a civilian.'

Vickers noticed a twitch of Onslow's eyebrows but Geraldine's smile remained in place.

'Glad you could make it at last, Mr Onslow,' Geraldine said. 'It's always nice to see an ENSA show.'

'And it's always nice to perform,' Onslow replied with a wink. He looked at Vickers. 'Any sign of the rest of my company?'

'They arrived two days ago and camped about half a mile south of here,' Vickers said. 'We're on the Luftwaffe's flight path to London and still getting shot up and bombed so they thought it best to be a little removed from the air station.'

'Brave troops, eh?' Onslow chuckled. 'I prefer a comfy bed.'

'I'll show you to your quarters shortly, but while we're over this way, you might as well have a look at where the show will be staged.' Vickers indicated a nearby hangar. 'I'm sure the wing commander and flight captain have bags of work to do.'

Parting pleasantries observed, Geraldine turned towards the Bedford lorry and Vickers led Onslow towards the hangar.

'I hear you're a comedian,' Matfield called.

Onslow didn't turn back. 'So I'm told.'

'I don't much care for professional comedians.'

'I don't much care for amateur—'

'Shall we?' Vickers cut across Onslow, hurrying him away.

Lizzie and the other ATA women sat in silence, being bounced around in the back of the Bedford as it negotiated the partly tarmacked gravel and earth perimeter track. She saw wariness in the eyes of the new women and had sensed a hostility towards them from the old since departing ATA HQ at White Waltham.

After the Ripper's killing spree had terrorised the air station and village, the women had tried to put it behind them and forget. But such wickedness can never be forgotten and the memories returned, often at the bottom of a third glass of sherry or whisky, sometimes in a noise half-heard on the wind, but always in nightmares. After everything they had been through, accepting new faces into their tight-knit group was never going to be easy.

In fact, the one place Lizzie felt truly free was in a cockpit, thousands of feet above the patchwork fields of England. Flying in the sun and among the clouds made her feel safe, despite her job becoming only marginally less dangerous since the end of the Battle of Britain. Barrage balloons and the weather still tried to bring down the unwary, enemy raiders continued to pick on lone aircraft during daylight hours, and the anti-aircraft boys were no less jittery and trigger-happy.

The Bedford jerked to a halt on the large semi-circle of gravel in front of the manor house used as the HQ and officers' quarters. The women heard the rattle of a chain and waited for the rear flap to drop open before rising from the bench seats and jumping to the ground. Lizzie felt giddy as her feet sank into the loose gravel. Fatigue and grief weighed her down.

Standing to one side, Geraldine addressed her pilots.

'As you are aware, ladies, our new pilots have finally arrived,' she said brightly. 'I hope you've started to get to know each other but we can continue that in the warm.' The smile fell from her face at the sight of the pilots' expressions. 'Has something happened?'

Lizzie looked sideways at Fizz and concentrated on controlling her breathing. The Scot, raising her chin defiantly, said, 'You *cannae* bring in any old whores to replace who we've lost.' The insult emerged as *auld hoors* as anger deepened her usually mild accent, and the new women stiffened as if ready for a fight. 'They were worth more than that.'

Geraldine's face hardened in a second. 'You two, wait inside,' she said, and waited for the new women to go in. She looked at Niamh, Agata and Lizzie with eyes that had lost their previous sparkle, before turning to Fizz. 'I don't much care for your opinions, Third Officer, especially expressed in such base terms.' She glanced at the others. 'I appreciate you still feel the loss of your colleagues, as do I, especially under such horrific circumstances. That does not mean you can denigrate new pilots on a whim. We need them and the reason for that is not their fault.'

She stepped back, took a deep breath and relaxed. 'Come on, I'll buy you all a drink and you can get to know each other, *nicely*. Take your minds off things.'

As she turned towards the door, Lizzie felt Geraldine's hand on her arm.

'Are you all right? You look pale.'

Lizzie wanted to express the sadness she felt about her friend at Duxford but the familiar band tightened across her chest. Anxiety attacks, and what psychologists had begun calling OCN – Obsessive Compulsive Neurosis – while she was still at university, had plagued her since her mother's riding accident, witnessed when she was a child. She had learned to live with her conditions, for the most part, but they did have the annoying habit of emerging at the most inconvenient times.

Lizzie shrugged. 'It's been a tiring day.'

As they followed the others into the lounge, Lizzie saw one of the comfy chairs and one of the sofas they had once regarded as their domain already occupied by the new arrivals. She felt like they'd walked into the saloon of a cowboy film as four RAF officers, sitting around a low table in the far corner, stopped chatting to look their way and the barman behind the counter that ran along one wall stopped polishing a pint glass. Tilly, the black and white cat adopted by the station as its mascot, jumped down from the arm of a chair and sauntered off. The rest of the lounge was empty.

Geraldine appeared to not notice the tension and strode across to order drinks, leaving the women to chat. The barman hung up the glass, the officers returned to their conversation and Lizzie half-expected a grizzled old-timer to resume bashing out a tune on a tinkly upright piano.

Despite their cool reception, the two seated women leant forward to greet the old team, their demeanour welcoming rather than threatening.

'We haven't really met properly. I'm Hazel Kennedy.' The woman with dark hair and bright, brown eyes looked up at Fizz.

'I don't care who you are,' Fizz growled. 'You're in my chair.'

Hazel looked puzzled for a moment then stood up, her nose two inches from Fizz's. 'That's not very friendly.'

'That's because I'm not your friend.' Fizz waited, unmoving.

Hazel held Fizz's gaze for several seconds before she smiled, as if realising something, and stepped aside to choose a seat on one of the nearby sofas.

Fizz flopped into the vacated easy chair as Agata and Niamh chose the two remaining chairs. 'We lost our friends to a maniac not long back and they were irreplaceable, so we're not best pleased you're here.'

Starting to feel the group tension permeating through her own chest, Lizzie sank onto the sofa and rolled her shoulders, trying to relax.

'Don't mind us,' she said. 'Fizz is right, we've had a bit of a rough time. I'm Lizzie Hayes, by the way. Where are you from?'

Hazel returned Lizzie's half-smile. 'Guildford, in Surrey. I've been working out of White Waltham but jumped at the chance to see somewhere different for more than an hour at a time.'

'Scotney's certainly different,' Lizzie said. 'What about you?'

The woman across from Lizzie guided her wavy, blonde hair behind her left ear. 'Yvonne Fournier, from St Omer in France.'

'Christ, a bloody Frog,' Fizz said dismissively, lighting a cigarette. 'It's getting like the League of Nations in here.'

Lizzie pulled a face. 'You've just met Fizz Mitchell. A Scot, as you can tell.' She nodded towards Niamh. 'That's Niamh McNulty, from the Emerald Isle.'

Niamh smiled. 'Pronounced *neeve* but—'

'Spelled N-I-A-M-H, would you believe?' Fizz interrupted. 'How many more times are you going to say that? No one cares.'

From the angry frown and gritted teeth, Lizzie saw that Niamh cared. She feared the Irishwoman would rise to the bait but Niamh sat back, glowering.

'I wouldn't set great store by Lizzie, either,' Fizz continued. 'She isn't quite normal at the best of times.'

Lizzie tensed. There it was again. The phrase that followed wherever she went and mocked her deep-rooted anxiety. But Fizz had already moved on.

'And Grumpy-face at the end is Agata Toroniska, a Polish refugee.'

'Sorry about Fizz, she has a problem with people,' Agata said, ignoring the glare from Fizz. 'She likes no one.' She gave Yvonne a nod that looked almost conspiratorial. 'I am from Polska. Nazis are in my country too. I want all Nazis destroyed.'

Yvonne's gaze met Agata's and she returned the nod.

Geraldine arrived with a tray of glasses and a half-full bottle of whisky.

'I hope you're all getting along, especially you two Celts. It's the Nazis we're fighting, remember?'

'Just getting to know each other, ma'am,' Fizz said, taking a final drag on her cigarette.

'We're both from passionate peoples, ma'am,' Niamh said.

'We can all be passionate.' Geraldine poured roughly equal measures in the glasses. 'As long as that passion is directed in the correct manner.' She looked at each woman with suspicion as they leant forward to claim a drink. 'We are a team of women in a man's world and that in itself is no slight challenge.' Geraldine looked at Fizz. 'You more than anyone should know what bad feeling can lead to, and if you are in any doubt, I suggest you relate the full story to the new girls. RAF Scotney should be our safe haven and anyone violating that sanctuary will no longer be welcome here.' She raised her glass. 'Back to work tomorrow, ladies. Your good health.'

Kember hung his fedora and raincoat on the coat-stand in the front office of Scotney Police Station, eased himself into the visitor's chair near Sergeant Wright's desk and pressed his fingers to his eyes. Wright placed his helmet on a two-drawer filing cabinet behind the door and sat heavily in his own chair.

'You all right, sir?'

Kember rubbed his hands over his face. 'Fine, thank you,' he said, feeling tired and far from fine. He'd always found ploughing straight into a case adequate camouflage for whatever he felt at any given time and now was no different. 'Before I telephone the chief inspector, I suggest you tell me everything he said.'

'Of course, sir,' Wright said, interlacing his fingers across his stomach. 'His sister-in-law, a Mrs Joyce Hartson, has been on the telephone to him, distraught with worry. Apparently, her daughter Evelyn, the chief inspector's niece, visited a family friend, who lives on a farm estate in Paddock Wood with her parents. She travelled there on Thursday, intending to return at lunchtime today.'

'But she never arrived?'

'She arrived, all right. Just never made it back home.'

Kember scratched the back of his neck. 'Did the chief inspector say anything else?'

'Only that he wanted to speak to you straight away and looked to you to get to the bottom of it, quickly, sir.'

'I'd better lance the boil, then,' Kember said as he reached for the telephone.

A moment later, Chief Inspector Hartson spoke over the operator as she connected the call.

'Kember, I want you to take charge and find my niece immediately. You're supposed to be a Scotland Yard detective and now's the time to prove it.'

Kember heard the operator tut in disapproval, and he spoke through gritted teeth.

'I'll do my best, sir. Have you anything for me to go on?'

'Of course I have,' Hartson snapped. 'Listen carefully. A car was sent to collect Evelyn from Tonbridge station as arranged but she wasn't on board. The driver checked with the guard who was adamant that only a young soldier in uniform and an elderly gentleman with his wife had boarded at Paddock Wood. I've got men tracing these people as we speak.'

'What about the family friend?'

'Joyce, my sister-in-law, telephoned the Edisons who suggested that Evelyn may have deviated or been delayed en route. I've checked, there have been no delays on the railway.'

Kember wrote down the address dictated by Hartson, and despite his superior officer's bullish attitude, he felt his detective's mind kick into gear.

'Could Miss Hartson have decided to visit another friend perhaps?'

'Absolutely not.'

'Or go shopping in Tonbridge before going home?'

'Shopping? Are you mad, Kember? Tonbridge isn't exactly the West End of London. And my niece is not in the habit of wandering off on her own without telling her parents.'

Kember bit his tongue. He'd met many families who thought they knew what their children got up to and were thinking. Circumstances had proved time and again how little parents really knew about their offspring, of any age.

'Merely exploring the possibilities, sir,' Kember said. 'As you may recall, I met your brother, Laurence, and his family a couple of years ago, when I was a part of the security detail at his home on the outskirts of Tonbridge. Miss Hartson seemed an intelligent and level-headed young lady, even then.'

'Of course, she was and still is,' Hartson said. 'Which makes this all the more disturbing.'

'Have you spoken to your brother?'

'Yes. He telephoned me from his office in the Ministry of Information. He stays at his club in London during the week but he's down here each weekend. I've told him to expect you first thing tomorrow.'

'Thank you, sir. That's helpful,' Kember said, and meant it. Getting in the same room with the likes of Laurence Hartson was never easy, even for a detective, and the chief inspector had saved him a lot of time. 'One more thing, sir. You haven't mentioned a ransom note or telephone call.'

'That's because there hasn't been any,' Hartson said. 'And no outsiders. If I hear you've roped in that woman to do the investigation for you, I'll have your warrant card before you can say quackery and witchcraft.'

'I'll do my best—'

'Is that clear?'

'Yes, sir.'

Kember heard a loud click as Hartson put his phone down. Kember followed suit.

His relationship with Hartson had always been sour but allowing Elizabeth Hayes to help during the Scotney Ripper case had curdled it further. Using her doctorate from Bedford College in London and her skills as a research psychologist specialising in crime and criminals, she had provided a psychological profile to the police that helped identify a serial murderer. Kember had realised the reputational repercussions for the police service, Kent County Constabulary in particular, and everyone involved, should Lizzie's involvement become widely known. Her persistence in the face of his own lack of progress at the time had persuaded him to take a chance. The outcome spoke for itself and he had no regrets. Now, through no fault of his own, it seemed his reputation and career were at stake, wrapped up in whatever fate had befallen the niece of his boss.

'The chief inspector has warned me not to bring in outsiders.' Kember gave Wright a weak smile. 'I'm not sure whether to take that as an endorsement of my abilities or not.'

He filled in those parts of the conversation unheard by Wright, who jotted in his notebook with a stubby pencil.

'Could she be a runaway?' Wright suggested. 'Plenty of those around at present.'

Kember leant back in his chair and shook his head. 'Her family may think she's a child but I believe she's of an age when running away doesn't have the same legal definition or standing. That said, in my experience there are two broad reasons why people go missing: intention and prevention.'

'The young lady has been missing for less than a day,' Wright said. 'There may be a perfectly reasonable explanation.'

'True, but Hartson's right. From my limited knowledge of Evelyn, she has never struck me as someone who would go off on a whim and omit to tell her parents. Of course, that doesn't exclude the possibility that the family friend is lying and Evelyn had secret plans to stay elsewhere last night, somewhere she believed her parents wouldn't approve of and so felt the need to deceive them.'

'With a sweetheart, you mean?'

Kember shrugged. 'Love is a powerful motive, and a man did go missing the same evening.'

'Aye, but as you said, there's no apparent connection,' Wright said. 'Could be coincidence.'

'I'm not a great supporter of coincidence, so we shouldn't rule out the possibility of elopement, until we can prove otherwise.'

Wright scribbled in his book.

'You mentioned prevention, sir. You fear the worst?'

'By prevention I mean death or detention. Without evidence of an alternative purpose or destination, or a clear indication that Miss Hartson wished to deceive her parents, we have to consider that she may be delayed in some way and unable to make contact to explain. She may have had a serious accident or someone may be holding her. Perhaps the missing man has her.'

Kember saw doubt in the furrows creasing Wright's forehead.

Wright cleared his throat. 'His name's Kenneth Jarvis, sir, and he's never struck me as one to run off either. Definitely not the type to kidnap. I know him, better than you know Miss Hartson.'

It was Kember's turn to frown.

'Evelyn Hartson is the daughter of a high-ranking government employee, and the niece of a senior police officer, so we can't rule out kidnap or murder by someone seeking revenge. But, if it is kidnap, you'd expect to see a ransom note by now and the chief inspector said nothing has been delivered. As for Kenneth Jarvis—'

A call from outside stopped Kember and a few seconds later a woman entered in a waft of cold air, the damp smell of winter clinging to her coat. Both policemen stood.

'Agnes, thank you for coming back,' said Wright. Kember raised questioning eyebrows. 'This is Mrs Agnes Jarvis,' Wright explained. 'It's her husband, Kenneth, who's missing.'

'Ah, I see,' Kember said apologetically as the woman's face creased with worry at the mention. 'Let's go through to the back room and get you a nice hot cup of tea, Mrs Jarvis.'

'Do excuse me,' Wright said as the telephone rang. He answered the call, exchanging pleasantries, and paused to listen before proffering the handset to Kember.

'It's Miss Hayes, sir.'

CHAPTER THREE

Lizzie wolfed down her dinner of Spam fritters, marvelling at how thin the mess staff could slice the tinned, spiced ham. She could often blag another piece from Fizz, who always complained it looked like someone had peeled a piece of skin from an arm, but not today. Now the adrenaline buzz of flying had dissipated, they were hungry and exhausted.

Lizzie put her cutlery down on her empty plate and massaged her temples. Despite it being almost the shortest day of the year, an intense schedule had seen Lizzie not only piloting the air taxi but also flying brand-new aircraft to front-line airfields and battle-scarred wrecks to repair centres farther inland. Coaxing barely airworthy, second-class warplanes into staying aloft sometimes took every ounce of her physical strength and mental concentration. But today had drained every type of emotional energy from her too.

Having spent most of the day alone in the air, the officers' lounge seemed too crowded so the women retired to the Hangar Round club. Consisting of a long games-room with a small, furnished lounge and a bar room off to one side, this was a women-only club made for themselves, mostly by themselves, in a disused wine cellar beneath the manor house. It provided a haven they could retreat to, when necessary, but that didn't mean they couldn't invite the men down occasionally. Today was not one of those days.

Agata brought bottled beer through from the bar and handed them around.

'This is nice,' Hazel said. 'How on earth did you manage it?'

'It was a strange summer.' Fizz took a bottle. 'I think they wanted us out of their hair as much as we wanted them out of ours.'

'Who's they?'

'Our brave commanding officer, Group Captain Dallington, for one.' Fizz sneered. 'He thinks all women should be at home, safe from nasty things like wars.'

'What, even when London's being bombed to bits?'

'Exactly.'

Agata swallowed a mouthful of beer. 'Matfield for two,' she said. 'The dashing wing commander you saw when we landed.'

'Ah,' said Yvonne. 'He did seem a little bit, shall I say, annoyed?'

'He's always a little bit annoyed.' Fizz laughed. 'And he's little better than Dallington but at least he doesn't try to get us thrown off the air station every day.'

'But still, letting you have your own club is no mean feat,' Hazel said, a hint of admiration in her voice.

'It was a joint effort, and good for all,' Agata said.

As the women chatted, Niamh gave Lizzie a mischievous smile. 'I've heard your detective still lives in the village.'

'He's not my detective,' Lizzie protested wearily, and took a swig from a bottle of light ale. She'd heard through the village gossip network that Kember had returned to his lodgings at the Castle pub following a stay in hospital, but his marriage situation was complicated. She didn't want to become part of someone else's problem when she had enough of her own to contend with. All the same, she believed their shared experience at the hands of the Scotney Ripper had brought them closer than mere colleagues.

'Give him a call and cheer yourself up, why don't you?' Niamh said.

Lizzie glanced at the wall clock. At this time on a Friday, with daylight already that murky, pre-dusk colour of dishwater, she knew Kember might have called it a day and gone home. But she also knew he wasn't one for keeping regular hours, especially during an investigation. If he was in the middle of a thorny case, he might still be at the police HQ in Tonbridge. He might even be at the police station in Scotney, and she wanted – needed – to talk to someone about her friend. Someone who understood.

She had offered her services to the police barely five months earlier, using her skill for getting into the minds of murderers to help solve an investigation led by Kember. He'd been injured and taken away by ambulance.

They hadn't spoken since, although she had telephoned the hospital to enquire about his health.

Lizzie looked at her fingers, her train of thought broken, puzzled for a moment by the whisky tumbler that had been thrust into her hand. She looked up as Agata raised a glass of the golden liquid in salute and downed it in one gulp. Lizzie raised her own drink to her lips and recoiled, catching the Glenmorangie's strong, sweet aroma, one she usually loved.

'Call him,' Niamh encouraged, with a wink.

Lizzie looked at her and the others, considering the suggestion but not for reasons of romance. Then she took a decision and knocked the whisky back in one go, the fire scouring her throat but warming her chest, giving her the instant hit of Dutch courage she needed. She plonked her empty glass on the table and left the lounge, accompanied by a big grin from Niamh and questions from the new girls. Ignoring them all, she went to the briefing room to telephone Kember.

Lizzie's finger hesitated, pressed into a hole of the telephone's rotary dial. She fought against the familiar feelings: sweaty palms, quick, shallow breath, pounding heart, dizziness, a sick feeling in her throat and the pit of her stomach. Her conditions always descended at inconvenient moments, but never affected her up in the air.

She concentrated on the large noticeboard fixed to the far wall, counting the number of drawing pins keeping papers fixed to the cloth-covered cork. Fourteen. She counted up through the numbers then back down again. Four times. Only on the last cycle did her mind get bored with holding her hostage and release her. She took a few deep breaths and allowed her finger to dial the operator.

Having been put through to Tonbridge Police HQ and been told Kember wasn't there, she tried again and asked for Scotney Police Station. Lizzie heard distant clicks on the line as the operator connected her call.

'Scotney Police Station. Sergeant Wright speaking.'

Lizzie heard the nervousness in her own voice as they exchanged greetings. She had seen Wright around the village many times in the past few months but Kember had remained busy in Tonbridge after his release from hospital. She felt awkward now, as she asked whether Wright would be so kind as to get a message to him.

Seconds later . . .

'Lizzie, how lovely to hear from you.'

Kember being there threw Lizzie's thoughts off balance, his voice welcoming but almost too bright.

'I did call before,' she said. 'Well – the hospital. A few times.'

'Really?' Kember replied. 'They never told me.'

'I didn't want them to trouble you.'

'Ah. That'll be why, then. I thought . . .'

His silent pause told her everything about what he'd thought. Whatever the state of his marriage, he was still legally wed, and a very busy Scotland Yard detective on secondment. She was the pushy woman pilot who had interfered in his investigation, caused him to end up in hospital, jeopardised his reputation and career. The one whose insights into criminal minds made her *not quite normal*.

'It seems odd to be ringing you now, after all these months, but . . .' Now her own hesitation turned into awkward silence.

Kember's tone changed to concern. 'Is there anything wrong?'

'Not really,' she said automatically. She bit her lip and frowned. 'Actually, yes. I had some news today that shook me up a bit. Someone I knew passed away recently.'

'Oh. I'm sorry to hear that. Were you close?'

'We trained together.' Lizzie fiddled with the telephone cord before deciding to just come out and say it. 'Passed away is not the right expression. She was murdered.'

'Ah. I'd not heard—'.

'Not around here. At Duxford. I'd like . . .' She took a breath. 'I *need* to talk to you about it because the circumstances are rather unusual.'

She sensed Kember's hesitation.

'*Serial murderer* unusual?' he said. 'You do know *he* is dead?'

Kember stating the obvious irked her but he'd quoted the term she'd used to describe the Scotney Ripper, giving her some small satisfaction that he'd remembered.

'Just like there's more than one burglar, there's more than one murderer,' Lizzie said. 'I don't want to explain on the telephone and calls still have a time limit.'

'Of course. Shall we meet?'

'The Castle pub in half an hour,' she blurted, kicking herself for seeming too blunt and eager. From the pause, she could imagine Kember looking at his watch and weighing up how much work he had left to do. She was about to tell him to not bother when he spoke.

'That should give me enough time to finish here. I'll see you over there.'

Replacing the handset after their goodbyes, she relaxed and allowed nervousness to flood back in.

She counted the pins again.

◆ ◆ ◆

Mrs Agnes Jarvis, sitting in the back room of Scotney Police Station, tightened the knot of her floral headscarf and returned to squeezing the life out of her black handbag. Kember sat opposite as Wright placed two mugs of tea on the table between them, waiting patiently as she pulled herself together.

Having crossed her path in recent months in various High Street shops, Kember could see her husband's sudden absence had taken a toll. Previously bright and animated, he thought she now looked older than the early fifties he knew her to be.

'I understand your husband didn't come home last night, Mrs Jarvis,' Kember began.

Her furrows of anguish deepened. 'That's right. He's normally home from the pub early because he can't take his drink any more.' She mouthed, *men's problems*, and glanced down to her lap. 'He has a couple of pints and comes home to listen to the wireless before bed.'

'Is there any reason not to think he's gone somewhere? To stay over, I mean?'

'Why would he do that?' Agnes twiddled her handbag strap between her fingers. 'He's never stayed away in twenty-two years of marriage, except when he's working up at Paddock Wood in the summer, so I don't know why he'd be wanting to do that now.'

Kember hesitated as his own recently failed marriage flashed into his mind. 'He gave no indication of being unsettled, upset or worried about anything?' he asked, rubbing his nose to hide his embarrassment.

'No, Inspector.'

'Nothing happened recently that might hint at something out of the ordinary going on?'

'No. We're simple folk.'

'What work does your husband do?'

'He was a platelayer on the Hawkhurst branch line, maintaining the track and suchlike, but he's not been able to do heavy work since his accident. He hurt his back and took odd jobs around the village for a while.'

'And now?' Kember pressed, feeling his own old back injury twinge, letting him know it was still there.

'Now he's a foreman over at Glassen Farm,' Agnes said. 'And up at Paddock Wood during hopping season. I take in laundry to make ends meet. Always have.'

To Kember, Kenneth Jarvis sounded like a nice, ordinary, local chap. But experience told him something always lurked beneath the surface if you scratched away the veneer.

'Could he be with friends or other family?' he said, noticing another squeeze of the handbag.

'Only family we've got is my sister Edith, in Wales,' Agnes said. 'All our friends are in the village.'

'Does he have any enemies? Owe anyone any money? Any recent arguments with anyone?'

'No, not my Ken.' Agnes shook her head. 'Gentle as a lamb, he is. We haven't got two ha'pennies to rub together most days so he sometimes goes out trapping rabbits to help us out a bit. Everyone's in the same boat, aren't they?' Agnes lifted her chin proudly. 'But we've never owed so much as a farthing.'

Kember nodded. There never seemed to be much to go on in this type of case, initially, but wives weren't always as much in the know as they thought they were.

'Sergeant Wright has a description and all the details, so thank you, Mrs Jarvis. We'll make some enquiries and let you know when we have something. Missing persons usually turn up with a good explanation,' he lied. 'So please don't fret.'

Kember accepted her thanks with what he hoped was a reassuring smile and waited while Wright showed Agnes to the front door and returned to the back room.

'What do you make of that? Do you know much about Agnes and Kenneth Jarvis?'

Wright shook his head. 'It's as she said, sir. He keeps himself to himself, a few jars in the pub, never any trouble, pretty decent worker but a rubbish trapper. He wouldn't have stayed out all night catching bunnies, especially not in this cold. She's a bit of a tittle-tattle, right in with Ethel Garner's gossip circle, but does a nice bit of laundry work. I use her for my uniform and shirts.' He hesitated and blushed. 'Not my smalls, like.'

Kember stifled a smile. 'Know anything about her sister in Wales?'

'Only what Ethel's told me,' Wright said with a sheepish grin. 'I was only a nipper when Edith ran away and I'd been up in London in the Metropolitan Police for a couple of years when all this between Agnes and her mother was going on, but Ethel's always a good source of local information.' He cocked his head and shrugged. 'Edith's eight years older than Agnes. Apparently, Edith fell in love with a railwayman herself when she was eighteen. Their mother and father didn't like railwaymen of any kind and forbade them to marry. Made no odds. They ran away back to his home town of Cardiff and got married anyway. Agnes was ten. Her father fought in the Great War but he never made it home alive. Died of

Spanish flu as he was on his way home from the Western Front. About the same time, Agnes met Ken in the village. He was a railwayman too and Agnes took to him straight away, perhaps because she'd seen her sister so happy with one. Of course, her mother forbade any courting but that winter brought an outbreak of Spanish flu and Agnes lost her mother to pneumonia and other complications. They say hundreds died, the hospitals were swamped and local doctors run off their feet. A shortage of coffins too. Being a poor man but good with his hands, Ken made the coffin himself, for Agnes's mother. She's buried in that part of the graveyard round the back of the church where they laid her father to rest. Agnes married Ken the following summer but she's never forgiven Edith for leaving her behind.'

Kember nodded thoughtfully. 'Why did the parents dislike railwaymen so much?'

'Thought they were beneath them, as far as I can tell,' Wright said.

'Any children?'

'Never happened for them.'

Kember took a small notebook from his pocket and scribbled a few lines. 'Thank you, Sergeant. That was most comprehensive, despite being hearsay from Mrs Garner.' He thought for a moment. If Edith's parents had disliked railwaymen so much that they forbade their daughters from marrying one, could others in the village have had a similar prejudice? Edith escaped to Cardiff but Agnes had stayed in Scotney. Had someone decided the time was right to teach her a lesson?

Wright twitched as Kember's notebook snapped shut.

'Right, it's a little late to start any legwork this evening so we've an early start tomorrow. I'll speak in person to Chief Inspector Hartson's brother and sister-in-law over at Tonbridge and to Evelyn's friend in Paddock Wood. You take statements from the

CHAPTER FOUR

Lizzie guided her black Norton motorbike to the kerb outside the Castle pub in Scotney High Street and turned off the ignition. She caught her breath when a figure detached itself from the shadows cast by protective sandbags piled high around the doorway but swallowed the waiting scream when she recognised Kember.

'It's lovely to see you again,' he said, as she removed her helmet and fluffed up her flattened hair. 'Although I'm not sure the circumstances are what I had in mind.'

'You scared the living daylights out of me,' she snapped. 'Lurking in the dark like that.'

'It's the blackout,' he complained.

'That's all well and good but it's not that long ago you could have been *him*, waiting to kill me.'

'You're right, I'm sorry,' he said. 'I do seem to have a knack for lurking.'

Despite the scare, she couldn't help a smile escaping as the half-moon's wintery light exposed Kember's apologetic frown. 'I've been meaning to telephone but . . .'

Kember nodded, hesitated. 'What time do you have to get back?'

'I've only got an hour and it's taken me ten minutes to get here.'

Another nod. 'Just time enough for a quick drink then. Shall we?' He indicated the door.

The smoky pub was full of Friday night regulars: Les and Alice Brannan holding court from behind the bar; Jim Corcoran the postman and part-time fireman, arguing some minor point about football with Brian Greenway the ARP warden and Bert Garner; even Elias Brown, captain of the local platoon of the Home Guard since the summer, had popped in after anti-invasion duty. Glances were thrown towards Kember and Lizzie as they pushed through the blackout curtain and took a recently vacated table. Seeing familiar faces, the men soon returned to nursing their respective drinks. Beer and discussion on a Friday night were far more interesting than anything Kember and Lizzie might be up to.

The heat from flaming logs crackling in the fireplace; ancient and musty crepe-paper Christmas decorations with fresh sprigs of holly and mistletoe slung from low ceilings; wooden beams adorned with pewter tankards and dried hop bines; the babble of conversation; tobacco smoke, sweaty bodies and beery breath: all combined into that weekend fug that seemed to make pubs so much more welcoming in the winter.

Lizzie waited impatiently while Kember got them each a half of best bitter, set down the drinks and sat opposite.

'No wine, I'm afraid,' Kember said.

Lizzie waved away the apology. 'They haven't had any for months. Apparently, the brewery only sent a few bottles to see if there was any demand for it, but they'd been in the cellar gathering dust because most people drink beer or cider around here. They were only brought up because my colleagues and I were invited to the summer dance and the Brannans thought that's what we'd like.'

'They were right,' Kember said, and took a mouthful of bitter.

Lizzie took two gulps of her own before taking the plunge. 'I needed to see you, to talk about my friend in Duxford. Catherine Summers.'

'That rings a bell,' Kember said, looking concerned, but in the professional way that Lizzie found inexplicably annoying. 'I think I read something about her murder in the *Police Gazette*. You said there was something unusual about it but the *Gazette* didn't speculate. Did the police say anything to you?'

'Yes and no.'

'That's clear then.'

Lizzie felt her cheeks flush and her chest tighten, rising anxiety gripping her throat. She tried to ignore it by distracting herself, allowing her OCN to come to the fore. She reached for her dimpled half-pint mug and aligned its handle parallel with the edge of the table. Not enough, so she did the same to Kember's. Still not enough. Her ultimate countermeasure was to sniff from a small, cobalt-blue glass jar of Vicks VapoRub she carried in her bag, but that was a bit obvious and there were other tricks to try first. She reached for a thick rubber band she'd slipped over her left wrist that morning and gave it a pull. The snap against her flesh jolted her mind and she repeated the action with a band on her right wrist. It worked. Her thoughts cleared and her eyes refocused on Kember, whose look of concern she now thought seemed more personal. She took a deep breath, let it out slowly and sipped her beer before continuing.

'Catherine and I trained together at White Waltham when we first joined the ATA. She was one of the quieter types. Didn't have a husband or regular boyfriend and disliked places too crowded so she avoided local dances, except on the air station. Even then, she made it very clear to all the boys right from the start that there would be no shenanigans. All good, clean, harmless fun.'

'So, what? You think one of her dance partners didn't understand the rules?'

'Not at all.' Lizzie took another mouthful of beer to settle herself. 'I was passing through RAF Duxford as part of my ferry duties when an orderly took me to one side. He'd been at White Waltham briefly, too, and was sure Catherine and I knew each other. He said the local Home Guard had come across something unusual while out on a routine patrol. They'd been that way before but hadn't noticed anything previously because it was just inside a copse of trees. This time, one of the men brought his Labrador along. The dog ran off into the trees, went straight to a mound of leaves and started scrabbling. When the men scraped away more leaves and removed a broken branch, they found the body of my friend. She'd been there for weeks, apparently.'

'I'm really sorry to hear that,' Kember said.

Lizzie waved away his platitude and took another gulp of beer.

'Did they say what happened to her?' he asked.

She took another deep, steadying breath.

'I spoke to the RAF Police at Duxford but they wouldn't say much at first because she was a civilian ATA pilot killed off station. I tried a little charm – not my forte – and they said they thought she'd had her throat cut before being dumped in a natural depression and hastily covered.' Lizzie clenched her jaw and pushed her tongue hard against the roof of her mouth to stop the tears she felt welling up.

'Unfortunately, quite common these days,' Kember said, shaking his head slowly. 'You'd think people would be more concerned with fighting Hitler than each other, but what with the blackout and Blitz and everyone looking to the skies for German paratroopers, very few people notice what's going on around them. That leaves them vulnerable.'

'That's what I thought,' Lizzie agreed, her emotions barely back under control. 'But we kept chatting and he let slip eventually that they'd found something unusual.'

Kember's left eyebrow twitched. 'In what way?'

Used to coming across bizarre murders during her PhD studies but not sure she could say it aloud about her friend, Lizzie took a moment to compose herself. This was proving a harder conversation to get through than she'd envisaged.

'Her hands were missing,' she said, eventually. Her voice almost a whisper.

From Kember's expression, Lizzie couldn't be sure whether he was shocked or had misheard. Their fingers touched briefly across the table before he withdrew his hand completely.

'I'm sorry,' Kember said. 'Knowing your friend had been outside that long, at the mercy of wild animals, must be awful.'

She took a breath, feeling tears welling up but not wanting to cry. 'From what I could gather, the Home Guard said her wrists looked like they'd been cut by something before the animals took an interest.'

Kember's expression changed almost imperceptibly but Lizzie noticed, as if a dial behind his eyes had been re-tuned from its sympathy setting to one of curiosity. She watched him take another mouthful of beer before continuing.

'She had everything on her: papers, ration book, purse, money. And she wasn't raped.' Lizzie knew the right time had come to give her opinion but still hesitated. 'I – I have a theory.'

'I thought you might,' Kember said. 'Don't tell me, if the murderer didn't rob or rape her, you think he took her hands as a souvenir. What did you call them last time? Trophies, that's it.'

'Yes, trophies. I can't think of any other reason why both her hands were missing completely and showed signs of cuts, not just gnawed by animals.'

'Perhaps she defended herself against the knife. Didn't you tell me serial murderers needed ritual? Where's the ritual here?'

Kember's matter-of-fact expression poked at Lizzie's frustration and she leant towards him, lowering her voice. 'Think back a few months. The murderer left his victims where they could be found, wanting his work to be seen, but he took a prize each time. As for rituals, that doesn't necessarily have to be at the scene of the crime.' She sat back in her chair. 'I told the police in Cambridge about my background and offered to help but I got short shrift.'

Lizzie could see Kember weighing up her argument.

'I'll tell you what I'll do,' he said. 'I'll telephone Cambridgeshire Constabulary in the morning to see what I can find out, but it's their investigation. They're not obliged to tell me anything so I may draw a blank. That's all I can do, I'm afraid.'

Lizzie relaxed. 'Thank you. Anything you can find out would be marvellous.' She finished the rest of her beer, noting that Kember had already finished his. 'I should be getting back. The roads are icy so I need to take it steady on the bike.'

She stood up, satisfied her job was done for now. While Kember took their glasses back to the bar, she headed for the door, buttoning her greatcoat as she went. She was outside beyond the sandbags, already donning her helmet as Kember emerged from the dark recess between the door and blackout curtain.

'If there is another madman out there, be careful,' he said.

'Don't worry.' She pulled on her leather gauntlets. 'Ben Vickers gave us a few lessons on unarmed combat after the last time.'

'Good,' he nodded. 'How is the flight sergeant?'

'Didn't you hear? He was promoted to flight lieutenant a few days after you were carted off in the ambulance.'

'Good for him, and well deserved,' Kember said. 'Look, I'll let you know if I find anything. I hope we can . . . ?'

She was glad of the blackout as he left the question hanging, feeling her cheeks flush. She started the engine to break the awkward silence, a thin strip of pale yellow appearing through the blackout mask over the headlight as she turned it on.

Over the loud grumble she said, 'If you don't call me, I'll call you,' and opened the throttle.

CHAPTER FIVE

First thing the following morning, having bought a newspaper and a stamp from the shop that served as a grocer's, newsagent and sub-post office, Kember closed the door behind him and headed for the police station. Before even reaching the kerb, he stopped sharp to let two young girls run past, giggling breathlessly while they chased the metal hoop from a barrel as it rolled and clattered along the High Street.

'Do you mind?'

Kember looked around to see who had thumped into his back like a fairground dodgem car and saw the hefty bulk of Mrs Ethel Garner, housewife and local gossip.

'Where's the fire?' she said, rubbing her hip as if she'd been rugby tackled.

'My apologies, Mrs Garner.' Kember touched the brim of his fedora, wondering why it was he who had apologised.

'Ah, Inspector. You still around? Where are you going all purposeful? Not another case, I hope. We all thought you'd stay in Tonbridge after your misfortunes. Mrs Jarvis said last week, there's not a lot around here for a man of the world like you. Seemed a bit stand-offish when I saw her this morning, though. Not that she's the life and soul of the party. Mind you, she's always partial to a bowl of my sherry trifle when it's on offer. I said to Mrs Tate, her in-growing toenail's no better, bless her. I said, I bet her Ken's up to no good. He's always been a one, if you know what I mean. He's a man, though, so what can you expect? No offence. Mrs Ware, her down the end, hasn't got a bad word to say about either of them, and she reckons she knows. Well, she would, wouldn't she? Anyway, I can't let you keep me here chatting. This basket won't fill itself.'

Kember walked on, amused at how often a brief encounter with Mrs Garner felt like a lengthy discussion. Sergeant Wright was on his knees before the fireplace in the front office when Kember entered the police station.

'Mug of tea on the table for you, sir,' Wright said. He selected a few lumps of black coal from the nearby scuttle and placed them on crumpled balls of newspaper and dry twigs arranged in the grate. 'You'll need something to fortify yourself before you set off to see the chief inspector's brother.'

'Thank you, Sergeant,' Kember said, intrigued by how Wright always had a pot of tea on the go and knew when he was coming.

He collected his notebook and pen from a drawer and slipped them into his jacket pocket before picking up the mug. Taking sips of the hot, brown sludge, he watched Wright light the paper with a match, momentarily mesmerised as the flames curled and caught the wood. Wright gave a grunt of satisfaction and held a sheet of newspaper across the fireplace to draw the flames. A roar came from behind the newspaper and he removed the sheet, sucking a cloud of grey smoke with it that rolled and curled towards the ceiling.

'My Maisie's not come home.'

The face of the man who suddenly filled the doorway crumpled into a mess of grief-lines and tears.

Wright stood, leading the man to his chair and sitting him down.

'Whatever's the matter, Derek?' Wright asked, his own face creased with concern. 'This is Derek Chapman,' he explained to Kember. 'The owner of Glassen Farm, east of the village.'

After a few awkward moments of hiccups and sobs, Chapman pulled himself together enough to carry on.

'Maisie. My daughter. She didn't come home last night and I've been worried sick.'

Kember glanced at Wright then back at Chapman. 'Could she be staying with friends or other family?' he asked, gently.

Chapman wiped his eyes on the ends of his jacket sleeves. 'We've got no family round here.' He shook his head. 'I've asked at a couple of farms, where she might have gone, to punish me like. Nobody's seen her.' His eyes darted, looking at Wright and Kember in turn.

Kember paused until Chapman next made eye contact. 'Why might she want to punish you, Mr Chapman?'

Chapman squeezed and twisted the cap in his hands. 'She helps around the farm but she's got ambitions. Wants to go to London, of all places. I told her, people like us don't go to The Smoke and I've already got my boys in the army. We had a bit of a set-to about it, the day before yesterday, and she stormed off.' He struggled for composure. 'I haven't seen her since, and I even checked the barn where she used to like sleeping sometimes, in the summer, when she was younger, but she wasn't there.'

Kember had seen his fair share of troubled youngsters over the years. In his experience, only the unlucky few turned up dead. Some ran away completely and weren't heard from again for years, if ever. Most reappeared within a week with their tails between their legs. Rural villages all over the country where farming was the main livelihood had seen their young people drifting towards the towns and cities, especially London: The Smoke. Hating the often harsh country life, especially in winter, they sought better-paid jobs with better working conditions. Many returned home disillusioned by the equally harsh conditions in factories and offices and the low pay for labourers and other unskilled workers, if they could find work at all. To Kember, a pretty village like Scotney set in rolling countryside with a nearby river, thriving farms and even a railway connecting it to almost anywhere else in the country, seemed idyllic. Then again, if anyone had asked him this time last year whether a serial murderer would choose a place like this to wreak havoc, he would have laughed them out of Kent.

'I take it she doesn't often stay away from home?'

'No, never.' Chapman shook his head. 'My Maisie's a good girl.'

Aren't they all? Kember thought, then chided himself silently for his lack of sympathy. 'You said Maisie was ambitious. Could she have gone to London, even for a day or two?'

Chapman shook his head again. 'We do all right on the farm, make enough to live and that, but we ain't rich, Inspector. We never have enough money to go swanning off to The Smoke. We always have to save up for things like new tools or even clothes. Maisie had to save up like the rest of us and she would never have wasted it on going to London where she knows no one and there's no work for her. She's been hurt, I know it.'

Kember could almost hear the farmer's heart breaking. He took a breath. 'What work does Maisie do for you, Mr Chapman?'

Chapman looked back at him with red-rimmed eyes and took a gulp of air. 'Looks after the sheep, she does. Was supposed to bring them strays in but . . .'

Kember felt a familiar shiver travel down the length of his spine. He couldn't even begin to guess how many mothers, fathers, spouses and sweethearts had sat before him hoping their loved ones were alive and no more than lost or injured in an accident, refusing to countenance the possibility of something worse. He glanced at the wall clock, suddenly realising he was running late.

'I'm going to leave you in the capable hands of Sergeant Wright.' Chapman stiffened but Kember nodded benevolently. 'He'll record all the details, of what she was wearing and suchlike, and take a statement from you.' He stood up. 'I'm sure she'll turn up, but in the meantime, you could help by checking her room, see if she's taken a bag or some clothes, maybe have another look around the farm.'

Kember gave Chapman a confident smile and gathered his coat and hat. He raised his eyebrows at Wright and received a wink and half-nod of reassurance in return.

Kember coaxed his Hillman Minx Tourer along a narrow dirt track in countryside not far from Tonbridge. His father had bought the two-door, soft-top brand-new in 1937, the car passing to Kember after his father died from a stroke, so he was careful not to scratch the British racing green paintwork. With all the road signs and marker posts having been removed to confuse an invading German army, Kember had taken several wrong turns already in an effort to find the home of Chief Inspector Hartson's brother. Evelyn Hartson had not been found nor had she made contact and Kember already feared the worst.

Finding his way from the dirt track back to the asphalt of the wider metalled lane, two magnificent stone gateposts topped with carved lions soon appeared around a bend. These marked a gap in an eight-foot-high wall that enclosed the Hartsons' estate. Black-painted iron gates, when open, gave access to a drive that swept through an avenue of apple and pear trees, long since bare of leaf and fruit, and pruned against winter's bite.

Kember halted the Minx at the gates and looked at his watch, relieved he'd managed to make up time after the morning's delays. He prepared to get out to ring through to the house when a labourer manoeuvred his beer-bellied bulk and wide-brimmed straw hat through a narrow doorway to one side of the main gate. Various tools hanging from a leather belt clunked as he approached.

'You Mr Kember?' the man asked.

'Detective Inspector Kember,' Kember replied. 'Here to see Mr and Mrs Hartson.' He held up his police warrant card.

'Aye. You're expected.'

The man retreated through the doorway and appeared behind the gates where he proceeded to undo two padlocks before swinging the gates wide for Kember to drive through. He ignored Kember's thank you while locking the gates again.

The Hartsons' Georgian mansion came into view, reminding him of Scotney Manor in many respects, minus two wings and an airfield. A set of stone steps led up to a portico supported by two white marble pillars protected by sandbags. A dozen upstairs windows, brown tape gummed across in X shapes against bomb blasts, suggested a large number of bedrooms and, if Scotney Manor was anything to go by, the ground floor would have a living room, drawing room, study, library and sundry other rooms. Another set of taped windows partially hidden by the ground level indicated a lower floor for the servants working in the kitchen, laundry and so on.

The large semi-circle in front of the house, where Kember brought the Minx to a halt, was reminiscent of Scotney Manor but surfaced with stone slabs rather than gravel. He guessed there'd be an ornamental pond and extensive gardens to the rear too. A man clearly too old to be in the army but possibly a survivor of the Great

War greeted Kember at the foot of the steps. He introduced himself as the Hartsons' butler and led Kember across a large hall with a central staircase into a lavishly decorated room filled with some fine pieces of furniture and exquisite ornaments. Kember shook his head at the arrogance of a family so convinced that their 'rightful' position in the world would protect them against bombing that precious objects had been left in situ. He sighed. Perhaps it was he who was arrogant to believe otherwise. A glance out of the window afforded a breathtaking view across a garden sleeping for winter, but still impressive, to gently undulating fields and trees beyond. He was shaking his head at the difference between this and his own lodgings at the Castle pub when a woman in a flowing floral dress, matching jewellery and with immaculate hair and make-up swept through the open double doors.

'Have you found her?'

Something about the woman's steady voice seemed at odds with her pained expression as she glanced over her shoulder. Without an introduction, Kember guessed this to be Joyce Hartson and gave her a small but deferential nod of his head.

'I'm afraid not,' he said.

'My brother-in-law asked me to give you a recent photograph of Evelyn,' Joyce said, holding out a piece of white card she'd been clutching to her chest.

'Thank you.' Kember took the card and turned it over, revealing a photograph of a pretty young woman holding a severe-looking doll.

'I understand you telephoned the home of your friend to ask after Miss Hartson.'

'Edison Farm.' Joyce nodded. 'They said she'd probably been delayed, but—'

Laurence Hartson, dressed in heavy twill breeches, a wine-coloured turtleneck jumper and Harris tweed riding jacket, strode into the room and stationed himself behind his wife, hands on her upper arms.

'Kempton, isn't it?' he said.

'Detective Inspector *Kember*, sir.' Kember didn't begrudge anyone their wealth, whether inherited or earned, but he did hate the presumption that this in some way equalled good breeding, intelligence and unquestionable superiority. He also deplored bad manners and rudeness. 'I'm here at the request of your brother, my chief inspector, to assist in the investigation of your daughter's disappearance.'

'Yes, yes,' Hartson said impatiently. 'Why are you here and not out looking for Evelyn?'

Kember could have returned the question but bit his tongue.

'We are doing all we can, sir, under current circumstances. Officers from Tonbridge have spoken to your daughter's friend in Paddock Wood but is there anywhere else she could have spent the night? Anyone else she might have stayed with?'

'Evelyn is not in the habit of spending the night away without prior arrangement.'

'What about her timekeeping? Has she ever made excuses for being late back or staying out beyond an agreed time?'

Hartson looked affronted. 'My daughter does not lie, Inspector.'

Kember understood the defensiveness of parents but never their reluctance to be totally honest, with themselves as well as with him.

'Does your daughter have other friends she might have spoken to? Anyone she might have confided in?'

'Only Ivy Edison at Paddock Wood,' Hartson said. 'We keep ourselves to ourselves here, Detective.'

Maybe your wife and daughter but not you, Kember thought. Laurence Hartson spent half his time in the corridors of government in London, or at his gentlemen's club. Hardly a recluse.

'What about Miss Hartson's habits and routines? Does she ever go into town on her own or for long walks, for example?'

'Evelyn goes to town with me,' said Joyce. 'She does go for walks, but only within the grounds of our estate. She has other interests.'

'Interests?' Kember said.

'Knitting and sewing, sometimes. She loves painting and learning the piano. She has a piano tutor once a week and practises very hard.'

'So, you wouldn't say she has troubles of any kind? Anything that might have been worrying her?' Kember couldn't be sure but thought he caught a flicker of Joyce Hartson's eyes. 'Perhaps it slipped her mind to inform you of a change of plan?'

Joyce Hartson looked down. 'Something terrible has happened to her.'

'What do you intend to do next?' Hartson said, rubbing his wife's arms slightly too vigorously in what Kember thought was a clumsy impression of giving comfort.

'People like your daughter do not go missing without there being at least one witness.' Lizzie's friend in Duxford flashed through his mind. 'It's a rural area but someone must have seen her leave her friend's house or arrive at Paddock Wood station for the return train journey. We'll have another word with your daughter's friend to establish timings, and make enquiries around the farm estate and at the station. It's a straightforward journey so she can't have deviated unintentionally.' He noticed another eyelid flicker from the mother. 'If she hasn't turned up here or elsewhere by this evening, we'll call in manpower from wherever we can, notify Scotland Yard and consider instigating a campaign of posters and newspaper appeals.'

Hartson visibly relaxed and Kember couldn't decide whether this signified he considered the plan satisfactory or if the mention of Scotland Yard had mollified him. After all, the commissioner and the Hartson family were old friends. In contrast, his wife remained stiff, her gaze lowered.

'Do excuse me,' Joyce said, flicking a glance at Kember before wheeling away and leaving the room.

Kember bowed his head as she left, frustrated he could not have spoken to her alone.

'I must be going too, sir,' he said, without extending a hand to Hartson, preferring to keep his hands clasped behind him as he too made to leave.

Hartson reached out and held Kember's arm as he passed. 'Find her, damn you.'

Kember looked at Hartson's hand until his grip was released, then left without another word.

◆ ◆ ◆

Lizzie looked left, right and up through the cockpit canopy to check for other aircraft encroaching on her airspace. She then glanced at the instrument panel before moving a T-handle to adjust the flaps. Throttling back further to reduce power encouraged the Anson to descend to the tarmac runway like it had hundreds of times before, its rubber tyres bumping and squealing before finding traction. Moments later, Lizzie trundled the Anson towards the old London Croydon Airport terminal building, now requisitioned as part of RAF Croydon, swung the nose to face out towards the airfield and cut the engines.

Agata opened the port-side door and stepped awkwardly onto the wing, her bulky parachute catching on the doorframe, before hopping lightly onto the tarmac. Yvonne Fournier followed her out, the arms and legs of her Sidcot flight suit and her wavy, blonde hair flicking in the cold breeze as she waited for Lizzie to hand out her parachute. Finally, Lizzie emerged without a parachute, hers being left in the pilot's seat she would reoccupy for the flight back to RAF Scotney.

'I hope Fizz and the new girls get along,' Agata said as they walked towards the entrance to the terminal building.

'So do I,' Lizzie said. 'We can't afford to have pilots grounded.' Her mind cast back a few months to when Fizz had been suspended following an argument.

'I was thinking they could put each other in hospital.' Agata shook her head, looking sad.

'I hope they're a bit more professional than that. Especially Fizz, after last time.'

'Why do you fight each other when there are Boche to kill?' Yvonne asked with a puzzled frown. 'Do you have more hatred for each other than the Nazis?'

They stopped at a sandbag-shrouded door into the terminal.

'We have people of all nationalities from around the world fighting with us,' Lizzie said. 'Five countries are represented in our ferry pool alone. Sometimes the frustration of being at war bubbles over.'

Yvonne shrugged. 'I don't know what you would do if your country was occupied.'

'In one way, snapping at each other, joking around and playing silly games relieves the tension.'

'I can think of better ways,' Yvonne said as she stepped through the door. 'In France we would make love.'

'Now there is an idea.' Agata grinned and followed her colleague.

Lizzie knew it would take twenty minutes at the most for the Anson to be refuelled and readied for her to return to Scotney. She intended to use the time productively.

All through the short flight from Scotney to Biggin Hill, Lizzie's mind had been on her friend's death in Duxford. She knew she couldn't begin to form a solid mental sketch without more information but something agitated at the back of her mind, warning her that such bizarre behaviour as removing the hands of your victim was so unusual and too specific to not be part of something larger and more sinister. If this was the type of murderer that she had been interested in throughout her time at London University's Bedford College, under pioneering female psychologist Beatrice Edgell, then there had to be more victims. The greater the number of victims, the greater the chance Lizzie had of forming an accurate profile. This fact upset her, as it always did, and she took a few deep breaths to relieve the tension building in her chest.

During stops at RAF stations Biggin Hill and Kenley to deposit the rest of their colleagues for ferrying duties, Lizzie's consternation had grown enough for her to speak to the respective RAF Police officers. Her enquiries had been purely speculative, to make her feel as though she was doing something to help, and as expected, she hadn't heard anything worth pursuing.

The Croydon RAF Police office was locked when she arrived but an aircraftsman pointed her towards the requisitioned Aerodrome Hotel standing on the north side of the terminal building and control tower. A flight of four Hawker Hurricanes from 605 Squadron stood at readiness close to the large, folding doors of the hotel and Lizzie could see a number of pilots inside. Some were reading or dozing, but they all looked so young.

Lizzie found Flight Lieutenant Lyle near the bar inside, and after formal introductions and the offer of a cup of tea, she decided the best way to broach the subject was to jump straight in.

'Although I'm here today as the ATA taxi pilot, that's our faithful Annie out there, I have another matter you may be able to help me with. Personal rather than official, at the moment.'

'Oh really?' Lyle said, extracting a cigarette from a packet of Woodbines before offering one to Lizzie, who declined.

'I had reason to be up at Duxford recently, on ATA business, and had some rather shocking news.' Lyle said nothing, looking mildly interested while lighting his cigarette. 'A friend of mine from our training days at White Waltham passed away.'

'I'm sorry to hear that,' Lyle said. blowing smoke at the ceiling.

'Thank you. I say passed away but, actually, the police believe she was murdered.'

That caught his full attention and he looked at her. 'That's terrible. Do they know who did it?'

Without revealing details about the hands, Lizzie went on to describe the circumstances of Catherine Summers' murder and asked Lyle if he had heard about anything similar. Her heart pounded, determined to escape through her ribs as she awaited his response and she could feel nervous perspiration gluing the collar of her shirt to the back of her neck. She struggled to remain focused, her mind about to take her into a full anxiety attack, until she remembered the rubber bands on her wrists.

As Lyle reached along the bar for a chunky ceramic ashtray, a few pings on the bands, snapping sharply against her flesh, brought her thoughts back to normality and she realised Lyle was speaking.

'. . . and there has been an incident, actually.'

'Oh?'

'We had a young girl working in the NAAFI canteen who went missing and turned up dead.' He tapped ash into the ashtray. 'Enright, I believe her name was. Dora.'

Lizzie could feel her chest tightening and she reached automatically to straighten the ashtray, aligning it with the edge of the polished bar to distract herself and appease her OCN. 'Where was she found, exactly?' she asked.

'In a ditch over by the trees at the edge of the field across the road from the aerodrome.'

'Did anyone see anything?'

'I don't believe so. Although the guards are extra alert during an air raid, we follow blackout rules religiously. Don't want to make it too easy for Jerry.'

'Was there anything unusual about the death?'

'You'd have to speak to the local police about any details, I'm afraid. Although regarded as a member of service personnel, the body wasn't found on RAF or War Office property. That means the civvies take precedence.'

'Surely there must be something you can tell me?' Lizzie frowned. 'Rumours, even?'

Lyle took a long, thoughtful drag on his cigarette. As he looked directly into Lizzie's eyes, she noticed a slight change in his demeanour. With a glance around at the nearest person, a pilot snoring in a padded armchair, he leant towards her, his left elbow resting on the bar.

'A local lad playing over by some trees found Dora. He ran across the field and reported it to one of my men, who's had the jitters ever since. We've been told to keep mum so as to not frighten the locals. You see, she had her throat cut and he's convinced she had no hands.'

Blood throbbed in Lizzie's temples but she tried to keep her face impassive. 'Really? That's interesting.'

'Bloody Nora.' Lyle flicked another glance at the snorer. 'Excuse my French, but that's a bit of an understatement. From his report, it looks like they were cut with a knife.' He hesitated before stubbing out the remainder of his cigarette. 'I shouldn't have told you all this. The War Office wants to keep morale up, not bring it crashing down. But in light of your friend . . .'

'Thank you,' Lizzie said.

'If you don't mind me asking,' Lyle said. 'The rubber bands. What's that all about?'

Damn. She'd thought he hadn't noticed.

'It's a habit. From schooldays.'

'Ah. Fair enough. Anyway, keep what I said under your hat or we'll both be for the high jump.'

'I can't be court-martialled, I'm a civilian,' Lizzie said.

'You can be thrown in the nick for sedition, though.'

Lizzie thought for a moment. 'In which case, I might as well be hanged for a sheep as a lamb.'

CHAPTER SIX

Kember drove along a lane through the farm estate belonging to the parents of Ivy Edison, still seething after being manhandled by Laurence Hartson. Line after line of upright poles supporting a criss-cross of horizontal strings that would have been covered in green hop bines a few months earlier now stood barren in the fields either side. A kink in the lane pointed him in a different direction and brought a substantial farmhouse into view. *Modest compared to the Hartsons' manor house but still smacking of affluence*, Kember thought. Climbing ivy covered part of the front wall, suggesting the inspiration for their daughter's name.

He stopped his Minx a stone's throw from the house, close but far enough away not to intrude on any privacy, hoping the engine noise would have alerted the occupants.

It had.

'Inspector Kember?'

Frances Edison, a tall woman, dressed for toil but looking bright and elegant all the same, strode from the front doorway and grasped his hand to shake. A different welcome to the one he'd experienced at the Hartsons'. Kember found himself hurried inside and he sat on a springy sofa opposite a sturdy girl perched on a stool. She was also dressed for farm work, with her strong-looking forearms showing.

Frances disappeared for a moment before reappearing with a tray of tea and cake from a scullery Kember could see through an open door.

'My husband, Elliot, is out in the fields I'm afraid, but this is Ivy.'

Kember gave a polite nod to Ivy as her mother sat in an armchair next to her daughter. After accepting a cup of tea but declining a slab of cake big enough to sink a battleship, Kember cleared his throat.

'There's no easy way to say this, Mrs Edison, but Miss Evelyn Hartson failed to return home yesterday morning and remains missing.'

'Oh!' Frances covered a gasp with her hand. 'Good grief.'

Ivy glanced at Kember but looked away just as quickly.

'Do you know where Evelyn may have gone?' Kember said, watching the young woman.

'I'm afraid I don't,' Frances said.

'Ivy?' Kember said.

'No, sir,' Ivy said, still refusing to hold his gaze.

Kember knew people took shocks in different ways, but he thought her mild response appeared out of keeping with the gravity of his news.

'I understand Mrs Hartson telephoned you yesterday. I'd—'

'No, Inspector,' Frances interrupted. 'I haven't spoken to Joyce for weeks.'

'I'm sorry?' Kember stared at Frances.

'Joyce Hartson and I last spoke about three weeks ago when we bumped into each other in Tunbridge Wells. She had Evelyn with her and I had Ivy. We had some tea and a little chat but I haven't seen either of them since.'

'That's curious because I've just come from seeing Mr and Mrs Hartson, and they were definitely under the impression that their daughter, Evelyn, had stayed here Thursday night.'

'Here?' Frances looked puzzled. 'Why would they say that?'

'Probably because that's what Miss Hartson told them.' Kember noticed Ivy drop her gaze to the floor but saw no deception in the face of Frances. 'Mrs Hartson was also adamant that she telephoned you yesterday.'

'That was me,' Ivy said. 'I spoke to Mrs Hartson when she rang. I said not to worry and that Evie had probably been delayed on the train or stopped off to see another friend on the way home.'

'You didn't tell me,' Frances said, looking aghast.

'Have you seen or spoken to her recently?' Kember asked.

'Not recently,' Ivy said. 'She was here a lot in the summer though. Stayed over.'

'What did you do when she visited?'

'Played with the animals: we have two dogs, a goat and chickens. We went for walks and helped in the fields.'

'I bet you talked a lot.'

'Of course, they did,' Frances said. 'They're young girls.'

Kember kept his eyes on Ivy. 'What did you talk about?'

'All sorts. Work, dancing, the war.' She glanced at him and blushed. 'Husbands.'

Kember glimpsed disquiet pass across Frances's face as she repeated her daughter's last word. He paused, seeing Ivy struggling to avoid looking at them both. When Ivy offered no explanation, Kember said, 'Potential future husbands, as in local lads? Maybe those you both liked?'

Ivy looked towards the scullery as if eyeing an escape route.

'Inspector,' Frances interrupted, clearly a little shaken. 'I hope you're not suggesting—'

'I'm not suggesting anything, Mrs Edison. If you say you haven't spoken to Mrs Hartson or seen Evelyn for a while, I believe you.' Kember looked back at Ivy. 'Ivy, I want you to think back to when you last saw Evelyn. Did she talk about anyone in particular that she liked?'

'I don't think so,' Ivy muttered, so softly that Kember strained to hear.

'Is there anywhere you two would frequent, perhaps? Maybe a tea shop in Paddock Wood or a favourite picnic spot?'

Ivy shook her head. 'No. We went all over.'

'Did you notice Evelyn taking a particular interest in anyone you spoke to on your rambles?'

Ivy shook her head again.

'What are you driving at, Inspector?' Frances said.

Kember sighed, still keeping his eyes on Ivy. 'I'm not accusing you or Evelyn of any mischief or impropriety. I'm merely trying to establish whether either of you came into contact with someone who may have taken an interest in you, whether wanted or not.' Kember paused. 'Ivy?'

'Not that I remember,' Ivy said.

'Do either of you know a man called Kenneth Jarvis?' he asked, keeping his expression impassive.

'If he's a hired labourer, my husband deals with that,' Frances said, without a flicker.

The corners of Ivy's mouth turned down and she shook her head.

If guilt could ever be said to be written on someone's face, Kember saw it there in block capitals on Ivy Edison's. But guilty of what?

'I think that will do for now, Mrs Edison,' he said as he stood. 'It seems clear that nothing untoward happened over the summer to be alarmed about. At least that clears up one line of inquiry.' He could lie with the best of them.

Kember allowed Frances to escort him to the front door.

'I may need to speak to your husband,' he said. 'If you hear from Evelyn, you will let me know?'

'Of course, Inspector, but please reciprocate. I must telephone poor Joyce.'

Kember left her at the porch, got into his Minx and glanced towards the house. If there was a simple explanation, part of that lay behind the closing front door.

◆ ◆ ◆

'This is rather odd behaviour for a lady,' Lyle called, standing by the open door of his RAF Police Austin parked at the side of the road.

Lizzie ignored him as she tried to keep her balance while slithering across a stretch of waterlogged grass on a field to the east of the aerodrome. It hadn't taken her long to persuade Lyle to take her to see the site where the young NAAFI woman had been found but he'd refused to get his boots muddy. She wasn't quite sure what she'd find or whether her skills would help reveal anything but she knew it was important to at least take a look.

It took her a few moments to cross the windswept, featureless field and reach the spot along a line of trees he'd pointed out. The narrow, shallow ditch just in front of her didn't look like much; more of a meandering depression where rainwater naturally drained from the field. With frequent patrols everywhere, especially around military bases, a murderer might have mistaken it as the perfect place for a dead body to lie undiscovered. But Lizzie knew, thinking of the boy who had discovered her, that this was a playground for adventure and make-believe.

Lizzie took a deep lungful of chilly air and relaxed her eyes as she exhaled, imagining the blackout engulfing the air station and nearby town of Croydon. Ten miles to the north, searchlight beams and bright bursts of exploding anti-aircraft shells signalled the return of the Luftwaffe to the East End of London yet again. Her mind adopting his way of thinking, Lizzie imagined persuading the young woman to go for a secluded walk; a young couple slipping away in the cold, dark night for a romantic liaison, just two shadows among many. No one would raise so much as an eyebrow.

Lizzie's eyes suddenly refocused and she lost the moment. Without information about how Dora Enright had died, her mind had raced forward and showed her the body lying in the ditch, skipping over the important part; the how and the why. She looked down at the grass, weeds and mud at her feet. Any useful marks would long since have been trampled by police from the town and aerodrome. Lyle had told her the woman had been found lying on her back in mud and water but a search of the area had revealed no discernible evidence.

Lizzie experienced the familiar stab of frustration at a dead end and turned back towards where Lyle leant against the car. She could take this no further without speaking to the local pathologist about his findings at the crime scene, but he'd never divulge information to her.

◆ ◆ ◆

Kember arrived back in Scotney village a few minutes after eleven to find Sergeant Wright poring over his notes in the front office. He slumped down onto the visitor's chair.

'How'd it go with the upper crust then, sir?' Wright asked.

Kember rubbed his eyes. 'As well as could be expected.' Wright gave a knowing nod as Kember continued. 'Both families were difficult in their own ways and clearly upset that Evelyn is missing, but I got the impression Joyce Hartson and Ivy Edison were less than forthcoming.'

'Families, eh?' Wright said.

Kember gave him a crooked smile. 'How was your morning?'

'Well, you'll never guess where Ken Jarvis worked over at Paddock Wood.' Kember raised a questioning eyebrow. 'Edison Farm, no less.'

Kember sat up, more alert. 'Mrs Edison didn't say anything when I mentioned his name.'

'No reason she should. The farm has many workers so it's probable she doesn't know him.'

'She did say her husband dealt with the hiring and firing.' Kember saw Wright hesitate. 'Sergeant?' he prompted.

'I thought I'd take the Wolseley for a run out to Edison Farm, after taking Derek Chapman home, but I didn't see the need to worry you about it, sir. In any case, I didn't get to meet Mrs Edison as there was no need. I came across a labourer well before I got to the house and he walked me over to a wooden hut where the farm manager was brewing up a pot of tea. He said Ken, they knew him as Kenny, had been a good worker, never late, never missed a day's work. In fact, he'd worked his way up to be in charge of a whole gang of hoppers who came down from London each year. He'd been managing the same families for a few years with never a cross word nor any reason to dock his pay.'

Kember rubbed his nose in thought. 'You said, had been?'

'Ken had a bit of a run-in with an itinerant worker, an agricultural labourer, over a job in the summer. The labourer came from outside the county and Ken knew times were hard so he persuaded the manager to take him on. The man was a wastrel, always asking for subs on his wages or scrounging food and cigarettes. His work was poor too, so Ken sacked him. Things started to go missing, like tools and one of the chickens by the house. Obviously, the work of the sacked man. The manager blamed Ken for getting him to take the labourer on and wanted him to sort out the problem.'

'What did he mean by that?'

'He wouldn't say. He just said things improved so he thought Ken must have solved it.'

'Has Ken been missed?'

'No, sir. The season's been over for a while. He divided his time between Edison Farm, where he managed the tending of the early hop bines then supervised the hoppers, and Glassen Farm, where he helped organise cropping, lambing, harvesting and such like. He did light repair work too, to fences and so on.'

'A hard worker, it seems.'

'And a good husband. The manager said he never saw Kenny so much as flirt with any of the women hoppers, even though their menfolk tended to stay in London because of their jobs.'

Kember let out a tired sigh.

'Anything else?'

'Aye. When I returned, I went straight back to Glassen Farm to speak to Derek Chapman.' Wright consulted his notebook. 'They called him Kenny too, but Chapman gave me a different story. He's been in dispute with Ken since he came back from hopping at Paddock Wood. The quality of his work went downhill and he kept sloping off early to meet with some floozy, as Chapman called her.'

'Did he say who the floozy was?'

'He didn't know but he thought she must be local because sometimes he'd go missing for an hour in the afternoon. Getting his end away, Chapman believed. Although his work was getting shoddy, they're short of manpower because of the war and they've missed him the last couple of days. He hadn't finished mending one of the sheep pens.'

While Wright went to make tea, Kember mulled things over. In his experience, men and women wanting to cover up illicit affairs became adept at playing their roles as faithful spouses and diligent workers, wanting to keep things as smooth and normal as possible. But it was notoriously difficult to sustain a double life, whatever class you came from. In fact, his own wife had soon tired of the subterfuge until she no longer bothered to conceal her affairs. Kenneth Jarvis had impressed the manager at Edison Farm with his sustained good work during hopping, but upset Derek Chapman with recent shoddy work and by skiving off to see a woman.

Kember knew young people tended to keep secrets from their families, to avoid confrontation with disapproving parents or make humdrum lives more interesting. The smallest defiant act became a bigger rebellion the higher up the class ladder you looked. Would a young woman such as Evelyn Hartson have considered a middle-aged man such as Kenneth Jarvis a suitable rebellion? Kember conceded love knew no bounds but the difference in ages and social backgrounds made it seem less likely that the two missing persons had eloped. Evelyn visited the Edison home frequently in the summer but had not done so for a few weeks. Chapman thought the 'floozy' to be local because of the timings and frequency of Kenneth Jarvis's absences. If that ruled out Jarvis as a potential suitor for Evelyn, who was the floozy, who had Evelyn gone to meet, and where the devil had everyone disappeared to?

When Wright came back with the tea, Kember said, 'Although I don't believe Evelyn and Jarvis were seeing each other we can't rule out elopement. However . . .'

'Are you thinking they've both come to harm?' Wright said.

'Possibly, either separately or together, and if their families do know more than they're saying I suspect it's because they don't want to be blamed for anything. It sounds like Jarvis began conducting an affair quite recently, maybe around October, so his wife might not know, or she might suspect but be lying to herself. If something has happened to Jarvis, five suspects present themselves: his wife, if she knew about the affair; the floozy, if perhaps Jarvis was going to end their affair; the husband of the floozy, if he had somehow discovered his wife playing away; the labourer he had angered by sacking him; and Derek Chapman.'

'Are you sure, sir? That's quite a list.' Wright took a slurp of his tea.

'That's why I need to go to Glassen Farm, to ask Chapman when exactly Jarvis skived off and speak to any workers I can find to see if anyone knows anything about the woman he was supposedly seeing. I think I may have to endure the unpleasant experience of asking Chief Inspector Hartson a few questions about his brother, sister-in-law and niece, too. Meanwhile, you should telephone the stationmasters at Tonbridge and Paddock Wood again.'

Both heads turned towards a polite knock and Wright opened the office door. An elderly gentleman with a thin face and grey hair under a flat cap, wearing a waxed jacket and carrying a leather binoculars case on a strap around his neck, stood hesitantly as though uncertain whether he had the right department at the county council offices. Two other elderly gentlemen in similar attire with worried expressions stood behind their friend.

'Can we help you?' Wright said.

'Hello, yes. We're from the Scotney and District Ornithology Club. We've been up at the pastures and woodland north-east of the village.'

'I thought everything but the robin had migrated by now,' Kember said.

The man gave him an indulgent smile. 'There are a number of finches, tits and thrushes that also prefer our shores in winter, Inspector.' His expression became solemn. 'We'd been out since early this morning and thought it time we came back for a spot of lunch.'

Kember saw Wright shoot him a glance that said *we've got a right one here.*

'You'll be needing the pub, then, not a police station.' Wright sniffed.

'No – no, you misunderstand. We took the eastern bank of the River Glassen up to the woods, crossed the footbridge and looped round, returning via the old shepherd's hut to Manor Lane.' The man took off his cap as if in a mark of respect. 'That's where we found the body, you see, and knew we should report it straight away.' The man took a half-step forward. 'The body of a young girl.'

CHAPTER SEVEN

'Lost Child, this is Cuckoo. Are you receiving me?'

Flying at two thousand feet, the countryside below was laid out like a large map, with each road, railway and village clearly discernible. Rivers and lakes shone in the wintery sun. Every field, regardless of size or shape, and enclosed by hedgerows on each side, looked like the knitted square of a giant patchwork bedspread. With five minutes' flying before her final approach to land, Lizzie could see the grass expanse of RAF Scotney in the middle distance. Even so, the urgent tone of the call from the Scotney control tower troubled her.

'Cuckoo, this is Lost Child,' she responded.

'Lost Child. Message from Sapper.' Lizzie stiffened. Sapper was the call-sign for Biggin Hill and she'd passed there some time ago. 'Four bandits, angels one-zero, vector two-seven-zero, range ten miles. Gannic reports tally-ho. Two bandits, angels three, vector three-five-five, range two-zero miles. Pancake, pancake, over.'

Lizzie felt her breath quicken.

'Roger, wilco. Pancake, pancake.'

Lizzie strained her eyes and could just discern vapour trails ten thousand feet above RAF Scotney where 92 Squadron from Biggin Hill, call-sign *Gannic*, had engaged the four German aircraft.

That left two more coming from the other direction at just three thousand feet which explained the urgent *pancake* order, to land immediately.

As Lizzie turned the controls to bring the Anson around, lining up for the RAF Scotney runway, she saw the flaming wreck of an aircraft plunging to earth, billowing smoke trailing behind. *That's bound to attract the other two*, she thought. The familiar, tinny voice squawking through her headphones made her jump.

'Lost Child this is Cuckoo. Pancake, for God's sake!'

The alarm in the voice made her pulse race. The two bandits must be close. Against all the rules, she put the Anson into a dive rather than follow a shallow glide-path landing. Wheels down, flaps lowered, Lizzie pulled back on the controls at the last minute, almost dropping the Anson onto the grass. The aircraft bounced high, threatening to tip sideways, then settled. Lizzie braked and steered for the protection of the blast pen. All around the airfield, anti-aircraft guns opened fire. From the pom-pom-pom of the Bofors guns, to the rattle of heavy machine guns, Lizzie found the cacophony both alarming and comforting.

A pair of Messerschmitt 109 fighters screamed overhead barely two hundred feet from the ground, three Spitfires from 92 Squadron in pursuit. The German cannon fire kicked up sprays of earth and blasted chunks from the dispersal hut. A stream of shell casings from spent ammunition fell across the Anson like hailstones. Lizzie's heart thumped but she remained outwardly calm and in control. She cut the engines and rolled the Anson to a halt inside its pen.

Silence.

As the Spitfires continued their pursuit of the unwanted visitors into the distance, the Scotney guns fell silent and personnel began emerging from wherever they had taken cover. Lizzie realised her hands had a slight tremble and she said a silent prayer for her narrow escape. Ground crew scuttled towards her and spun the Anson 180 degrees. With chocks applied to wheels, men began checking the airframe and a fuel bowser appeared.

Normal service resumed.

Lizzie decided to walk across to the manor house but turned at the sound of a call. She recognised the form of Martin Onslow striding towards her from the direction of the hangar where the pantomime would be performed and waited for him to catch up.

'Miss Hayes, isn't it?' Onslow said, with a grin.

'Mr Onslow,' Lizzie greeted.

'You flew me in from Rochester yesterday.'

'I did.' She didn't think much of him, far too brash and cocky, but she smiled anyway.

'That was a superb bit of flying, if I may say so.'

'Thank you,' Lizzie said, pretty sure he wouldn't know good flying from bad even if it came with a glowing review in *The Stage* newspaper and an Oscar nomination. 'Just obeying orders from the tower.'

'I'm not sure the tower could have instructed you how to do that. It looked like instinctive flying to me.'

Lizzie suppressed a laugh. His accent held some allure but the smarmy attempt at charm made her cringe inside.

'I was about to get a cup of tea at the house,' Onslow said. 'Can I tempt you?'

Her smile almost faltered but she managed to keep it in place. 'I'm parched, actually.'

In truth, Lizzie was desperate for a hot drink and in need of rejuvenation after her morning's flying. She had no desire for company, male or female, but could see no immediate way to slake her thirst without either accepting Onslow's invitation or offending him. He performed a sweeping bow and gestured towards the manor house. She took the hint to begin walking across the grass but he suddenly took her arm and linked it with his. Too surprised to pull away, Lizzie had to do a little skip to get in step and was annoyed at herself for allowing a man to guide her when she was perfectly capable of walking unaided.

Their entrance into the lounge together did not go unnoticed by the steward but Lizzie's blazing look soon wiped the soppy grin from his face. Her mood was not improved by being forced to sit in the lounge, still in her Sidcot flying suit, hot, sweaty, smelling faintly of engines, and her hair a bird's-nest mess from the flying helmet. Sitting with the other women all looking like this after a hard day's ferrying was one thing, being bought tea while he sat there with neatly trimmed hair, immaculate shirt and tie, and a self-satisfied Clark Gable smile, was another. Onslow clicked his fingers at the steward and ordered for them both, without any consideration for what she might like. This threatened to tip her over the edge but she needed that drink and thought spending twenty minutes in his company was just about achievable.

'How long have you been flying?' Onslow smoothed his hair back with his hands and flashed another Hollywood smile. 'You must have had a good teacher.'

'My father taught me a few years ago.' Lizzie stared out of the window rather than meet his piercing stare. She knew he was working towards a chat-up and didn't have the energy to meet it head on, deciding instead to let it wash over her.

'He did an excellent job. The ATA are lucky to have you.'

She smiled politely and wondered whether staying silent would put him off. Unfortunately, the smile seemed only to encourage him. He sat forward, his hand resting on the tablecloth, poised to touch her own should she leave it there.

'Your mother must have been a very beautiful woman.'

Lizzie's smile waned. Perhaps twenty minutes would be too long to endure after all. She sat back, withdrawing her hand as his moved to touch her fingers.

'Will you be coming to the show?'

The steward returned with their tea, a small jug of milk, and a bowl containing about half a teaspoon of rationed sugar each. The gradual tightness forming in Lizzie's chest eased when she saw he'd already poured the tea into two cups. Onslow frowned but she glanced up and saw the steward wink. She knew that by pouring the tea and not leaving a pot, the steward was trying to help her by shortening the time she might be obliged to spend in Onslow's company without bruising his ego. If she was happy, they could always ask for a top-up. Although appreciative of a gesture most would find gallant, she still found the implication that she needed a man to rescue her from another, while in public in broad daylight, mildly insulting.

The unexpected absence of a teapot – Onslow was looking over his shoulder at the retreating steward – gave her the opportunity to change the subject without him noticing.

'I understand the rest of your theatre company arrived three days ago,' Lizzie said. 'Didn't you want to come with them?'

Onslow looked back at her with a half-smile. 'And spend several hours in the back of a draughty lorry with that rabble?' Onslow shook his head. 'I spend enough time with them as it is.'

'You never travel together?' Lizzie gritted her teeth as Onslow poured milk into her cup without asking.

He laughed. 'Not if I can help it. I prefer to fly in and out.'

'What do you do after the others move on?'

'I stay behind after the last show and wait until the company are settled before I waltz in to direct them once again in the subtle art of performing.'

'I bet they don't take kindly to that.'

Onslow shrugged. 'Those who wish to make a career out of being on the stage, or the radio for that matter, take notice of people like me who have greater experience. If they wish to learn, I teach.' His eyes narrowed suggestively and she avoided his gaze, pretending to not notice. 'If they think they know it all, I let them sink or swim. Mostly they sink.'

'That's a harsh outlook.' Lizzie took a sip of hot tea and almost grimaced at the amount of milk.

'Being a director of a troupe is a bit like being the group captain in charge of this airfield. Decisions have to be made for the good of all.'

'You sound like you don't think much of your colleagues.'

'It's not a case of liking them. In the theatre, especially a touring group like an ENSA company, you only need to have a passing tolerance for those around you. If you don't like a town or the building you're playing in, you'll be gone in the morning. If you don't like the people who come to see your show, or they don't like you, there's always the next performance with a more discerning audience. If you don't like the second-rate juggler that you're sharing a dressing room with, chances are you'll only be together for a short tour anyway. Whatever the problem, there's always next time. In the meantime, you can always draw on your memories of outstanding performances by skilled fellow performers, appreciative audiences who laugh at your every utterance, and nights spent in comfortable digs after a successful show.'

Lizzie thought the philosophical response sounded at odds with his behaviour. If Onslow was so resigned to the life of a travelling entertainer, why did he avoid his colleagues by hanging back each time?

'What do you do while you're waiting for the others to get to the next stop?' she asked. 'I don't suppose you get to see the sights when you visit a town, and there's nothing to see around here.'

Lizzie reached for the sugar to improve the milky tea and found his hand there, ready to grasp her own.

'On the contrary,' Onslow said, with a smile. 'I have all the sights I could wish for right in front of me.'

Lizzie pulled her hand away and groaned inwardly, feeling her shoulders sag as another ounce of energy leeched away. She supposed men found her attractive enough, and someone had to make the first move, but even the most genuine approaches could be obvious, unsubtle and downright clumsy. Sometimes all a girl wanted really was just a cup of tea.

'Ah, there you are, Lizzie. I've been looking for you.'

Lizzie looked up to see Geraldine standing over them.

'Sorry ma'am.' She stood. 'I've not long returned and Mr Onslow offered to buy me some tea.'

Geraldine looked at Onslow and smiled sweetly. 'How thoughtful, but I must spirit Miss Hayes away. Duty calls, I'm afraid.'

Onslow rose from his chair. 'Of course.'

Still thirsty, Lizzie picked up her cup and drained it down to the tea dust, trying not to shudder at the milky contents.

'Thank you for the tea, Mr Onslow. Good luck with the pantomime.'

Onslow looked disappointed but gave them a half-bow, half-nod as they left.

'You looked as though you needed saving,' Geraldine said, as they emerged from the lounge into the hall.

'I had him under control,' Lizzie replied, feeling the heat rise in her cheeks.

'It didn't look like that to me. He's quite the charmer.'

The steward's assumption that she might need rescuing was irritating enough, but her flight captain, a woman, coming to the same conclusion about her ability to fend off unwanted advances was doubly annoying. They entered the empty ATA ops room where Geraldine stopped in front of the main desk, motioning for Lizzie to sit. An angry frown had replaced the sweet smile deployed on Onslow and Lizzie's own anger subsided as she wondered what had caused such a sudden change of expression.

'A message has been relayed to me from DI Kember asking for my permission to allow him to employ you again, citing your unique skills as justification.'

'I'm sure I could be a great help,' Lizzie said, as calmly as she could manage, although she felt energised as though electricity had suddenly coursed through her body.

'I'm sure you could,' Geraldine said with a cool edge to her voice. 'But your participation last time caused no end of problems with Group Captain Dallington and Wing Commander Matfield.'

'The situation would be different this time,' Lizzie said, not knowing how that could possibly be the case but hoping Geraldine would see it that way. She held her gaze as Geraldine studied her through narrowed eyes, convinced the thumping of her heart could be heard beyond her chest.

Geraldine sighed.

'I am torn. We both know how difficult the senior officers can be on a good day, and the threat of our withdrawal, redeployment or even disbandment still hangs over our heads. However, I cannot deny that your input brought the previous situation to a head and undoubtedly saved lives. It would be wrong of me to refuse a Scotland Yard detective inspector access to your skills and talents. So, somewhat reluctantly, I find myself unable to refuse you permission to assist the police again in your capacity as an experienced . . .'

'Criminal psychologist, ma'am,' Lizzie obliged, her mind already racing.

'Yes, that. DI Kember has two investigations running that may be linked; one a possible kidnap, the other a murder case. I don't know how much of your time he expects me to grant but let me make this clear: nothing you do for him will impinge on the work you do for me. Understood?'

'Yes, ma'am.'

'All right. Carry on.'

Lizzie felt the tone of the discussion warranted a formal ending so she stood and saluted before stepping towards the door.

'Oh, Lizzie?'

Lizzie paused and turned.

'I hope it goes without saying, the least the group captain and wing commander hear of this, the better.' Geraldine raised her eyebrows questioningly.

Lizzie nodded. 'Understood, ma'am.'

CHAPTER EIGHT

Dr Headley, formerly a surgeon at St Bart's Hospital in London but now a Home Office-approved pathologist at Pembury Hospital, half-crouched in a drainage ditch at the edge of a field. He let the broken remnants of a cigarette end drop into a paper evidence bag, handed it to a police constable and pocketed his medical tweezers. Dressed in wellington boots and winter coat, knees cracking as he straightened up, Headley narrowly avoided slipping over into the twelve inches of cold, muddy water at the bottom.

'This cold weather doesn't agree with me, Kember.' Headley grimaced and stretched out a hand for assistance. 'As I recall, it wasn't so long ago we met over the body of a dead woman as it tipped down with rain.'

'What can I say?' Kember said, pulling the doctor from the ditch. 'I have no more control over death or the weather than I do my own assignments.'

'Ha, me neither, more's the pity.' Headley stamped mud, water and weeds from his boots. 'We've had a thousand patients crammed into Pembury Hospital since our boys made it home from Dunkirk, and I can't move for all the medical staff they evacuated from Guy's. Do you know, they put the poor nurses in bell-tents for months while they built dozens of wooden huts? They've ended up living in the old workhouse building.'

'Well, there is a war on.' Kember looked up as a flight of three Spitfires buzzed overhead. 'Still looking for strays, I see.'

Headley scowled. 'Bloody nuisance, if you ask me.' He sat on a large box containing instruments and items used for forensic recovery, and began taking off his boots. 'I've finished what I can here.'

Kember looked down at the body of the young woman found by the birdwatchers and his heart sank a little lower at the futility of life and permanence of death. In London before the war, he'd seen the picture of the drowning Ophelia painted by the pre-Raphaelite, John Everett Millais. No such romanticism here, just pale skin, dirty, sodden clothing, a cut throat, and both her hands missing.

'Why are people still killing their own in a time of war?' he said, to himself more than anyone else.

Headley snorted. 'Because man is inherently wicked.'

Kember found he couldn't disagree. 'Any indication of how and when she died?'

'I was waiting for that. I'm not a clairvoyant, Kember.' Headley reached for his shoes. 'There are bruises around her lips and cheeks that look like finger marks. Suggests someone gripped her very hard, but given all the blood, I think it unlikely that suffocation or strangulation was the cause of death. All I can say, pure speculation at this point, is she appears to have died from the cut to her throat. I'll have to check for signs of drowning, water in the trachea and lungs and so forth.'

Kember's mind flashed back five months and his heart thumped harder. 'Has she been . . . ?'

Headley looked up from tying his shoelaces and peered at him through thick, round spectacles. 'I know what you're thinking: do we have a Scotney Ripper copycat?' He shook his head. 'Her hands have been removed with a sharp implement, but apart from that, this appears completely different. Her clothes and the rest of her body haven't been touched as far as I can tell. I'd say she was put in the ditch for concealment, not display.' He tied the last lace and stood up. 'I'll check for semen and all the rest. Standard procedure. Virtually impossible to give you a time of death though, I'm afraid. Rigor mortis is complete but it's been near freezing lately and the ditch is full of icy water. I'd estimate she's been in there for a good few hours at least, certainly overnight, but probably not much more than a day.' He blew his nose into a handkerchief with a loud snort. 'I can't assess lividity while she's floating in muck, but from the amount of blood on the bank, I'd hazard a guess she was attacked right here before being tipped in. Usual caveat: quote me and I'll deny everything.' Headley put his tweezers in the box. 'No doubt you had a quick rummage around before I got here?'

'The ground has been hard from the start of the cold weather,' Kember said, as he walked with Headley towards the doctor's car. 'All the footprints we've found are probably days old and not the murderer's. Couldn't see any signs of a struggle in the surroundings. No telling whether she was with someone she knew, taken by surprise, or lured to her death.'

'She's dressed in a smock but that's a common garment for farm workers and all sorts around here,' Headley said.

Kember nodded. 'I noticed that, and we had a report today of a missing person. A shepherdess. Did you notice anything else that might help? I know you like discovering these little details.' He saw Headley's lips twitch as if the doctor had been waiting for a dramatic finale.

'There is one curious anomaly you'll be interested in,' Headley said. 'She had the remains of a cigarette crushed inside her mouth. The advertising mark was for the Craven A brand.' He got into his car, closed the door and wound down the window. 'I'll let you know all the usual bits and bobs later on but, in the meantime, you're the detective. Cheaper than sending for the real Scotland Yard, no doubt.'

◆ ◆ ◆

Lizzie turned her black Norton motorbike into the field, through the gap left as a constable opened a five-bar gate, and stopped next to an old, battered Wolseley with the word 'Police' on a sign fixed to its front grille. She slipped off her black gauntlets and helmet and fluffed up her flattened, brown hair. Sergeant Wright had his back to her as she walked over to where Kember stood.

'Can we move young Maisie yet, sir? It's perishing cold out here.' Wright cupped his hands and blew warm air into them for emphasis.

'But I've only just got here.'

Wright spun around. 'We—'

Lizzie waved away his stuttering explanation. Her smile faded upon seeing Kember's solemn expression.

'I got your message,' Lizzie said. 'What's so urgent?' She swept an arm to indicate the assembled police presence. 'What's all this?'

'They sent more men over from Tonbridge but we've only got them for a couple of hours. You've not long missed Dr Headley.'

'Why, what's happened?'

Lizzie noted Kember's look reflected in every other face present and felt the tightening in her chest that usually signalled an oncoming anxiety attack. This time it came with a sense of foreboding and sadness, the trinity she recognised as the manifestation of empathic loss. Something very bad had happened here. No one was meeting the gaze of another and even Wright looked as if he'd rather be anywhere else at that moment, and not because of the cold. She followed as Kember beckoned and they moved a few yards further along the hedge.

Lizzie's thoughts flashed momentarily to her friend in Duxford as Kember stopped by where the woman's body still lay in the waterlogged ditch, and her eyes were drawn to the stumps of her arms. She'd seen dead bodies before, in a far worse condition, but it never ceased to cause her dismay at best and revulsion at worst. She turned away for a moment, thinking about the dead woman in Croydon, summoning her professionalism before turning back having regained full control over her body and mind, for now. She rattled off a list of questions, avoiding the obvious as she studied the scene. Kember responded, giving her almost everything he and Headley had discovered in this corner of frozen field.

'Sergeant Wright is certain she's a local shepherdess called Maisie Chapman,' Kember said. 'The killer's taken the hands with him.'

Lizzie looked at him sharply. 'You haven't found them?'

'I'm afraid not. That's two bodies now with the hands missing and I'd be none the wiser if the other hadn't been your friend.'

Lizzie saw compassion for her loss in Kember's eyes but assumptions about how she might be feeling, whether right or wrong, often made her determined to show the opposite. To be more resolute, somehow.

'Two women killed in the open and mutilated in the same way,' Kember said. 'How many bodies does it take to be a serial murderer?'

'More than two.' She looked at the body.

Kember scratched the end of his nose in thought. 'I realise there's quite a distance between the two deaths but it seems too unusual, too much of a coincidence for there to be no connection.' She looked up when he hesitated. 'I thought you'd be interested, given your area of expertise.'

'I didn't say I wasn't interested,' Lizzie said, aware it had come out harsher and quicker than she'd intended. 'I thought Chief

Inspector Hartson considered me *persona non grata* after last time. You're taking a risk involving me.'

'I'd better not tell him then,' Kember said with the hint of a smile.

'Sir.' A young constable picked his way towards them from further along the ditch. He held a long, thin object at arm's length as it dripped water. 'We found this.' The constable handed Kember a wooden staff with an insert of curved ram's horn at one end.

'A shepherd's crook. Thank you, Constable.' He turned it over, studying its full length. 'It's wet from being in the ditch but it's not sodden. It can't have been there long. It's in good condition, too. Worn at the point but not broken and no sign of rotting. My guess is it's the crook Maisie Chapman was using before she was killed.'

'Fits with her clothing and the sheep droppings around here,' Lizzie observed. 'Could it be the murder weapon?'

'We'll have to wait for Dr Headley's post-mortem report before we can say how she died. There is bruising around her mouth but he seemed to think the cut to her throat killed her.'

Kember called Sergeant Wright to secure a waxed paper bag over the curved end of the crook. 'The body can be moved now, Sergeant. Make sure this crook stays with it and gets to Dr Headley right away.'

'Yes, sir,' Wright said. 'By the way, that old shepherd's hut over yonder you wanted checking?'

Lizzie followed Kember's gaze and could just see the roof of a low building somewhere beyond the next field.

'One of the lads from Tonbridge says it's locked up,' Wright continued. 'I'm not surprised, old man Glassen bought these fields from the manor after the Great War. The place hasn't been used since and I expect the roof leaks like a sieve.' He waved to an ambulance just arriving. 'Excuse me, sir.' He waved again and walked over to where the crew were trying to reverse their vehicle through the gate.

Lizzie's attention was already back on the woman in the ditch. 'Did you find anything else unusual?'

'As it happens, there is one other thing,' Kember said to Lizzie but looking at the woman in the ditch. 'She had a cigarette crammed inside her mouth. Craven A.'

Lizzie's heart gave another thump, her mind leaping to conclusions. 'You don't think it could be the Ripper again?'

Kember looked at her sharply. 'Of course not. But you're the second person to ask me that.' He shrugged. 'You needed to know everything we found, that's all.'

Lizzie couldn't tell whether Kember was lying or not and that irked her. She could usually read expressions and body language but maybe he was getting used to her and becoming guarded. She heard his voice and realised she'd been staring at him.

'Can you glean anything from this?' he said, again.

Lizzie looked at Kember for a few seconds, thinking how much more information was present here than at Croydon, before looking down at the dead woman. She imagined her coaxing a flock of wayward sheep along the path across the field. The gate gave access to the field from the road and she imagined the killer standing nearby, cigarette in hand, maybe a car parked just out of sight. The land seemed deserted and quiet except for the bleating of sheep as they approached. No other soul around. No witnesses but the animals.

Lizzie performed a slow 360-degree turn, taking in the location and landscape, near and far, and imagined the shepherdess approaching.

What drove him to kill her? Lust? Sexual jealousy? No. He overpowered her easily enough and could have raped her but didn't. Anger at some slight, rebuff or some wrong, either real or imagined?

No. She wasn't beaten, either in hot, savage rage or cold, calculated revenge. Avarice then? But she was a lowly shepherdess. What could she possibly have that he wanted?

With the real world around her disappearing further into an enveloping, red haze, Lizzie looked again at the woman in the ditch and imagined a shadowy figure standing beside her. 'You killed her,' she said, softly. 'Quietly and efficiently, quickly and powerfully, by grabbing her mouth to stifle any cry.' She nodded. 'Crushing the cigarette in the process.'

Lizzie imagined herself holding the hands of the shepherdess standing in front of her, turning her hands over and back, showing her wrists, looking at the smooth skin. 'She has slender arms so her hands must also be slender, and beautiful. They aren't trophies to be prized, kept and looked at from time to time, are they? No, the hands are not fortuitous trophies from a vicious kill, like others might take.' She felt the hands being tugged away but held on. 'You wanted them for a reason, a higher purpose, but what? Why not take something else, like her hair? What could you possibly want with the hands of a shepherdess?'

'Sir?'

The voice of Sergeant Wright brought Lizzie's mind back to the real world and she saw a pained expression on Kember's face.

'You can let go now, Lizzie,' he said, softly.

She looked down and realised she had hold of Kember's wrists, her fingernails digging into the flesh. She let go, dropped her hands to her sides and took a deep breath, feeling an exertion headache creeping across behind her eyes.

'Sir,' Wright said again. 'The ambulance crew are ready to recover the body.'

Kember nodded and said, 'Carry on, Sergeant,' guiding Lizzie in the direction of her motorbike.

'Sorry,' she said, remembering the previous case. 'I seem to be making a habit of trying to hurt you.'

'I'll live.' Kember gave her a comforting smile. 'You were there again, weren't you? In the land of murderers?'

She nodded.

'This doesn't fit any pattern I worked on in Oxford but I think you're right to be concerned about the similarities. I just can't make sense of it at the moment. Catherine and this woman are – were – both beautiful but I don't see how they can be connected in any direct way. Then again, it would be unique for two killers to be after the same thing as unusual as hands. The manner of their deaths tells me they weren't afraid. My friend seems to have gone willingly into the countryside and I think the sheep would've alerted the shepherdess to anyone approaching her from behind. She must have let him get close enough from the front to grab her face. The murderer didn't kill in a frenzy or wilfully disfigure them so I'm starting to think the hands have a greater significance than mere trophies.'

They stopped by Lizzie's motorbike.

'For sick fantasies, probably,' Kember said.

'Sick fantasies are not a reason by themselves, they're a symptom of something else going on in the mind.'

'I know we can't see it yet but I have to consider a physical connection. Criminals don't recognise police-force jurisdiction and it's not unheard of for burglars or smugglers to strike in different areas. Why not murderers?'

Lizzie's chest tightened again and she found it difficult to look Kember in the eye. She realised now was the time to tell him about her own investigations but knew he'd not be happy with her going off on her own accord.

'I've not been entirely honest with you.' She looked up when he didn't respond straight away.

Kember's lips were pressed into a thin line. 'What do you mean?'

'I flew to Biggin Hill, Kenley and Croydon today and spoke to the RAF Police at each air station. I asked about unusual deaths on their patches.'

'You did what?' Kember's face clouded. 'I'm the detective here, remember? What right do you think you have to go asking questions like that? You know Hartson wasn't best pleased when I involved you last time and I've already had another warning from him.'

Lizzie put a placating hand on his chest and told him about her discussions with the three RAF Police officers and the death of Dora Enright at Croydon. He listened intently, raising his eyebrows and frowning at certain points as she spoke about death, ditches and severed hands. After she finished, it was several seconds before he spoke and she could see his professional curiosity overcoming any displeasure.

'You're certain about all this?'

'That's what the flight lieutenant told me. It all fits with this girl's murder but Catherine was found in a dry natural dip. There might be some deeper significance, of course, but I think it more likely he chooses ditches and streams to hide the bodies rather than risk spending precious time digging graves.'

Kember sighed. 'If they *are* all connected, this investigation just became a lot more complex.'

Lizzie pulled on her helmet and gauntlets, swung her leg over the Norton and slipped it off its stand. 'As you've said before, you can't rule something out, or in, unless there's a good reason to do so. I'm unable to separate the three deaths we know of. The problem I have is how someone can kill so far apart, over such a wide area, and why they'd want to do that. Like burglars and other criminals, serial murderers usually have a patch and stick to a tight area most of the time. But I'm pragmatic too.'

'Go on,' he said.

'There's a war on, which in many ways makes travel quite difficult. Checkpoints and petrol rationing and so on. But it can also make it easier in some respects. What with all the troop and other military movements, food distribution, bombings, evacuations and God knows what else, one man wouldn't be noticed amongst all that confusion.'

Kember nodded. 'As long as you've got the right papers and a good story, you could go anywhere that's not a restricted zone.'

Lizzie kick-started the Norton and turned it in a semi-circle to face the gate. She leant towards Kember to speak over the engine noise.

'You need to speak to the police in Cambridge as soon as you can. Either three killers with the same ritual of removing hands have spontaneously emerged at the same time or we've unearthed another serial murderer. If the hands from these three women were taken by one man he won't stop now, and there's no telling where he'll strike next.'

CHAPTER NINE

Sitting in the passenger seat as Wright eased the police Wolseley through the five-bar gate to exit from the field, Kember held up his hand. 'Wait a moment, Sergeant.'

'Sir?' Wright stopped the car.

Kember recalled Wright saying a concert party from ENSA had rolled up in a convoy of lorries three days ago and had erected their tents in a paddock beside the road leading to the air station.

'I've changed my mind. Turn right,' Kember said.

'To the air station?'

'Towards it, yes, but I want to stop at the ENSA camp.'

'You think one of them might have seen something?' Wright gave Kember a sideways glance. 'Apart from putting up posters for the pantomime, they've pretty much kept themselves to themselves.'

'It's worth asking though, I'd say.'

Wright acknowledged with a nod, swung the wheel and pulled the car into the lane heading north. In less than five minutes, he steered the Wolseley through another open gate, only a few fields from where the dead woman had been found, and parked next to a line of three Bedford lorries and a Morris truck. Kember and Wright got out and surveyed the camp spread before them.

Canvas tents of various sizes and shapes, in dull tones of green, brown, khaki, olive drab, beige and dirty white, punctuated the perimeter of the field. What appeared to be the living quarters stretched to the left, following the line of the lane before turning along the far side of the paddock to the furthest corner. Two large tents had been erected under a cluster of trees near the centre of the field. Kember supposed a group reading aloud on the far side, beneath a simple canopy, were performers rehearsing. A scattering of larger accommodation tents lay directly ahead between the lane and the far hedgerow.

Some of the tents looked to Kember like they had been issued from government stores, being somehow more robust and utilitarian than their counterparts. Others had the look of pre-war about them, possibly used for peacetime pursuits such as holidays, fishing expeditions and Scout camps. These were less rugged, thinner, probably a lot chillier to sleep in and no doubt requisitioned from many a garden shed.

Netting, branches and strips of cloth dyed green and brown adorned each tent; an attempt at camouflage by breaking up the uniform outlines. Some of these efforts had been more successful than others but the overall effect appeared fortuitously haphazard, adding to the disguise. Even with personnel dressed in uniforms emblazoned with ENSA shoulder flashes, the camp looked more like a random peacetime gathering than a military encampment.

A small group were ferrying stores from one of the lorries to a straight-sided storage tent. Two of them dragged large hessian sacks of potatoes from the back of a lorry onto their shoulders and Kember hurriedly sidestepped as one staggered back.

'Have a care, lad,' Wright called, banging his fist on the side of the lorry.

'If you think I'm a lad, you need your eyes testing, love.'

Wright's mouth dropped open as a woman with short, dark hair turned around.

'And stop banging my lorry,' she said. 'I'm responsible for that.'

'Our mistake,' Kember said, touching the brim of his fedora.

'Oh, hello,' she said, and flashed a smile. 'Are you responsible for this oaf?' She nodded at Wright.

'We're looking for the commanding officer, if that's the right term,' he said, stepping forward as Wright's face clouded over. 'I'm Detective Inspector Kember.'

'Won't I do? I'm Paula . . . Unwin.'

'Not unless you're in charge, Miss Unwin,' he said, feeling heat in his cheeks. Kember estimated the woman to be no older than early thirties, quite slim beneath her greatcoat, and wearing very little make-up. Naturally attractive, then, despite the dark patches beneath her eyes being a sign of fatigue.

The woman adjusted the sack on her shoulder.

'You look like you could do with some more help,' he suggested, to hide his embarrassment more than anything else, but he mentally kicked himself as soon as the words left his mouth.

Unwin's face fell and she glared at him.

'Don't mistake tiredness with weakness, Inspector. I suffer from lack of sleep, not muscle wastage.' She jerked her head in the direction of a cluster of larger tents. 'Over there.'

'Thank you,' Kember said.

Wright leant back out of range as the woman swung around with her burden and strode off in pursuit of the other sack-bearer.

'They look like a right shower if you ask me,' Wright said with an air of disdain.

Kember ignored a small group smoking to his left and headed for the open-sided, marquee-sized cooking tent under the trees from which wispy smoke and the odd profanity emanated. As they approached, he saw an even larger mess tent behind, where someone looking a bit like a commanding officer was speaking to another. It was towards this that Kember led Sergeant Wright.

'Have you never enjoyed the theatre or music hall, Sergeant?'

'I have, sir, and I've heard some beautiful singers in my time but I can't help thinking actors are a rum bunch. All that dressing up and pretending. It can't be good for you.'

Kember smiled at Wright's grimace and made eye contact with the officer-type, who stood as the two policemen approached.

'Can I help you, gentlemen?' he said.

Kember flashed his warrant card. 'Are you the commanding officer?'

The man laughed. 'You could call me that but we have no military ranks in ENSA. I'm merely the assistant director of this rabble of an entertainments group.'

'Ah, I thought . . .' Kember looked the man up and down.

'Don't let the uniforms fool you. We were given these when we went to entertain the troops in northern France. They were just for show in case we got captured by the enemy. That way we couldn't be shot as spies. Got us a place on military transport too, when the Germans invaded and we were evacuated.'

'They had some benefit then.'

'Equally as important, they granted us officer status. Even without a formal rank, it means every one of us is allowed in the officers' mess.'

This drew another grimace from Wright, who elected to remain standing while Kember accepted the offer of an unstable folding chair by the rickety camping table.

'I'm Bertrand Coates but call me Bertie,' said the man, shaking hands with Kember. He nodded at the other man. 'That's Tanner. Not his real name and nothing to do with leather. He's always betting people sixpence that he can do something better than they can. Lost a lot of tanners haven't you?'

'Not to you I haven't,' Tanner said.

Kember wasn't sure the jovial riposte, said with an unconvincing smile, didn't hide an underlying animosity, but that wasn't his concern. 'If Tanner is your nickname, what's your real one?' he asked, feeling a tug at his patience.

Tanner identified himself as Charles Thorogood and Kember introduced Wright before he led straight into a few general questions as a warm up before turning to the real issue.

'I'm afraid I have something more serious to discuss,' Kember said. 'A young woman was found dead this morning in a field between here and the village.'

'Dead?' Coates said, looking wide-eyed at Thorogood. 'What on earth happened?'

'We believe she was murdered.'

'Good God!' The look of shock on Coates' face seemed equally as genuine as that on Thorogood's. 'That's an awful tragedy, but what's it to do with us, Inspector?'

Kember noticed Coates' gaze flicker towards Thorogood and back to him.

'My sergeant says some of your people have been putting posters up in the village.'

'That's right. We're performing a pantomime on the air station early this evening, in one of the hangars, and again on Christmas Eve in Scotney village hall.'

'Is it usual for an ENSA party to stay several days in one place?'

'It's not unusual. We usually flit in and out again but it depends on what's booked and where we're needed. ENSA and the War Office decided it would be good for public relations if we stayed on after the air-station show to entertain the villagers.'

Kember nodded. 'The girl was wearing a light-coloured smock and carrying a shepherd's crook. I was wondering whether anyone from your company, especially those who visited the village, may have seen a shepherdess between here and the village sometime yesterday, or have noticed anything out of the ordinary since your arrival?'

Coates looked quizzically at Kember. 'I'm not sure we'd know what you mean by *out of the ordinary*. Most of us come from beyond Kent, so we wouldn't know what normal was around here and what was not.'

Kember tried to ignore Coates' insensitivity and keep his tone even. 'I'm sure suspicious activity looks suspicious wherever you come from. I'm sure you'll agree that camping in a field not too far from where the body was found makes each one of your people as good a potential witness as any.' Kember felt a measure of satisfaction as colour tinged the embarrassed assistant director's cheeks. The gravity of the situation was finally getting through. 'The murdered girl was last seen Thursday evening. Any information you can give us could be of vital importance.'

Coates looked up and to one side, frowning in thought and taking his time. 'Almost everyone was rehearsing for most of yesterday, apart from Sparky and Chippy.' He hesitated at Kember's raised eyebrow. 'The company's electrician and carpenter,' Coates explained. 'They were off performing minor miracles of lighting and set design on the air station. Some of our actors did go down to the village in the morning but I'm sure they were back in time for lunch. That's another benefit of being in ENSA. We get well paid and fed, even when we camp beyond the reach of the officers' mess.' Coates looked at his watch. 'It's lunchtime now, in fact. This tent will be full in five minutes.'

Kember decided to take the hint and stood to leave, indicating to Wright that he should lead the way out. Back in the wintery sunshine, Kember stopped and turned to Coates.

'How many went to the village?'

Coates counted on his fingers. 'George Wilkes, Vera Butterfield, Tubby Saunders, Betty Fisher and Shorty McNee.'

Out of the corner of his eye, Kember noticed Wright lick the end of his pencil and make a few notes. 'It took five of you to put up posters in a small village?'

'Many hands make light work, Inspector.'

'Were they gone for long?'

'They all came back after . . .' The corners of Coates' mouth turned down as he threw a questioning look at Thorogood. 'About an hour or two?'

Thorogood shrugged then nodded his agreement.

'How did they get to the village and back?' Kember asked. 'They may have passed where the body was found and seen something important.'

Coates looked over Kember's shoulder. 'You can ask them yourself. That's them over there.'

Kember looked across and saw the group of smokers they'd passed on their way through the camp. Coates pushed past Thorogood to return to his table, without a handshake or goodbye. Thorogood looked apologetic but followed his boss.

Making their way back to the smokers, Kember said, 'What do you make of that?'

'Looked to me like they weren't the best of friends,' Wright said.

'Hmm, and he's not the most accommodating of men, our Mr Coates.'

'They're all fly-by-nights, if you ask me.' Wright scowled. 'Can't be trusted.'

Kember looked sideways at Wright. 'Do you have something in particular against entertainers, Sergeant?'

Wright frowned as they kept walking. 'I was courting a chorus girl for five months when I was working in London. She ran off with an actor; an understudy from the Theatre Royal where she worked. Broke my heart, she did.'

'I'm truly sorry to hear that—'

Kember navigated around an impromptu football match, avoided a flying football, and made his way towards the group of smokers. They huddled around a brazier, the orange flames licking over the top creating a bright splash of colour against the khaki greatcoats and drab tents, and he could smell the mingled cigarette and wood smoke several yards away. As he and Wright approached, one of them pointed two fingers holding a cigarette at another.

'It's the rozzers, Tubby, they've finally caught up with you. Not that that's difficult.'

The smokers all laughed, even the butt of the joke whose ENSA uniform looked like it had needed to be let out to accommodate his bulk. Kember kept his serious face and the laughter faded.

'Any of you called George Wilkes?'

'That's me,' the joker said. 'Have I done something wrong?'

'I don't know, have you?'

Wilkes' grin faltered.

'Don't mind him,' said a tall man who Kember guessed to be at least six foot five. 'He thinks he's the camp comedian but he's just a second-rate actor like the rest of us.'

'Oi, you speak for yourself.'

Kember and Wright turned to find another woman, cigarette in mouth, coat over her arm, carrying a full crate of beer atop another, stepping towards him. 'And you are?' he said.

'Betty Fisher.' She put down the crates and held out a cigarette packet. 'Fag?' She shrugged when Kember declined, put the packet in her pocket and donned her greatcoat. 'That's James McNee. We call him Knee High or Shorty, obviously.' She waved a hand at the large man, 'Graham, Tubby Saunders to one and all,' then at a woman of medium build wearing small, round-framed spectacles. 'And Vera Butterfield on the end.'

Kember nodded to each, admitting to himself that Wright's assessment of the camp's inhabitants might not be far wrong. You'd be hard-pressed to find a group looking less like professional actors. But this was wartime.

'I understand from your assistant director that you spent some time in the village, putting up posters.' Kember caught the flicker of a glance from Saunders to Fisher but she didn't seem to notice.

'You understand correctly,' Wilkes said. 'Advertising for the pantomime in the village hall on Christmas Eve.'

'I do hope you're coming?' Fisher said, with a wink.

'How long were you there?' Kember said, ignoring her question.

'A couple of hours,' Wilkes replied. 'People like to chat when they see our posters, and especially when they realise it's free.' He turned to Butterfield. 'Vera?'

Butterfield dug into her coat pocket, drew out a thick rectangle of paper and handed it to Kember. He unfolded the poster and looked at the illustration of Cinderella and Prince Charming, finding it garish, almost childlike.

Butterfield shrugged. 'A bit crude I'm afraid but it does get the punters in.'

Kember noted that the date, time and venue for the pantomime performance in the village had been handwritten in a white space at the bottom.

'I remember seeing some of you,' Wright said. 'Did you do the whole village?'

Wilkes nodded. 'Of course.'

'How did you get there and back?'

'Walked. We can't be wasting petrol. There is a war on, Inspector.' Wilkes looked at the last remains of his cigarette and took a long drag.

Butterfield smirked and Wright gave her a hard stare.

'What's up, Inspector?' Fisher asked, smiling. 'Are we in trouble?'

'Not unless you're responsible for the body of a young shepherdess discovered near here this morning,' Kember said.

The effect was instant: Fisher, Wilkes and Butterfield looked embarrassed by their previous levity; the faces of Saunders and McNee paled with shock.

'She was last seen on Thursday, wearing a light-coloured smock and carrying a crook,' Kember continued. 'Did you see her yesterday, either on her own or with anyone?' All shook their heads. 'Did you notice anything you might regard as unusual or suspicious on your travels to and from the village?'

Heads shook again and Kember realised this was getting them nowhere.

'I'm afraid we're little more than cheap entertainment,' Fisher said. 'We learn our lines, perform and move on to the next town, keeping our blinkers on against the real world. Half this troupe probably wouldn't recognise a real dead body if they tripped over one and spilt their G and Ts. The other half would be too drunk to notice.'

She gave Kember a smile that told him her brief moment of contrition was over, and Wilkes had turned his attention to lighting a fresh cigarette from the embers of his previous one.

It seemed to Kember that war had eroded the deference once shown to the police. It used to be little street urchins in the city or apple scrumpers in the countryside who showed contempt for the law but now everyone seemed less afraid of the police. Perhaps uncertainty about whether one would survive the war or be dead in the next air raid had changed people's perceptions and attitudes. Whatever the cause, with able men taken by the armed forces, the police service was bolstered by reservists, recalls from retirement and the unfit-for-active-duty. Not exactly an elite organisation commanding respect at any time, and especially during a war.

'That's all for now,' Kember said, handing the poster back to Butterfield. 'But we might need to speak to you again.'

He nodded and left the smokers to their smirking and muttering. Wright followed, a scowl still entrenched on his face.

'And now I have the difficult task of delivering the bad news to Mr and Mrs Chapman,' Kember said.

As they passed the line of lorries on the way back to the car, someone called through the open door of a cab.

'Inspector.'

Kember looked over as Unwin stopped cleaning a revolver with a cloth and reached into her pocket.

'It seems I've forgiven you,' she said. 'Would you like a conciliatory cigarette?' She held up her packet.

'No thank you.' Kember held up a hand and carried on walking. 'Duty calls.'

'Well, you know where to find me.' She winked. 'Until Christmas Day.'

'I'd like to bang their heads together, the lot of 'em,' Wright said, as Unwin turned away. 'Knock some sense into their thick heads.'

'Oh, I think they've got sense, Sergeant.' Kember glanced back at the smokers, still talking and looking their way. 'They certainly didn't tell us everything, and did you notice that everyone here appears to smoke Craven A?'

CHAPTER TEN

Lizzie sneaked into the ATA operations room to check the work board, scanning the allocations for her name until she saw with relief that an air taxi from another ferry pool would be bringing back the Scotney pilots later in the day. Her next job would be at first light in the morning. No aircraft had been named, which usually meant they didn't know yet or it was a bit hush-hush. The women of the ATA always lost out to the men when anything exciting was in the offing so this was bound to be another mangled Miles Magister or tatty Tiger Moth.

She scraped a chair towards her and slumped onto it, closing her eyes for a rest but her mind deciding otherwise. A film played against the back of her eyelids, her friend walking happily with a man she couldn't quite see, along a country path up a hill to a copse of trees. Lizzie shook her head and the film changed to a shepherdess with a small flock passing by a five-bar gate, but the copse swum into focus again, her friend being laid gently on the ground into a shallow depression. No, not her friend. The shepherdess.

Lizzie opened her eyes and tried to take a deep lungful of air but it felt like someone had sat on her chest, pressing down and preventing her breathing. She shivered as if outside without a coat but as she rubbed her hands together, she felt their clammy moisture.

Lizzie knew the whole situation was stupid. She was alone but safe, and although concerned about the recent murders, not under pressure or stressed in the way she had been during the terror of the Scotney Ripper. Still her eyes widened involuntarily and the walls seemed to close in, the edge of her vision blurred red.

Over the last few years, Lizzie had developed a number of countermeasures to combat her anxiety attacks, the first of which was to distance herself from whatever possible cause she could identify. She could think of no trigger around her except the pictures in her head and even she couldn't run from her own thoughts. This made the second countermeasure, clasping her hands together tightly and focusing her mind on anything other than how she was feeling, equally ineffective. Lizzie turned to the third option. Sitting there, in the same office where her last anxiety attack had occurred, again counting the number of drawing pins she could see on the noticeboards, had a slight effect, so she persisted. After counting up to twenty-seven, she counted down to one, doing this three times.

Although her breathing began to slow and her vision to return to normal, tears still flooded her eyes and coursed down her cheeks. Conscious that someone might come in at any moment, Lizzie fumbled for her handkerchief, blew her nose and wiped her eyes. As she took the square of embroidered linen away from her face the looming shadow of a person made her jump.

'I do apologise. I didn't mean to make you jump. I did knock.'

Lizzie pulled herself together and gave Vickers a thin smile. 'It's my fault. I was miles away.'

'I could see that.' He drew up a chair. 'Problem?'

Lizzie hesitated, wondering whether to discuss the murders with him. Ben Vickers had been a great help to both Kember and herself during the Ripper investigation so it wasn't as if he was a stranger to her skills and method for catching killers. She took a deep breath, decided, and sighed.

'I have – had – a friend, in Duxford, but she was murdered.' She saw his expression change but waved away any sympathy. 'I asked Kember to let me know if the police in Cambridge found out anything else or caught her murderer. He said he'd look into it but while I was on air-taxi duties this morning, I asked around at Biggin Hill, Kenley and Croydon. I wanted to do something but didn't expect anything to come of it. I found out Croydon had a similar death, quite recently.'

Vickers whistled. 'If you're back in contact with Kember, you don't think we've got another loony on our hands, do you?'

Lizzie winced at the term. 'Actually, I do.' She reached into her bag and brought out a crumpled cigarette packet, clearly empty. She accepted a Woodbine proffered by Vickers and sucked down nicotine as he extinguished his match with a wave. His face had taken on an expression of concerned interest but he remained silent.

Lizzie blew a smoke cloud at the ceiling.

'When I got back, I found a message from Kember asking me to meet him in a field between here and the village. I was curious but didn't know a woman had been murdered until I got there. Knowing how my friend died, Kember thought her death and the one here in Scotney too similar to be coincidence. He hoped I could use my insight to interpret the scene. He was upset when I told him about my own investigation but agreed we might have another serial murderer traipsing around the country.'

'What makes you think they're all connected?' Vickers asked, speaking through smoke.

'Because they all had their throats cut and were left in shallow depressions or ditches.' She looked him straight in the eyes, sensing the victims' pain, trying to convey in one look the sense of loss their families and friends must be feeling. Feeling it herself. 'They all had their hands taken.'

Vickers choked on his smoke and stared at her. 'You *are* joking?'

Lizzie shook her head. 'I told Kember, I think someone's taking them for a reason. Not as trophies but for a specific purpose.'

'Which is . . . ?'

Lizzie looked away to hide her frustration and anguish. 'I don't know. What I do know is, the killer placed the bodies into their graves. They weren't just dumped. Why would you do that? Why would you deliberately target and kill someone, cut off their hands and leave the bodies in open graves but position them so carefully? It's as if the killer feels he has no choice but to kill, but in doing so, wishes it to be as painless and dignified as possible before taking what he needs, what he can get no other way.'

'Sex, you mean?'

'No. I don't think this is about sexual excitement, or money. It's about . . . I don't know yet.'

'Well, if there's anything I can do to help, but it's not my jurisdiction or area of expertise.'

Lizzie paused. 'There is something you can do. You must know other RAF policemen?'

'Of course—'

'Can you ring around, to other air stations, to see whether they've had any similar murders in their area?'

Vickers nodded. 'I'll see what I can do.'

Lizzie's mood lifted. Vickers' contacts would cover a lot more of the country in one go than she could get to herself. She'd wanted to confide in her ATA friends, to get them to help, but even though her original colleagues knew her quirks and skills by now, she knew they would take any suggestion of another serial murderer as a sign of paranoia. The last thing she needed at that moment was to be placed under the air station's MO. Even though Medical Officer Dr Sam Davies had lived with them through the nightmare reign of the Scotney Ripper, he might also refuse to believe another killer could be at large, in the same year, on his patch.

'Could you ask around discreetly?' Lizzie said. 'Perhaps say it's part of a wider investigation?' She watched Vickers studying the glowing end of his cigarette. 'I don't want people asking awkward questions, especially if I'm barking up the wrong tree.'

At university, Lizzie's studies had included psychological reactions to traumatic events. Some civilian survivors of coal-mine accidents suffered ongoing symptoms of what the medical profession was beginning to call Acute Stress Reaction. Many ex-soldiers were still suffering from the artillery bombardments of the Great War, but shellshock had been re-labelled Combat Stress Reaction. She couldn't take the risk of being labelled with ASR or CSR because Dallington and Matfield would jump at any chance to use signs of weakness to have all of the ATA withdrawn again. The head of the Women's Section, Pauline Gower, had fought hard for women to fly and Lizzie wouldn't be letting her down any time soon. If Davies signed her off sick, she'd be grounded indefinitely and her livelihood, career and any chance of finding the killer would evaporate in one go.

Vickers took a lungful of smoke and exhaled through his nose. 'I'll try,' he agreed.

'Thank you.' She glanced at her watch. *All the police activity should have concluded by now*, she thought, as the urge to find out more became too great to resist. She stood up. 'And now, I need to go back to that field.'

◆ ◆ ◆

After returning from the ENSA camp, Kember left Wright in the village before collecting his Minx and driving over to Glassen Farm. Squawking hens scattered as he pulled into the farmyard and stopped near the house. Two middle-aged men, thick-necked, flat-capped, hands and faces tanned and toughened like leather from working all year outdoors, looked across at the commotion.

Kember acknowledged them with a nod as he stepped from his car, noticing a broken-open shotgun resting in the crook of the taller man's right arm, and a scythe held blade up like the Grim Reaper by the stockier of the two. He showed his warrant card and saw the familiar look of guilt and suspicion cross their faces, one that even the innocent seemed to display whenever he introduced himself.

'Is Mr Chapman in?' Kember asked.

Stocky nodded.

'Are you the only workers around?'

'Aye,' Shotgun said. 'All the summer and harvest workers have moved on long since.' He inclined his head towards his mate. 'We work here all year.'

'You'll know Kenneth Jarvis, then?'

Kember saw a look of contempt pass between the two men.

'Used to be an all-right bloke who worked hard,' said Stocky. 'Until recently.'

'Aye,' Shotgun agreed. 'A decent foreman was Kenny. Firm but fair. And good with his hands.'

Stocky nodded. 'Would turn his hands to anything, as long as it didn't aggravate his bad back.'

'Why until recently?' Kember asked.

'Been going downhill these past few months. Couldn't be trusted to so much as close a gate never mind mend one, so good riddance to bad rubbish.'

'Any idea what happened?' Kember asked, keeping an eye on the farmhouse for signs of Chapman.

Stocky gave him a crooked smile. 'Same as it always is when these things happen. A woman. The *floozy*.'

Kember asked a few more questions but it was clear they didn't know who it was. Jarvis sometimes came back smelling of a woman's perfume but never let on who he'd seen. As far as Shotgun and Stocky could recall, Jarvis disappeared at all times during the day. Sometimes it was for half an hour in the morning, sometimes for a two-hour lunch, and he often left between twenty minutes and an hour before he should at the end of the day. The last they saw of Jarvis was Thursday afternoon when Chapman told him to get back to work. Jarvis had stuck two fingers up and carried on walking away.

Kember thanked the men and let them return to their jobs.

It didn't make sense.

Could Evelyn Hartson really be considered a floozy? Would she have taken up with an older man, or he with a young girl? Could Shotgun, Stocky or even Chapman have killed Jarvis over something as trivial as a dispute about him pulling his weight on the farm?

Out of the corner of his eye, Kember noticed a curtain twitch at a downstairs window. He sighed. Telling someone their loved one had passed away would never and could never be an easy or pleasant duty. He bit the bullet and was about to knock when the door was yanked open and a tiny, pale-cheeked woman stood there rubbing her hands dry on a thin towel. Kember guessed this to be Mrs Chapman, an assumption reinforced when Derek appeared behind her with an expectant look. Kember didn't have time to even open his mouth before Mrs Chapman read his expression and howled, her face collapsing with grief. Her husband pulled her to him, blocking the door so Kember couldn't enter.

Kember recited all the usual platitudes about being very sorry and he'd do all he could to bring her murderer to justice but they sounded hollow even to himself. He glanced over his shoulder but the two workers had gone, which was a blessing. Grief should be private, he felt. Through Mrs Chapman's sobs, Kember offered to arrange with Dr Headley for the Chapmans to see their daughter over at Pembury Hospital. Derek nodded, reached out a hand and pushed the front door closed.

As he drove back down the farm track and onto Glassen Lane, his thoughts turned to his own daughter in the WAAF and his son flying fighters in the RAF. He really should telephone them, especially because they'd visited him in hospital a few months ago as he recovered from the shrapnel injuries that he'd received at the hands of the Scotney Ripper.

The window on his side suddenly shattered and he thought he'd hit a low branch but a sharp crack echoed across the field and a metallic thud came from his door. *Messerschmitts,* he thought, so he floored the accelerator and the Minx surged forward behind the meagre protection of a hedgerow, its tangled mass of twigs laid bare by winter. He accelerated towards where he knew a tunnel had formed from the entwining branches of trees on either side of the lane, forgetting the humpback bridge over the River Glassen. It seemed to Kember as if the Minx became airborne for a heart-stopping moment before sinking heavily onto its suspension and slaloming as he fought for control. Reaching the parade of sentinel trunks supporting a leafless but nonetheless protective canopy of thick branches, he gripped the wheel and stamped on the brake, skidding the car to a halt.

CHAPTER ELEVEN

In the field where Maisie Chapman's body had been found, Lizzie began to let her subconscious take control. All the earlier police presence had dwindled to nothing, and if it wasn't for her lying on her back on the ground, avoiding the blood-stained grass where Maisie Chapman had died, this corner of the field would have looked much the same as it had for a century or more. With arms by her sides and eyes closed, she could feel cold permeating through her hair, touching her scalp. Lizzie shivered, her fingers numbing, the cold-hardened ground leaching the warmth from her body through her greatcoat. Her mind relaxed further, conscious thoughts mingling with subconscious, her mind beginning to see the dreadful possibilities of what had happened here rather than the harsh reality of the aftermath.

'You've taken my life,' she said aloud, her speech visible until swirled away by a breath of wind. 'But I wasn't beaten.' There had been no signs of a struggle. 'You got close, befriended me, kept me calm.' Lizzie could see someone in the corner of her mind. She opened her eyes and turned her head. No one there. 'You haven't touched me, not like a man touches a woman he wants. Am I not pretty enough?' She turned her head back and held up her hands, looking at them. 'I had no jewellery, only my pretty nails. I had nothing but my body to give you yet you took only my hands. Why? I'm known in the village so taking my fingerprints did not conceal who I am.'

She closed her eyes again and the elusive shadow stepped farther away. 'What is it about them, the hands of women, that draws you? For what purpose do you need them but not the rest of their bodies? Did you kill me so I wouldn't suffer as you took my hands from me?' Lizzie made fists. 'Some take a prize to relive the moment of killing, but hands perish.'

Lizzie sat up, her body shivering automatically but her mind now oblivious to the cold ground and chill wind. She opened her hands, spreading her fingers.

'That is why you can't stop killing. You need to keep collecting, to replace them.'

Sitting in the Minx with the engine running, Kember realised he hadn't heard aero engines or the chatter of machine guns. He'd heard only two shots and remembered the shotgun carried by the tall man back at Glassen Farm.

He opened his door and stepped out, wary and frowning. He'd expected to find the driver's side peppered with holes from shotgun pellets but his door showed one neat, round bullet hole. *Bastards*. With rising anger, he thought for a moment about going back to investigate but without a gun he would be exposed. The attempted assassin would most probably have fled by now, but that carried no guarantee. His best option had to be escape and survive.

The hands of the clock on the squat tower above the village hall had already eased past one o'clock and Kember's temper had cooled by the time he parked outside the police station, where Sergeant Wright stood talking to the village postman. Jim Corcoran was wearing a stripey, triple-length woollen scarf wrapped around his neck and tucked into the front of his red-trimmed navy-blue General Post Office overcoat. He had secured his beige canvas pouch and steel air-raid helmet, both stamped with GPO, to the front rack of his Post Office-red bicycle. Kember noted the flattened pouch, suggesting Corcoran had completed his morning round of deliveries.

'Corky here has been telling me about that ENSA lot camped near the air station,' Wright said to Kember without any preliminary greeting.

'It's Jim,' Corcoran said. '*Jim.*'

'Tell the inspector what you just told me,' Wright said, ignoring Corcoran's protest.

Corcoran sighed. 'Well, it's a bloody cheek, if you ask me. It's all right that I have my rounds to do, that's my job, but the lazy beggars wanted me to hand out their posters too. For free. Down here in the village, they were, so I told them it wasn't my job and they could get on and do it themselves.'

'How many were there?' Kember asked, his mind cast back to the smoking group at the camp.

'Two, as I recall,' Corcoran said, holding up two fingers for emphasis.

'Only two?' Kember was interested in what had happened to the other three from ENSA who Coates had said were handing out posters. 'Can you describe them?'

'I gave what description I could to Scrumpy Wright.'

'It's Sergeant, not Scrumpy,' Wright complained.

'It's what we called him when we were kids. Quite the apple scrumper, he was.'

'We aren't kids now.'

Corcoran winked at Kember. 'He still is.'

Kember couldn't conceal a brief smile at the gentle ribbing, but said in a firm, authoritative voice, 'I would prefer you to tell me, Mr Corcoran.'

'Of course.' Corcoran nodded, no longer joking. 'They were both of medium height and the woman wore glasses. Round wire ones. They were wearing ENSA uniforms but the man looked like the buttons on his greatcoat needed help, if you catch my drift. At least all his buttons matched, though, unlike Elias Brown's.' His face became serious. 'In actual fact, I know those two got up my nose but I'd be more concerned about Elias's pillboxes, if I was you.'

'Oh, really?' Kember said, his mind on the two characters that Corcoran had just described. 'Why is that?'

''Cos he's never there. We might have won the Battle of Britain but Jerry could still invade tomorrow and walk straight in.'

'I'm sure he's got his orders.'

'Aye. Don't mean he follows them, though. He's another lazy sod, like those actors. Anyhow, I've got a postbag to collect off the next train so I'm going to have to love you and leave you.'

Corcoran put his left foot on a pedal, pushed off with his right and swung his leg over the saddle. 'Give my love to Gladys,' he called, pedalling towards the railway station with a tinkle of his bicycle's bell.

'You and Gladys still courting?' Kember asked.

'Any joy over at Glassen, sir?' Wright said, as if he hadn't heard the question.

Kember gave a faint nod. 'Quite right, Sergeant. None of my business.' He beckoned Wright around to the driver's side of his car. 'Unlike whoever took a potshot at me earlier.'

Wright let out a curse as he saw the bullet hole and shattered window.

'Did you see who did it?'

'I was too busy putting my foot down to get away.'

'You were lucky there, sir,' Wright said, bending to inspect the bullet hole. 'A few inches different and you'd be a customer of Dr Headley.'

Kember knew he'd cheated death again. The difference was, he usually knew who wanted him dead.

Retiring to the front office out of the cold, Wright said, 'There's one in the pot,' and held up his own mug of tea. Kember waved away the offer and related more details of his eventful visit to Glassen Farm. Wright listened, nodding at various points, and Kember gave him an *I don't know* shrug to the repeated question of who might have tried to kill him. There had not been enough time for the worker outside the farmhouse to reach where he'd been attacked and the bullet hole in his car door had not been made by a shotgun. Kember could think of no other suspect than whoever had killed Maisie Chapman, but he was a long way off discovering who that was.

'Any success with the stationmasters?' Kember asked, grateful to change the subject.

Wright swallowed tea and put down his mug.

'Tonbridge confirmed that a lady of Miss Hartson's appearance bought a return ticket eastbound for Paddock Wood on Thursday. She did get on the train but never returned, either Thursday or Friday. Staff at Paddock Wood remembered her alighting because a young soldier was kind enough to help her off the train. He then assisted an old couple board the same carriage before boarding himself. The staff said Miss Hartson bought another ticket from the office and I feared she might have taken the northbound line to Maidstone. However, they're adamant she bought a single to Hawkhurst.'

Kember sat forward, intrigued. 'Go on.'

'There are only five stations on the branch line, not counting Paddock Wood, so I worked my way up from the terminus at Hawkhurst, to Cranbrook, then Goudhurst and Horsmonden. As it happened, a train was at the platform at Horsmonden and they managed to get the conductor to the telephone. He remembered clipping a young lady's ticket just before she got off.'

'For God's sake, where, man?'

Wright hesitated, his face holding a pained expression.

'The only station I didn't telephone,' he said. 'Scotney.'

◆　◆　◆

'You're not how I imagined you'd look.'

Holding up a dog-eared photograph for him to see, the black and white image faded at the edges and with a fold creasing the centre, a man in shadow took a long drag on a cigarette and inhaled deeply.

He stared back beneath eyelids heavy with pain and fatigue, watched the man lower the photo and blow smoke at the rafters. On a small, square, woodworm-riddled table pushed against the rotting wood of the end wall lay an open packet, half-empty, next to a solitary candle dripping wax into a dirty, chipped saucer. He too needed a cigarette desperately, to let the warmth swirl in his lungs to get the maximum benefit and perhaps ease his pain. Dog-tired but determined to stay awake, he remained motionless, tied to a hard, wooden chair. With his back resting on the rotting wooden wall and legs outstretched, his boots and those of the man almost touched. He watched him take a final pull on the cigarette, crush the smouldering end underfoot and sigh, smoke billowing like morning fog.

'It's not your fault, of course.'

The man sat forward, elbows on knees, eyes raised, studying him, and he saw his bespectacled, moustachioed face for the first time.

'This is an old photograph but there is a resemblance.' The moustache twitched. 'Enough, I think, to make this worthwhile.'

He remained motionless.

'I know,' the man said, nodding. 'I know what you're thinking. Not all pieces of the jigsaw fit. Am I correct?' The man nodded again. 'You're right, of course. I should have chosen with more care but they looked good before. More than good.'

Shadows jerked and shrugged.

He saw a flicker of alarm in the eyes behind the spectacles as the pale-yellow flame fluttered in a draught. The man stood and moved across to the window set into the wall to the right of the door from their perspective. His own eyes followed the movement, feeling as though they were being gouged out by spoons. The man listened for a moment before lifting a corner of the two layers of heavy sackcloth hanging across the cracked glass panes made translucent by dust and frost. The man replaced the makeshift curtain and checked its positioning before moving across to where a rickety wooden bed-frame had been pushed into a corner. A tarpaulin sheet hung on the wall behind, and he just about managed to see the man pull it aside and put his ear to what looked like a wooden board.

The man shivered despite a thick greatcoat buttoned tight against the winter's bite, breath blooming like smoke from the recent cigarette, and turned back to him. He suspected his captor would never feel as cold as he felt now, with every muscle seized, every joint frozen and his face numb. His thoughts becoming laboured and difficult to marshal, drifted towards the people he loved.

'Still not talking to me?' the man asked.

He stared back, unsmiling.

How deranged is this madman? he thought, his brain working slower now. Bandaged stumps where his hands should be, held captive, kept barely alive with sips of water, trussed up on a wooden chair unable to change position. Was it any wonder he remained unmoving and silent?

His captor sat again and squinted through the curl of smoke irritating his eyes.

'Can't say I blame you.' The man averted his eyes. 'Don't look at me like that. I thought I had the right one this time. She looked perfect for you but I hadn't reckoned on the harsh lives they lead out in the sticks. Her hands were smooth and gorgeous on the back but . . .' The man took a drag on his cigarette and exhaled through his nostrils. 'The calluses must have come from holding that crook all day. How was I to know? I'm a city dweller at heart.'

The new hands lay displayed in his lap, flesh pinned to his bandages to keep them in place, one cupped in the other, palms upturned as if waiting for the wafer at evening Mass, or like Oliver Twist. *Please, sir, can I have some more?*

The man opposite him leant back, resting his head on the wall and rubbed his temples as if to relieve a headache. A sprinkling of ash fell on his sleeve like the first snow of winter. He rubbed the white flecks away and flicked ash from his cigarette into the chipped saucer, probably considering his next move.

The two layers of heavy sackcloth hanging across the window billowed in a sudden gust through the broken glass.

'This can't be good for my health.' The man shivered. 'Flu, bronchitis, pleurisy, even chilblains. You can catch all sorts out here. City dwellers don't do well in the country. The city is for people, the countryside should be left to animals.'

He wanted to tell the man to fuck off home then, but could barely keep his eyes open, let alone speak.

The man looked back at him.

'All right, I give in,' the man said, stubbing out the remains of his cigarette in the saucer. They both watched as a piece of stray tobacco still smouldered, its glow fading until finally extinguished. Like life. 'I'll have to find another one. Perhaps the one on that motorbike would be a good match. She didn't look like a woman who works in the fields. In fact, she didn't much look like she'd completed a decent day's work in all her life.'

Oh, dear God, he thought. *No one else, please.*

He felt no fear for himself but another wave of despair weighed on him at the thought of another young life to be taken needlessly.

The man leant forward to pat his knee.

'It's the Christmas show tonight, on the air station, so she's bound to be there. I'm sure she rode off in that direction and why would you do that if you weren't enlisted?'

The man smiled as he stood and placed the photograph face-down on the table, taking two blankets draped over the back of the chair. The man wrapped them around him with care, but although grateful for the little warmth they afforded, he really wanted to be released or allowed to die and wondered why he was being kept alive.

'That's settled then,' the man said, as if they'd been having a quiet, civilised discussion over a beer. 'There's still plenty of time, and if Mary Shelley's anything to go by, we'll get this right eventually.'

His head slowly tilted to one side but without the strength to right it. He realised he hadn't taken a breath for a while but hadn't missed it, hadn't needed it. So, so tired. So, so cold. The man stepped forward and straightened his head, taking care to prop it in position so it wouldn't move again. He watched as the man turned away and snuffed out the candle before opening the wooden door of the hut.

Never had he wanted to kill someone so much.

With no hope or strength left, he allowed himself to close his eyes, hearing the footsteps fade until he was left alone again, and fell asleep, forever.

◆ ◆ ◆

Collecting a dustpan and brush on the way outside to inspect the damage to his car, Kember instructed Sergeant Wright to interview the Scotney stationmaster and telephone his contact in the records office at New Scotland Yard. His own stock not being of great value, he hoped Wright would be able to cajole the Yard into checking for unsolved murder cases involving missing body parts but suspected it being a Saturday afternoon might throw a spanner in the works.

Kember cleared as much glass as he could find from the seats and floor of the Minx but could find no bullet. The window needed replacing quickly and he was fortunate in knowing someone in Tonbridge who could do that for him. His inspection of the door was more fruitful. Some putty and paint for the hole would do for now. The bullet had gone straight through and made a hole in the driver's seat, two inches below where his right buttock had been. He sighed. Another of his nine lives gone. There couldn't be that many left.

He pushed his finger into the hole in the seat and managed to fish out a hard piece of metal. Ballistics wasn't his forte but he did know about a few familiar weapons and a careful inspection of the deformed lump told him it was probably a .455 bullet. Smith & Wesson and Colt had made handguns of that calibre, but by far the most common gun he knew that fired .455 was the British army-issue Webley revolver of Great War vintage, not unlike the two .38 calibre police-issue specimens Wright had locked up inside.

It was probable that some had been kept by old soldiers as souvenirs and possible that a few had found their way onto the black market.

Kember wondered whether the killer of Maisie Chapman was trying to get him off the case, permanently. He shrugged to himself. Or maybe he'd managed to get in the way of someone shooting at rabbits.

He retired to the back room of the police station and ate his lunch, provided thoughtfully by the Taplow sisters. Each bite of the crusty bread roll sent spiky shards cascading into his lap, the filling of bloater fish paste coated the roof of his mouth, and a mug of insipid tea barely washed away the pungent taste. Since the war began, he found tea had degenerated into two versions: sludge and dishwater.

He was about to rejoin Wright when he heard him end a telephone call in the front office just before the front door closed.

Twenty minutes later, having left a message for Chief Inspector Hartson at Tonbridge Police Station and spoken to the Cambridge Constabulary, Kember put the telephone down following his third call of the afternoon. He closed his notebook with a snap and a frown, and turned to face Wright as he re-entered the front office.

The burly sergeant shed his helmet and greatcoat before plonking down in the visitor's chair. 'Any joy your end, sir?'

From the look in Wright's eyes, Kember suspected he'd found out something useful in the last half an hour but decided to share his findings first.

'I've just spoken to Cardiff City Police,' Kember said. 'John Davies and his wife Edith were killed on the seventh of August in an air raid on Cardiff. A bomb hit next door to their terraced house which also destroyed the houses either side and blew out windows down the whole street. The bodies pulled from the rubble were identified by their ration books and neighbours.'

'So that's that then?' Wright said, stroking his beard.

'As far as Cardiff goes, yes. Duxford is a different matter. On the promise of a pint next time we meet, I spoke to my counterpart in the Cambridge Constabulary, whom I happen to know from a previous posting. He said they're sure the woman found in the copse had her throat cut there, because of the amount of blood on the ground. They found no evidence of drag marks, scuffling feet or a struggle. Far easier for the killer to either walk with a willing but unsuspecting victim or meet her there before doing the deed. He also said it looked as though someone had laid the woman down with some care, in a natural depression rather than a shallow grave, and putting her legs together and her arms by her sides as if she was in bed.'

'Or a coffin?' Wright suggested.

'Maybe,' Kember said, rubbing his eyes. 'The pathologist found animal teeth marks on the exposed flesh of her legs and wrists, and the bones of her forearms. There are other marks on those bones he said were commensurate with having been cut with a very sharp blade, such as a butcher's boning knife or one used for fish filleting.'

A sound from the hallway had their heads snapping in that direction. The door opened and standing there bedraggled with wet hair clinging to the sides of her face, was Lizzie.

CHAPTER TWELVE

Just after four o'clock and already the light was fading fast.

And it was very cold.

She could still make out the shapes of Scotney residents hurrying about their business before the natural light disappeared completely. No street lamps. Blackout curtains and shutters sliding and banging into place. No one had the time or inclination to pay her any attention.

Holding her cigarette between thumb and index finger, reversed to conceal the glow of the tip in the cup of her hand like she'd seen the Home Guard do, she passed the door of the grocer's. The last customers called back to the shopkeeper, bell tinkling as they left, and pulled the door closed, squawking away like a gaggle of geese.

She dropped the remains of the cigarette, crushing it with her heel, pulled her collar higher and her thick beret unfashionably lower. Keeping a discreet distance, she followed the women down the High Street, past the police station and the memorial to the fallen of the Great War until opposite the deserted car garage. A minute later, the women waddled around the corner into Meadowbank Lane. She adjusted her woollen neck scarf and turned in the opposite direction, towards Acorn Street.

Labourers' cottages, erected by local landowners for their workers and looking so tiny against the lofty backdrop of ancient woodland, seemed to shrink into the darkness. The dwellings became less huddled, finally petering out as the street became a track of stone and then half-frozen mud and grass. Beyond lay a small paddock surrounded on three sides by a thick wood.

Only a final few yards to reach the warmth of her own home, next door but one to the last house in the line.

She felt her progress check as her scarf tightened, fearing she'd snagged it on something. Then her head yanked violently backwards. Fear coursed through her, a sharp pain silencing the scream forming in her throat. Warmth seeped into her scarf and across her chest. She couldn't move or catch her breath, such an all-pervading tiredness making her arms heavy and her legs weak.

She could see her front door swimming before her and had never wanted to reach home so much as she did now.

A journey never completed.

'Lizzie, what are you doing here?' Kember stood and brought her into the warmth of the police station's front office. 'Your hair's wet and you're shivering.'

Lizzie took the seat offered by Wright and thanked him when he fetched a blanket.

'I couldn't get my friend in Duxford and the girl down here out of my head so I went back to the field while it was quiet,' Lizzie began. 'I walked around a little, stood by the gate for a while and lay down next to where she was found in the ditch.'

'Lay down?' Wright said. 'Whatever for?'

'To know her as the victim,' Lizzie said, suddenly concerned they'd think she was mad. 'Putting myself in a victim's position, physically, helps me understand their perspective, and can some-times reveal the killer's.'

'I thought you'd done all you could in that field,' Kember said.

She saw concern in his expression. Concern as much for her sanity as her physical well-being because he knew her methods from the Ripper case.

'I needed to feel it,' she said. 'To walk through it, be there on my own. I needed to become a victim to ask myself: Why there? Why then? Why her? For what purpose?'

'Because he's a madman, if you ask me,' Wright said with a curl of his lip.

A weight of expectation settled on Lizzie's chest. Whenever something horrific or equally inexplicable to the minds of the decent happened, people turned to simple explanations of evil and madness. This, she knew from experience, could close a mind to understanding the rationale behind a killer's modus operandi and their individual rituals and needs.

She shook her head.

'He's looking for something. Serial murderers usually are. Not wealth or sex because the women weren't robbed or raped. He didn't beat or disfigure them. Why? Because that's not his purpose. You beat someone out of rage or revenge or to exert power and control, to gain information or their submission. He didn't do that: he sub-dued Maisie Chapman and Catherine without a struggle, probably Dora Enright too. He either enticed Catherine to the copse or met her there. A place of seclusion, of execution. The same for Dora. I'm not sure but I think meeting Maisie, a shepherdess working alone, might have been fortuitous, for him. A chance meeting in another secluded place that he took advantage of. Far better for his victims to be willing than not, and far better for them to be out of sight than not.'

Kember rubbed the end of his nose. 'If I'm following, you're saying he became friendly towards these women so they would walk to their deaths, and killed them in as quick and efficient a way as possible.'

'By cutting their throats.' Lizzie nodded. 'A silent way to die.'

Lizzie saw the looks on their faces and knew she had to explain carefully or lose their trust. She shivered and drew the blanket tighter around her shoulders.

'You don't plan a death and commit murder without a reason. There has to be some driving force urging you to kill and kill again. Perhaps he's trying to repeat a feeling of euphoria or superiority. Perhaps there's a deeper meaning to the rituals he performs. Even if meeting the shepherdess was a happy accident for him, his method remained pretty much the same, but that's not his ritual. The ritual is their hands and the way he takes them.'

'Cambridge Police said the pathologist suggested a fish-filleting or meat-boning knife might have been used.' Kember looked thoughtful. 'He wants to preserve them intact.'

'Exactly. He doesn't hack at them, he removes them. Why would you do that?'

'To collect them?'

'I don't know.' Lizzie shrugged. 'The serial murderers I've studied took smaller trophies like personal possessions, nail clippings or locks of hair. I'm more inclined to believe he's looking for something else. Something that can only be found on the hands.'

Kember glanced at Lizzie's hands. 'Like rings and bracelets, do you mean?'

'Not jewellery,' Lizzie said, unable to suppress a sigh of irritation. 'Meaning. He wants whole, beautiful, feminine hands because they're important to him.'

'Your girls not back yet?'

Geraldine looked away from a pantomime poster taped to the lounge door as Onslow entered the hall.

'Any time now.' She smiled. 'They've not flown far afield today. How about you? All ready for this evening's performance?'

'Absolutely. I'm looking forward to it.' He nodded at the poster. 'I take it your ladies will be there too?'

'Absolutely,' Geraldine said, inwardly cringing at having copied him. 'I want my old girls and new recruits to get to know each other as soon as possible, and a Christmas pantomime is the perfect opportunity.'

'That's great. If I've learned nothing else, it's that we all need a little fun now and then,' Onslow said with a wink.

Geraldine forced out a weak smile, unsure whether this was his usual behaviour towards everyone, part of his cheeky-chap stage persona, or his flirting technique. Either way, it made her neck prickle with discomfort.

'You can't wind people to breaking point without releasing a little of the tension from time to time,' Onslow continued.

Geraldine caught movement by the front door.

'Talking of tension,' she murmured, relieved by the interruption but looking with trepidation over Onslow's shoulder at the approaching Wing Commander Matfield. Ben Vickers followed him through the door.

'Cinderella,' Matfield sneered as he reached them. 'Nothing too childish in it, I trust?'

'What would be the point otherwise?' Onslow said, with a smile. 'I've always loved a good panto and hope as many personnel as possible get to watch. I've been in the RAF long enough to know you Europeans can be a little uptight about enjoying yourselves.'

Matfield's expression fell like a landslide.

'I'll have you know we're British,' he snapped.

Geraldine fought to suppress a smile.

Onslow ignored the retort. 'I take it arrangements are in place: security, logistics, defence plan, and so on? It's a lot of people to gather together at the same time.'

'All taken care of,' Matfield said, looking affronted. 'Flight Lieutenant Vickers is on the ball. If there's an air raid tonight, we'll be ready.'

'Glad to hear it. Well, don't let us keep you from your preparations.'

Matfield looked confused as if unaccustomed to being brushed aside by someone he considered a nobody. His gaze flicked back and forth between them, his mouth open but any words seemingly caught in his throat. Geraldine could see the struggle to comprehend going on behind his eyes and she tensed, ready for the backlash. None came. Instead, Matfield said, 'Carry on,' before turning on his heels and taking the stairs up to the first floor towards where his office faced Dallington's.

Geraldine considered the man in front of her through fresh eyes. Beneath the humour and tough exterior needed by every comedian appeared to lie an even harder centre capable of rebuffing one of the two men who made her life uncomfortable on an almost daily basis. She wasn't sure how she felt about that.

'I'm terribly sorry,' Vickers said. 'I'd like to say, I'm sure he didn't mean to be rude, but . . .' He shrugged.

Onslow held his hands up, palms out, placating.

'I know – I'm a big brash Yank who thinks a good time is more important than work.' He smiled. 'At least, that's what Group Captain Dallington told me.'

'But you're Canadian,' Vickers said.

'That's what I keep telling them.'

Vickers returned the smile. 'Matfield and the CO have some funny ways but you'll get used to them. Their bark's worse than their bite.'

'But they bark a lot, right?'

'Oh yes.'

◆　◆　◆

Kember blew air through puffed-out cheeks.

Whatever happened to the good honest villains out to make a few quid? he thought. He hated violence but could understand why those seeking to make a quick and sometimes substantial profit would use it. What he'd never understand was this seemingly new breed of murderer who sought something intangible that money couldn't buy. Perhaps they weren't new and had always been around. What if they always would be? The thought depressed him and he looked up sharply when Wright gave a discreet cough.

'Here's a hot sweet tea to perk you up, Miss Hayes,' Wright said. 'You'll be right as rain in no time.'

'Thank you,' Lizzie said, taking the steaming brew.

'About the other matter, sir. I spoke to Alf Lewis, the station-master, like you asked.'

Kember nodded. 'Ah, yes. What did he have to say?'

'I showed him the photograph and he recognised Evelyn Hartson.' Wright consulted his notebook. 'Alf remembered that particular young lady getting off the train from Paddock Wood because he thought it were unusual.'

'Unusual, why?'

'Said he didn't get many young ladies dressed up to the nines passing through his station on their own before the war, and even less since war broke out. These days he gets all sorts in uniforms coming through so you can't tell if someone was born with a silver spoon in their mouth or not, until they speak. But he remembers this one because she wasn't in uniform, wore expensive-looking clothes and seemed anxious.'

'Anxious as in scared?' Kember asked, opening his pocket book and looking up at Wright. 'Was she being forced or followed?'

'Neither.' Wright tapped his notebook with a pencil. 'According to Alf she looked excited but nervous, as if she were looking forward to meeting someone but worried about it at the same time. Kept looking around and over her shoulder.'

'Did Alf notice anything else? Who she met, perhaps?'

'He did.' Wright gave a knowing nod. 'He collected her ticket at the gate and saw her hurry across to a man standing by the road. Said he was dressed like he was off to church. You know, smart, Sunday best, but not a toff. Alf had to take tickets from the other passengers so he didn't see where they went but he's sure they walked because he didn't hear an engine or the rumble of cartwheels.'

Kember made an entry in his book.

Wright flicked over another page of his own notebook. 'If Alf's eyes told him the truth, amid the distraction of ticket collecting, the man was young looking, in his twenties perhaps, of slim build and with a full head of thick dark hair. Couldn't see his face though.'

'Doesn't sound like our missing Mr Jarvis.'

'No, sir.'

'But it does sound like dozens of young men around here,' Lizzie said.

Kember rubbed his neck and pinched the bridge of his nose in thought. 'If Evelyn Hartson wasn't meeting Kenneth Jarvis, we're still left with several questions. Who is the young man? Why were they meeting? Where did they go and where are they now?'

'Not forgetting, where is Kenneth Jarvis and who killed Maisie Chapman?' Lizzie said.

'Exactly.' Kember gave Wright an apologetic smile. 'I know it's Saturday and getting a bit late but can you have a quick trot down to Meadowbank Lane and Acorn Street?' Despite a twinge of guilt when he saw Wright flick a look of dismay at the wall clock, he knew time was pressing if Evelyn was in danger. 'If Alf reckons the couple walked from the station, they must be close by. Someone might have noticed a well-dressed young lady on the arm of a young man in his Sunday best, especially neighbours. We might get lucky.'

'Aye sir,' Wright said, reaching for his helmet and greatcoat as he left the room.

Kember was relieved to see the colour returning to Lizzie's face but his train of thought was broken a few moments later by a knock. At Kember's called response, the door opened, revealing a woman standing unsteadily in the office doorway, leaning against the frame. She looked at Kember through eyes glistening with unshed tears and lined at the corners with worry. He stood and ushered her to his chair, offering tea she refused.

With her wavy hair bleached blonde and cut shorter in the 1930s style, he judged her to be in her late forties. Not the usual visitor to a village police station.

Turning her face away from Lizzie and dabbing her eyes with a small handkerchief as the tears finally fell, the woman said, 'I was looking for Sergeant Wright. I've come to report a missing person.'

Kember's interest piqued in an instant.

'And who might that be?' he asked.

'Well, it's all a bit delicate.'

Kember saw the hand holding the handkerchief squeeze it tighter. The other drew her handbag closer as if for protection.

'Unless a crime has been committed, whatever you say will remain confidential, I assure you.'

The woman glanced at Lizzie cocooned in her blanket.

'Let's start with names,' Kember urged. 'I'm Detective Inspector Kember and this is Miss Hayes. She's seconded to us.' He almost winced at how easy that lie came again. 'And you are?'

The woman narrowed her watery eyes as if assessing Kember's statement, then relaxed a little and took a breath.

'My name is Janice Bateman and I live in a small cottage off the Lamberhurst road. I've' – she gave a nervous cough – 'been seeing a gentleman for a while. I'm a widow, you see, and times can be hard, lonely, especially in wartime. We've become quite close.'

Kember could sense how close. 'And what is it about this gentleman's absence that gives you cause for concern?' he asked.

'He's a foreman on the farms so work is seasonal. He goes where the work is most of the year but the winter months are spent around here, near Scotney. That's when I get to see him most, you understand? When he's here we can spend more time together, but . . .'

Kember nodded as Mrs Bateman's voice tailed off. 'How long since you last heard from him?'

'Two days.' She gave her handkerchief another squeeze. 'He was supposed to come to the cottage for some supper but he never arrived. He always lets me know if he can't come so I thought he might get a message to me this morning. Certainly, by early this afternoon.'

Kember made a show of writing a note in his book. 'Have you tried contacting him?' he asked.

She shot Kember a pained look. 'He has a wife, in the village. Our arrangement has to be very discreet, but it's most unlike him not to let me know. I'm worried about him.'

Kember found his compassion evaporating. On the one hand was a distraught woman looking for her lover but on the other was a man who had been cheating on his wife. Having been kicked out himself by his adulterous wife five months ago, he was less inclined to be sympathetic.

'Why should you be worried? What do you think has happened?'

'I don't know, but he had a serious argument with the owner where he works and I know his workmates were upset too, about him taking time off to see me.'

Realisation turned to a feeling of dread radiating outward from Kember's chest. 'What is the name of your gentleman friend?'

Janice Bateman hesitated before replying. 'Jarvis. Kenneth Jarvis,' she said. 'And there's no telling what his wife's done if she's found out.'

Kember and Lizzie exchanged a glance.

'His wife?' Kember said, remembering Agnes Jarvis sitting there the previous evening, wringing her hands in a similar way.

'Have you never heard the rumours? They say her parents refused to let them marry so she killed them and married anyway.'

Kember regarded the woman in front of him. She appeared terrified of the man's wife and employer but had been carrying on an affair for several months at least, regardless of the potential consequences. Clearly, she had the wherewithal to be both secretive and strong minded. From what she'd just said, she was the so-called floozy they'd been looking for, but she was a widow which meant no jealous husband in the picture. If the mysterious Kenneth Jarvis really was no more, that left four suspects: his wife, the sacked labourer from Paddock Wood, Derek Chapman, and Janice Bateman herself.

Kember decided not to mention the visit from Agnes Jarvis. Instead, he took all the particulars and filled in a missing-person report, promising that Kent's finest officers would be right onto it.

He declined to mention those officers consisted only of himself and Sergeant Wright.

◆ ◆ ◆

Flight Lieutenant Vickers sat back from his mound of paper-work and rubbed his eyes. When he'd joined the RAF Police, he'd thought a life of excitement and adventure lay ahead. No such luck. The days were mainly filled with routine and boredom, inspections and paperwork, punctuated infrequently by brief bursts of activity and the odd petty offence by one of the men. Still, at least he wasn't flying bombers through clouds of flak over Germany.

He looked at his in-tray again and leant forward for the next sheet of paper in the pile, a circular, warning against the dangers of Fifth Column agents helping the Nazi cause. He shook his head dismissively. Scotney was too tight-knit a community to let German agents roam around. He jotted a note on the circular and put it in his out-tray just as the harsh ring of the telephone shattered his thoughts. He stretched out a weary hand for the receiver and listened. The conversation was brief; one of his RAF pals returning his call with the information he'd requested. He signed off with the promise of a beer whenever they next had the good fortune to meet, and hung up. In one way the news was good but he suspected it added nothing to Lizzie's investigation.

He sighed and reached for the next document.

◆ ◆ ◆

'You need to get back to the air station and get some rest,' Kember said, once Janice Bateman had left. 'You look exhausted.'

Lizzie returned a half-smile. 'So do you, but I'll be all right. My next assignment isn't until early tomorrow, if I get anything at all. We're almost back to full complement so the flight captain said she'll keep giving the new girls the first chits so us old girls can have a bit of a rest.'

'Quite right, too.'

She saw him chew his lip before his professional drive got the better of him.

'Before you go, did you get a sense of whether she was telling the truth?'

Lizzie ran her hands back through her damp hair before rubbing them together. Her own professionalism took over and she held herself differently, automatically, as if she now sat before magistrates in a court.

'Mrs Bateman was obviously distraught. It's possible to act that upset for a while but difficult to sustain the pretence in such close proximity to other people, especially people in authority like the police. Little things can give you away but I believe I saw genuine tears and anguish. You could feel her distress, see it in the way her knees almost buckled when she leant against the door and how she almost wrung the life out of her handkerchief. You could hear it in the crack in her voice and the way random sobs broke up her speech. Did you notice the way she always referred to him in the present tense, never the past, as if he's missing but still alive?'

Kember nodded. 'That's not unusual, surely?'

'No, it isn't. Loved ones almost always refer to the deceased in that way, especially for the first few days or until after the funeral, because they find it difficult to believe they've gone. Families need to grieve to achieve that acceptance. That's difficult to fake without slipping up. Mrs Bateman may have argued with Kenneth Jarvis and feel guilty because of that, or because of the whole love affair, but I'd be very surprised if she had anything to do with his disappearance.'

'I admit I got that impression too,' Kember murmured.

Lizzie almost smiled at Kember's look of grudging acceptance. He understood as well as her that most victims knew or had met their murderers, but he also knew she had a way of reading people that made it difficult for them to conceal their true selves for long. She glanced at the clock and stood abruptly, bringing Kember to his feet also.

'I'd better go. The ENSA troupe are performing their Christmas show at the air station tonight. As long as Jerry doesn't pay us a visit, it should be a good evening.' She moved to the door and felt a tightness in her chest as an idea came to her. 'You can come if you like,' she said, and left quickly before he could turn her down.

◆ ◆ ◆

Flight Lieutenant Vickers lifted the receiver of his office telephone for the fourth time in an hour and greeted a familiar voice on the other end. Grunting at irregular points, he made jottings on a scrap of paper until he replaced the receiver and stared at it without seeing, the information passed over being something of a relief.

War he could cope with. War he could understand. War was structured and understandable as a concept. One army against another. You had the bad guys who wanted something, and the good guys who were there to stop it being taken. Nice and simple. Chasing murderers, on the other hand . . .

◆ ◆ ◆

As Kember stared at the place Lizzie's smile had been, his frown returned, more in embarrassment than annoyance as he felt his cheeks burn. He sat down and consulted his notebook.

He typed up his scribbled notes and made a fresh pot of tea as he mulled over their conversation. It seemed the disappearance of Evelyn Hartson had little or nothing to do with the disappearance of Kenneth Jarvis. That the two incidents had happened around the same time could be one of those rare occurrences that policemen are loath to entertain; a coincidence. But when you added Maisie Chapman to the mix along with Catherine Summers and Dora Enright . . . Some coincidences were just that, while others were nothing less than truths converging.

Kember had just sat back at Wright's desk when the telephone rang.

'Scotney Police Station,' he answered. 'DI Kember speaking.'

Kember listened to the caller, sometimes making noises of acknowledgement but mostly just listening. After a few moments he thanked the caller and put the Bakelite handset back on its cradle, only for the harsh ringing of the telephone bell to make him snatch it up again.

'Yes?' he snapped, irritated by the interruption. His tone softened and he apologised when he recognised the voice of Chief Inspector Hartson. He thanked his superior officer for ringing back and proceeded to ask him about his niece. While Hartson was adamant that she was not courting, he could not verify she had no suitors at present. Hartson became outraged at Kember's suggestion that Evelyn might have arranged to meet someone secretly in Scotney, a new friend perhaps, male or female, and one unknown to the family, incensed at the suggestion his niece could be in any way deceitful. 'This is the English countryside not the East End of London,' he spluttered, threatening to suspend Kember with a view to throwing him off the force altogether. In his mind's eye, Kember could see Hartson's face becoming redder and redder, eyes widening in further outrage, and could sense little benefit in continuing the interview. He emphasised that all they had so far were unreliable sightings and circumstantial evidence before changing the subject.

'In the course of my investigations into the murdered woman, two similar deaths have come to light in Duxford and Croydon, both near to the air stations.' Kember heard Hartson take a deep breath as he continued. 'All three had their throats cut and their hands cut off. I think we should notify Scotland Yard as soon as possible and draft in more men, sir, because it's possible we have a serial murderer hunting young women in the south-east for their hands.'

Hartson's hollow laugh told him everything.

'Firstly, if you weren't already seconded to us from the Yard, I dare say they'd send you anyway, so you'd better get on with your job. Secondly, I order you to steer clear of that crazy woman who keeps filling your head with nonsense. I'll not have her interfering with my officers while they're investigating.'

'But—'

'And you can't have more men!'

Hartson grunted and rang off, leaving Kember fuming at the rebuff. Surely three dead women with missing hands was strong enough evidence for anyone that a serial murderer was at work?

◆　◆　◆

'Ah, Lizzie. I'm glad I caught you.'

Lizzie spun at the sound of her name and waited for Vickers to cross the hall.

'Are you all right? You look a bit flushed,' she said.

'I must say, you're not looking very chipper yourself,' he replied.

Lizzie's explanation died on her lips as Vickers put his hand on her elbow and she found herself guided through the blackout curtains covering the lounge door. Although the blackout was in force across the air station, a half-moon shed enough pale illumination between the clouds for her to see across the darkened terrace.

'What's wrong?' she hissed, alarmed by his grip and the furtive glances he'd shot at drinkers as they'd passed through the lounge.

'I've been on the blower to the contacts you asked me to call,' he said, keeping his voice low.

Lizzie's focus snapped to attention. 'Go on.'

Vickers glanced around again as they sat at a table. 'I did a quick ring round to as many RAF mates as I could get away with before Dallington and Matfield got suspicious,' he said. 'I've also got a pal in the army, based in Catterick, and another in the Royal Navy, stationed at Portsmouth.'

Lizzie's heart sank, the familiar ache of dread flooding her chest. 'And?'

'Only one said he'd heard of an odd death in the last few months. He'd recently been posted away from Croydon but said he knew about the girl in the NAAFI canteen there.'

Her heart thumped harder with relief. She would have taken no pleasure in being right because it would have meant more dead women. Even so, she could feel the change begin. Soon, the familiar throat tightening and chest-crushing anxiety fought to the surface. Being exposed on the terrace, and in the presence of Vickers, compounded the effects of the rising anxiety attack. She saw him reaching for his packet of cigarettes and snatched the opportunity to reach for the countermeasure in her tunic pocket. Normally, she would take herself away from the trigger incident and use a count-up and count-down method of distraction followed by the sharp shock of pinging the band against her wrist. This time the onset was more rapid and she feared collapsing in front of Vickers.

She opened her eyes, vaguely noticed Vickers indicating his cigarettes and nodded. While he put two between his lips and struck a match, she unscrewed the lid of the Vicks jar and inhaled deeply. The mixture of camphor, eucalyptus oil and menthol did its job instantly, knocking the unnatural rhythm of her breathing and negative cycle of her brain back to something akin to normality.

She gave Vickers a wan smile and accepted a lit cigarette, hoping he hadn't noticed her momentary loss of control. She took a long, steadying drag, blew a stream of smoke skyward and crossed her legs.

'Thank Christ it's not more, Ben,' Lizzie said, and shivered as the frosty night air penetrated her uniform. 'That still leaves three murdered women though.'

CHAPTER THIRTEEN

Sergeant Wright breezed back into the front office, bringing in cold air and the smell of outdoors on his clothes. Kember, whose temper had returned to something akin to normal after his brush with Hartson, looked up expectantly as Wright shed his greatcoat and helmet and sat in the visitor's chair.

'I take it from your face that you had no luck?' Kember said.

'Yes and no, sir,' Wright replied.

That expression always irritated Kember. Either you had some luck, good or bad, or you didn't. He realised his face had assumed a frown, and cursed the march of each decade of age which brought increasing levels of grumpiness, pedantry and intolerance.

'Sir?'

'Sorry, Sergeant,' Kember said. 'Carry on.'

'I checked all the houses down Meadowbank Lane, where two young lads live, and Acorn Street where two others live. I know most of the families there anyway but I knocked on every door like you said. Two doors weren't answered but only one where a young lad lives with his mother. I know the young woman who lives in the other one, she looks after her elderly mother there. Three of the lads have reserved occupations, two of them working at local farms and another on the railway. The fourth is unfit for active service, problems with his arm. He works for Les Brannan at the pub.'

The *unfit for active service* letter he'd received from the War Office flashed into Kember's mind and he remembered the feeling of being crushed, all while his son went off to join the RAF and his daughter the WAAFs.

'Did the neighbours shed any light?'

Wright shook his head thoughtfully. 'Nobody saw a thing. The three lads I spoke to are all nice enough. Can't see what the chief inspector's niece would see in them though.'

'Well, make a note. We might need to bring them in for a chat at some stage.'

'Right-o, sir.'

Kember waved a hand vaguely at his notebook. 'You had a visitor while you were out.'

'Really?' Wright's eyebrows emphasised his surprise.

'A middle-aged woman by the name of Janice Bateman came asking for you.'

'Janice Bateman?' Wright frowned. 'Janice Bateman. Is that she who has a place on the Lamberhurst Road?'

'The very same.'

'And she wanted me?'

'Relax, Sergeant. She wanted the police and yours was a name she knew. She was rather keen to find her missing gentleman friend.'

'Did she give a name, or a reason why she thinks he's missing?'

Kember gave Wright the gist of his conversation with Janice Bateman and watched expressions of surprise, concern and interest pass across his face.

'And there's more,' Kember said. 'Your contact at the Yard came back to us. The murder rate across the whole country has gone up since the blackout started, but only one murder has been reported to them that fitted the description you gave, Dora Enright in Croydon.'

'Bloody hell, that's a relief – excuse my French,' Wright said.

'I take it you smoothed things over because he gave me the details without asking any questions. He also gave me a telephone number to ring, unaware I already knew the DI on the case.'

'That's another favour I owe him,' Wright said, with a theatrical sigh. 'I think I need a cuppa.'

◆ ◆ ◆

Still feeling shaky after narrowly averting an anxiety attack, Lizzie finished her cigarette with Vickers and retired to her room upstairs in the manor house. The thought of the women suffering muti-lation, albeit after their deaths, sickened her. She sat on her bed, back against the wall, and linked her fingers behind her head. She stared at her chair as if someone sat there, and relaxed her eyes as she let her thoughts wander, trying to wriggle into the mind of the predator.

'What is it about their hands that drives you?' Lizzie said, softly. 'You take care, removing them whole, intact, feminine, and position the bodies tenderly, as if they have given you a precious gift and you are grateful for their sacrifice.'

She closed her eyes to focus her mind, still conversing with the killer as if he sat in the nearby chair.

'Hands are too big and rot like meat left out of cold storage. I'd take something they owned that I could treasure, like a lock of hair. Unless . . .'

Lizzie opened her eyes again, took her hands from behind her head and looked at them.

'Do they represent someone taken from your life, or the one who did the taking?'

Seeing but not seeing as the edges of her vision blurred, her thoughts swam together and the dark-shrouded figure of a man sat on a chair at the centre.

'You're searching for someone very important to you, but whatever these young women have, it doesn't measure up to your expectations, does it? Their hands seem perfect, until you have them for yourself and see them close up.'

Lizzie's eyes, still focused on that indefinable, inexplicable place existing between daydream and reality, widened as a realisation hit her.

'They all have a fatal imperfection, a blemish that renders them useless.'

Lizzie pressed her hands to her chest as her breaths came quick and shallow.

'But is there such a thing as perfection? If not, you'll always be looking!'

Lizzie sat bolt upright, her eyes staring and her heart thumping.

A harsh sound from the door had startled her and it took her a few seconds to realise someone was knocking. She moved to the door, composed herself and opened it a few inches, the concerned face of Geraldine appearing in the gap.

'Is there something wrong?' Lizzie said as calmly as she could.

'The group captain wants to see us right away,' said Geraldine.

'All right. Give me a minute to freshen up.'

Lizzie closed the door and took a deep breath, feeling her heart rate returning to normal.

Having retired to the back room, Kember had just sat down while Wright put the kettle on to boil when someone called from along the hallway. Wright answered and the mop of fair hair and youthful face of Reverend Giles Wilson, vicar of St Matthew's Church, appeared in the doorway.

Kember indicated the chair opposite him and Wright automatically pulled another cup from the cupboard. Wilson sat but declined the tea.

'What can we do for you, Reverend?' Kember asked.

He had first met Wilson during the Scotney Ripper case. An ex-merchant navy man with a penchant for strong rum, Wilson suffered from deep remorse, having killed a man accidentally while at sea.

'I have something for you I think may be of interest,' Wilson said. 'What with the glut of policemen that passed through the village this morning and Sergeant Wright knocking on people's doors, tongues have been set wagging, as you can imagine. The village is rife with rumours about another murderer.'

'That isn't helpful—'

'I know.' Wilson held up his hands. 'But you can't stop people talking in a place like this, and they're worried after what happened last time.'

'I can assure you, that's not happening again.' Kember knew he could give no such assurance and his heart gave an extra hard beat.

'Maybe not, but the gentlemen of the birdwatchers' club frightened Miss Finch in the tea shop with gruesome tales of missing hands.'

Kember saw Wright look across from his tea-making, alarm on his face and his mouth open to speak.

'I'm sure Sergeant Wright will reassure her and the other villagers later on. What is it you have for us?'

'Ah, yes. I've not long been speaking to Jennifer Ward on the telephone.' Wilson's gaze flicked between the two policemen. 'You must remember her.'

Kember remembered Jenny Ward very well, having met her years before when she was training to be a nurse and he was a young constable. He had asked her about Wilson as part of the investigation into the Scotney Ripper murders. Kember nodded, his face giving nothing away. 'Lovely telephone voice.'

'Lovely lady all round,' Wilson agreed. 'Well, she gave me a little piece of information, I'm loath to call it gossip, about an incident at the Chatham naval dockyard.'

'Here we go again,' Wright said with a frown.

'It's probably outside your investigation but I had to tell you, given this morning's activity. The secretary in the chaplain's office at the dockyard rang the Rochester Diocesan Office to report the disappearance of one of the chaplain's assistants, Lance Atkinson, a curate in his own right who had volunteered to minister to the armed forces when war was declared. When Jenny took the call, the secretary also told her the dockyard police had found a body of a young woman. Angela Caxton was a cook in the NAAFI canteen, she said.'

Kember was on full alert now. 'Where was she found?'

'By the dockyard buildings right next to the river,' Wilson explained. 'Underneath a pile of rubble caused by a bomb last weekend. The navy has claimed jurisdiction, stating she was killed during the air raid, but the secretary told Jenny she didn't believe a word of it.'

'Why not?'

Wilson took a breath. 'Because her throat was cut and her hands were missing.'

Kember had feared as much. In the moment's silence after the revelation, the kettle startled them by whistling loudly. Wright took it off the gas ring by its handle, used a cloth to twist the whistle from the spout, and poured hot water into the teapot.

'I thought there were striking similarities to the young girl in the field,' Wilson explained.

'So why are the authorities saying it was a bomb?' Kember asked, wondering how Hartson would take the news.

'To stop panic, I would think. You don't want a murderer among you when you're trying to fight a war. They're saying that modern bombs can kill you in more ways than blowing you up or shredding you with shrapnel. There have been cases reported in the papers where the air has been sucked from people's lungs by the bomb blast and people have been found half-naked, virtually bald or without ears and hands.'

'God Almighty,' Wright said, sadly. 'What are we doing to this world?'

'Indeed,' Wilson agreed.

Kember had often joked with colleagues about his head being a giant paper room where the files of thoughts and past experiences were kept. A little man with a tan overcoat and flat cap, who would rummage through his brain to retrieve a memory or make a connection, resided there. Kember sensed the little man rising from his chair.

'What happened to the young curate?' he asked.

Wilson's eyebrows descended into a slight frown. 'Ah, he wasn't a *young* curate. He found his calling in later life, so I'm told. Jenny said they're still looking for him, apparently, but the dockyard police blame the air raids too.'

Kember found the suggestion of a cover-up not so far-fetched. Truth was always in short supply in wartime and that did little to help his investigation, or his mood. Could it be the same murderer? Wartime restrictions suggested you couldn't go very far without papers and a travel warrant, but the country was awash with movement, and papers could be forged.

'Thought you should know anyway,' Wilson said, standing to go.

'Thank you for telling us,' Kember said. 'I'll have a word with the dockyard police myself.'

Wilson's mouth twitched a brief smile as he shook the hands of Kember and Wright. 'Good day, officers. Perhaps I'll see you at tonight's pantomime, up at the air station.'

'Over my dead body,' Wright said with a grimace, once Wilson had left. 'Sorry, sir.' He looked at Kember. 'Poor choice of words.'

Kember sighed.

'The War Office wants to avoid hitting morale so has put pressure on the local police in Croydon to downplay the murder there. The navy has claimed jurisdiction at the dockyard so Scotland Yard will be kept in the dark about that one. The Yard knows about Lizzie's friend in Duxford but Hartson doesn't want them involved in what we have down here.' He shook his head. 'This is ridiculous.'

'Four poor lasses dead,' Wright said, his voice cracking with emotion. 'What kind of evil are we up against this time?'

◆ ◆ ◆

'That was a bloody damn fool landing,' Dallington said, thumping his fist on his desk.

Lizzie remained standing to attention next to Geraldine. Neither woman flinched. Dallington picked up his pipe from its carved wooden stand and frowned at the empty bowl.

'I've never seen one of our aircraft dive on its own air station then slap onto the runway with a bounce like a tennis ball.'

Holding the bowl of the pipe, he thrust the stem at Lizzie. 'What on earth were you thinking?'

Out of the corner of her eye, Lizzie caught the look of disdain that crossed Geraldine's face.

'Sorry, sir,' Lizzie said. 'The tower ordered me to pancake the Anson.'

'Pancake, yes. Not dog's dinner. Any more flying like that and I'll have you thrown off my air station. Is that clear?'

'Perfectly, sir,' said Lizzie, hoping to escape with no more than a dressing-down.

'If I may speak, sir,' Geraldine said.

Lizzie flicked a sideways glance at her flight captain, who had remained silent until now, and could see from the colour in her cheeks that she had no intention of letting the matter lie.

'As I understand it, the order to pancake came directly from Scotney control tower in response to a warning from Biggin Hill control room.'

'And your point is?' Dallington said with a puzzled look.

Geraldine looked down at the seated RAF man for the first time since entering his office. 'My point is that both Biggin Hill and Scotney were aware of a dangerous situation developing and ordered Third Officer Hayes to land, not only immediately but with haste.'

'Correct but—'.

'There can be no but, sir. Third Officer Hayes is a talented and experienced pilot who used all her flying skills to carry out a direct order from the tower in the most effective and efficient manner she could.'

'Yes but—'

'Unless Third Officer Hayes has disobeyed an order or con-travened any flying regulations, I cannot see what problem has arisen.'

Lizzie could see Dallington's temper beginning to fray by the deepening colour of his face and the way he jabbed his glasses back up to the bridge of his nose.

'You know as well as I that it is my responsibility to ensure the safety and security of this air station and its personnel,' Dallington said, almost with a growl. 'That means even you women.'

'And we appreciate your efforts, sir,' Geraldine said. 'But I have a particular responsibility to ATA headquarters and the women under my command. Third Officer Hayes, through quick thinking, skill and dexterity, not only ensured her own safety and that of the aircraft she was piloting but also the continued viability of this air station by maintaining the continuity of my detachment.'

Everyone who came into contact with Dallington could be in no doubt that he hated having the ATA women, any women, associated with his air station. He thought they should remain in the home, or at least the factories, and had been put in harm's way unnecessarily. He still called the Air Ministry on a regular basis to see if he could have them withdrawn, as he had done since the ATA arrived five months ago at the start of the Battle of Britain. But he was also pragmatic and both Geraldine and Lizzie knew he was fully aware that the detachment had been the saviour of him and what he considered to be *his* airfield.

If her continued employment by the ATA hadn't been at stake, Lizzie could have found the power play between the two officers almost amusing. As it was, she found it fascinating and could sense a shift in Dallington's mood as he scooped a wad of Old Holborn tobacco from a tin into the blackened bowl of his pipe. His complexion had begun to return to normal by the time he struck a match and emitted clouds of blue-tinged smoke.

'As no physical harm has been done on this occasion, I will leave the matter in your hands, Flight Captain,' he said, as if that had been his decision all along.

Lizzie felt the tension leave her shoulders.

'Thank you, sir,' Geraldine said, saluting to end the hearing before Dallington could continue. 'Very wise.' She turned on her heel and left the room.

Lizzie quickly followed suit and closed the door behind her before Dallington could recall them. Geraldine said nothing as they left the anteroom and strode along the corridor but stopped at the top of the main staircase in the hall.

'What does landing like a "dog's dinner" actually look like?' she said.

Despite the admonishment, the image of her landing looking literally like a dog's dinner popped into Lizzie's head and she couldn't help smiling.

◆ ◆ ◆

'Sorry to disturb you, sir,' Wright said. 'I found this scruffy lad loitering outside the front door. He's one of the young lads I told you about earlier.'

Kember had just put the receiver down on a call to the Royal Marine Police at Chatham Royal Navy Dockyard, arranging a meeting for the following morning. He looked up at the young man dressed in baggy trousers, loose shirt, waistcoat and flat cap, the traditional garb of an agricultural labourer. Kember motioned for the man to sit and waited as he folded his overcoat neatly across his knees.

'Thank you for coming in,' Kember began. 'What do we call you?'

'Yates, sir. Peter Yates.'

'And where do you live, Peter?'

'Down Meadowbank Lane, sir, with Mum. It's a bit pokey, like, but it's all right. I do my best to keep it fixed while Dad's away.'

'I'm sure. And what is it you do?'

'Do?'

'As a job, for a living?'

'I'm a farmhand, sir. Nothing skilled, just general labouring and that. I can't join up because growing food is a reserved occupation. I've joined the Home Guard though. Wanted to do my bit somehow.'

Kember could see the disappointment as the young man spoke and it was obvious that he had wanted to fight for his country. He gave a nod of understanding. 'Do you know why we wanted to speak to you?'

'Something about a missing girl, Mum said. But I haven't got a girl. Got no time see, what with early starts and late nights. Crops and cows and that.'

'That's not quite what I meant. Have you seen any strangers in or around the village? A young girl perhaps, in her early twenties?'

Yates frowned in thought. 'No, sir. Plenty of strangers in all sorts of uniforms all over the place these days. And then there's that acting lot in the field beyond the village.'

'Do you work every day?' Kember asked.

'Pretty much. I get the odd afternoon off, and time for church, of course, but there ain't much to do around here and I can't get over to Tonbridge much so I stays home mostly, when I'm not on parade with the Guard.'

'What about other young men in the village? Do you meet with any of those?'

'Sometimes. We grew up together and went to the same school but I keep myself to myself mostly . . .' Yates stopped, dipped his head slightly and half-raised his hand. 'Hold on. Was this young 'un in civvies?'

Kember caught a look from Wright. 'She would have been, yes. Well-dressed, I'd say. Why do you ask?'

''Cos Chapman sent me to the railway station last Friday to collect new ploughshares that were being sent from London. Jogged my memory, that has. I remember now, I did see a young lady, dressed in finery, being escorted arm-in-arm away from the station by a gentleman.'

Kember rested his elbow on the desk and leant towards Yates. 'Did you see who it was or what he looked like?'

Yates looked Kember straight in the eyes. ''Fraid not, sir. I had to get back with the parts before I had my wages docked.'

Kember almost swore in frustration. 'Did you see which way they went? Did they get into a car or a carriage of any sort?'

Kember's face was close and Yates leant back to increase the distance. 'As I said, sir, I wasn't taking much notice. There *was* a car and a couple of carriages near the station but I don't know who owned 'em or whether they got in one.'

Kember sat back and looked up at Wright for inspiration but, as usual, the sergeant merely shrugged and Kember felt the case was outrunning them again.

'All right, Peter. Thank you for coming in to talk to us. We appreciate you taking the time rather than waiting for us to come looking for you again. If you see a young civilian woman not from this village, or you remember more detail of the encounter at the station, please let us know as soon as you can.'

Yates stood and shrugged into his overcoat. 'I will, sir, thank you.'

Kember waited for him to leave the police station before speaking again. 'What do you make of that?'

Wright shook his head. 'No better than I got from Alf Lewis, although it corroborates the story that the young lady walked away from the station willingly, with a smartly dressed gentleman.'

'Yates lives in Meadowbank Lane so I suppose he would have noticed if Evelyn and this man had headed that way. Is it possible then that our mystery suitor lives in Acorn Street?'

'Seems a fair bet, sir. I'll make further enquiries in the morning.'

CHAPTER FOURTEEN

With Lizzie still smarting from her dressing-down, Geraldine insisted on buying them both a pick-me-up. They chose a window table in the almost deserted officers' lounge on the ground floor of the manor house and ordered tea, which came swiftly. As Lizzie poured two cups, she noticed the airfield runway lights flick on. They were answered seconds later by the distant landing light of an aircraft on its final approach to land, bringing the ATA pilots back home. She clinked the pot back on the tray and offered milk.

'So, what are your first impressions of the new girls?' Geraldine said, pouring a splash of milk into her cup. 'Do you think they're up to scratch?'

Lizzie took a few sips of her tea, almost scalding her top lip in the process but needing to give herself a few seconds to reply.

'I don't know much about their flying abilities but I assume the ATA wouldn't let them join if they couldn't fly well.'

Geraldine eyed Lizzie over the rim of her cup. 'That's not quite what I meant.'

Lizzie knew that. Ever since revealing herself to be a psychologist she'd had Geraldine and the other ATA women asking for her opinion on various situations and potential boyfriends. She enjoyed being able to use her skills to help where she could but her reputation as someone who could understand the way that a murderer's mind works had somehow become transformed into her being a sage or soothsayer, or some kind of mind reader. Recently, her professional speciality, the serious domain of the criminal mind, seemed to have been forgotten and she'd begun to feel like a cheap party trick.

Geraldine was still waiting for a reply and Lizzie sighed in resignation.

'First impressions only, then,' Lizzie said. 'Hazel seems a good egg, and strong willed so she can stand up for herself.' She put down her cup. 'Yvonne is very pretty but smart with it. She's also French. Fizz is a Scot.'

'Meaning?'

'They say the Scots and French are old allies but you saw what happened when the new girls arrived.' When Geraldine said nothing, Lizzie continued. 'Yvonne has Gallic blood, Fizz has Celtic, both fiery temperaments when riled, which could give them common ground to bond or . . .'

'Or clash like two warring tribes.' Geraldine nodded.

Lizzie shrugged one shoulder. 'Could go either way.'

'Fizz and Niamh haven't killed each other yet.'

'Hmm.' *Yet*, she thought.

'And how are you?' Geraldine asked. 'The news of your friend being killed must have been a shock.'

Lizzie felt a twinge of anxiety at the sudden change of tack and pinged the rubber band on her wrist, hoping her face hadn't given her away.

'I'm fine. It *was* a shock but DI Kember's investigation is an interesting distraction and I think I'm helping.' Lizzie felt Geraldine's eyes boring into her.

'You're fully aware that I disapprove of your extra-curricular activities,' Geraldine said, a cool edge to her tone. 'I made that clear last time. However, as long as Dallington and Matfield don't find out and you keep yourself safe . . .'

Lizzie knew she could offer no guarantee, but gave Geraldine her most reassuring smile.

Flight Lieutenant Ben Vickers eyed the convoy of civilian lorries with suspicion as they entered RAF Scotney through the entrance created by the raised red and white barrier. In one way, he was looking forward to the ENSA pantomime being put on in little under two hours. On the other hand, every performer was capable of deception through their acting skills, representing an unnecessary and unwanted security risk.

Led by one of Vickers' men on a motorbike, a Morris truck had already started its journey around the perimeter track towards the performance hangar by the time the barrier closed behind the last of three Bedford lorries. Vickers did a double take of the driver: the face of a beautiful, dark-haired woman grinned back at him. He looked over the shoulder of the warder on gate duty and watched him tick off the last of the expected names.

Vickers looked back at the cab but the lorry was already grumbling past. *Dallington won't like that*, he thought, sliding into the passenger seat of an RAF blue Austin and nodding for the driver to follow the convoy. He had instructed his guard force to be on full alert tonight, until the last of the interlopers could be shepherded off the premises and the station made secure once again.

'With a madman on the loose,' he muttered more to himself than the driver, 'what better way to keep everyone safe than to gather strangers together in the dark?'

Watching the ENSA troupe's arrival from the darkness of a first-floor office, Group Captain Dallington turned away from the window criss-crossed with bomb-blast tape and cleared his throat loudly. Geraldine smiled at his discomfort and noted another of Onslow's sly winks at her.

Dallington noticed too.

'I suppose this is your influence, *Mister* Onslow.'

'How so, sir?'

'Your lot. The Americans.' Dallington's lips pressed forward in a petulant pout. 'Pantomimes, indeed.'

Onslow returned a disarming smile.

'I think you'll find the pantomime tradition originated from the Greeks and Romans. The English took characters from Italian *Commedia dell'arte* street theatre in the sixteenth century for their comic plays. To cut a long story short, the English stole the concept and took it to America.' Onslow smiled disarmingly before adding, 'And I believe us *Canadians* refined it. Sir.'

Geraldine had never seen Dallington's expression so dark, not even at the height of the Battle of Britain, and winced as he jammed his unlit pipe in his mouth.

'I'll be glad when this charade is over,' Dallington mumbled out of the side of his mouth before striding across the room and banging the door behind him.

Geraldine saw an RAF staff car peel away from the lorry convoy and stop on the gravel by the manor house. Vickers' head appeared at the passenger window and he waved at her.

Geraldine held up her hand in acknowledgement. 'Your ride's here,' she said to Onslow, letting out the breath she hadn't realised she'd been holding. 'Did you have to antagonise him?'

'Dallington?' Onslow shrugged. 'I'm helping out in a time of crisis. You'd think he'd be grateful for the support and give a little back.'

'That's not his way.' Geraldine fixed the blackout curtain back in place and turned on a banker's-style desk lamp. 'Get used to that and your brief stay here will be all the more pleasant for it. Trust me.'

'I'm here only for a few days to put on a couple of shows. I love pleasing a crowd, making the troops laugh, so Dallington's personal opinions of me, or Matfield's, come to that' – Onslow shook his head – 'don't matter at all.'

◆ ◆ ◆

Even in the blackout, Kember recognised the bulk of Ethel Garner barrelling along the pavement towards him.

'Mrs Garner,' he called, 'how are you this evening?'

'Don't you *how are you* me,' she said. 'I want to know what you're doing about that poor woman found up in that field.'

Kember took a step back from the face thrust at him. 'You know I can't discuss police investigations. It wouldn't be right.'

'I'll tell you what's not right, keeping us in the dark about what's going on, that's what.'

'All I can say is we're doing all we can.'

'That hardly makes me feel any better.' Ethel pouted. 'It took you a while to get to grips with things last time, didn't it? Mrs Ware said they're calling him the Handyman, according to her Tom who spends too much time in the pub if you ask me. Handyman. I ask you, whatever next? Have we got to have eyes in the back of our heads to look out for odd-job men now?'

'I can assure you, we're on top of the case,' Kember said, aware that he was giving shaky assurances rather too frequently today.

'If you want my opinion,' Ethel continued, 'you should be looking closer at the Jarvis sisters. Rumour has it, it wasn't the

Spanish flu that did for their parents. Folk reckon they killed their mum and dad so they could marry their sweethearts.'

'That's just hearsay, Mrs Garner,' Kember said, remembering his conversation with Wright. 'You know we can't work with that. Anyway, I thought Agnes was a friend of yours; a member of your gossip circle.'

'What do you mean, gossip circle?' she bristled. 'Cheeky sod. You know the old saying, no smoke without fire, as well as me. They've never denied it, you know.'

'Why should they if they've not done anything wrong?'

'How do you know if you haven't interrogated them? And where's that Ken Jarvis run off to? That's what I'd like to know.'

'We don't interrogate, we interview.'

'Well get off and interview, then. I tell you, something's not right there.'

'Mrs Garner,' Kember soothed. 'You know we've got everything in hand so I suggest you get yourself indoors, safe and warm, for a hot cup of cocoa. Doesn't look like Jerry will be over any time soon so you can settle down for a nice evening listening to the wireless.'

Kember could feel Mrs Garner's glare boring into him and was grateful when she pulled back and muttered something, no doubt derogatory, before striding away towards her house.

◆ ◆ ◆

In spite of the earlier altercation between Fizz and the new girls, Lizzie felt optimistic about the new recruits. They seemed to have a lot of experience and could certainly stand up for themselves against the often acid-tongued Scot. Hopefully, new friendships would form and the horrors of July could be put to the back of their minds.

Standing on the darkened terrace, looking across the ornamental gardens to where the airfield, hangars, trees and sky almost but not quite blended together, Lizzie found herself unable to relax. She should be calm and looking forward to the show but even the nicotine hit from her cigarette failed to settle her.

At the back of her mind, connections were forming, trying to tell her about something she'd missed. She'd had this feeling before and knew to stop worrying at it, to let her subconscious do the work for her. It would let her know the outcome in due course. She forced her consciousness away from the problem and found her mind instantaneously filled with thoughts of Kember. Not only would she be glad to see him again but she should tell him about Ben's enquiries.

Lizzie shivered and glanced at her watch, able to make out the time by the faint glow from its luminous hands. He should be arriving soon so she nipped off the smouldering end of her cigarette, placed the stub back in the packet and went to get ready. As she opened the door to slip through, the suction of air pulled at the blackout curtain, allowing a shard of light to cut through the thick material into the garden.

For a moment, she could have sworn she saw something briefly illuminated, an animal perhaps, gliding behind a bush and back into shadow.

CHAPTER FIFTEEN

As Lizzie descended the steps to the Hangar Round club, nodding to a ground-crew flight sergeant roped in as door security, she heard her colleagues laughing above the chorus of 'Santa Claus is Coming to Town' playing on their newly acquired record player. She joined them in the bar room, where to her relief she saw that Fizz and the new girls seemed to have called a Christmas truce. That was not to say Fizz wasn't airing her opinions, but her targets for tonight were the Germans for starting a war that had begun to deprive her of luxuries such as fine food, stylish clothing and some of her favourite single-malt Scotch whiskies.

In spite of shortages, alcohol appeared to be flowing freely enough and a flight engineer stood behind the bar, dispensing drinks with the dexterity of a juggler and making the limited tipples go further with judicious use of lemonade, tonic and fruit cordials. Lizzie accepted the gin and tonic that Niamh thrust her way, no ice or lemon available, and was soon deep in discussion with Hazel and Agata about leave coming up after Christmas and the potential for a New Year's Eve party.

Moments later, Lizzie caught sight of Kember at the same time as Agata, as he entered the games room through the vestibule.

'Your young man looks for you,' Agata said with a glance back, smiling as Lizzie's cheeks coloured.

'How many more times, he's not—'

'Ah, I do like a love story,' Yvonne interrupted.

'So do I,' Hazel said. 'He looks a bit of all right, so if you're not interested . . .'

'Oh, she's interested,' Niamh assured. 'She's a bit backward about coming forward, that's all. Come to think of it, so is he.'

All the women laughed and Lizzie took the good-natured ribbing for what it was, stepping forward to intercept Kember. Although his smile was a welcome sight, Lizzie's first thought was to discuss the case further. She bought him a bottle of light ale and they picked their way back through a throng of officers hanging around in the games room. Lizzie spotted Vickers and inclined her head for him to follow them.

Outside, Kember reached out a hand. 'Ben.'

'Jonathan.' Vickers grasped it in his own as a brief look of surprise crossed Kember's face at the unfamiliar use of his forename. 'I haven't seen you for a while.'

'Work,' Kember said. 'You know how it is.' He looked at the pips on Vickers' epaulettes. 'I see you've been promoted.'

'It seems they had a sudden vacancy a few months ago.' He smiled. 'It's nice to see you again.'

'And y—'

'We haven't got long,' Lizzie interrupted, as two RAF warders approached the steps. 'They'll be calling for us to make our way over to the hangar shortly.'

'Of course,' Kember said, apologetically.

Despite the cold, several people were milling about. Too many for Lizzie's liking. She led them back into the hall of the manor house, along a corridor and into the empty darkness of the briefing room, where Vickers flicked one switch to give them enough light to see each other.

'Why have you dragged us in here?' Kember asked.

'I – we – needed to tell you something,' Lizzie said.

Kember gave her and Vickers a puzzled look.

'We've been looking into recent deaths on or near military bases,' Lizzie explained.

'You've been turning detective on your own again?' Kember's voice held an edge of disapproval. 'You do remember what happened last time? I told you I don't want you looking for trouble and getting hurt.'

'As I recall, it was you who looked for trouble and got hurt.' Lizzie felt her mood darken in an instant at the implied suggestion that she couldn't take care of herself. 'But that's irrelevant. I'm trying to find out what happened to my friend, so if you'll just listen.'

The tone of Kember's voice and his attitude had started a ball of anxiety rolling inside Lizzie and she felt a twinge of resentment that he was able to elicit such a response from her. She tried to ping the thick rubber band on her wrist without drawing attention but both Kember and Vickers heard the snap. No matter, they'd seen it before, and her mind refocused as it did the trick.

'You already know about my friend at Duxford, the woman I discovered had been killed at Croydon, and Maisie Chapman, all found dead with their hands taken. Well, I persuaded Ben to ask around, to see if he could find out about any more suspicious deaths on military bases.'

She saw Kember's interest and nodded for Vickers to take over.

'I saw no harm in asking so I did a little ring round,' Vickers said. 'I called in a few favours and asked some old mates posted around the country. Only one of them had heard of any unusual deaths; the one at Croydon.'

'If it's true that there haven't been any others, it means my friend was his first victim,' Lizzie said. 'Which could be significant.'

Kember gave a heavy sigh and sat on a chair in the front row.

'I'm not pleased you went off and did this on your own, but we also did some digging. I got Sergeant Wright to call Scotland Yard about suspicious deaths involving missing hands. The only one reported to them was your friend at Duxford.'

A flicker of satisfaction passed through Lizzie but then she felt the familiar cold grip on her chest and she knew something was coming.

'But that doesn't include another one within the last week at Chatham Dockyard that Reverend Wilson told me about today,' Kember said.

'Christ Almighty,' Vickers said, running a hand through his hair.

'The reverend?' Lizzie said, intrigued. 'How did he find out?'

'He heard through the diocesan office. A woman working as a cook in the NAAFI was found dead with no hands. And a curate working for the dockyard chaplain is missing.'

'Jesus Christ,' Vickers said, sitting on a chair two along from Kember. 'That's three missing and four bodies with no hands. What the hell is going on?' He shook his head. 'I thought we'd left nightmares like this behind months ago.'

Lizzie saw the gaze of both Kember and Vickers alight on her and felt her face begin to colour up again.

'So did I,' she said, putting her hand to her throat automatically as if to protect herself. She caught herself in the act and lowered her hand as unobtrusively as she could, feeling her cheeks burn. At the sound of a shout, she checked her watch, grateful for the distraction. 'We have to go. They've called for us to go over to the hangar for the show.'

Kember stood and turned to Vickers. 'I'm off to see the Royal Marine Police and the chaplain at the dockyard tomorrow morning.

Reverend Wilson is coming with me after his morning church service and I'd like you to come too, if you can wangle it.'

Vickers also stood. 'I can't do that, I'm afraid. Dallington would have a fit.'

'Oh well, just a thought,' Kember said, moving to the door. 'Best not keep the concert party waiting then.'

As they filed out and joined the throng waiting to be ferried in vehicles over to the hangar, Lizzie thought she saw movement out of the corner of her eye. She turned her head to look up and caught the scowling face of Dallington, smoke billowing from his pipe, before he ducked back behind the blackout curtains.

◆　◆　◆

The first hour of the show went smoothly enough. In fact, Kember thought the ragtag bunch he'd seen lounging around the assorted tents of the ENSA encampment actually had a modicum of talent. Allowance had to be made for the temporary nature of the stage and auditorium, but the troupe were making a very good fist of it.

Pleased to see Lizzie enjoying herself, he smiled as the ATA women sitting to his left snorted and squealed with laughter at some topical joke. On a raised stage made from interlocking hollow wooden sections, the Cinderella pantomime played out in a riot of colour, lavish costumes, outrageous make-up and double entendres. After the Battle of Britain and now the ongoing Blitz, all endured in grey, the dull, earth tones of camouflage and the pitch-darkness of the blackout, the audience lapped it up. In spite of costume changes and the thick greasepaint make-up worn by the troupe, Kember easily picked out the performers who had posted flyers in the village.

The short, rotund figure of Tubby Saunders had been paired for comic effect with the six-foot-five Shorty McKnee as the Ugly

Sisters, and the constantly joking George Wilkes had landed the role of Buttons. Not only was Betty Fisher playing Dandini with thigh-slapping camp but also the Wicked Stepmother, with the aid of a wig and dress worn over her male costume. The greatest revelation was the spectacle-free Vera Butterfield who had undergone a transformation into a beautiful and captivating Cinderella. Kember didn't recognise the actors playing Prince Charming or a series of incidental characters, but Martin Onslow, whom Vickers had pointed out earlier, was hard to miss as a cigar-smoking Fairy Godmother who teased howls of laughter from the audience.

Although enjoying the show, Kember began to fidget and welcomed the arrival of the interval. He stood up and arched his aching back to ease his old injury, and saw a figure on the other side of the hangar jerk the theatre curtain back into place to disguise that they had been spying on the audience. Kember was intrigued. He looked around but no one else seemed to have noticed, or at least had thought nothing of it. He turned to mention it to Lizzie but she had declared her need to visit the lavatory and was already leaving the hangar through the haze of several hundred cigarettes being lit.

◆　◆　◆

Lizzie needed the loo badly. She left the hangar and took the most direct route towards the bulky shadow of the manor house, straight across the airfield, her breath condensing around her in the chilly air.

Reaching the trees and tall hedges near the house, she called a quick greeting in passing to one of Vickers' warders before crunching along the paths through the ornamental gardens and hurrying up the steps to the terrace. She slipped in through the unlocked doors and threw a loose salute to the startled Dallington, who was enjoying a quiet whisky at the dimly lit bar, before threading through to the lavatory.

◆ ◆ ◆

Kember watched from outside the hangar, wishing he'd escorted Lizzie as she walked across the airfield and disappeared into the dark.

Many audience members, including officers and lower ranks alike, gathered outside for fresh air, cigarettes and a leg stretch. Their murmuring conversations were all that disturbed the otherwise tranquil night. She'd been wearing nothing warmer than her tunic and he hoped she'd hurry back before she caught her death of cold.

Out of the corner of his eye, a movement caught his attention at the far end of the hangar, down low where the corrugated-iron roof met the concrete base. As usual, curiosity got the better of him and he tried to look casual as he went to take a look.

Nothing moved.

He knew shadows could play tricks on your eyes, especially at night when the periphery of your vision was a better detector of black and white than the colour-catching centre. But he felt sure someone or something had been there. He strolled along the length of the hangar, ears straining for any unusual sounds until he reached the far end. The clunk of scenery changes and the raised but muffled voices of actors in disagreement filtered through the crack in a door. Kember took a step forward.

'Halt!'

Kember jumped back as if punched, his heart racing, and saw a gun pointing at his stomach.

Retracing her journey at a more leisurely pace, her eyes readjusting to the enveloping darkness after the harsh glare of the lavatory light bulb, Lizzie picked her way carefully across the terrace slabs and down the frost-slick steps to the garden. The deep shadows around her kept changing appearance as her position moved, but she had a feeling that not all of them were behaving in the same way.

She paused and lit a warming cigarette, protecting the telltale glow in the cup of her hand, hoping the misbehaving shadows might take the hint and leave her imagination alone. In striking the match, she ruined her night vision further, plunging the area around her into an even deeper black. She tipped her head back and blew a lungful of smoke at the sky.

The pain in her neck was instantaneous as the shadow in front of her, gripping her throat, cut off air and stifled any cry.

Lizzie panicked, pushed her hands up between the shadow's arms but could not break the grip. Her cigarette dropped in a shower of sparks and lay trampled underfoot in the scuffle. Vickers' training flashed through her mind and she brought her arms up and over, smashing down to bend her assailant's arms at the elbows and break the tension. Their heads were thrown together, clashing and scattering her thoughts. That wasn't supposed to happen.

Through a swirling mass of twinkling speckles, Lizzie thought she saw a head with no hat, angular in shape, almost cube-like. The face had been covered but she couldn't tell with what. Her attacker spun her around and her head snapped back as an arm clamped across her throat from behind. She kicked out and heard a cry as it connected with a leg. She tried again but the attacker had dragged her back at an angle and her heel met nothing but air. With red mist now blurring her vision and her lungs bursting for want of oxygen, Lizzie groped for and found a gloved hand, scrabbling to catch hold of a finger and bend it back. The attacker yelped again and the arm released her but the respite was short-lived. A blow to the back of her head took the strength from Lizzie's legs as her brain began to shut down.

◆ ◆ ◆

'Christ Almighty, Ben,' Kember said, making a show of covering his chest where his heart would be. 'Give a chap a heart attack, why don't you?'

Vickers grinned as he holstered his gun. 'Serves you right for creeping around an air station in the dead of night. I thought you were a prowler.'

'A prowler? You've got all your guards on high alert and a hangar full of military personnel. Why would a prowler come anywhere near here?'

'Good question, so what are you doing back here?'

In the daylight, Vickers would have seen Kember's face redden as he muttered, 'I thought I saw . . .'

'A prowler?' Vickers finished.

Kember gave a sheepish grin and they started walking back to the front of the hangar.

'I thought I saw someone looking around the curtain at the audience earlier,' Kember said. 'Maybe checking who was sitting where.'

'Could have been one of the troupe making sure they had a decent audience,' Vickers suggested. 'You know what these actor types are like. They love to be loved.'

'Probably,' Kember said, but he wasn't so sure.

'The only people on this air station tonight are those with legitimate reasons for being here,' Vickers said as they reached the hangar door. 'I know what you're thinking. You think the Handyman's here tonight.'

'Not you as well?' Kember groaned and couldn't keep the look of distaste from his face.

'A couple of lads heard it in the village this afternoon. The killer must have made quite an impact to get a nickname.'

Kember could almost feel his blood pressure go back up. 'I hope it doesn't get back to Chief Inspector Hartson or he'll have something to say to me about it.'

◆ ◆ ◆

When Lizzie's consciousness rose up from the depths, she saw a group of worried faces arranged in a circle in front of her. Only when her senses began to return did she feel the cold gravel path digging into her back and realised the faces were above her.

Her ability to decipher sounds returned suddenly and she heard a babble of worried voices firing questions about her well-being. She assured her friends she was fine as they sat her up, although she felt far from all right. Her head throbbed, she suspected her neck would be bruised, and the bone-numbing cold made her feel as though she'd been sleeping on a block of ice for hours. As Niamh and Hazel helped her up, her legs momentarily refused to cooperate but eventually bore her weight and she felt her strength returning.

'What happened?' Fizz asked.

'It is your investigations again, yes?' Agata said aggressively, as if some unseen assailant could hear.

'I think I fainted.' Lizzie's first instinct was to keep the truth to herself to avoid a mass panic. She looked around: maybe he'd fled when her friends had appeared. She felt numb. Had she hit her head?

'You look a bit wobbly,' said Hazel. 'Do you want to go inside?'

'Did you hurt yourself?' Yvonne asked, rubbing Lizzie's arm like a mother soothing a child.

Lizzie noted the shift away from thoughts of an attacker to it being her fault.

'I bumped my head when I fell but I'll be all right.' *Some bump*, she thought.

'We should tell your man,' Niamh said, looking across the airfield as if anything could be discerned in such darkness.

'There's really no need,' Lizzie said, in as reassuring a voice as she could manage.

Head pounding like the beat of the show's opening number but insisting she didn't have concussion and wanting to go back to the hangar, Lizzie allowed the women to guide and escort her back across the airfield. She agreed that Kember should be told but wasn't looking forward to that conversation. She'd been alone in the dark when she knew a killer was on the loose looking for pretty women with nice hands, even though she'd never thought of herself as pretty. By not taking basic precautions she'd allowed herself to become a target, even though there had been no indication that the killer was someone on the air station. Kember would be worried, angry and protective, and although she understood all those emotions she didn't want or need them. They would undermine her standing as a modern, independent, intelligent and free-thinking woman. Dallington and Matfield would have a field day if Lizzie insisted that they stop the pantomime and use the attack as an excuse to get rid of the ATA again.

She could not allow that to happen.

But nor could she let this dangerous man get away.

◆ ◆ ◆

Kember glanced across the airfield and could just make out the swaying blob of what could only be the returning ATA women. Lizzie should be among them and something held tense inside him finally relaxed. Only then did he acknowledge how concerned for her welfare he had been.

But as they approached, the way Lizzie held herself, with her friends clustered around her, told him something was wrong. The other women threw looks of worry and concern at her as she walked towards him and Vickers, leaving them to carry on to the hangar.

'What's happened?' he asked, trying to keep his voice soft and calm while his heart raced.

Standing on the edge of the ink-black airfield a few yards from the hangar, Lizzie accepted the offer of a Woodbine from Vickers. She waited for him to strike a match, shielded by his greatcoat, and light both their cigarettes. She took a long drag, cupping the glowing end in her hand, and sighed through a cloud of almost luminescent smoke.

'I told the girls I fainted, but . . .' She winced as she pushed up the sleeve of her tunic, revealing a short, shallow cut on the back of her right wrist still oozing beads of blood.

'What in God's name happened?' Kember hissed.

She pulled her arm away. 'I may have been . . . grabbed,' she said, a tremor in her voice.

'Grabbed?' Vickers said, the lines of his frown visible in a brief wash of moonlight. 'What does that mean? Who by? Why—'

'Stop,' Lizzie said, resting a hand on Vickers' chest. 'It was after I'd been to the loo and left the manor house to come back.'

'Why didn't you scream for help?'

'He didn't exactly let me. It was pitch-dark and he was long gone by the time I came to.'

Kember turned her towards him. 'Came to?' he snapped, a sick feeling in his chest that he hadn't been there to protect her, aware of others looking their way.

'I'm fine. I got a fright and a bump on the head. Nothing serious.'

'Nothing ser—? Jesus Christ.' Vickers took another pull on his cigarette and gestured to his flight sergeant who was standing by the hangar.

'Why did he knock you out rather than kill you?' Kember said.

'I suppose the girls came out of the manor house and scared him off,' Lizzie said. 'I was out for a few seconds at most, and woke up with them all standing over me and fussing. The bigger question is: why did he attack me in a place like this? One swarming with all sorts of people?'

The flight sergeant appeared.

'What did he look like?' Vickers asked Lizzie.

'All I remember seeing is a squarish head, and he was wearing some kind of a mask or scarf over his face. I think he was medium height and build but he had a dark overcoat so I can't be sure.'

Vickers ordered his flight sergeant to alert the gatehouse and pass the word to his RAF Police warders to challenge anyone not in the hangar.

The flight sergeant barked 'Yes sir,' saluted and wheeled away.

'Can we stop the show?' Kember asked, anxious about having a madman loose in the dark.

'If I had my way, I would, but there are too many of the top brass in there,' Vickers said. 'There'd be merry hell to pay.'

'You can't stop the show,' Lizzie said. 'Dallington's just waiting for an excuse like this to kick the ATA off the air station.'

Kember rubbed his nose with frustration. 'At least he knows we're onto him now and is unlikely to try again tonight. I hope. We should get you to the MO. Where is Dr Davies?'

Lizzie held up her right hand, still cupping the cigarette, really seeing the wound for the first time. She touched the dark line curving around her wrist and pulled away the sliced remains of the rubber band, her fingers coated with black-looking, congealing blood. 'I'm all right. No need to bother him now. I'll see him after the show.'

Vickers threw his cigarette to the ground and crushed it underfoot. 'I have to go but wait for me at the manor house after the show.'

The small ENSA band was already playing welcome music for the second half of the performance as Lizzie rejoined her friends and entered the hangar. Kember waited as they filed into their row, sitting just as Buttons made an appearance onstage. Even though the Prince fluffed a couple of lines and Dandini kept dropping her cane, earning titters from the audience, the performers quickly settled down and got into their characters again.

But Kember wasn't paying attention to the stage.

◆　◆　◆

At the end of the show, with the performers having milked every last drop of applause, the audience began threading through the blackout curtains. With low cloud still reluctant to let much moonlight filter through, the area outside the hangar doors became a galaxy of twinkling flecks, the dancing lights of masked torches shedding just enough light to enable their owners to find their way to the waiting cars and lorries or to walk back to the barrack blocks and manor house.

While the other ATA women rode in a lorry around the perimeter track, Lizzie chose to walk with Kember, hoping the cold air would help the throbbing in her head and neck. She had her greatcoat on now, and Kember his overcoat, as they strode in silence directly towards the manor house, across grass crispy with frost.

They stopped on the manor-house terrace and Lizzie saw the look of worry in Kember's eyes. She felt guilty, even though she couldn't have known she'd been putting herself in danger in the middle of the air station. She wanted to say it wasn't his fault either and that she was all right, really, but the words wouldn't come. Instead, she moved towards him and felt tears pricking her eyes as he stepped towards her and wrapped his arms around her. She buried her face in his shoulder, determined not to cry but welcoming someone else's strength enveloping her instead of always having to rely on her own.

She pulled away hastily as the terrace door opened and Vickers joined them, hoping the dark concealed the flush in her cheeks.

'My men conducted a search and didn't find anyone who shouldn't have been exactly where they were,' he said. 'They're busy escorting all ENSA and civilian personnel from the air station now, but due to the late hour and blackout, all the pantomime kit and scenery has been left in the hangar for collection tomorrow morning.'

'Unless you've had a perimeter breach, whoever attacked me must still be here,' Lizzie said. She didn't think he'd try twice in one night now the Wardens were on the lookout but the very thought that someone who had tried to kill her for her hands was still on the air station, perhaps even watching them now, made her shudder.

Vickers nodded. 'We've already checked the fence. You know I'll have to tell Dallington and your flight captain, don't you? I'll also need to organise a search for the morning, witness interviews, all the usual.'

'Thank you,' Kember said. 'Virtually everyone not on duty was at the show and stayed by the hangar during the interval. They wouldn't have seen a thing. Your best bet is the ATA women who scared him off and any of your warders in the immediate area.'

'I didn't have a man stationed over here,' Vickers said.

Lizzie frowned. 'But I saw one by the gardens as I passed that way,' she said, realising as soon as she spoke that he must have been the Handyman lying in wait.

'That settles it,' Kember said to Vickers. 'I'll come up early tomorrow to help, but don't forget I'm going to Chatham Dockyard with Reverend Wilson after his church service. I'll leave the details with Sergeant Wright in case you need me.'

'What about me?' Lizzie said. 'I'm coming with you.'

'But I thought—'

'You thought I'd be too scared to leave the air station?' The insinuation irked her. 'I've just been attacked here so I'd say a naval dockyard is as safe as anywhere, wouldn't you? I'll get the MO to sign me off and I'll see you out the front tomorrow, after church parade.'

CHAPTER SIXTEEN

'Why the blazes wasn't I told about this last night?'

Dallington threw his cap onto his desk but it skittered to the floor sending Tilly the cat scuttling into the corner of the office. Vickers stood to attention alongside Geraldine, neither of whom had been invited to sit, unlike Matfield who lowered himself as usual into the visitor's chair. Dallington's foul mood had been triggered by the revelation of the assault on Lizzie the previous evening and Vickers knew they were in for a bumpy few minutes. They waited while Dallington sat, popped open a new tin of Old Holborn, scooped a generous wad of tobacco into the bowl of his pipe and lit it with a match that seemed to fizz in sympathy with the CO's temper.

'It was too dark to see very much but I had my men search the station, sir,' Vickers answered. 'We found no intruders and Third Officer Hayes was not seriously hurt, so I thought it could wait until this morning rather than wake you unnecessarily, sir.'

'But I'm the commanding officer of this dump, damn you!' Dallington's frown became so pronounced that Vickers wasn't sure where the deep furrows of his brow ended and the bridge of his nose began. 'You didn't even deem it necessary to inform Wing

Commander Matfield, who was at the show and presumably wide awake.'

Vickers squirmed at this. Dallington was right, of course. He should have at least given some indication to Matfield that an incident had taken place but that would have meant cancelling the show and enduring the wrath of the top brass as well as all this kerfuffle last night when everyone was already tired.

'I'm sure the flight lieutenant had the base secure, sir,' Matfield said. 'I saw his men checking the ENSA troupe and civilians out through the gate and as far as I'm aware there were no perimeter breaches.'

'And you think that makes it all right, do you?' Dallington's mouthful of smoke hung like a barrier curtain between him and the others. Matfield's eyes narrowed and his jaw muscles clenched as Dallington continued. 'If someone who shouldn't have been on my air station last night didn't get in through the fences, that means they walked in through the front gate under your very noses or, and this is almost worse, they are one of us and still here.'

'If it's any consolation, sir,' Geraldine said, 'I've spoken to Third Officer Hayes and she believes she may have been deliberately targeted because of her association with Detective Inspector Kember. As a result, she is confident that no one else on the air station is at risk.'

Dallington's face grew ever darker.

'*She* is confident?' Dallington pointed the stem of his pipe at Geraldine. 'You're telling me I can let this scoundrel have the run of my air station because one of your little girls is *confident* and thinks she's so far above the rest of us that he couldn't possibly want to do anyone else any harm?'

Vickers saw anger flash in Geraldine's eyes and worried she might snap back. Unexpectedly, Matfield intervened.

'I think what the flight captain and flight lieutenant are trying to say is that we have the situation back under control and everyone is on the lookout. Speaking as your second-in-command, I believe we can leave the flight lieutenant and DI Kember to get on with their jobs.'

Dallington's furrows retreated as he cradled the bowl of his pipe in his hand and sucked the stem, creating a series of small blue-tinged clouds. Vickers watched realisation dawn on the CO that the main responsibility lay with the three officers in front of him and any blame could be laid at their feet.

'Very well,' Dallington said. 'Get out, all of you. And bloody well keep me informed!'

◆ ◆ ◆

Kember arrived at RAF Scotney to be greeted by Vickers on the gravel parking area by the manor house. He had mulled over the events of the previous day and achieved little sleep as a result, hoping their investigations this morning would bear fruit and that Lizzie was in a better frame of mind. That he had antagonised her through his open display of concern was self-evident and suggesting she be left behind for today had compounded his mistake. But he had conceded, at least to himself in front of the shaving mirror that morning, that he did need her help at the dockyard, and her valuable insights elsewhere.

'How's the clear-up going?' Kember said as he closed the door of his Minx.

'Not bad,' Vickers said. 'The ENSA lorries arrived back about half an hour ago and I think they've pretty much finished. As for last night's drama, come with me.'

Kember followed Vickers into the portico entrance, across the hall, through the officers' lounge and onto the terrace. The

RAF man pointed to a line of men walking slowly across the airfield.

'We'll search the hangar once ENSA's gone,' Vickers said. 'In the meantime, we're looking for anything that may have been dropped on the airfield last night. We check routinely anyway, for anything hazardous to aircraft, but we're looking extra close today.'

The men had almost finished the sweep across the grass.

'Have you looked at the garden?'

'Not yet. Geraldine and I were summoned to a set-to with Dallington earlier this morning. More of a dressing-down, actually.'

'Oh?' Kember raised an eyebrow.

'I needed to tell Dallington and Matfield about the assault but Lizzie and I told Geraldine and the others first. They were shocked, of course, but understood why she said nothing last night, in case Dallington and Matfield used it as an excuse to have the ATA posted elsewhere. Geraldine insisted she went with me to share the burden.'

'And did she?'

'Thankfully, yes. Matfield was there, of course, and Geraldine assured them that Lizzie was relatively unharmed. Matfield came to our aid in fact, and persuaded Dallington to let you and me get on with our jobs.'

'Kind of him, I'm sure.'

Vickers grinned at the sarcasm.

No sooner had Vickers' men entered the ornamental gardens to continue their search than a shout went up. One of the men stood with an arm raised to indicate a find of some kind. Vickers and Kember hurried down the steps and along a gravel path to meet him. The warder pointed to the end of a smoothly rounded piece of wood protruding from a knee-high hedge before standing well back.

Kember eased apart the small, tightly compacted leaves of the evergreen box shrub to reveal a foot-long, slightly battered handle. Vickers slipped on a pair of thin leather gloves and held the end by thumb and forefinger to extract it from the hedge, laying it on the top of a nearby stone wall for further inspection. At one end, the handle joined a metal head formed into a blade on one side and a flat hammer on the other.

'An axe.' Kember felt the blade. 'Razor sharp. Look here, it's been recently honed.'

'Think this is what he attacked Lizzie with?'

Kember noticed where gravel from the path had been displaced from its usual level, some of it spilling under the box border. 'Seems likely. Lizzie was a bit vague about how and where in the garden she was attacked but there may have been a scuffle here.' He felt his pockets and pulled a large paper evidence bag from his pocket.

'I'll have a word with the groundsman to see if he's missing any tools,' Vickers said, feeding the axe into the bag. 'Lizzie's attending the Sunday service in the chapel but if you want to speak to the other ATA women, you'll have to be quick. They're due to fly off in their Annie shortly.'

'Annie?' Kember queried.

'Avro Anson,' Vickers explained. 'The Scotney ATA use one as their air taxi since they lost the use of their Airspeed Oxford.'

Kember nodded his understanding and gestured towards the manor house.

'I take it they'll be in the briefing room getting their daily chits?'

Vickers glanced at his watch. 'Probably over at dispersal now. We'll have to hurry.'

The chapel of Scotney Manor was a church in all but name. It had once been a stone building of modest size but as the estate had grown so had the chapel. It had been extended along both sides and at both ends, a small steeple-topped bell tower being the latest addition completed fifty years ago. After all, the spiritual needs of the expanding workforce had needed tending and the small village church couldn't accommodate everyone.

Today, only a dozen civilian staff huddled together on one pew while RAF personnel on the weekly and obligatory church parade filled the remainder of the chapel's plain but cavernous interior. The number of estate workers had diminished considerably due to conscription and the giving over of pastures and fields to local farmers for essential food production.

Lizzie sat at the far end of the last pew occupied by NAAFI women from the mess and kitchen, resting her head against the cold stone wall, trying to marshal her thoughts. Going over the attack had caused her as much of a headache as the blow to the nape of her neck, and the flashes of shadows and gloved hands, of a mask and an almost angular head didn't make any sense. No one she'd ever seen looked like that in real life. *Mind you*, she thought, *it could as easily have been a scarf and hood as anything else in the dark.* She ran a finger along the bandage on her right wrist. Dr Davies had insisted on the dressing even though she thought it unnecessary, attracting unwanted attention to something she considered no more than a scratch.

The volume of greatcoat-clad bodies in the chapel warmed the air and combined with the drone of the station chaplain's sermon to create a soporific effect. Lizzie's mind wandered, slipping into its familiar daydream-like state, her thoughts becoming those of her attacker. She watched herself leave the manor house through the terrace doors and descend the steps to the garden, heard the crunch of her regulation shoes on the gravel path, saw the flare of a match as she lit a cigarette.

Her hand reached forward to grip her own throat and everything became a blur. The ensuing fight, struggle for breath, an unintentional head butt, kicking, flailing, the final blow. And she shouted—

'Oh!'

'—things bright and beautiful . . .'

Lizzie's mind jolted into the present. Who was singing?

'. . . All creatures great and small . . .'

Dear God, Lizzie cringed. The standing congregation were singing, the NAAFI women looking down at her with concern.

'. . . All things wise and wonderful . . .'

Lizzie took a deep breath to clear her head.

'. . . The Lord God made them all.'

The congregation sat and Lizzie stared straight ahead, too embarrassed to even glance at the other women. A tightening across her chest had her reaching automatically for the rubber band on her right wrist, but her fingers touched bandage. With anxiety threatening to turn up another notch, Lizzie felt for the band on her other wrist and gave it a sharp snap. That and another curious glance from the NAAFI cook sat next to her focused her mind for the next few minutes until the end of the service. She hoped they'd think she'd been asleep and dreaming and wouldn't ask questions. It worried her, slipping so easily into the killer's mind while in company, and such a large group of people too. Only Kember and her old university tutor, Beatrice Edgell, had ever witnessed her do that, and she considered even those times unfortunate.

Lizzie fled from the chapel as soon as she could, nodding politely to the chaplain as she left. She knew Kember would be waiting by now so she hurried towards the manor house where his Minx would be parked.

Kember drove Vickers around the perimeter track of the airfield to the dispersal, where the aircraft were parked, in his Minx, leaving Vickers' men to resume searching the garden. He didn't expect anything further to be found because he thought an axe would have been the perfect tool to knock Lizzie unconscious and cut off her hands. But then again, something she'd said niggled him. She was right about the place she'd been attacked; so risky for the killer. And he'd used a different MO: cutting her wrist but not her throat. What did that mean?

He found the ATA women gathered around the twin-engine Anson, dressed in their khaki Sidcot flying suits. Leather helmets and goggles dangled from the fingers of Agata and Fizz. Hazel and Yvonne each clutched a piece of white paper detailing the day's ferrying duties. Niamh's head appeared in the open door of the fuselage as Geraldine called for the women to wait.

'How can we help, Inspector?' Geraldine asked. 'My women know about last night but I'm not sure they saw anything helpful.'

Kember took off his hat and held it in one hand.

'Thank you. I'll be brief.' He addressed the women. 'Third Officer Hayes was attacked in the gardens last night during the interval of the pantomime I believe you all attended. I—'

'She lied,' Agata interrupted. 'She told us she fainted. How can we protect ourselves if we don't know what's happening?'

'Is he back?' Fizz asked, stern faced.

The question took Kember by surprise but he knew who she meant and the worried expressions of all the women told him they'd been discussing that very topic.

'Absolutely not,' Kember assured with all the gravitas he could muster.

'So, there's another one?' Niamh said from the doorway. 'Really?'

'Ladies.' Geraldine clapped her hands. 'Let the inspector ask his questions. You have aircraft to fly.'

Kember gave Geraldine an appreciative nod.

'All we know so far is that the assailant used the cover of the blackout and patchy moonlight to attack Miss Hayes as she returned from a brief visit to the manor house.'

'She went to the toilet,' Agata said. 'We all did. We found her in the garden when we came out.'

'We're interested in what happened either side of that moment,' Vickers said. 'For example, how long after Miss Hayes left the house did you all leave?'

'Two minutes,' Fizz said. 'Less, probably. We used the ladies' loo on the ground floor and Lizzie was washing her hands as we arrived. The interval wasn't long so we rushed to get done and back.'

'Did Miss Hayes not wait for you?' Vickers asked.

'For a moment but she wanted to get back to the inspector.' Agata grinned.

Kember covered his discomfort with another question.

'I believe you left together after her, through the terrace doors and down the steps. Did you notice anyone running away or hear anything at all that might help? Did Miss Hayes scream or the attacker shout, for example?'

'We didn't hear a scream but were laughing and joking with each other as we left,' Hazel said. 'Making such a racket that we wouldn't have heard a thing until we were right on top of them.'

'We had no idea until Yvonne stumbled over a bundle on the ground,' Niamh said. 'Which turned out to be Lizzie lying there. She was a bit groggy.'

'We couldn't get much sense out of her to start with,' Yvonne said. 'Then she insisted we take her back to the hangar. She told us she'd fainted and played it down.'

'If this is the Handyman, should we be worried?' Fizz asked.

Kember glanced at Geraldine and saw the same question in her expression.

'The truth is, we don't know who did this yet and assigning someone a nickname only serves to give them a power they shouldn't have and a presence they don't deserve.'

'We appreciate that, but he's not killing men, is he?' said Fizz. 'Whatever you want to call him, he's still trying to cut our hands off while you and your sergeant are running around in circles in the dark.'

While unable to disagree with Fizz's assessment, Kember knew the likelihood of more manpower being assigned was negligible. Although seconded to Tonbridge, in essence he was a New Scotland Yard detective inspector and needed to exude the confidence and authority of his rank.

'This is just another man trying to hurt people,' he said, putting on his fedora. He indicated Vickers. 'I'm working closely with the flight lieutenant and his men to ensure whoever is doing this is caught as soon as possible. Some of you know me so you'll believe me when I say I'll be doing all I can. In the meantime, you should remain vigilant and look out for each other.'

He turned to Geraldine and nodded his thanks as the women grumbled among themselves and resumed boarding the Anson.

'Thank you for allowing Miss Hayes to accompany us today. Her knowledge really will be a great help.'

'She gave me little choice,' Geraldine said.

Kember heard the steel in Geraldine's voice and almost shivered at the chill from her icy stare.

'She insisted on helping you again,' Geraldine said. 'And as we're still one short of a full complement, I cannot afford to sack her. But take heed of this. If the group captain or wing commander get wind that Miss Hayes is off station with you, I will have no compunction in laying the blame firmly at both your doors.'

'Understood.' Kember nodded.

As they returned to the Minx and opened the doors, Kember stopped and turned at the call of his name. Geraldine's head and shoulders were framed by the open door of the Anson.

'Miss Hayes suffered a serious blow to her head last night so the MO grounded her for forty-eight hours. Please ensure that is sufficient.' She slammed the door.

On the drive back to the manor house, Vickers said, 'We double-checked the perimeter fence this morning and there were no signs of a breach so it wasn't an intruder. That means Lizzie's attacker was among the legitimate personnel present on the air station last night.'

'It must have been someone inside the hangar or nearby who wouldn't be missed during the interval,' Kember said. 'He must have followed her and waited until she came back out from the house.'

'I've already spoken to a number of those who were in the hangar, including the ATA women. When they came out onto the terrace shortly after Lizzie, making quite a noise, they must have scared away whoever was in the process of cutting off her hands.'

'That's something that bothers me,' Kember said. 'Lizzie's friend in Duxford had her throat cut and hands severed with something very sharp, like a butcher's knife. Maisie Chapman also had her throat cut. Why would the killer change to something as imprecise as an axe, however much it had been honed?'

'Perhaps he threw the knife away, or lost it,' Vickers suggested.

Kember wasn't convinced. Lizzie had only been knocked unconscious and the cut on the back of her wrist appeared superficial, so what the hell was the killer playing at? His job was to solve crimes and protect people but he had never felt so helpless. There had been hundreds of people in the hangar and he had no clue where to start.

◆ ◆ ◆

Having been dropped off near the portico when Kember picked up Lizzie, Vickers strode through the house and gardens and across the lawn. He approached a utility hut beyond the operations block where the head groundsman sat outside on an old milking stool, sharpening a sickle resting on his knees.

'Good morning,' Vickers said. The man stopped honing to look up at him. 'I wondered if you'd had any tools go missing, specifically, an axe.'

The man put down the sickle and whetstone, took off his cloth cap and wiped the crown of his bald head with a piece of cloth before standing.

'Nay, lad,' he said.

'Are you sure?' Vickers opened the evidence bag.

'Course I am.' The groundsman peered inside. 'And that's not an axe.'

Vickers felt a twinge of impatience. 'What is it then?'

'An axe has a bevelled edge to the bit, cutting edge to the likes of you, and a long handle for two-handed work. If that were a hand axe, it'd be the same but with a short handle. What you've got there's a hatchet. See how the blade and bit is smooth on both sides and sharpened to a fine edge? The blade's got a slight flare at the bottom and a hammer head on the butt end too. Like I said, a hatchet.'

Vickers detected no smugness or humour from the man but still wasn't sure whether to be irritated or thankful for the lesson.

'And all yours are accounted for?' he pressed. The man didn't answer and his face remained impassive. 'Who else would use a hatchet?'

The man shrugged. 'A carpenter, a roofer for shingles, someone wanting to chop firewood into kindling, anyone working with wood, really.' The man stretched before picking up his sickle and whetstone again.

'Well, if you find you are one short, please let me know immediately.'

The man gave Vickers a sideways glance before sitting down to resume his work. 'Aye,' was all he said.

'Thank you,' Vickers said, nodding to the man, but the rasp of stone on steel had already begun again.

Helpful in one way but not another, Vickers thought, as he turned back towards the manor house. Lizzie had been attacked with a hatchet but not one belonging to the manor house.

Who the hell did it belong to then?

Having been too tired to polish his boots before going to bed the night before, Sergeant Wright had decided they would pass all but the closest scrutiny until his mid-morning tea break. Even so, a dull smear on the toe of his right boot had bothered him all morning. With the kettle set on the stove to boil, he took the wooden box containing his shoe-cleaning kit from its home in a cupboard and sat down to polish. He selected the rag he used for cleaning away the worst debris and gave his boots the once-over. Frowning when the offending smear remained, he pushed his finger into the rag, spat on it and worked at the smear with a circular motion. He grunted in satisfaction as that did the trick, following up with a dab of black polish, a swift going-over with a polishing brush and then a buff up with a yellow duster. The shine pleased him as much as the boiling kettle whistling its readiness and he rose to make himself a brew.

Returning to the table moments later with his steaming mug, Wright gathered his shoe kit together to pack away but froze when he glimpsed a dab of scarlet on the cleaning rag. He reached for it and there, sure enough, was an oval of red where his finger had been. He looked at his right forefinger expecting a wound but it wasn't even scratched. He rubbed a smear of the red substance between his finger and thumb, then sniffed it. His conclusion gave him a jolt: it was someone else's blood.

CHAPTER SEVENTEEN

An hour and a half after leaving the air station, Kember drove Lizzie and Reverend Wilson up to the barrier across the imposing archway of the main gate leading into the Chatham Royal Navy Dockyard. A Royal Marine Police constable directed him to a space to park his Minx. Dr Davies may have stopped Lizzie flying but fortunately hadn't said she couldn't leave the air station. She had slept for most of the journey so at least she had taken heed of his advice to get some rest, even if the back seat of a car wasn't the most comfortable bed.

The original Tudor dockyard had been the birthplace of HMS Victory, Nelson's flagship at the Battle of Trafalgar, and now extended as far as the eye could see. Cranes fussed over a mine-sweeper ship in a dry dock, tarpaulin-covered lorries ground along in low gear towards the covered slipways beyond, and the radio masts of warships docked in the main basins could just about be glimpsed in the distance through gaps in the buildings. Sailors in navy-blue uniforms strode along in twos and threes, jacketed civilians darted in and out of buildings, the entrances protected by stacks of sandbags, and overall-clad ship-workers, some carrying boxes or bags, scuttled back and forth. Anti-aircraft guns pointed at the eastern sky, the gunners keeping vigilant watch for enemy bombers. A hiss of steam and the whistle of an unseen steam train, the screech of metal on metal, barked orders, and the general bustle of a busy dockyard at war created a wall of sound.

Another RMP officer met them as they got out of the car and Kember noticed Lizzie's stiff stance, square shoulders and slightly bowed head as she looked warily at the two RMP officers. She stood between him and Wilson but noticeably a few inches behind them. After seeing Lizzie so confident on the air station, it shocked Kember to witness her looking so subordinate and subservient, almost submissive.

The RMP sergeant, wearing glasses with thick lenses, began the introductions, and afterwards said, 'You have to be escorted but I'm afraid I haven't the time to show you where the bodies were found, which I believe is one of your requests.'

'Bodies?' Kember said, returning Wilson's glance. 'You found the curate?'

'Did no one inform you?' the sergeant said with the hint of a frown.

'We were told he was missing.'

'Well, they found him in one of the old parts of the dockyard, in a room used for general storage. Constable Morgan will show you. The chaplain is busy in the church at present so I can take Reverend Wilson over and you can join him later. Hayes can wait in your car or the gatehouse.'

In that sentence, Kember saw something in the sergeant more sinister than anything he'd witnessed in Dallington or Matfield. Something automatically dismissive and condescending as if women, even those in uniform, were somehow lower than any male naval rating or dock-worker. Now he understood Lizzie's demeanour, Kember fought to conceal a flare of temper and confined himself to staring into the eyes of the sergeant.

'*Third Officer* Hayes is seconded to my investigation and *will* be accompanying me.'

'That won't be poss—'

'I am a Scotland Yard detective and your chief inspector said I could speak to him at any time if I encountered a problem.'

The sergeant stared back.

'Is there a problem?' Kember challenged.

It seemed like the sergeant would refuse to back down but he looked at his constable after a few seconds.

'Constable, take the inspector and Third Officer Hayes to see where the bodies were found.' Lizzie's rank was said with a sneer. He turned to Wilson. 'Reverend, if you'll come with me?'

Kember watched the retreating backs of Wilson and the sergeant.

'What was that about?' he asked.

'I apologise, sir, ma'am,' Morgan said. 'He has terrible eyesight which kept him from becoming a sailor like his father. Can't see a thing without his glasses. It's made him rather bitter.'

'Being bitter against circumstance, I can understand. Being rude to officers in uniform for no good reason is unforgivable.'

'Don't worry about it,' Lizzie said. 'I know which battles to fight and which to let others fight for me.'

Kember admitted to himself that she looked more resigned than upset, and Morgan looked uncomfortable but wasn't responsible for his sergeant's behaviour. He decided to let it go.

'Please lead on, Constable.'

A few minutes' walk took them to a brick building with a solid-wood door where Kember noticed the paint looked new on the frame of a window to one side. He pressed his finger against the frame, leaving an impression in the soft material and a smear of tacky paint on his finger.

'The putty and paint are fresh,' Kember said. 'Have these windows been replaced recently?'

'Yes, sir,' Morgan confirmed. 'The windows blew in during an air raid about a week ago. It was the glazier who found the chaplain's assistant earlier today.'

Kember took in the scene as he and Lizzie followed Morgan into the room. A pile of rope-handled wooden crates and what looked like tea chests huddled in one corner while metal-framed racks creaked under the weight of cardboard boxes of various sizes stuffed onto bowing wooden shelves. Hessian sacks lay stacked haphazardly against the far wall. All had reference numbers stencilled in black.

'Who attended the scene after the glazier found the curate?' Kember asked.

'I did, sir,' Morgan replied.

'Can you describe what you saw?'

Morgan moved further into the room.

'It looked pretty much how you see it now. The windows had shattered and glass was all over the floor. A few packages from the rack closest to the window had been dislodged, some fallen to the floor. Apart from that, it looked to have escaped the full blast.'

'Where did you find the body?'

'Behind here.' Morgan pointed behind the last rack.

Kember and Lizzie moved around to see.

'It was horrible,' Morgan continued. 'He was sat on a crate, leaning back against the wall. His face was as white as his dog collar, but that's not surprising given he had no hands and had bled all over the floor. Took two men half a day to scrub it off.'

Kember saw Lizzie shudder and look at him. A shiver started at his own neck and travelled down his spine. 'Did you find his hands?' he asked.

'No, sir.' Morgan shook his head. 'Rats probably got 'em. They'd had a nibble at the body too. As I said: horrible. That's not to say we didn't find any hands.'

Kember stopped inspecting a small box he'd selected from one of the shelves. 'What do you mean?'

'We found a pair of women's hands – or what was left of 'em. Pretty gruesome. One over there.' Morgan pointed to the sacks. 'The other under there.' He pointed under the lowest shelf of the nearest rack.

'And that didn't strike you as unusual?' Kember raised his eyebrows at Morgan, astonished at how blasé the constable appeared.

Morgan shrugged. 'Got at by rats. Probably dragged 'em back here to eat.'

'From the woman found beneath the bomb rubble? How far was that?'

'Not far. Maybe a hundred yards.'

Kember almost laughed at the notion that rats would have brought the woman's hands a hundred yards to this storeroom before moving on to the curate's.

'Were there any other wounds?' he asked, deciding to let Morgan off his uncomfortable hook.

'Ah, yes.' Morgan felt in his pocket and handed Kember a folded piece of paper. 'From the medical report, sir. Thought you'd be interested.'

Kember unfolded the sheet and read aloud.

'"Dead about a week. Large contusion on back of head." So, he did have another mark. "Hands missing, probably severed by flying glass. A severe ring of bruising above both elbows. Cause of death: exsanguination."' Kember looked up from the paper. 'Death by loss of blood,' he added for Morgan's benefit. 'That's odd, wouldn't you say? This room couldn't have caught the full bomb blast because only a few boxes were blown off the first shelf.

Glass shards big enough to sever bodily extremities wouldn't get past the other shelves and, in any case, it would be an odd thing for both hands to be cut off leaving no other lacerations on his body. And what caused the blow to his head if there wasn't any debris?'

'Bomb blasts can do strange things,' Morgan said.

'I don't dispute that, but it would be less problematical if the curate had been caught out in the open.'

Kember could see from Morgan's face that he was wrestling with a decision, the mask of indifference slipping.

'If you have any information that might help us understand what went on here, it will remain completely confidential.'

Morgan remained silent for several seconds before saying, 'The original I copied that from had a line crossed out, almost scrubbed out. I thought that was very odd.'

'Go on,' Kember encouraged.

'I shouldn't be saying anything but . . . I could barely make out the words: bone, cut and scalpel, with a question mark.'

A jolt went through Kember. If the curate had been cut with a scalpel, could one have been used on Catherine Summers instead of a boning knife? And what about Maisie Chapman and the woman at RAF Croydon? He looked at Lizzie and saw the significance had not escaped her either.

'Thank you, that's helpful,' Kember said to Morgan, not wishing to make more of it and get the man in serious trouble with the navy authorities. 'It still doesn't explain why you found the woman's hands but not his.'

'I'm at a loss, sir,' Morgan said apologetically.

Kember glanced around the interior again. 'Do you know what he was doing in here?'

'No idea, sir. Not many people come down this way. Perhaps he was drinking or having a crafty smoke.'

'Unlikely to come all the way down here for that, I'd have thought. Were cigarettes and drink found with him?'

'Actually, no.' Morgan squirmed. 'Maybe he wanted a moment's peace.'

Kember wasn't convinced. 'He was a man of God. Surely he'd find peace in the church?'

'I meant peace and quiet,' Morgan said, with a sideways glance at Kember. 'Away from the hustle and bustle, not spiritual peace.'

'How was she positioned?' Lizzie asked, looking at the constable. 'The woman: was she laid flat on her back, curled up, on her front splayed out?'

It was the first time Lizzie had spoken since Wilson had left with the sergeant. All the while Kember had been asking questions, she had been wandering here and there, looking at the window and door, inspecting the shelves and sacks. Now she stood in front of the crate positioned behind the last shelf.

'On her back, ma'am,' Morgan said. 'With her arms by her sides like she was having a nap. I don't see—'

'And the curate?'

'He was sat on that crate with a sack either side of him, all cosy, like.'

Kember could see Lizzie itching to do her thing so he turned to the constable with an apologetic smile. 'Do you mind leaving us alone for a moment so we can have a good look around and a think?'

The constable looked at Lizzie with a doubtful expression before saying, 'The sergeant wouldn't like it but I'll step outside for a two-minute smoke.'

Sergeant Wright looked to see who had knocked on his office door and felt a warmth rise in his cheeks when he saw a woman in her mid-forties standing in the doorway.

'Gladys,' Wright said, surprised to see her. He knew they were alone but still he looked around in case. 'What are you doing here?'

'That's a nice welcome,' she said. 'Aren't you pleased to see me?'

Gladys Finch, who Wright thought had lost none of her teenage looks, stepped into the room. She undid the top button of her thick coat but left her crocheted cloche hat in place. Despite all public protestations to the contrary, Wright had been sweet on Gladys for over a year. Knowing his feelings had started to be reciprocated made it no easier for him to relax and he always felt awkward in her company.

'I am. Of course, I am,' Wright said, regaining some of his composure. 'But I'm on duty.'

'You're a policeman, Dennis.' She smiled. 'You're always on duty.'

'Aye, true enou—'

Wright swallowed as Gladys took a step forward and he realised his desk was the furthest he could retreat to. She came close enough for him to smell her floral perfume.

'Don't look so scared, Dennis, I won't eat you. I thought I'd bring you a little something.' She took half a step away and held out a small package. 'I know you love my bread pudding.'

Despite the waxed-paper wrapping, Wright fancied he could smell the spiced fruit and his stomach growled.

'Ah, well,' Wright managed. 'Thank you.'

He reached for the package but Gladys put her other hand on his, trapping it there.

'I've got to get on but I'll see you this evening,' she said. 'In the Castle, perhaps?'

Wright felt his cheeks warming again.

'I don't know, Gladys. We've got a big case on at the moment and the inspector needs me.'

'I'm sure he could spare you for one small drink.'

'Cooee,' came a call from the hallway and Wright pulled his hand away as if given an electric shock.

Ethel Garner appeared in the doorway and eyed them suspiciously, her jaw set and mouth pressed into a thin line as if she had recently chewed an unripe gooseberry.

'Hello, Gladys. I thought I saw you come in here,' Ethel said, clutching her shopping bag to her chest. 'Something wrong?'

'Not at all.' Gladys smiled. 'My Dennis needs to keep his strength up so I thought I'd bring him some of my bread pudding.'

'Yes, well,' Ethel said, with a curl of her lip. 'When I saw the closed sign on your tea-shop door and you slinking in here, I thought I'd better see what's what.'

'And what is it?' Gladys teased.

'What? Oh – well, what you get up to, outside of work, is your own affair but I was wanting a piece myself.'

Gladys smirked.

'Of bread pudding,' Ethel emphasised, frowning indignantly. 'Are you going to give him that then?'

Gladys handed Wright the waxed-paper package with a smile. 'See you later, Dennis.' She eased past Ethel and left with a goodbye flutter of her fingers. Wright sighed with relief and put the package in a drawer in his desk.

'You want to be careful of that hussy,' Ethel said, watching Gladys through the office window as she walked back to her tea shop. 'Mrs Ware, her Tom fell off a ladder yesterday but it was only the bottom rung, says she's no better than she should be, and she's never far wrong. We've seen the way she looks at you, ready to get her claws in. That's just like Gladys all over, leaving her tea shop in the middle of the day like that. You're a good man, Dennis

Wright, and you could do much better than the likes of her. Mrs Tate, she can't get the doctor out to her feet for love nor money, said Gladys has had a hard life but haven't we all. I know you haven't any money but I know her type and it makes no difference. You mark my words; she'll take you for what she can get and leave you broken-hearted. And that's another bad lot, if you ask me.' She pointed to a flyer lying on Wright's desk. 'I saw three of them skiving off and leaving that poor couple to do all the work for them. I said to my Albert, "Albert," I said—'

'Ethel.' Wright put his hand on Ethel's arm to stop her in mid-flow.

'What is it?' Ethel looked up at him in puzzlement.

'What did you mean, you saw those three skiving off? Which three?'

'You must have seen them. They were sticking up posters all over the village for that pantomime on Christmas Eve.'

'From ENSA?' Wright remembered the smoking group saying they had distributed posters; he had seen them himself. Now he thought about it, he'd only seen two of them.

Ethel nodded. 'I thought it was a cheek when three of them went off and left the others to it.'

'Can you describe them?'

'Not really, except one was tall. Towered over the other two.'

'What about the ones that were left?'

Ethel pouted in thought.

'The man was unfit for active duty, if you know what I mean. Around the waistline. The other was a woman with glasses. Small round ones, they were. That's all I remember.' She frowned. 'Why are you interested all of a sudden? Is it one of them that did for that poor girl?'

Wright ignored the question. Ethel's memory matched his own which meant the three ENSA performers had abandoned their duty

199

and hadn't mentioned they'd split up. Kember had known they were lying but he wouldn't be back for a while and Wright thought Flight Lieutenant Vickers would want to know straight away.

'Thank you for helping with our inquiries, Ethel,' he said, taking her elbow to steer her towards the front door. 'But I really must get on. The inspector's left me a pile of work to do.'

'Oh. Well, I suppose I should get over to the tea shop, then. Before Gladys gives away all the bread pudding.'

◆ ◆ ◆

'What do you think of that?' Kember said, as soon as Constable Morgan had shut the door. 'Could the killer be using a scalpel?'

'That's something to ask Dr Headley,' Lizzie said. 'A scalpel would be perfect for taking the hands intact. The ring of bruising above the elbows could well have been from tourniquets, designed to stem the bleeding and keep him alive for a while. Would that make him a medical man?'

'Maybe, or someone with access to medical supplies? I'll get onto the pathologists in Croydon and Duxford as soon as we get back to Scotney. I'd better ask Headley about Maisie Chapman, too.'

Kember began a thorough look around the storeroom, bending to examine the floor. 'It's been cleaned up in here but you can still see flecks of glass on the floor near the window,' he said.

'As you'd expect?' Lizzie asked, as she sat on the crate where the curate had been found.

'Yes, but there isn't any glass near the far wall, which ties in with Morgan's report that the bomb blast had pretty much dissipated by the time it reached here. Packages were blown off the shelves nearest the window, absorbing the weakened blast, and debris didn't get past the first couple of shelves. Because no blood was found anywhere outside, or inside near the window, I think we can rule out any wounds being inflicted as a result of the bomb. He was smacked on the back of his head, dragged in here and had his hands cut off, possibly with a scalpel. But why?'

'I don't know, but I'm sure it's the same man who killed the others.' Lizzie assumed the slightly slumped position of someone semi-conscious and muttered, 'Hands. Your hands. Her hands. Where are your hands? Why bring hers here?'

'Pardon?' Kember said.

Lizzie didn't respond, feeling her breathing become fast and shallow as she almost felt the presence of the killer beside her.

Kember returned his attention to inspecting wooden crates with rope handles.

'Without proper treatment for his wrists, the curate could have lasted a couple of days at most,' he said. 'Slowly bleeding to death.'

'He had his hands removed while unconscious – couldn't struggle or cry out – but was still alive when whoever did this seated him on this crate.' Lizzie pulled two bulging but surprisingly lightweight sacks in close to her sides. 'Not just seated – propped up and posed.'

'If this is a serial murderer, what's he trying to do?' Kember moved on to search a pile of stuffed sacks. 'I still don't understand the rationale behind wanting to cut the hands from random victims.'

Lizzie relaxed her eyes, her point of focus somewhere beyond the confines of the storeroom walls, and allowed herself to drift towards the state she could only ever describe as daydreaming. She began to imagine herself caught in an air raid but hit by someone, not a bomb. She felt herself being seated on the crate, slumping, and having sacks wedged either side. A figure, indistinct and unidentifiable, appeared before her, holding – no – caressing a feminine pair of hands.

'This isn't random or unplanned.' Lizzie sat upright. 'Killers like this choose their victims very carefully, to fit set requirements. He's choosing his victims for a specific reason, a higher purpose, not to cut their hands off for the fun of it.'

'I understand you saying there's more to this than wanton mutilation after the abduction.' Kember turned to investigate a neat stack of large tins containing creosote. 'But if that's true, where do the hands of the NAAFI cook fit in?'

'Angela Caxton? I'm not sure yet.' A heaviness clutched at Lizzie's heart. She knew something significant was staring her in the face but her subconscious had yet to make a connection. 'It's puzzling why the curate was brought to this room but she was left outside underneath building rubble. The sites are only a hundred yards apart but he deliberately brought her hands, only her hands, here to where he'd hidden the curate. And where are *his* hands? The constable said they hadn't been found.'

'You think that's significant?'

'Of course, until proved otherwise. This crate, the sacks, the pose. This isn't someone unlucky enough to be in the wrong place at the wrong time. This is an important person, a chosen one, being given the best seat in the house and made comfortable. The cook must have been less important to him or else she would have been brought inside, but even she was laid out and covered. Protected. It looks to be violent on the surface but there's no anger or malice here. It's love.'

◆　◆　◆

Wright's irritation when the telephone's jangling announced an incoming call soon vanished when he heard the familiar voice of Vickers. 'I was just about to call you,' Wright said, before listening with interest as the flight lieutenant described the discovery of the hatchet and his conversation with the head groundsman.

'Any ideas?' Vickers asked at the end.

'It's as the groundsman said,' Wright replied. 'All sorts use hatchets around here.'

'Not everyone was on the air station, though.'

'Very true, sir. Have you an inkling?'

'Not really,' Vickers said. 'I can check all the RAF personnel were where they were supposed to be and if we rule out visiting dignitaries and guests of officers, all of whom would have been escorted, who are we left with?'

'What about one of that ENSA mob?' Wright suggested. 'We know five of them were sent to the village to hand out posters and flyers but I have a witness who says not all of them actually did that. Three of them were seen sneaking off and leaving the others to it.'

'Oh, really,' Vickers said. 'Do you know who they are?'

'That I do, sir. I have their names in my notebook.'

'Excellent,' Vickers said. 'Can you meet me at the camp in twenty minutes? While Kember is in Chatham with Miss Hayes, I think we'd better have a word with our ENSA friends.'

◆ ◆ ◆

Back outside in the winter's cold, Kember watched Lizzie crouch by the area where Angela Caxton had been found under a partially collapsed wall. The rubble had been cleared a few days before and wooden scaffolding erected to brace the rest until it could be repaired.

'What is it you said she does?' Constable Morgan asked.

Kember ignored the question, instead watching Lizzie as she walked over to the river wall and looked across the murky Medway.

'Er, you, boys,' Morgan suddenly shouted at a young lad whose wheelbarrow had overturned, tipping its load of tins across the tarmac. Another lad, who had been handing the tins down from the back of a cart, stood laughing at the other's misfortune. 'Excuse me a moment,' he said, striding towards the commotion.

Lizzie walked back from the wall, her coat buttoned up against the cold wind that whipped in from the river and tugged at her hair. Kember turned up his own collar.

'Water definitely has nothing to do with this,' Lizzie said. 'The river's only a few yards away yet he took the time to cover her up rather than take the easy option and dump her body in the water. I think he uses whatever's close by to give them a decent resting place.'

'You think being buried under building debris is a decent resting place?'

Kember saw Lizzie's expression change and knew his mistake as he spoke. Even he recognised the connection and realised the cook hadn't been covered in a hurry just for concealment.

'He laid her out, placed her arms close into her sides and covered her,' Lizzie said, a hard edge to her voice. 'This is solid concrete and tarmac.' She stamped her foot twice. 'You can't dig a grave here, and there are no channels nearby to use as one, so he did the best he could under the circumstances.' She walked back to the scaffolding and turned to look at him, frowning. 'I don't understand why he shows them reverence but then abandons them.'

'Inspector Kember!'

Kember turned at the call from his left and saw Reverend Wilson approaching with the RMP sergeant.

'Have you finished?' the sergeant asked.

'Just waiting for Constable Morgan,' Kember said.

'Blast,' the sergeant said, and strode off towards where Morgan was still gesticulating at the two boys as they reloaded the wheelbarrow.

Lizzie joined Kember and Wilson.

'What did the chaplain say?' she asked.

'Nothing less than I expected,' said Wilson. 'Reverend Pearson said that Lance Atkinson was a good man with no enemies that he knew of, was hard-working, a credit to the church, and not one person has ever had a bad word to say about him.'

'Coming from a chaplain, I suppose we can accept that account at face value,' Kember said. 'But I couldn't begin to count the times I've heard something similar said by mothers about their sons.'

'That's a cynical view, Inspector, but I take your point. However, I did speak to others in the church before I came back and they had the same opinions. I also managed to get this.' Wilson handed Kember a photograph. 'I don't know if it helps but it was taken quite recently.'

Kember studied the photograph and saw a middle-aged man in uniform wearing the dog collar of a clergyman. Although his hair had begun to recede, he had a strong jawline and an expression of contentment, of a man who was exactly where he wanted to be.

'A handsome man,' Kember said, turning the photograph over and reading *Lance Atkinson* written in pencil. 'And he doesn't look like someone who made enemies easily.'

'I thought so too.' Wilson shook his head as Kember offered him the photograph back. 'The chaplain said you could take it with you.'

Kember slid it into his jacket pocket as the scowling RMP sergeant strode towards them with Constable Morgan. 'Time to go, I think.'

CHAPTER EIGHTEEN

Vickers steered his RAF blue Austin through the rutted, muddy entrance to the field where the ENSA encampment stood and parked next to Wright, who was just emerging from his police Wolseley.

'Perishing cold out here,' Wright said when Vickers joined him. 'I don't know how these people do it.' He pulled up his collar to cover his neck.

'They're used to it,' Vickers said. 'They go all over the country, mostly staying in billets and draughty barracks, but sometimes camping.'

'More fool them.'

'I think Group Captain Dallington may have had a hand in keeping them off the air station,' Vickers said, with a thin smile. 'You know what he thinks of women in that regard, but he's not too fond of performers either. The presence of actresses must have given him heartburn.'

'Aye, he's a right one.' Wright nodded towards a group sitting around a trestle table inside the mess tent, nursing cups of tea. 'So are they, if my witness is right.'

Vickers looked across to the group. 'Who is your spy?' he asked, slightly intrigued by Wright's cloak and dagger approach.

'Mrs Garner, who lives opposite the church.'

Vickers nodded. He vaguely remembered the name from Kember's previous murder investigation.

Wright extracted his book from his overcoat pocket and read out descriptions of the poster group.

'According to my notes, Vera Butterfield and Graham Saunders were seen in the village,' Wright said. 'I saw them myself and took a flyer. George Wilkes, Betty Fisher and James McNee were seen by Mrs Garner turning back before they even got started, leaving all the work to the other two.'

'We'd better rattle their cage a bit, then,' Vickers said.

The conversation around the mess table died as the two policemen approached and Vickers saw a look of concern on two of the faces. From the descriptions related by Wright a moment ago, he guessed those to be Butterfield and Saunders but it was the others who interested him.

'Sergeant Wright,' said Wilkes, brightly. 'Brought a different friend this time, I see.'

'Mr Wilkes considers himself a joker,' Wright said, deadpan.

'George, please,' Wilkes said. 'And I'm a professional joker, I'll have you know.'

'That's debatable,' said Betty, with a grin. She looked at Vickers. 'I'm Betty Fisher by the way. I remember you from the hangar yesterday, at the pantomime.'

'That's correct. I'm Flight Lieutenant Vickers, in charge of the RAF Scotney Police.' Vickers saw Vera Butterfield and Graham Saunders exchange a glance. 'We're here to ask you a few questions about the run up to the performance.'

'Oh, really?' she said. 'Is it to do with the attack on that poor woman?'

'Well, Miss Fisher—'

'Mrs, actually.'

'I beg your pardon.' Vickers glanced around at their faces. 'I'd assumed you were all unmarried. Because of the lifestyle.'

'George and I are the only two married,' Betty said. 'My husband is in the Royal Navy so things do get a bit strained at times, and George's better half is looking after his two children somewhere up north.'

'Stoke-on-Trent,' George confirmed.

Vickers nodded his understanding and heard the scratch of Wright's pencil in his notebook.

'Sergeant Wright tells me you were in the village putting up posters and handing out flyers.'

'That's right,' Wilkes said. 'We're giving a repeat performance for the villagers in the hall on Christmas Eve so we needed to advertise.'

'How long did it take you?'

'Not long. It's not a big village.'

'Did you stick together or split up?'

Betty opened a packet of Craven A and handed out the cigarettes. Vickers and Wright declined the offer but all those around the table took one and made an issue of lighting theirs. Even with his limited experience, Vickers recognised it as a delaying tactic to allow them thinking time. Betty blew smoke at the canvas roof before answering.

'We split into two groups, as I recall. I teamed up with George and Shorty. Vera went with Tubby.'

Vickers saw Saunders flick a glance at Vera before returning to his study of the tabletop. He found it curious that they and Shorty McNee hadn't looked in his direction since their first introductions.

'And whereabouts did your group deliver their leaflets?'

'Oh, it was pretty willy-nilly.' Betty smiled through smoke. 'We didn't really have a plan.'

'But enough of a plan to split the work between two groups.'

'What's your point, Flight Lieutenant?' Wilkes said, flicking ash into a tin mug.

Vickers saw the corners of his mouth quiver as if with the strain of keeping a smile fixed in place.

'My point is, you three were seen turning back and leaving the village before the leafleting had begun. And we know from Inspector Kember's previous visit that you didn't arrive back separately because . . .' Vickers turned to Wright.

'Messrs Coates and Thorogood, sir,' Wright confirmed.

'Coates and Thorogood,' Vickers echoed, looking at each of the actors in turn. 'They confirmed you arrived back in camp together after an hour or so.'

He noted Vera and Saunders looked increasingly worried. McNee's face remained impassive. The smile had deserted Wilkes. Betty seemed engrossed in her smoking.

'That's easily explained,' Wilkes said. 'We didn't fancy the job, to be honest, so we persuaded Vera and Tubby to do ours for us. Gave them a few extra ciggies, didn't we, Tubby?'

Tubby gave a staccato nod and took a nervous pull on his cigarette.

'Wouldn't it have been quicker to stick together?' Wright asked.

'Too boring,' said Wilkes. 'Why do it yourself when you can get someone to do it for you. As an officer, you must appreciate that?' His smirk returned.

'Where did you go when you parted company with the real workers?'

'We've been working flat out recently so we had a well-earned rest in a field before we met up on the way back,' Betty explained.

'A rest in a field?' Wright scoffed. 'With frost on the ground and a cold wind.'

'Nothing a blanket couldn't cope with, Sergeant. And hedgerows make perfect windbreaks.'

Vickers wasn't convinced and he could see by the muscles of Wright's jaw tensing that neither was the sergeant. At worst, they were lying. At that moment, Vickers and Wright looked at each other as the rasp of a saw on wood echoed across the camp.

They excused themselves and strode towards the source of the sawing: the ENSA carpenter standing inside a large tent with one side open to the elements. Several lengths of wood lay across a trestle table that served as a workbench, a number of tools protruded from a canvas bag and two sizes of spirit level were visible inside a wooden box. The carpenter wore a thick leather apron and stood in an area of pale sawdust, the toes of his work boots coated as if it had snowed nowhere else but on him.

'Can I help you?' the carpenter asked.

'Flight Lieutenant Vickers of the RAF Police and Sergeant Wright of the Kent County Constabulary,' Vickers said, noting no reaction from the man. 'Would you mind answering a couple of questions?'

'I'm a bit busy but what can I help you with?' He put down his saw and blew sawdust from the cut he had just made, sending flecks over Vickers' greatcoat.

'You must have quite a number of cutting tools in your line of work,' Vickers said.

'Of course,' the carpenter said, interested now. 'Couldn't do my job otherwise.'

The carpenter's response came out in a wheeze which turned into a full-blown coughing fit. He grabbed a dirty square of cloth from his workbench, covered his mouth until the coughing stopped, and wiped tears from his eyes.

'Sorry 'bout that.'

Vickers eyed the man's toolboxes. 'The sergeant and I wondered if you possessed a hatchet.'

'I have an axe, a hand axe and a hatchet.' He nodded to Wright. 'Are you a country man, Sergeant?'

'Born and bred,' Wright said, puffing out his chest.

'Then you'll know they do different jobs.'

'Ah, really?' Vickers said before Wright could reply. 'Could you show me the difference?'

The carpenter eyed them both then searched through his tools and produced two axes: one with a long handle and a one with a short handle.

'Where the devil is my hatchet?'

'Have you misplaced it?' Vickers suggested. 'Maybe you lent it to someone?'

'No one touches my tools of the trade and I don't touch theirs.' He rummaged some more. 'It always lives in this box so it must be here somewhere.' He pulled out what looked like a bundle of cloth and unravelled it. 'What in God's name is this?' He held it up for them to see.

'I think I know what that is,' Wright said, taking the item from the carpenter. 'It looks like something I've seen at the cinema. It's from a Frankenstein costume.'

'We haven't done Frankenstein in almost a year,' the carpenter said, scratching his head. 'What's it doing in my toolbox?'

'It's made of dyed cloth and wool, sewn and stuffed to make the head and hair appear like a block.' Wright opened it out to show the shape. 'That's how Lizzie described her attacker, as having a square head.'

'What are you saying?' The carpenter looked at them in alarm and backed away. 'It isn't mine. It's one of the actors' costumes.'

'I'm afraid Inspector Kember will want a word with you.' Wright brandished his handcuffs and took hold of the carpenter's arm.

'I didn't take it. What would I want with it?' The man made to pull away but Vickers had already stepped around the table and

211

Wright's powerful grip convinced him to submit. 'I don't know how it got in my toolbox. Someone must have put it there.'

'The same someone who took your hatchet to a poor lass, I suppose?' Wright tightened the handcuffs.

Vickers saw alarm turn to shock and fear as realisation of what he was being accused of registered on the carpenter's face.

'I don't know where my hatchet has gone,' the man whined plaintively. 'Whoever put that in there must have taken it.'

'Why would they do that?' Vickers asked.

'I don't know, do I? I didn't even know that was in there.'

Wright finally had the handcuffs fixed to his satisfaction and placed his hand on the shoulder of the carpenter.

'Right, I'm arresting you on suspicion of assault committed on the night of Saturday the twenty-first of December. We'll be taking you to Scotney Police Station to await the return of DI Kember.'

CHAPTER NINETEEN

Lizzie's mind wandered as Kember took the Minx out of Chatham on the main road south, over the chalk ridge of the North Downs and down Bluebell Hill. Progress through Maidstone had been slow due to the number of checkpoints, and the presence of a policeman, pilot and vicar had made little impression on the Home Guard. Only when they had negotiated their way through the town and into the country lanes beyond did everyone relax as the journey became smoother with fewer interruptions.

'It's all about the connection between the curate and the cook,' Lizzie said, after a while.

'I'm not sure I follow,' Wilson said, from the rear seat.

'Lance Atkinson had been posed, taken care of as if respected,' Lizzie explained. 'Angela Caxton and the other women were carefully laid out in sheltered places, or protected.'

'I don't see that cutting someone's hands off shows much respect.'

'That's a different issue. A necessity. A detail. The bodies left behind are treated reverently, in contrast to the violence displayed in removing the hands, which I believe is for a specific purpose. All the women were found in sheltered places. In the case of Angela Caxton, she had been covered with debris as protection. We aren't looking for some maniacal, wide-eyed killer foaming at the mouth. Our man will be outwardly calm and ordered, someone who is comfortable with their surroundings, but not necessarily reserved. He might well be a charmer, enabling him to get close to his victims, but not in the sense of true intimacy.' She looked at Kember. 'Have you got your notebook? I'll write this down.'

The book was retrieved from Kember's coat lying on the back seat next to Wilson, and Lizzie wrote:

Calm, Ordered, Tidy

Comfortable with surroundings

A charmer

'You said the curate and the cook had a connection,' Kember said. 'Not a relationship?'

'That's right.' Lizzie waved his pen at him. 'But our man did. He met these people in life and caused their deaths to achieve a higher purpose, another kind of relationship. There may be an underlying anger in the blows and throat cutting that I can't explain yet, but he takes the hands of the women very carefully, and Atkinson was propped upright. It's almost as if he hates them and loves them at the same time.' She wrote:

Loves (and hates?) his victims

'Inwardly, he'll be anxious and confused about where the boundaries lie between himself and others. Despite his charm, that confusion creates difficulties forming friendships, especially close ones. The knock-on effect is mistrust of others and a suspicion about

their behaviour causing a misinterpretation of their motivations.'
She wrote:

Anxious/Suspicious

'That's not to say he won't have a friend, two at most, but these will be a carefully cultivated smokescreen against his anxiety and true nature, like his charming of those around him and those he meets. My guess is he'll be single; most likely, never married.' She wrote:

Unmarried

'Many conditions affecting how the brain works and the mind thinks cause specific behaviours to begin emerging at quite a young age, usually well before children become young men and women. I saw evidence of this many times during my research at Bedford College and in Oxford Prison. But this is very specific behaviour. The young don't have the freedom to travel around the country in wartime like the killer does, and as far as we know, my friend was his first victim. I believe he must be someone older who might be suffering a reactive depression brought on by some kind of loss. Someone killed in the bombing, perhaps. That's why all the murders, at least those we know about, have been in recent months.'

'If he's lost someone, I don't understand why he'd start killing people himself?' Wilson said.

'If I'm right, it's a psychotic reaction to trauma,' Lizzie said. 'But we know he's old enough to be able to travel around the country, committing these murders in private, in both the quiet countryside and busy places like the dockyard. That points to someone at least in their early twenties but I think the level of planning and detail means he might be older, perhaps up to mid-thirties. My friend in Duxford would never have gone out with anyone older than that.' She wrote:

Man, 20–35, Traveller

'Good Lord,' Wilson said. 'If I had all that going through my head it'd give me sleepless nights.'

Lizzie nodded and wrote:

Insomnia

'Unfortunately, that's still a wide field,' Kember said, with a wry smile. 'A youngish, normal-looking, charming bachelor who wouldn't say boo to a goose, and has trouble sleeping while there's a war on.'

Kember entered the back room of Scotney Police Station and was relieved to see a fire burning in the grate, the coals seeming to ripple with a welcoming orange glow. He was grateful to see a pot of tea on the go too, but narrowed his eyes in puzzlement when he saw Vickers sitting close to the fire, holding a toasting fork with a thick slice of slowly browning bread speared on its prongs.

'Welcome back,' Wright said, removing a padded cosy from the teapot and pouring the steaming liquid through a strainer into mugs. 'No Reverend Wilson?'

'He went straight home,' Kember said, as he and Lizzie shed their overcoats. 'I think discussing serial murderers on the way back from Chatham may have disturbed him.'

Wright splashed milk into their teas before handing one each to Kember and Lizzie.

'I didn't expect to see you here.' Kember nodded to Vickers.

'Sergeant Wright and I have been taking care of a little business that couldn't wait for your return,' Vickers said, pushing a plate of hot toast towards Wright before impaling another slice of bread.

'Oh?' Kember raised an eyebrow, thinking he'd had enough excitement for one day. 'What was so important?'

Wright began smearing slices of toast with margarine. 'I've arrested a Mr Arthur Allen, for assaulting Miss Hayes, sir. He's the ENSA carpenter.'

'You did what?' Kember put his mug on the table rather too heavily.

'New evidence came to light while you were away so the flight lieutenant and I met at the camp to make some enquiries, and one thing led to another.' He held up a plate for Kember. 'Toast, sir?'

Kember took the offering, annoyed that Wright hadn't waited for his return. He'd once told Lizzie off for forging ahead and asking questions, but Wright was a policeman. Even so . . .

'I hope I did the right thing,' Wright said.

Kember could feel the eyes of Lizzie and Vickers on him as he regained his composure. 'I think you'd better explain,' he said to Wright.

'Well, sir,' Wright said, handing plates of toast to Lizzie and Vickers. 'I had a visit from Mrs Garner. She was rabbiting on as usual and inadvertently revealed that the ENSA mob had split up before they started their work. When pressed, she described Vera Butterfield and Tubby Saunders as the only two who did the distribution of leaflets and posters. This corresponded to sightings by Jim Corcoran the postie, myself and others. Mrs Garner saw the other three turning back in the direction of the camp before they even fully entered the village.'

'The assistant director we first spoke to said they came back together,' Kember said, feeling his irritation dissipate at this new revelation.

'They did,' Wright said, wiping his hands on a tea cloth. 'They met on the way back after all the leaflets and posters had been given out. Anyway, not long after Mrs Garner left, Flight Lieutenant Vickers telephoned and told me about the discovery of the hatchet.'

'Ah, yes,' Vickers said. 'The head groundsman confirmed we'd found a hatchet, not an axe.' He put down his mug. 'It has a tapered cutting edge on one side and a flat hammer-like end on the other, for banging in nails and tacks and so on. It's not really designed for heavy-duty chopping but more as a tool used for working with wood in a more refined way.' Vickers held up a hand to Wright. 'Sorry, Sergeant. Please carry on.'

'Anyway.' Wright lifted his chin to stretch his neck. 'I told the flight lieutenant about what I'd learnt, and as you weren't due back for some time, we thought it practical to meet at the camp and question the poster group again. They were as difficult as last time, especially Wilkes and Fisher, but the three that deserted their colleagues did say they retired to a nearby field to have what they called a well-earned rest. It all sounded highly suspicious to me, especially it being so cold, but then . . .' He nodded to Vickers, offering for him to take up the narrative.

Vickers obliged.

'We asked the carpenter whether he had a hatchet and if we could see it. Mr Arthur Allen was as stand-offish as the rest but did admit to possessing a hatchet. He made a show of rummaging in his toolbox but said he'd either lost it or it had been stolen, something the sergeant and I didn't believe.'

'Not only had he lost his hatchet but we found this,' Wright said, and took a canvas bag from a hook behind the door. He reached inside, removed the contents and held it up to display the shape.

Lizzie gasped as Wright rotated the Frankenstein headpiece.

'That looks like the head of the man who attacked me,' she said. 'It was dark, of course, but I'll never forget it.'

'The carpenter said they do all sorts of shows but haven't performed Frankenstein for a year,' Wright said, putting the headpiece back in the bag. 'He also said he has no idea how it got there so I had no choice other than to arrest him on suspicion of assault. He's downstairs awaiting questioning, sir.'

'Good work, gentlemen,' Kember said. 'Sergeant, I hope you—'

'A carpenter?' Lizzie interrupted, frowning. 'What did his workshop look like?'

'No more than a glorified tent, miss,' Wright said.

'I meant was it ordered or chaotic? Did he keep it tidy or was it messy?'

'Oh, I see,' Wright said. 'I'd say it were in a right state: tools all over the place, dirty rags, sawdust blown everywhere, and he was standing on a carpet of wood shavings.'

'Did he seem anxious, or suspicious of your motive?'

'Wouldn't you if you'd been caught?' Wright said.

'How old is he?'

'Late thirties, I'd say. Maybe forty.'

'It isn't him,' Lizzie announced.

Kember's eyebrows rose in surprise. 'But what about the headpiece?'

'I can't explain that but our man craves order. He leaves his victims laid out serenely. Carpenters can be as tidy as the next man, cleaning as they go, but your Mr Allen sounds a lot more chaotic. It isn't him.'

The three men looked at Lizzie until Wright cleared his throat to break the awkward silence.

'I've preserved any evidence, sir, and I telephoned Dr Headley to expect an urgent delivery, to work his magic on whatever stray hairs and the like may be stuck on the headpiece and hatchet.'

'Well done, Sergeant,' Kember said. 'He should be able to tell us if it's the weapon used to murder Maisie Chapman, too.'

'I'll drop them both off to Alf before I go to Acorn Street.' Wright glanced at the wall clock. 'There are still people to talk to about Kenneth Jarvis and Miss Hartson, and they might be in at this time on a Sunday.'

'Good man.' Kember moved towards the door. 'Meanwhile, we have a suspect to question.'

◆ ◆ ◆

Kember ushered Lizzie to the front office and shut the door. Then he collected the handcuffed carpenter from the cells, took him to the back room and left him under the watchful eye of Vickers. Returning to the office, he prepared to face Lizzie's ire.

'Why have I been put in here like a naughty child?' she snapped, as soon as he entered.

'Sorry.' Kember closed the door. 'I don't want you in the room when we question him.'

'Why not?' She drew away from him. 'What's wrong with me observing?'

'Think about this rationally.' He knew he had to tread carefully when he saw her face harden at the implication that she was being irrational. 'You're a victim and a witness, and he's my prime suspect. Given the suspension I received after last time, I can't have you confronting him across the table. Anyway, even if that wasn't the case, this man's a carpenter, a tradesman, salt of the earth, and you're a woman in uniform. I want him to talk and he might not take kindly to having a woman there.'

'Not every man is like Dallington,' she scoffed.

'True, but even you must admit it's a possibility.'

Kember saw the tension in her face and posture ease as she thought it through. He would have loved to have her sit in, watching the carpenter's every move, listening to his every word, waiting for her insight that would support guilt or innocence. But it was impossible and they both knew it.

'You're right, of course.' Lizzie sat in Wright's chair and sighed.

He looked at her for a moment but she avoided his gaze.

'Just make sure you take plenty of notes,' she said, and turned to stare at the things on Wright's desk.

He clicked the door shut behind him as he left, and sighed.

Sergeant Wright strode back from delivering the packaged headpiece and hatchet to the stationmaster and turned left into Acorn Street. The young woman he sought to question, the one who hadn't answered the door the previous evening, was called Dorothy Ingram, and so was her elderly mother. To distinguish the two in conversation, Dorothy the elder had always been known as Dot and her daughter as Dottie. Dot suffered from bad ankles, a martyr to them, she often said, so Wright wasn't surprised no one had answered the door. Dottie had probably been cleaning up in the scullery before helping her mother up to bed and hadn't heard his knock.

As Wright approached the Ingrams' front gate, something unusual on the ground caught his eye. Knees cracking as he crouched, he dabbed at what looked like a large, dark stain amid other splashes on the muddy ground. He thought it looked like motor oil but vehicles never ventured this far down Acorn Street and oil usually shimmered in rainbow colours. This was dull and gloopy. He rubbed the icy substance between finger and thumb and saw the same effect as when he'd cleaned his boots, giving him a similar jolt.

His head snapped up at the sound of shouting to see two boys, about ten years old, dressed in baggy trousers and winter coats, running full pelt around some bushes at the end of the street. Wright stood as they ran into the muddy lane and caught the first around the waist as he went to run past. His mate skidded to a halt, sending a splatter of mud over Wright's boots.

'Where's the fire, boys?' Wright said, with a friendly smile.

'It ain't a fire,' said the boy in Wright's clutches, his eyes wide and darting. 'It's a dead body.'

'Now don't you be telling me no lies, Billy Driscoll.' Wright's smile faded. 'You've been caught out like that before.'

'But it's true.' Billy squirmed out of Wright's hold. 'Ask Davey.'

Wright looked at the other boy.

'It's a corpse all right,' said Davey, his eyes as wide as his friend's. 'Dead as a dodo.'

Wright frowned. These two boys were notorious for playing pranks like Knock Down Ginger, knocking on doors and running away, but something in their eyes and the way they glanced back nervously towards the bushes told him they were scared.

And that substance on the ground – was blood.

◆ ◆ ◆

Kember took a seat next to Vickers, ignoring the angry stare of the carpenter from across the large oak table. He opened his notebook and readied his pen, making each action slow and deliberate before he met the man's gaze.

'Mr Allen, my name is Detective Inspector Kember of the Kent County Constabulary. I believe you've been introduced to Flight Lieutenant Vickers of the RAF Police.'

'Thank God,' Allen said, seemingly relieved. 'A copper with a bit of clout behind him. When can I go back to work?'

Kember ignored the question. 'Where were you during the pantomime on the air station last night?'

'In the hangar, of course. All night. Anyone will tell you.'

'What about all day Friday?'

'Friday?' Allen frowned. 'I was in the camp preparing props for the show most of the day, and in the hangar all evening setting up scenery. Why?'

Kember thought he detected genuine puzzlement in Allen's voice as if the man thought he should have known. That wasn't what he'd expected.

'The body of Maisie Chapman was found in a field near the ENSA camp on Saturday morning. She'd been murdered.'

'What?' Allen's mouth fell open. 'Murder? Now look, I don't even know who that is. Why would I want to hurt her?'

He sounded a little wheezy to Kember. Could that be shock?

'We found a hatchet in the bushes next to where it was used to attack an ATA pilot. How do you explain that?'

'I can't,' Allen said, his gaze flicking between the two police-men. 'I didn't even realise it was missing until you' – he nodded at Vickers – 'and the sergeant turned up. Why would I hit someone with my own hatchet and leave it behind for you lot to find?' The exact same thought had been at the back of Kember's mind, and Allen didn't strike him as being slow-witted enough to make such a mistake. Nor did he appear to think so much of himself that he could deliberately leave a clue and still get away with it. But evidence was evidence.

'We also found a Frankenstein headpiece in your toolbox,' Vickers said.

'I know.' Allen's wheezing turned into a full coughing fit that he smothered with a threadbare handkerchief pulled from his pocket. 'I found it when you and the sergeant turned up, but it's not mine. I'm not an actor and I don't even touch the costumes. Mostly, they're made for one person, and very particular about who touches their things, are actors.'

Kember made a note. Could the mask belong to just one of the troupe? He'd have to get Wright onto that. 'What about during the shows. You ever help with costume changes?'

'No. It's not part of my job.'

'What do you class as part of your job, Mr Allen? Killing help-less women in the dark?'

'Good God.' Realisation spread across Allen's face. 'You think I'm the Handyman.' Kember winced at the nickname. 'Look, I was in the hangar the whole time and most of the company can vouch for me. I'm a carpenter and all I touch is wood, nails and paint.'

Kember could feel the interview getting away from him. The hatchet would have Allen's fingerprints on it because it was his, and Wright had witnessed Allen handling the headpiece when he took it from his toolbox. They had no real evidence to say it was him and if the troupe confirmed his alibi . . .

He noticed a movement by the door and almost did a double take when he saw Lizzie beckoning to him. Rising from his chair, he asked Allen and Vickers to excuse him for a moment and went into the hallway.

◆ ◆ ◆

Lizzie could tell Wright and Vickers had made a mistake. Superficially, the physical evidence suggested Allen could be the killer but there were other interpretations and everything else was wrong. She had to do something before this went too far so she waved from behind the crack in the door, caught Kember's attention and retreated to the front office.

'What do you think you're doing?' Kember hissed as soon as he walked through the door. 'I told you to stay in here.'

'It's not him,' she hissed back, angry at the suggestion that she'd been told, not asked, to stay out of sight.

'Why not? Isn't he a man who fits your profile in terms of age, looks and behaviour? And he travels with ENSA.'

'You could probably pick another five like him out of the troupe.' She flung an arm in the rough direction of the camp, annoyed at herself for undermining her own profiling. 'But did you really look at him?' She pointed towards the back room. 'Yes, he's scared, but wouldn't you be if you'd been arrested for something you didn't do? Look into his eyes. He's no confident charmer.'

'He looks as scared as any guilty man I've ever met who's been found out,' Kember said. 'After all, we found his hatchet in the hedge and the headpiece in his toolbox.' Kember held out his hands. 'And he had the means and opportunity.'

Lizzie shook her head. 'Like he said, why would he throw his own hatchet into the hedge when he's just used it on me? And having done that, why would he keep the headpiece when he must've known you'd find the hatchet and search his belongings?'

'I must admit, the logic baffles me,' Kember said looking tired all of a sudden.

'Exactly,' Lizzie said, feeling she was getting somewhere. 'The killer didn't want my hands at all. I think he wanted to kill two birds with one stone, so to speak. I think he attacked me on the air station to frighten me off, knowing there would be others around to see what he'd done to me. Then he deflected attention away from himself by dropping the hatchet and planting the headpiece to implicate Allen.'

'I can see how he might have panicked and dropped the hatchet when your friends disturbed him but hiding the mask in his tool-box seems inordinately stupid. Mr Allen does not strike me as stupid.' He rubbed the end of his nose. 'I don't think it's him, either.'

Lizzie was taken aback at the sudden turnaround and the fact that he'd come to the same conclusion as her.

'You told me the killer likes calm and order.' Kember held up a hand. 'I know, despite the nature of their work, carpenters generally keep their workshops tidy, but the inside of Mr Allen's tent was a mess.'

'Exactly,' Lizzie said. 'The killer would hate that. It isn't Allen.'

'But how does that square with all the bludgeoning and cutting and blood?' Kember said. 'That's not calm and ordered.'

Lizzie gazed out of the window.

'A necessary means to an end,' she said. 'But he leaves the bodies posed and protected, cleaned and tidied.'

'The problem is, you know I can't base my decisions on theories and supposition alone. Chief Inspector Hartson would have a fit if he knew I'd spoken to you and I ignored the obvious. Even though the hatchet and mask could have been left deliberately to implicate Allen, I have to hold him at least until we corroborate his account with the rest of the troupe.'

Lizzie turned back to face Kember. 'Trust me. It's not him.'

Her thoughts raced and tumbled as Kember turned the door-knob and made to leave. She couldn't bear to let an innocent man remain locked up a minute longer than necessary.

'Ask him about his family and home life,' she said. Kember paused in the doorway. 'If he's your man, he'll be unmarried and fastidiously tidy. And his profession: he's a skilled carpenter. Why isn't he in the army or a reserved occupation? Ask him about the performance schedule.'

Kember shut the office door behind him and Lizzie waited for a count of thirty before returning to her vantage point outside the back-room door.

◆ ◆ ◆

Wright followed the two boys past the end of Acorn Street to the small paddock beyond. The path continued on towards a stile at the far corner, but they veered off to their right, heading towards the woods where the trees stood stripped bare for winter. There was a path of sorts, originally worn by nocturnal animals but made more defined by the children who played there. Wright tried to keep his bearings as the boys led him through the trees and a knot of blackberry bushes, around a campsite made from hefty logs, branches and salvaged planks of wood, beneath a rickety tree house that would be concealed behind summer's foliage, and past two rope swings slung from low branches. The smell of damp earth and leaf mould filled his nostrils.

Following the trail along icy ground still covered in autumn's leaf fall, like walking on a carpet of cornflakes, he realised they were making their way deeper into the thicker woodland behind the houses of the High Street. After a few minutes, he noticed that some lower branches were broken from the trees and the trunks bore signs of having had their bark ripped off. He recognised the signs of a bomb blast and knew exactly where they were. This was the site of a close shave when a stray bomb had fallen during a Luftwaffe attack on RAF Scotney a few months earlier during the Battle of Britain.

Suddenly, the boys stopped at an artificial clearing, the one made by the Nazi bomb.

The smell of earth and leaves had given way to one of rotting wood and stagnant water. All the trees here were broken or bore the scars made by the high-explosive blast and deadly flying shrapnel. Wright supposed it had become a favourite place for the children to play, hunt for shards of bomb casing, and throw stones into the crater full to the brim with muddy water.

'Over there,' Billy shouted, and pointed.

Wright's gaze followed the line of Billy's outstretched arm towards where Davey stood on the broken stump of a tree that had fallen. The root end remained partially fixed to the earth, the other disappearing beneath the surface of the water. He couldn't see anything from this side so he inched his way around the slippery perimeter, holding on to trees for support, until he could see behind the tree trunk.

He took a sharp intake of breath and fought to keep his half-digested lunch down.

He forced himself to look and saw the body of a woman lying in the water between the trunk and the bank as if deliberately wedged there. Her open eyes and almost white face gave her a ghostly appearance. He thought he recognised her but she wore a military-style greatcoat with an ENSA shoulder flash. An ugly gash across her throat told him everything he needed to know about how she'd died, but it was her missing hands that brought the bile to his throat again.

'Davey, Billy, come away now,' Wright called.

He returned to the trail, slithering and sliding as the two boys bounded over fallen branches like young deer. *Oh, to be a nipper again*, he thought, and led them back through the woods, stopping where the path leading to Acorn Street emerged from the trees into the open paddock.

'I need you two boys to stay here until I get back,' Wright said, putting as much authority into his voice as he could. 'Tell anyone who tries to use this path that I said they mustn't.'

'Like you're the sheriff and we're your deputies,' said Davey, eyes bright at the prospect of adventure.

'Exactly like that.' He knew he'd have to be quick. Not everyone would take the boys' word for it and there were other ways into this area of the woods.

Davey grinned at Billy, who pulled a home-made tin star from his pocket and pinned it to his coat.

'Right you are, sheriff,' Billy said, in a poor American accent.

Wright gave them as big a smile as he could muster but it fell from his face as soon as he turned away.

Kember was tempted to ignore Lizzie's advice and charge Arthur Allen with assaulting her, but doubt plagued him. He usually trusted his instincts, and wasn't sure whether the irritation that bubbled up was because Lizzie might be wrong about Allen or because he knew she was right. He sighed. There could be no harm in asking a few more questions.

Returning to the table in the back room, Kember looked directly into Allen's eyes as the man raised his gaze from the handcuffs that restrained his wrists.

'Do you have family, Mr Allen?' Kember asked.

'I've got a lass in Wakefield.' Allen's wheeze was back. 'Two kids: a boy aged five and a girl two years older.'

Kember wrote in his notebook.

'But you chose to leave them at home and travel around the country with ENSA.'

'It wasn't much of a choice,' Allen said, sadly. 'I had tuberculosis when I was a kid so I couldn't enlist. My lungs are shot to bits. I worked in a local woodworker's doing joinery and the like, but the old man died and the young'un got called up after Dunkirk. Even the factories don't want someone who's weak and has fits of coughing. ENSA offered me a job with a proper uniform, and decent money. I have my self-respect back, earn a wage, and I still get to go home every few weeks.'

Damn, thought Kember. A man whose childhood TB had left him with damaged lungs and obvious breathing problems didn't sound like someone who would have smoked Craven A cigarettes with Maisie Chapman or crept up on Lizzie.

'Everything all right at home, is it?'

Allen shot Kember a sharp look. 'Of course, it is. I love my family and I'd do anything for them. The wife gets the arse-ache with me now and then. Same as in every home, I shouldn't wonder. She thinks I make a mess wherever I go, traipsing mud and woodchips into the house, but we've been together since we left school. We know which side our bread's buttered.'

Kember felt deflated. When Wright had presented his report, he'd thought it a decent lead. Now, he wasn't so sure. He rubbed his eyes with his thumb and forefinger and looked at the carpenter again. Lizzie was right. He seemed small, frightened and sad, not at all like a vicious killer.

'Where were you last Saturday and Sunday?'

'I was in Wakefield,' Allen said. 'There's only a few actors and workers in the company who have kids and we were allowed to go home for the weekend because we were going to miss Christmas. I went home on the Friday and came back Monday, in time for the first of two shows at the dockyard.'

'You missed the air raid?'

'Oh, aye. I was lucky. Mind you, from what I hear, the place was too hot for the Jerries and they scarpered before they could do much damage.'

'Where did the troupe perform before the dockyard shows?'

'We did one for the Royal Engineers at Brompton Barracks on the Saturday, but as I said, I was at home.' Allen felt inside his coat pocket, pulled out his identity card and opened it. Inside was a folded piece of paper which he handed to Kember. 'That's our six-month schedule from July through to the new year. You can keep it, if it's any good to you.'

Kember unfolded the paper and put it on the table. 'All right, Mr Allen. Unless the flight lieutenant has any questions . . .' He looked at Vickers who pouted and shook his head. 'Then I thank you for helping us with our enquires, and you can go now.' Kember leant forward and unlocked the handcuffs.

'Is that it?' Allen rubbed his wrists and looked at both officers with an expression of relief.

Kember nodded. 'We may need to speak to you again, of course, but for now you can go back to your work at the ENSA camp. One of us can give you a lift.'

Allen waved away the offer. 'I'll walk, if it's all the same to you.'

Kember escorted Allen to the front door, noting the door to the front office was ajar, and watched him buttoning up his coat as he strode off towards the north end of the village and the ENSA camp half a mile or so beyond.

Kember suspected Lizzie had eavesdropped again, but no sooner had he stepped into the front office than Wright hurried in, sporting an anxious look and sweating despite the cold.

'Sorry to interrupt, sir,' Wright said. 'You'd better come quick. We've got another body.'

CHAPTER TWENTY

Kember stood with Lizzie and Wright at the edge of the water-filled bomb crater. He'd hoped he wouldn't have to watch Dr Headley pick over the remains of another dead body: wishful thinking in his chosen line of work.

'Dorothy Ingram, called Dottie round here,' Wright said, breaking the silence. 'She's named after her mother, known as Dot, who's just returned home from visiting her sister in Maidstone. I've got a neighbour comforting her.'

Thank God it's not Evelyn Hartson, Kember thought, and immediately felt a heavy weight of guilt descend.

'I thought I recognised her,' Wright continued. 'Her beret and knitted scarf confirmed it. Mother and daughter live together at the end of Acorn Street, where I found blood splashes on the ground just before the boys came running over.'

'That's quite a way from there to here,' Lizzie said.

'Aye, I don't understand that. I don't understand why she's wearing an ENSA greatcoat over her own coat, neither.'

'Perhaps she met someone from the troupe that she liked, got cold and he gallantly offered up his coat,' Kember said, not really believing it.

'Before slitting her throat?' Lizzie shook her head. 'No. It's definitely the same killer, but this is a deviation. They've not met somewhere else and walked to the place he wants to kill her. Three women were killed in fields: two of those must have been meeting someone romantically, one while tending sheep. Angela Caxton and Lance Atkinson were killed in or near a scarce-used part of a dockyard warehouse. They seem random but they're all out-of-sight places in their own ways. Outside a row of cottages in Acorn Street is public, dangerous.' She looked at the trees surrounding them. 'The cutting of the hands is still as neat and tidy as he can make it, but make no mistake, this is an escalation.'

Dr Headley let out a growl as his foot slipped and plunged into the icy water, filling his wellington boot in the process. Wright grabbed the doctor's hand and pulled him up to the rim of the bomb crater, where he then sat dejectedly on his box of forensic instruments and struggled to remove his boot. In any other circumstance, Kember would have laughed, but even gallows humour seemed inappropriate.

'What is it with you and muddy water, Kember?' Headley moaned, as he emptied his boot of brown sludge. 'Can't you find a body somewhere warm and dry for a change?'

'I'd prefer not to find any bodies at all,' Kember said, flatly. 'It's not my preferred way of spending a Sunday afternoon.'

'Nor mine,' Headley agreed.

Kember looked down at the young woman still lying in the water, wedged between the tree and bank. If you were to take a close-up photograph, this could be Maisie Chapman in the ditch at the edge of the field.

'Apart from the obvious, are there any other injuries?' Kember asked.

Headley shook his head. 'Not that I can see. I'll do the usual checks for signs of drowning and so on when I get her back to the mortuary but I can't see any bruising around her neck. And before you ask, there's nothing in her mouth or pockets either. The blood on her two coats is rather confusing, though.'

'Oh?' Kember waited patiently for Headley to remove his sodden sock and wring water from it.

'She does have a lot of blood on the chest area and sleeves of her overcoat as I'd expect, given the wounds to her neck and wrists,' Headley continued. 'But she also has considerable staining over the left shoulder and down the back of the greatcoat.'

'And that means – what?'

'It means I should get paid double for doing your job as well as mine.' Headley groaned with distaste as he put his wet sock back on. 'Given the traces of blood on branches over there, and what Sergeant Wright said about blood on the ground, I'd say she was killed in Acorn Street with a cut to her throat and carried here before having her hands removed.' He pushed his foot back into the wellington with a grimace. 'Picking up the limp body of a recalcitrant child is difficult enough, but moving the unconscious or dead body of an adult is bloody awkward. The limp body folds over and slips through your grasp and the limbs flop everywhere and stick out, catching on things as you pass.'

'You don't have to tell me,' Kember said. 'I've moved my fair share of Saturday night drunks.'

'Exactly, so I don't have to tell you that carrying the deadweight of an adult any distance is backbreaking work.'

'What about . . . ?' Kember said, with no need to finish. He knew Headley expected the question.

Headley wrinkled his nose and removed his glasses. 'I'll not bore you with the usual details about rigor mortis and freezing water, but I'd say she's been dead since late yesterday evening at least. Maybe a few hours earlier.' He cleaned brown splashes from the lenses and replaced his glasses.

'Sometime between blackout and bedtime, then,' Wright said. 'Four 'til ten.'

'Really?' Headley said, hooking the arms of his glasses behind his ears. 'That's closer than I can estimate.'

'I doubt the murderer would have struck in daylight,' Wright said, 'and according to Dottie's mother, she always listens to the nine o'clock news on the wireless before taking a mug of Horlicks up to bed. We can't know for certain that she did that last night but Brian Greenway would have been on his ARP rounds at ten o'clock. He'd have said if he'd seen anyone or anything.'

Headley threw Wright a glance and grunted an acknowledgement.

'I'd appreciate a small favour, Doctor,' Kember said.

'Do your job, do you mean?' Headley replied.

'Not exactly. I wondered if you could check with your professional colleagues at Duxford and Croydon, to compare notes about the type of weapon that might have been used. The question would be much better coming from you.' Kember knew that stroking Headley's ego was never a waste of time.

'You know very well that we wouldn't be able to say definitively,' Headley said.

'Speculatively would be sufficient for now.'

'Hmm.' Headley stood with a groan.

Kember turned to Lizzie. 'You said this is a deviation. Could it be his first real mistake? Killing her in the street outside her home was opportunistic but highly dangerous, even in the blackout. Something must have happened to provoke another attack.' Kember frowned. 'Our investigation, perhaps? Maybe we're getting close.'

Lizzie shook her head. 'It's not a mistake because he isn't concealing his crimes. He leaves the bodies comfortable and protected, like I said before. And I don't think it's anything we did. It's him.

His desire to find whatever he's seeking is pushing him to kill more frequently and take more risks.'

Headley tripped and stumbled his way around the back of their little group, well away from the water's edge, his bag in one hand and his box swinging wildly from its strap over his shoulder.

'If you get the poor girl out of the water, I'll send the ambulance crew through,' Headley called. 'And I'll let you know the usual bits and bobs in due course.'

Kember wanted to emphasise the urgency of conducting a post-mortem but knew better than to try to hurry the doctor. He sighed and rubbed his eyes. Two dead and two missing on his patch in four days, including Chief Inspector Hartson's niece, and however hard he worked he'd still get lambasted from above. Some days being a copper just wasn't worth the money or sorrow.

◆　◆　◆

In the warmth of the back room of the police station where Sergeant Wright was using a sheet of newspaper held across the fireplace to draw the fire back to life, Lizzie paced up and down like a caged animal. Kember sat at the table, toying with the photograph of the curate. Vickers sat next to him, comparing two pieces of paper.

'They match,' Vickers said, quietly, almost to himself. He looked up at the others and said louder, 'They only bloody well match.'

Kember leant across and looked at the papers. Lizzie stopped pacing and peered between their shoulders.

'The ENSA schedule matches the list of dead and missing we compiled,' Vickers said. 'Look.' He pointed. 'The tour dates for Duxford, Croydon, Chatham and Scotney correspond with the known deaths. I say known because the only stop on the tour so far without a murder that we know of is RAF North Weald between Duxford and Croydon.' He glanced at Kember, then up at Lizzie.

'What about one of the three from the poster group?' Kember said, looking over at Sergeant Wright.

'Saunders, McNee and Wilkes,' Wright said, getting up from his crouch by the fireplace. 'Didn't like any of them, especially Wilkes. He's got the gift of the gab and could charm the ladies. Mind you, it could be any of that ENSA mob, if you ask me.'

Kember nodded. 'Coates and Thorogood weren't the easiest men to talk to, either.'

'I'd throw Martin Onslow in there, too,' Lizzie said. 'He's already turned the charm on for me and the flight captain.' She ignored the sharp look of jealousy that Kember gave her and began pacing again. 'The killer must have known we'd make the connection sooner rather than later. That's why he tried to frame the carpenter.'

She stopped by the blackboard, snatched up a piece of white chalk and made a rough sketch of Acorn Street, the woods and the bomb crater.

'He carried her,' Lizzie said. 'He had to kill her right outside her home, before she went in, but then he didn't drag her like a piece of meat, he carried her carefully all the way.' She drew a line from the murder site and through the woods to where Dorothy Ingram had been found. 'From here to here.' She turned suddenly and pointed the chalk at Kember. 'That explains the blood on the greatcoat. He was wearing it when he put her over his shoulder.'

'And he left it with her because he couldn't clean off that much blood or wear the coat back to the camp?' Vickers suggested.

Lizzie looked above their heads, visualising the scene. 'He didn't just leave it with her, he gave it to her. Made her warmer.'

Hearing Wright scoff, she felt the usual clash of opinions coming.

'I'm sorry but that makes no sense,' Wright said. 'Why would he want to make her warmer when she's already dead?'

Good question, Lizzie thought. 'Because he's grateful to her.'

'Grateful for what? The poor lass hardly had much of a choice.'

'No, but *he* did and he chose her deliberately. She gave her life and her hands to him; giving her his coat was the least he could do.'

'A coat stained with her own blood that he doesn't want to be seen wearing?' Wright's short laugh was cold. 'He was getting rid of evidence. Pure and simple.'

Lizzie shook her head. 'There are better ways. Burning, burying. He could have weighted it with stones and sunk it in the crater but he chose to take the time to put it on her, and make sure she didn't sink under the water. All the victims were posed and made comfortable. He sees each death as a sacrifice, an act of love, and he respects that.'

'That's not my idea of love,' Wright said, folding the sheet of newspaper. 'Anyone for a cuppa?' As he passed behind Vickers and Kember, he stopped and reached for the photo in Kember's hands. 'May I, sir?'

Kember held the black and white image higher and Wright took it, looking at it intently for a few seconds.

'You say this is the curate from the dockyard?' Wright asked.

'Yes,' Kember confirmed. 'The dockyard chaplain gave the photo to Reverend Wilson.'

'Well, it's uncanny. If it wasn't for the dog collar, I'd say this was a picture of Kenneth Jarvis.'

Kember snatched back the photograph and stared at it with Lizzie.

'The headpiece!' Lizzie said, suddenly. 'Frankenstein's creation was seen as a monster.' She scrubbed the map off the blackboard with a rag. 'I think the killer might be looking for someone who's harmed him in some way; a real monster he can't find or get to.' She chalked the word *Monster* on the board and underlined it.

'How does killing the others get at the monster?' Kember asked. 'And where does love come into it?'

'If I'm right, he wants retribution and an end to his own suffering.' Lizzie wrote the names *Catherine, Dora, Angela, Maisie* and *Dorothy* in a column as she spoke. 'He thinks the only way he can do that is to create a good-enough likeness so he can kill it, and the monster with it.' She added *Lance* and *Ken*. 'Lance Atkinson was found alone in a room but with the hands of a woman killed nearby. Kenneth Jarvis looks very much like him and we now have two women in Scotney whose hands have been removed. That must be the connection. He finds men who look like the monster, but they aren't perfect replicas.' She pointed to the photograph. 'Look at the those long, slim fingers. He needs feminine hands, a woman's hands.'

Kember looked. 'Are you saying he applied the tourniquets to the curate's arms to keep him alive long enough to find a hand match, and to then kill him?'

'Exactly. He needs the likeness to be perfect to rid himself of the monster in his mind. Until then, he tries to treat the donors as respectfully as he can.'

'Donors?' Wright said, grimacing. 'Sorry, miss, but that's sick. He'll never get a woman's hands to match a man's body.'

'That's what I mean. Each attempt can never achieve the perfection he's after. He has to keep looking and keep killing.'

'That means Jarvis and Miss Hartson could be . . .'

'He won't stop until he's caught,' Kember said.

'He can't stop,' Lizzie said.

The bell from the telephone in the front office jangled loudly and Kember held up his hand for them to wait.

◆ ◆ ◆

Sitting at Wright's desk in the front office, Kember listened to the sergeant from Cardiff City Police. The information seemed to have little bearing on his case of missing persons but the final snippet made his eyebrows shoot up. He thanked the sergeant and put the handset in its cradle.

The phone rang again immediately.

'Scotney Police Station,' Kember said, and winced as Chief Inspector Hartson shouted down the line.

'What the bloody hell do you think you're playing at, Kember? How many times must I tell you not to employ that bloody woman to do your job for you? You're still a Scotland Yard detective so I expect more from you than mere dilly-dallying.'

'Dilly-dallying, sir?' Hartson's attitude already had the hackles rising on Kember's neck.

'You don't appear to have made any progress whatsoever on finding my niece, you have bodies piling up in your backyard again, and I've heard you've turned to that bloody clairvoyant to commune with the dead.'

'She's not a—'

'Word has reached the chief constable and he's already expressed his displeasure. You and I both know that when the chief constable is displeased, he's actually apoplectic. I'm not far off that myself.'

Kember gritted his teeth at the irony of how angry Hartson could be, having risen to chief inspector on the back of other people's efforts and never having caught a murderer or confronted a knife-wielding maniac in his life. And how in hell's name did he always know what was going on?

'We have made progress, actually, sir,' Kember said. 'We've managed to narrow our search for your niece based on a lead we're following and strongly believe she is alive and safe. We hope to have a resolution soon.'

'Soon? What does that—?'

'We've also discovered other murders in the south-east,' Kember carried on. 'I believe they're connected to the Scotney murders.'

He outlined the deaths they'd discovered and put forward the theory about the killer's driving force.

'It would really help to have another man or two at my disposal, sir,' Kember concluded.

Whereas the news about Evelyn had begun to calm Hartson, the Handyman theory reignited his temper.

'No, you bloody well can't have any more coppers down there! It's only a piddling little village. You can walk the entire length of the high street in five minutes, for Christ's sake. You're supposed to be a highly trained Scotland Yard detective, so start behaving like one and stop making excuses about lack of manpower. As for your theory about hands and bodies, that will get you locked up in the loony bin if you're not careful. There's only so much I can do to protect you.'

Kember couldn't prevent a short laugh escaping. He'd never felt any protection from Hartson. Quite the opposite.

'And who in God's name gave him a nickname? Makes him sound like some bloody folk hero. We're the police. *We* should be the folk heroes.'

'Yes, sir.'

'Yes, sir? I don't want "yes sirs", I want results. I expect you to get on top of all this with the utmost urgency because if you don't find my niece and stop this murderer, there'll be no Christmas cheer for any of us. And get rid of that bloody woman!'

'Yes—' Kember jerked the receiver away from his ear at the sound of Hartson slamming down his phone.

He took a moment to get his breathing under control and put Hartson to the back of his mind, turning its attention to the information from Cardiff. It seemed he and Vickers had a mutual acquaintance, with a secret.

◆ ◆ ◆

Lizzie had the photograph of Lance Atkinson in her hand as Kember returned from the office but she put it down when he sat at the table, his jaw set in anger.

'Hartson's just given me another rocket for not finding his niece or the killer,' he said, bitterness in his voice. 'Apparently, the chief constable's not happy either.'

'Isn't that par for the course?' Vickers said.

Kember relayed the essence of Hartson's displeasure but Lizzie saw in his eyes and crossed arms that there was more to come.

'I thought I heard two phone calls,' she said.

He shook his head and Lizzie saw the anger fall away to reveal the face of the inquisitive detective she knew so well.

'Sergeant Wright told me about Agnes Jarvis and her sister, Edith, and Cardiff City Police filled in the gaps,' Kember said. 'We know that Edith ran away with John Davies to his home town to get away from the disapproval of her parents, Frank and June Robinson, leaving Agnes behind. Both parents died later, around the time Spanish flu was sweeping the country, and we thought maybe some bad feeling might have resurfaced, either between Agnes and Edith or among the villagers. John and Edith married and had a son but it was believed they all died when a bomb hit the house next door during an air raid on Cardiff docks on the seventh of August, meaning they couldn't be involved in our cases.'

'Was believed?' Wright said.

'That first call just now was Cardiff calling me back with some new information. It appears one of the bodies they thought was the son was later identified as someone else who was visiting next door.'

'So, the son is still alive?'

'He is.' Kember looked at Vickers. 'He's a medical officer in the RAF called Samuel.'

'Samuel?' Lizzie frowned. 'As in Sam Davies the Scotney MO?'

'The one and only,' Kember said.

Vickers sat bolt upright. 'You think he has something to do with all this?'

'I don't know what to think, but I'd like to know why he's never mentioned he was born here and has an aunt living down the road.' He stood. 'I think we'll have to forego the tea, Sergeant. We'll hold off telling Agnes about her sister until the flight lieutenant and Lizzie have spoken to Sam Davies. Meanwhile, you and I should speak to the poster group again. I want to know exactly what they were up to when they shunned their duties, and what, if anything, they saw.'

CHAPTER TWENTY-ONE

Night was already casting its shroud over the east as Kember eased his Minx through the five-bar gate, a look of distaste already on Wright's face, and pulled up next to one of the ENSA transport lorries by the encampment. He realised their return might elicit an even less favourable response than last time but he was surprised to hear no sounds of rehearsals, sawing wood, cooking or even conversation. It was as if their arrival had flicked an invisible off-switch.

On the way to the marquee tent with Wright, Kember noticed dark looks from those they passed and felt eyes boring into his back. Coates and Thorogood sat at the same table as during their first encounter, but this time the troupe's director, Martin Onslow, sat with them.

'Inspector,' Coates said. None of the men stood up. 'Have you come to arrest more of us?'

'For bad acting, perhaps?' Onslow smiled.

Wright scoffed and Kember flashed him a warning look.

'Actually, the pantomime was better than I expected,' Kember said.

'Any closer to solving the case?'

'I thought you were staying at the manor house,' Kember said, avoiding Onslow's question.

Onslow smiled. 'I am but we have another performance to put on for the villagers in two days' time. The show must go on.'

'Talking of shows.' Kember reached in his coat pocket and drew out Allen's note. 'We checked your troupe's performance schedule against a series of unexplained deaths that have occurred around the country.' He noted Onslow's smile slip for the first time. 'They match.'

'Good Lord,' Thorogood gasped, the blood draining from his face.

Onslow's mouth dropped open but no sound emerged and Coates looked as though the ceiling had fallen in.

'Do you suspect one of us?' Thorogood said, his voice rasping.

'Of course, he doesn't.' Onslow regained his composure and puffed out his chest. 'I'm sure it's just a coincidence. After all, there is a war on and we're in the middle of the Blitz.'

Kember glared at him. 'Even in wartime, I wouldn't expect men and women to have their hands cut off, be propped up as if on display or be laid out as if in a coffin.' He could feel the pull of a tic beginning at the corner of his mouth. 'And when matched with your schedule . . .'

The ice in his voice had a visible effect on the three men. Coates and Thorogood were unable to look him in the eye, while Onslow seemed to shrink before him.

'Indeed, Inspector.' Onslow sighed. 'How can we help?'

His rapid deflation from Dallington-like pomposity to world-weary actor took Kember by surprise. He'd expected more resistance and had come prepared for a battle of wills. He could see all of them for what they were: ordinary men who were unable or unwilling to fight a war, men who were under the illusion that they could do their normal jobs in extraordinary circumstances with no consequences, men for whom the violence of real life had suddenly thrown a spotlight on their inadequacies.

'I'd like another word with Betty Fisher, George Wilkes and James McNee,' Kember said.

The two assistants looked to their director for approval. Onslow nodded and Thorogood strode off towards the tent where Kember had first questioned the poster group. He returned two minutes later with the three actors.

'Gentlemen, could you give us some privacy for a few moments?' Kember ignored the disgruntled looks from Onslow and his assistants as they rose from their chairs, seemingly performing the hardest task in the world. He looked at Wright. 'Sergeant, do you mind taking Mr McNee somewhere quiet for a chat?'

'My pleasure, sir,' Wright said.

Kember noted the furtive looks exchanged by all three, and waited for everyone to walk out of earshot before inviting Betty Fisher and George Wilkes to sit down.

'I'm not here to cause you trouble,' Kember began. 'But I am investigating several horrific murders and need answers so I can catch the lunatic doing this.'

'But we don't know anything,' Betty said, looking at Wilkes as if for confirmation.

'Betty's right,' Wilkes said. 'We haven't seen or heard a dicky bird about what's going on.'

Criminals lied. Frightened people lied. People did things they wanted kept secret even if they weren't illegal. Most of the time, Kember knew which kind of person sat in front of him and he didn't need Lizzie to tell him that these two had a secret. He remembered when Lizzie had once demonstrated how a person's way of sitting and gesturing said as much as the words they spoke. Betty sat close to Wilkes, leaning towards him, legs crossed, her gaze darting from his face to Kember's. The bravado of the first meeting had vanished.

'When Sergeant Wright last spoke to you, you said you'd abandoned your leafleting duties and went to a field to have a rest. Is that correct?'

'Yes,' Wilkes said.

'Why didn't you just come back to your tents?'

Betty looked away, a slight flush appearing on her cheeks. Wilkes raised his chin defiantly. Kember had seen this kind of behaviour before. She was embarrassed, he was protective. The conclusion was obvious.

'How long have you been having an affair?' Kember asked.

Wilkes shot to his feet. 'Now, look here—'

'Sit down, Mr Wilkes,' Kember said, quietly but firmly.

Wilkes remained standing for a moment longer, trying to look indignant. Betty put her hand on his arm and coaxed him to sit.

'People's lives are at risk so I need to know what you two were doing in that field for the hour or so it took Graham Saunders and Vera Butterfield to deliver all the posters and leaflets. At the moment, you two and Mr McNee are high on my list of murder suspects, so anything you think might be inconvenient or embarrassing is really not.'

Betty squeezed Wilkes' arm. 'We might as well tell him, George,' she said, quietly.

Wilkes looked away as if struggling to make a decision. Then he turned his head back and looked Kember in the eye. 'Can we keep this between us?' he said, his composure regained.

Kember was inclined to say no and make them both squirm but his thoughts flashed to his own crumbling marriage. He realised any animosity he felt towards Betty and Wilkes was due more to his own humiliation and sense of failure than to any secret liaisons the two might have been enjoying.

He nodded. 'If I can.'

Wilkes relaxed and leant forward. 'Betty and I are in love but things are a bit complicated.'

Kember almost smiled. 'I should imagine being already married does complicate things,' he said, feeling little sympathy as Betty's face turned a deeper red and Wilkes' mouth opened in surprise. 'You told my sergeant when he was last here, and once I'd thought about your disappearance, I suspected you'd been meeting in secret.'

'My husband is in the Royal Navy and he'd kill the both of us if he found out,' Betty said, gripping Wilkes' arm.

'To be frank, I'm not concerned about your affair. I'm trying to find a killer and I need to know if you saw anyone or anything while you were in the fields, or wherever you went. And I need to know what Mr McNee was doing all that time.'

'He wasn't doing anything,' Wilkes said. 'Vera and Tubby agreed to get rid of the posters and leaflets on their own, reluctantly. Shorty, being six foot five, could see over the hedgerow so he said he'd keep a lookout for us.'

'What was in it for them?' Kember asked, feeling another interview slipping away.

'We said we'd give them some of our fags and booze, and do the same for them if they ever needed it.'

Kember sighed. Adultery had always been more prevalent than people realised and for three hundred years had been allowable as the sole grounds for a man to divorce his wife. Women had achieved the same right less than two decades ago. At a cost. In his experience, adultery, often the catalyst for angry, jealousy-fuelled murder in the home, had never been a precursor to senseless serial murder beyond the front door.

'One last question,' Kember said. 'Did you see anyone in the fields at any point or was anyone acting suspiciously on the night of the air-station pantomime?'

'Not that I noticed,' Betty said, looking at Wilkes. 'George?'

'Sorry, no,' Wilkes said.

Kember saw Wright lurking outside the marquee and decided he'd heard enough. He thanked the two actors and left, joining Wright for the walk back to the car. Wright revealed he'd also had time to ask Vera Butterfield and Graham Saunders a couple of questions after talking to James McNee. Each version of events roughly tallied, but not precisely enough to suggest a concoction.

'There is one curious fact, sir,' Wright said. 'Miss Butterfield told me that certain actors take on particular roles in their productions. The Frankenstein headpiece was made specifically for Mrs Fisher.'

◆ ◆ ◆

Lizzie and Vickers caught up with Dr Davies outside the air-station hospital building and they all squeezed into his broom cupboard-sized office.

Lizzie began to feel a little claustrophobic, the memory of being attacked and having been so close to the man who had wanted her dead causing her throat to constrict. She felt her face flush and feared the men would notice at any moment. The thought made the rising anxiety attack take hold of her chest, squeezing the air from her lungs. She tried to focus on her countermeasures but the restricted space, proximity of the men, and impending conversation ruled out all but the rubber bands and VapoRub. Dr Davies had already thrown her a curious look so she took the cobalt-blue jar from her pocket and unscrewed the lid. She took a deep breath and the mixture of camphor, eucalyptus and menthol brought her mind back into sharp focus.

'Do you have a cold, Miss Hayes?' Davies asked.

'A slight sniffle,' Lizzie lied, returning the jar to her pocket.

The presence of Vickers was some comfort, but he'd been seething for most of the journey back to the air station, muttering about how you couldn't even trust a doctor these days. In contrast, Davies looked relaxed but perplexed by the obvious aggression seeping from Vickers. He sat back in his chair and put his fingertips together, acting neither anxious nor smug. These weren't the actions of a man with something to hide and Lizzie began to fear they were barking up another wrong tree.

'Then what can I do for you?' Davies said. 'You mentioned some new information.'

'DI Kember, Sergeant Wright and I have been speaking to potential witnesses about the recent murders and disappearances,' Vickers said. 'This has thrown up some new questions.'

Davies looked interested but unflustered. 'I don't see how that involves me but fire away.'

'Where were you yesterday evening between sixteen-hundred hours and twenty-hundred hours?'

'On duty until eighteen-hundred.' Davies thought for a moment. 'Then at dinner and in the lounge.'

'Any witnesses?'

Davies frowned and he sat forward. 'Everyone else eating and drinking, for a start, and my shift will be recorded in the hospital log.'

'What about during the pantomime?' Vickers pressed.

Davies' frown deepened. 'I was in the hangar with everyone else, all evening.'

Lizzie noticed Davies take up his pen and start to fidget with it, his expression darkening.

'Why?' Davies asked. 'What is all this? I thought you'd brought new information, not accusations.'

'Do you know anything about the disappearance of Kenneth Jarvis or Evelyn Hartson?' Vickers continued.

'I don't even know who those people are.' Davies crossed his arms defensively. The two men glared at each other across the desk. Lizzie knew she had to step in before one of them punched the other. She sat forward and spoke quietly.

'One of the witnesses gave us some information about John and Edith Davies,' she said.

'My parents?' Davies' gaze flickered between Lizzie and Vickers. 'What information? Are they all right?'

'Why didn't you tell anyone your family came from Scotney?'

'Because they don't.'

'The witness says different,' Vickers snapped.

'Then they're lying,' Davies snapped back. 'Or mistaken.'

Davies looked confused and Lizzie was a little annoyed at the interjection. She placed a hand gently on Vickers' arm, urging him to sit back and let her take the lead.

'Your grandparents, Frank and June Robinson, hated railwaymen and your father, John, worked on the Hawkhurst line down here,' Lizzie said. 'He and your mother fell in love and ran away to his home town of Cardiff to get married. That's when they had you. Your mother's younger sister, Agnes, was furious at being left behind and when your grandparents died of Spanish flu, she married another railwayman, Kenneth Jarvis.'

Each revelation took more wind out of Davies' sails until he slumped back in his chair. Vickers was looking at Davies through narrowed eyes.

'We don't know what went on between your mother and your aunt,' Lizzie continued. 'But Cardiff City Police confirmed the family connections.'

'Cardiff City Police?' said Davies. 'Why are they involved?'

Lizzie took a breath and exchanged a glance with Vickers.

'What is it?' Davies sat forward. 'What's wrong?'

'DI Kember contacted them to confirm that John and Edith lived there but they gave us some bad news, I'm afraid,' Lizzie explained. 'I'm sorry, but they were killed in an air raid on Cardiff docks in August.'

Davies doubled over as though he'd been kicked in the stomach and Lizzie thought he might be sick so she carried on quickly.

'The police mistakenly identified one of the bodies as yours, which is why no one contacted you about your parents. Did you really not know your family came from Scotney?'

'How could I?' Davies looked up, eyes brimful of tears but chin held high to prevent crying.

That bloody English stiff upper lip again, Lizzie thought. If only everyone had a damn good cry now and then the world might be a better place. Perhaps he would later, in private, after the shock had worn off.

'I was born in Cardiff and my parents never mentioned Scotney at all,' Davies continued with a steady voice but looking dazed as if struck by a blow in a boxing ring. 'Is Agnes still alive?'

'She is,' Vickers said. 'But she reported her husband missing two days ago. That's why your failure to tell anyone about your connection to Scotney looked suspicious. We thought you might be involved.'

Davies shook his head, his eyes unfocused as if seeing beyond the walls. 'I had no idea about any of this.'

Lizzie was relieved that Vickers' attitude had mellowed. She'd studied Davies' every move but found nothing in any gesture or expression to suggest he was being anything other than totally truthful. She felt for him. Being wrongly accused of conspiracy to murder and kidnap was enough to knock anyone off kilter, never mind the recent death of both of your parents and hearing about your family history for the first time. The man's thoughts must be in turmoil.

Davies stood suddenly, taking Lizzie by surprise.

'With respect, I'd like you to leave, if you don't mind. I need to phone Cardiff.'

'Of course,' Vickers said, looking contrite. 'We have other matters to attend to.'

'I'm sorry to be the bearer of such news,' Lizzie said.

Davies nodded.

Grateful to escape the stuffy confines of the office, she left the hospital building with Vickers and walked towards the manor house in the rapidly fading light.

'What other matters?' Lizzie asked.

'Nothing,' Vickers said. 'I just wanted to get out of there. I was sure we were onto something. Turns out, he's just another casualty of war.'

Lizzie had almost given up hope of getting through to Scotney Police Station and was about to put down the telephone receiver when Sergeant Wright answered. After a few more seconds, Kember came on the line.

'I don't think Dr Davies has anything to do with anything,' she blurted out.

'And a good evening to you, Lizzie,' Kember said.

'He had no idea that his family came from Scotney,' she continued, ignoring his remark as her thoughts tumbled inside her head again. She took a pen from the ops-room desk and scribbled *John, Edith* and *Sam* on the back of an envelope. 'As far as he was aware, he was born and bred in Cardiff, and being posted here was one of those random coincidences you hate so much. The police hadn't even informed him of his parents' death.'

'That's understandable, given that they've only just correctly identified the body they thought was his. How did he react?'

'Shocked, hurt, saddened, angry.'

'As you'd expect?'

'I'd say so.' She wrote *Agnes* and *Ken* on the envelope. 'He didn't look like a man who had deliberately kept a secret for so many years.' She wrote *Frank* and *June*. 'But that begs the question: why didn't his parents tell him where they came from?' She drew lines from Edith and Agnes to their parents. 'Even though they ran away and Agnes was upset at being left behind, Frank and June were dead so why wouldn't they tell him he had an aunt still living in Scotney?'

'You think there's more to this than meets the eye?'

'I don't think Agnes has told us the whole story.' Lizzie drew a heavy ring around *Frank*. 'I know family feuds can go on forever but you'd think once she and Kenneth got together that she'd at least write to her sister. After all, they both wanted happiness and found it in the end.'

'True, but it's not so rosy now,' Kember said. 'We know Janice Bateman was having an affair with Jarvis, and she reckons there are rumours that his wife, Agnes, killed her parents because they refused to let her marry Kenneth, and then she married him anyway. That can't be true, though. Agnes's father, Frank Robinson, died of Spanish flu while still in the army and her mother, June, succumbed shortly after, to pneumonia brought on by the flu.'

'That doesn't mean she didn't give it a helping hand.' She underlined *June*. 'I still say Janice wasn't play-acting when she came to report Ken missing. She looked apprehensive and clearly believed the rumours.'

'If it's true that Agnes took advantage of the wave of Spanish flu that swept through the village in the winter of 1918, using it as an excuse to get rid of her controlling mother, there's no way to prove it.'

'Dig her up.' She ticked June's name, shocked by her own bluntness in making the suggestion.

'What?'

She took a breath. 'Exhume the body of June Robinson and get Dr Headley to have a good look.' She heard a gasp of incredulity from down the line. 'The death certificate will only show pneumonia or flu as the cause of death. You'll have to dig her up.'

'She's been in the ground too long. A pile of old bones won't confirm the flu.'

'There might be nothing to see. But what if there is? Didn't I hear you or Sergeant Wright say that Ken made the coffin?'

'Yes.'

'Convenient, don't you think?'

CHAPTER
TWENTY-TWO

The blackout was in full effect by the time Kember walked around the corner from Scotney Police Station and stood outside the tiny, terraced house of Agnes Jarvis in Meadowbank Lane. He'd left Wright to get on the telephone, searching for the death records of Frank and June Robinson. Exhumation was a serious business and he hoped desperately for an outcome that wouldn't require digging up the graveyard of St Matthew's Church. The paltry light from the slit in his blacked-out torch picked out the door knocker and he gave it a rap.

The door opened and he threw up an arm to protect his eyes from a sudden, blinding light within. 'Mrs Jarvis?' he said, holding his torch out as if defending himself with a sword.

'Inspector,' he heard. 'Do come in.'

The bright light vanished but a white disc remained imprinted on his vision, distorting the face of Agnes Jarvis. She ushered him in, closed the door and switched on the hall light. The dim 40 watts eradicated the pitch-black but turned the floating disc to a slowly dissipating black shadow.

'I'm so sorry,' Agnes said, placing her torch on a hall table. 'You can't be too careful in the blackout.'

And therein lies a lesson for me, Kember thought, still blinking away the dot from his vision.

He followed her through to the living room and accepted the invitation to sit in an armchair behind which stood a standard lamp with a tasselled shade, allowing the occupier to read by its light. The room was like millions of others around the country, a few of which he'd had cause to visit in the course of his many investigations. Logs glowed orange and threw out a comforting warmth from the fireplace; ornaments and a framed photograph of a man he recognised as Kenneth Jarvis adorned the mantelpiece; a wireless set and a carriage clock stood on a sideboard against one wall; a woven rug lay on the floor between Kember's armchair and another; and a blackout screen was just visible through a gap in floral-patterned curtains. Among the home-made Christmas decorations, Kember noted a cardboard tree, the result of a decree from the Ministry of Supply that wood was required for the war effort. He declined the offer of tea and motioned for Agnes to take the other seat.

'Have you any news of Ken?' she asked.

Kember noticed her grip the arms of her chair. 'I'm afraid not,' he replied, 'but I do have a few more questions, if you wouldn't mind?'

He saw the hope drain from her face as she nodded and relaxed her grip on the chair, placing her hands in her lap.

'Can you tell me why your sister, Edith, felt she had to run away?' he said softly.

Agnes sighed. 'My father was very strict,' she said. 'He didn't want his girls marrying anyone he considered beneath them. He said railwaymen were nothing but common labourers who couldn't give us a settled home because they had to go where the work took them. No one was going to drag his daughters all over the country.

John was a railwayman and the only way Edie could marry him was to run away. He came from Cardiff, so . . .'

'If your father was the problem, why didn't Edith and John come back after he died?'

'I suppose they'd settled. Anyway, our mother was almost as bad.'

'Oh, really?' Kember caught the edge of bitterness in Agnes's voice and tried to look mildly surprised. 'Is that why you waited until after your mother died to marry Kenneth?'

Agnes looked down to her left. 'Something like that.'

Lying, thought Kember. 'And Edith came to your wedding?'

'Edie wasn't invited. We didn't even write to each other very much. I was angry when she left – when she left me behind. I was only young and felt abandoned. I never told her our mother had died, or I was getting married. It was my way of revenge.'

'Might she have come back?' he said. 'If you'd asked?'

'I don't know.' She shrugged. 'I don't care.'

'Were you there when your mother died?' Kember asked.

Agnes looked away. 'Yes,' she whispered, dropping her gaze to her lap. 'She had pneumonia on top of Spanish flu and passed away one night, in the early hours.'

'I believe Kenneth made the coffin for the funeral.'

She looked up sharply. 'Yes.'

Kember saw something in her expression, behind the sadness and anger. Fear, maybe? Guilt, perhaps?

'Why was that?' he asked. 'If she disliked railwaymen as much as your father and prevented you from marrying one, why would your future husband, a railwayman, spend time making her coffin?'

'Because we're not made of money,' Agnes snapped. 'She hurt me but still needed a Christian burial, Inspector. Ken's always been good with his hands so he got hold of some wood and made it himself. Made a good job of it, too.'

The anger in her voice surprised him.

'Do you have the death certificates for your parents, that I could see?' he asked.

She went to a cupboard drawer, rummaged through its contents and handed him some papers.

'Thank you,' he said, unfolding the papers.

Kember read the certificates of Frank and June Robinson, both certifying death by Spanish influenza and pneumonia. The third paper was the most interesting. It detailed the results of a post-mortem performed on Frank in a military hospital by the army due to concerns that he may have contracted diseases other than just flu, such as cholera, typhoid or even dengue. Frank had experienced sudden and excessive bleeding from his nose and ears and, after he died, the small, red spots of petechial haemorrhages in the skin were seen. When opened up, the doctors also found he'd bled from his stomach and intestine. A footnote confirmed the same symptoms, sometimes even more violent and widespread, had become one of the signatures of the infection.

After reading that, he felt a moment of reluctance but decided there was no good time to break the bad news. A sadness had descended on Agnes, displayed in the slight downturn at the corners of her mouth and the dullness in her eyes, but he needed to see how she reacted.

'I asked for these because I needed to establish familial links and next of kin. You see, I'm afraid to tell you that John and Edith were killed in an air raid four months ago.'

Agnes jerked a handkerchief from the sleeve of her cardigan as her face crumpled and tears flowed. Now this was a reaction that Kember believed. The sudden shock looked as real as anything he'd seen in his career and it was clear that, for all the anger and hurt, Agnes had still loved her sister. Kember recalled Wright saying Agnes had never had children. That might make what he was about to say ten times more shocking. He waited for the sobs to subside.

'Are you aware that Edith had a son with John?'

Agnes stared at him, more tears in her eyes. 'I had no idea.'

'Their son, Samuel, your nephew, wasn't at home when the bomb hit.' Kember took a breath. 'We discovered he's a doctor in the RAF, stationed at RAF Scotney.' He saw another jolt pass through Agnes. 'He was told about his parents earlier, and you too, and had no idea he had relatives here.'

'He's here?' Agnes croaked. 'In Scotney?' The blood had drained from her face but her eyes were eager. 'I can't believe it. Can I see him?' she said, squeezing her hankie. 'Does he want to see me?'

'That's all with the RAF Police at the moment but I'm sure they'll be in contact very soon.'

Kember decided to hold the questioning there, taking the papers with him and leaving the grateful Mrs Jarvis still thanking him from her front door as he strode into the blackout. The family revelations had come as a genuine shock to her, but her reaction to his questions about her mother and the coffin had clearly touched a nerve. There was more to Agnes than met the eye, and the prospect of something other than a romantic link between Kenneth Jarvis and Evelyn Hartson was starting to twist in his gut. It was looking like they would need to apply for an exhumation order, and he needed to question the Edison family again tomorrow morning, this time with Lizzie.

Wright could hear a muffled conversation on the other end of the line, then the sound of the receiver being picked up and a rasping breath.

'Dr Smith?' Wright said. 'I'm sorry to bother you but you might have something to help me with an investigation.'

'It's very peculiar to get a call from you after all this time,' Dr Smith wheezed. 'I've retired, you know?'

'Aye, Doctor. I was at your retirement party in the village hall last year.' The doctor's wheezing made Wright clear his own throat. 'I know you kept meticulous records and wondered if you still had them for 1918, from during the flu epidemic.'

'Of course. I never threw anything away, you know.'

'That's a relief. I'm looking for the circumstances surrounding the death of Mrs June Robinson.'

'Oh, I don't need to look at my books for that. I remember it well—'

Wright held the receiver away from his ear as Smith was consumed by a fit of coughing. When he came back on the line, his voice was much clearer.

'Ah, that's better. Now, what was I saying? Oh, yes. Troops were still arriving home from France after the end of the Great War and many died of the Spanish flu or other diseases, and their wounds. The flu tore through the village like cannon fire and everyone had to wear masks for weeks, not just hospital doctors and nurses. I did what I could but so many died.'

'And Mrs Robinson?' Wright asked.

'She'd lost her husband to Spanish flu only a few months before. Terribly sad for Agnes to lose her mother in the same year. Edith had run away, you know?'

'Aye, Doctor. I know. Can you tell me the circumstances of Mrs Robinson's passing?'

'Nothing much to tell,' Smith said. 'Agnes knocked on my door one morning to say her mother had passed away in the night. She'd developed pneumonia after catching the flu. It wasn't unexpected so I went to certify the death. And there she was, laid out.'

'Laid out?' Wright asked, his ears pricking up.

'In a coffin,' Smith said. 'I thought it odd at the time, and that's why it stuck in my mind, but Agnes explained that a chap she was courting had started making coffins because there was a shortage, so he had one handy.'

'She was already in the coffin when you went round?' Wright asked, puzzled. He'd heard the story before but had always assumed Mrs Robinson was in her bed when the doctor had called. The business of the dead and coffins was the domain of undertakers.

'Yes.' Smith coughed again. 'Spanish flu was highly infectious and families were burying their dead as soon as they could. I believe there were three burials at St Matthew's on one horrific day. Mrs Robinson's buried with her husband in the churchyard, you know?'

'Aye, Doctor. I do know. Is there anything else at all that you saw during your examination?'

'I saw a smear of blood on Mrs Robinson's lips as if she'd had her face and mouth wiped with a damp cloth. With the amount of coughing that flu victims suffered, flecks of blood from the rupture of tiny blood vessels in the throat were common. I have a pink tinge to my spittle, too.'

Wright grimaced and made a note. 'Well, that's all I need so I thank you for your time and bid you a good evening.'

'I never knew his name, you know? The coffin maker, I mean.'

I know the coffin maker, Wright thought, as he put his receiver down. *Ken Jarvis*.

CHAPTER
TWENTY-THREE

Kember had not slept well.

Any attack on RAF Scotney meant a threat to the nearby village and he had descended to the pub cellar with Les and Alice Brannan around midnight, as soon as the sirens began. He had spent several hours with a pillow and blanket from his room trying to ignore the chilly air, but pub cellars were designed to keep beer cool and therefore not conducive to restful sleep in the middle of winter. The muted sounds of bombing had seemed distant, but still the danger to Lizzie had occupied his thoughts.

On the wireless, the early morning BBC news reported air raids all over the country and Kember surmised that a Luftwaffe squadron, finding London's defences a bit too hot to handle, had hit the air station on their way home.

Crossing to the police station from his lodgings at the pub, the plumes of black smoke rising in the direction of the air station to the north drew his thoughts to Lizzie again and he felt great relief when Wright relayed a message that she was safe. The airfield itself had been heavily damaged and put out of action. That meant no flying for the ATA and she could meet him at Edison Farm to question Ivy as he'd hoped.

Kember listened with growing interest as Wright reported his conversation with the retired Scotney doctor, thinking it highly irregular for a doctor to issue a death certificate without examining the deceased first, even during an epidemic. For that person to already be laid out in a coffin, especially a home-made one, was cause for suspicion, in his book. That simple act had discouraged and hindered a proper examination and he had to find out what they'd been hiding.

But first, he needed to pay visits to Dr Headley and Chief Inspector Hartson.

Within the hour, Kember stood in the reception of Pembury Hospital, appreciating the cleanliness but not the aroma of carbolic soap. He'd seen the inside of hospitals far too much in his career and walking into one was never a pleasant experience. He'd shown his warrant card on arrival but noticed the nurse behind the desk still eyeing him suspiciously. With any luck, Dr Headley wouldn't be much longer.

The reception-desk telephone rang a few moments later and the nurse gave him directions to meet Headley. The smell of disinfectant got stronger the deeper he went into the maze of corridors and his breathing became shallow as he tried not to take it into his lungs. Hospitals had seemed deathly quiet on some of his visits but Pembury hummed and clattered with noise and bustled with people. Kember saw what Headley had meant about the number of patients and medical staff crowding the wards and corridors. He had to sidestep often, narrowly missing doctors with white coats flapping, nurses wheeling squeaking drip-stands, and walking-wounded patients on crutches sporting bandaged heads and limbs.

Kember reached the mortuary and knocked on the door. It was soon answered by an assistant whose white hat matched the white hair that sprouted from beneath it. The rest of his outfit consisted of a white rubber apron over a white gown, and white galoshes. He ushered Kember through to where Headley, dressed in similar attire, was pulling on a pair of white rubber gloves.

'Ah, Kember,' said Headley. 'I'm honoured. I expected a telephone call rather than a personal visit.'

'I'm on my way to interview potential witnesses so I thought I'd check progress on Dorothy Ingram's post-mortem.'

'Huh,' Headley scoffed. 'Do you really think I've been working all weekend? I do have a life outside of medicine.'

Kember raised his eyebrows in amusement. 'Do you?'

Headley frowned. 'Of course I don't. Come through.'

Kember followed Headley into the mortuary room and caught his breath. The smell of bodies undergoing examination, mixed with formalin and strong disinfectant, was a heady mixture he'd never managed to get used to. Some mortuaries he'd seen looked positively medieval both outside and in, but here the vivid whiteness of everything hurt his eyes. The bright overhead lights reflected off everything: from Headley's white attire to the white wall tiles, from the white porcelain post-mortem tables to a huge white-fronted refrigerator that took up one side of the room, where the bodies were kept on metal trays.

Kember shuddered. Far too early in his career, he'd accompanied his inspector to a rural mortuary where he'd seen a body stuck so fast to a tray with the cold that it had to be removed by the mortuary assistant pouring hot water around it. Sights such as those never left you.

The shapes made by white sheets draped over the two porcelain tables told Kember that bodies lay beneath, and he almost turned away as the mortuary assistant uncovered one to reveal the pale, blotchy body of Dorothy Ingram. Another waft of body smells and chemicals filled his nostrils. Seeing a dead body at the scene of a murder made him flush with anger, and seeing it stripped, cleaned, picked over and depersonalised always lowered his spirits. But he realised the process was necessary and knew the feeling would be temporary, to be replaced with cold anger and a resolve to get the evil killer responsible.

'As I said at the scene, the cause of death was the cut to her throat,' Headley said, breaking into Kember's thoughts. 'There was no water in her lungs and I found nothing in her mouth, no sign of sexual assault or a struggle, and no other marks on her body.'

'Except her missing hands,' Kember said, seeing Headley shoot him a dark look.

'I was coming to that,' Headley said. 'Her hands were removed after she died, as we suspected, but I discovered something on the radius and ulna of her forearm that you might find interesting.' Headley picked up a scalpel and used it to point to the two exposed bones of her left arm. 'See here?'

Kember bent to take a closer look at where Dorothy Ingram's hand should have been. 'What am I supposed to be looking for?'

'Not there, here,' Headley said, pointing to the top of the bones with his scalpel. 'Obviously, a cut severed the hand from the wrist but look at this. There are two other cuts, one on each bone.'

Now Kember could see. 'They look more like nicks than cuts.'

'Granted, they are both shallow, but I found similar marks on her other wrist. Look at this.'

Kember followed Headley across to the other table.

'This is Maisie Chapman,' Headley said, as the assistant pulled back another white sheet. He pointed his scalpel at the end of her right arm where her hand should have been. 'I found the same marks on both her wrists.'

Kember looked away. 'Definitely the same killer, then?' he said, sickened by the sight but relieved by the confirmation.

'It would suggest so, but that's not my point. There are no bone shards or percussion marks suggestive of hacking or chopping, like one might expect to see when a murderer tries to dismember a victim for disposal. These cuts have a very narrow V-shape from the edge of a very sharp knife, rather than the square-bottomed cut made by a serrated or saw-toothed blade.'

'He didn't use the hatchet we asked you to look at?'

'I did find a couple of hairs on the flat butt of the hatchet, suggesting that's what hit Miss Hayes, but nothing on the blade itself, apart from some wood resin and light oil, which you'd expect of a woodworking tool. In any case, the cuts were made with a blade very much thinner than that of a hatchet, however honed it might have been. In addition, they don't go all the way around. Normally, I'd say they were what we call false starts, like you might make on a block of cheese until you've chosen the right amount you want to cut.'

'Normally?' Kember said, feeling queasy at Headley's description and fearing whatever it was that he might consider abnormal.

'Despite the marks on the bones, this is cleaner than many a butcher's cut.' Headley pulled the white sheet back over the body of Maisie Chapman. 'It's almost surgical, as if he wanted to preserve the hand, including the flesh, in as pristine a condition as possible. And while we're on the subject,' Headley continued, before Kember could ask the question, 'I managed to speak to the pathologists serving Duxford and Croydon. They were very curious why I wanted to know but both reported the same cuts to the radius and ulna.'

The confirmation was satisfying but depressing in equal measure.

'Lizzie did say she thought the killer wanted the hands intact, maybe for some ritualistic purpose,' Kember said.

'Clever girl is Miss Hayes,' Headley said as he covered Dorothy Ingram. 'I don't know about ritual but it was certainly clinical. I wouldn't be surprised if the man you're looking for had some medical knowledge.'

Kember's thoughts flashed back to the medical report on the curate, and he stared at Headley. 'Could the killer be a doctor or surgeon?'

Headley raised his eyebrows. 'Do you want to swap hats, Kember? Or shall we stick to our own specialities?'

'I'm just asking for your personal opinion. I won't hold you to it.'

Headley sniffed. 'All I'm prepared to say is that the cuts are so narrow that in this instance I wouldn't be surprised if the killer ran one of these' – he held up his scalpel – 'around the wrist to cut the flesh and expose the bone before pushing down through the joint.' He nodded at his assistant to return the bodies to their refrigerator compartments.

That was good enough for Kember, but who on earth in the ENSA troupe would have any medical knowledge beyond basic first aid? He'd already discounted the only one skilled in the use of cutting tools.

'I hardly dare to ask,' he said, 'but did you have a chance to look at the mask?'

'You don't want much, do you?' Headley stripped off a rubber glove. 'Actually, I did. The hairs I found inside were nothing unusual. Brown, mid-length, female.'

'Female? You can tell?' Kember was intrigued.

'In this case, I believe so.' He pulled off his other glove. 'I would expect a man's hair to have nothing on it except maybe some Brylcreem or hair oil, and a woman's hair might display a number of chemicals used in styling.' He selected a fresh pair of gloves from a metal tray and began pulling them on. 'Setting lotion is scarce these days and very expensive so women are using sugar-water on damp hair as an alternative, to keep their waves and curls in place. The hairs from the mask show signs of having such a solution applied.'

'You really are an extraordinary man, Headley,' Kember said, shaking his head.

'It has been said,' Headley agreed, without any sign of modesty. 'I'm happy to do half your job for you, as always.'

Kember reached into his jacket and offered the death certificates and post-mortem reports. Headley read all three and handed them back.

'I'm going to ask for an exhumation of June Robinson,' Kember said.

Headley gave Kember a sharp look. 'That won't go down well with the powers that be. You do know I can't confirm the presence of influenza if all you find are bones? Come to that, I won't be able to detect many other diseases or poisons. A knife might have left a mark on a bone or two if she was stabbed. What are you hoping to find?'

'Anything.' Kember shrugged. 'I have a feeling her death was somewhat more violent than succumbing to disease.'

'A feeling?' Headley scoffed again, turning away. 'I thought our respective occupations had robbed us of those a while ago.'

Headley's attention was already on another job as Kember became suddenly aware of the disinfectant smell again. He turned and pushed through the mortuary doors into the corridor, eager to get outside and breathe fresh air. Headley's use of the words 'surgical' and 'clinical' turned his thoughts to Dr Sam Davies again, bringing with it suspicions about Agnes Jarvis and the death of June Robinson. There was more here than met the eye, but how did that tie in with the deaths of the women laid out before him in the mortuary, the others around the country, and the disappearance of Ken Jarvis and Evelyn Hartson?

◆　◆　◆

Less than an hour later, Kember stood in Chief Inspector Hartson's office, awaiting an invitation to sit but aware he was being made to stand as a show of authority and displeasure. It was an unnecessary game, and one that irked him a little more each time.

Many years of memorabilia accumulated by several senior police officers adorned the wall behind the desk where Hartson sat. Kember knew that of all the framed badges, certificates and photographs, Hartson had contributed only one: a photograph of himself receiving a commendation from Chief Constable Davison for his leadership during the Scotney Ripper investigation. The award had come as no surprise to Kember but still rankled, as did the knowledge that the presentation had taken place while he lay in hospital, having been injured in the line of duty while trying to apprehend the killer. Even so, given Hartson's stated opinion of the 'gaudy array of pretentiousness' behind him, it amused Kember to note the prominent position taken by the photograph, and he failed to suppress a smirk.

'I'm glad you find this funny, Kember,' Hartson growled.

Kember concentrated on the way Hartson's moustache moved almost independently of his top lip, overshadowed by his bulbous red nose, and brought his own facial expression under control. This seemed to satisfy Hartson and he barked the order to sit. Kember made a show of trying to get comfortable on a chair patently designed and utilised to discourage an extended audience, which further displeased his senior officer.

'Stop fidgeting, for God's sake, man,' Hartson said. 'I'd rather hoped all your energies would be brought to bear on finding my niece.'

Kember stopped moving and fixed Hartson with a stare.

'It's my priority to find Miss Hartson, sir, but I also have the disappearance of a local man, a possible historical murder and an active serial murderer to contend with. At New Scotland Yard—'

'This is Kent, not London,' Hartson interrupted. 'We do things differently. Properly, most likely.'

'But with fewer resources,' Kember said, bitterness rising and showing in his cheeks. 'I have one sergeant, and help from an RAF Police officer.'

'And that bloody woman, too, no doubt. What's she said to you now, hmm? That her crystal ball told her the Tooth Fairy did it?'

'Third Officer Hayes was invaluable last time and a useful member of—'

'Don't give me that.' Hartson glared across the desk. 'I warned you about getting others to do your job for you, especially her, so think on.'

Kember bit his tongue and tried to change the subject.

'Regarding the murdered women, sir,' he said. 'I've not long been to visit Dr Headley at the mortuary. He, the pathologists covering Duxford and Croydon, plus the medical report of the deaths at Chatham Dockyard all corroborate my suspicions about the use of a scalpel to remove the hands. We think the killer might be a medical man collecting them for a specific purpose.'

'Are you still on about that?' Hartson exploded. 'I suppose it's that bloody woman putting stupid ideas into your head again. Do you really think we've got another Burke and Hare roaming the streets?'

'No, sir, but—'

'Then stop chasing shadows and find my niece. I've had every available man on high alert, looking for sight or sound of her, but I have tasked you – you, Kember – with the job of finding and returning her safely home. You brought Scotland Yard up, so I suggest you forget all this witchcraft and put your so-called world-renowned training and expertise to better use.'

Kember clenched his jaw to prevent saying something that would get him suspended again or dismissed, but held Hartson in a savage glare, seeing his discomfort as the senior man looked away. Hartson liked a good shout but baulked at the idea of his officers standing up to his challenge.

An awkward silence followed before Hartson looked back and spoke softly.

'I don't think you realise the high regard in which my brother is held within government circles. He has influence and friends in high places. One word from him and I'll have the Home Secretary breathing down my neck, for God's sake. I implore you to get your act together and find her.'

Kember's anger began to subside at the realisation of the pressure his superior officer must be under. It couldn't be easy having a brother more successful than him, and one so ready to bring out the big guns if necessary.

'I'll ensure we redouble our efforts, sir,' Kember said. 'We have a number of sightings and lines of enquiry to pursue, and I'll be speaking to your brother's family and the Edisons again as soon as I leave here.'

'Then I suggest you get to it.' Hartson nodded. 'Carry on.'

Kember rose from the chair and turned towards the door, but hesitated and turned back. He couldn't leave without asking the most important question.

'There is one other matter in which your help would be appreciated, sir,' Kember said, reluctant to reignite Hartson's temper but certain of the necessity to ask. 'I mentioned the possibility that a murder took place in Scotney village which has lain undetected for a number of years, and therefore remains unsolved. On the understanding that it does not impinge on my priority of finding Miss Hartson, I would like to request permission to seek an exhumation order for St Matthew's Church.'

'Exhumation?' Hartson's mouth opened in shock. 'We're in the middle of a war and burying hundreds of people every day, and you want to dig one of them up?'

'I wouldn't ask unless I felt it absolutely vital to the investigation, sir.'

Hartson's eyebrows knitted together and his moustache twitched with the internal struggle Kember knew he would be going through. An exhumation, even when proven to be necessary, was never a course of action to be taken lightly. The Church of England was uncomfortable with the idea of disturbing the dead, especially on consecrated ground, and could sometimes be uncooperative. The police shied away from asking unless it was the last resort. Kember finished outlining the reasons for his request and waited for the backlash. Surprisingly, none came.

'Very well,' Hartson said at last. 'As long as it's not at the behest of that cranky woman. Give me the details and I'll get someone to telephone the magistrate and the Rochester Diocesan Office.'

'Thank you, sir.' Kember retrieved a folded sheet of paper from his inside jacket pocket, but as Hartson reached to take it, Kember kept hold of his end. 'It's Christmas Eve tomorrow, sir. For the sake of propriety and to soothe religious sensitivities, I would be most grateful if this matter could be expedited.'

'You push your luck sometimes, Kember,' Hartson snarled, pulling the paper from Kember's fingers. 'Very well, I'll see what I can do.'

Kember felt a release of tension across his shoulders with the relief of knowing he had Hartson's rare backing. As he left and closed the door, he heard Hartson call out.

'And Kember. You'd better be right about this.'

CHAPTER
TWENTY-FOUR

As Lizzie approached the entrance to the Hartsons' country estate, she could see Kember already waiting in his Minx. His window wound down as she braked her Norton alongside and pulled the black scarf away from her mouth.

'Everything all right?' she asked, and listened while Kember told her about his visit to the mortuary, the discoveries made by Dr Headley, and his questioning of Agnes Jarvis.

A labourer carrying a large hammer and a wood saw appeared behind the padlocked double gates. Despite the man's battered straw hat, Lizzie thought the dark-brown overcoat he wore made him look very much like a bear. He looked through the bars, seemed to recognise Kember, and deftly unlocked two padlocks before dragging the gates open.

As she followed Kember's Minx up the driveway to the mansion, her thoughts came thick and fast again. It didn't make sense. Surely the killer had to be someone who travelled around the country, someone in ENSA? If not the carpenter, then who? The possible exhumation of Agnes Jarvis's parents made her blood run cold. Watching people who had been given Christian burials being dug up was not on her list of favourite pastimes, and she was certain the deaths weren't linked. How could they be? The Robinsons had died twenty-two years ago, but if Agnes's missing husband, Kenneth Jarvis, looked as much like Lance Atkinson as Sergeant Wright suggested, was he dead too? And what of Evelyn Hartson? Could she be yet another victim?

Lizzie had a sense of déjà vu as the driveway curved slightly and the Hartson house came into sight. Smaller than Scotney Manor, its stuccoed frontage, taped-up windows and sandbagged portico reminded her so much of the place that had become her home earlier in the year.

Lizzie stopped her Norton behind Kember's Minx, pulled the motorbike onto its stand and removed her helmet. She walked with him across the large semi-circle of neatly laid stone slabs to where an elderly gentleman awaited them between the marble columns of the portico. They were asked to follow and were shown into an impressive room leading off an equally impressive central hall. Everywhere, the decor was certainly opulent and so unlike the stripped-down interior of the requisitioned Scotney Manor. She took in the view through the windows and nodded appreciatively. No hangars, anti-aircraft guns or Nissen huts here. *Looks much better without an airfield*, she thought.

'Is there any news?' said a woman as she burst through the double doors.

To Lizzie, the expensive jewellery and coiffured hair were incongruous with the riding breeches and green waxed gilet she wore, but there was no mistaking the lines of worry on her face.

'I'm afraid not, Mrs Hartson, but we are making progress with our enquiries,' Kember said. 'That's why I've brought along my colleague, Miss Hayes. She's assisting with the search for your daughter.'

Lizzie felt Joyce Hartson's gaze sear into her, as if she were the one who posed a threat to Evelyn rather than whoever had taken her.

'I only have a few questions, Mrs Hartson,' Kember said. 'Have you had any thoughts about whether Miss Hartson may have arranged to meet someone other than Ivy Edison, last Thursday?'

Lizzie saw Joyce's eyelids flicker and noticed her fingers picking nervously at the skin around her thumbnails.

'My husband is at work and won't return until Friday evening, I'm afraid,' Joyce said.

Lizzie thought it curious that she'd answered an unsolicited question about her husband, not the one asked about her daughter.

'Excuse me, Mrs Hartson,' Lizzie said. 'Would it be possible to have a quick look in Evelyn's room?'

'What? I—'

'It would be very useful for me to understand the kind of girl that Evelyn is, from a woman's perspective.' Lizzie smiled, disarmingly.

Joyce frowned. 'I suppose so. If it helps.' She turned and rang a bell, answered by the elderly butler appearing at the doors. 'Please show Miss Hayes to Evelyn's room,' she commanded.

Lizzie followed the butler to Evelyn's room and was struck immediately by the disparity between the age she knew her to be and what was on display. In front of an oval mirror on the dressing table lay a hairbrush and hand-mirror set, decorated with embroidered baby rabbits. The counterpane covering the bed also had a design incorporating baby animals. Porcelain-faced dolls in Victorian dresses and layered petticoats stood on one shelf and furry bears on another. A number of forest creatures carved from wood, highly polished farm animals made of painted lead, and porcelain figurines of ladies in layered dresses and wide-brimmed bonnets had been arranged on a chest of drawers beside which stood a black-painted Victorian doll's pram. Three framed watercolour paintings of Beatrix Potter characters adorned the walls: Mr Jeremy Fisher, Mrs Tiggy-Winkle and Squirrel Nutkin. The contents of the drawers and a large wardrobe were as one might expect of a young lady of Evelyn's class, but still Lizzie found the whole room strangely unsettling.

Having seen enough, she began to return downstairs with the butler and got an unexpected snapshot view through a door slightly ajar, into another bedroom that looked the same as Evelyn's.

Back in the room where they'd left Kember and Joyce Hartson, now sipping tea, Lizzie asked, 'Where did Evelyn go to school, Mrs Hartson?'

Joyce frowned. 'She had a private tutor. My husband thought her education would be better served that way.'

'Does she ever go into Tonbridge or Tunbridge Wells, for tea or shopping?'

'Of course. We go all the time.'

'I meant with her friends.' Lizzie saw the thumb-picking begin again.

'She always goes with me,' Joyce said. 'It's my husband's wishes.'

'You have only one child?'

Joyce dropped her gaze to the floor. 'Yes.'

'Only . . . I noticed another child's bedroom on my way down.'

Joyce trembled as if about to cry and Lizzie exchanged a concerned glance with Kember.

'Evelyn had a twin but she caught measles when she was six.' Joyce looked up, eyes glistening. 'There were complications and she died of pneumonia.'

'I am so sorry, Mrs Hartson. I didn't mean to pry.'

Lizzie had never thought about having children but a lump formed in her throat as Joyce took a handkerchief and dabbed a tear from the corner of her eye. Her thoughts shifted and she saw a six-year-old girl, distraught at the death of her twin sister, roaming the large mansion on her own, but never really allowed to be alone.

'How does Evelyn feel about spending all her time here?' Lizzie said, softly.

'She visits her friend Ivy each summer and the Edisons come for lunch each Christmas,' Joyce said in a tremulous voice. 'But she often says she is bored.'

'Bored enough to seek adventure, perhaps?'

Joyce buried her face in her handkerchief and her shoulders shook. 'This will be such a scandal,' she said through her sobs. 'I think you'd better go.'

Lizzie wanted to ask more questions, convinced there was more to this, but Kember said their goodbyes and ushered her out towards his car.

'What was that all about?' he said, clearly annoyed.

'Evelyn's bedroom,' Lizzie said. 'As soon as I stepped inside, it all felt wrong.'

'What do you mean, wrong? How can a bedroom be wrong?'

Lizzie began to pace up and down as she fought to keep her thoughts in order. 'She has lots of toys and dolls on display and bed-covers with twee animals embroidered on them, but there are no cosmetics, no perfumes, no ornate hairbrushes with floral designs.'

'I don't understand,' Kember said. 'What's wrong with that?'

Lizzie stopped pacing.

'All the trappings of a young woman are missing. Evelyn is – what? Twenty-one, twenty-two? But I've just seen a child's bedroom. There is nothing to say a young woman sleeps there.'

'Maybe it appears that way but—'

'I think the loss of Evelyn's sister devastated them so much that they can't let her grow up. They want to keep her locked on this estate, safe, forever their little girl.'

'That's their business,' Kember said, opening the door of his Minx.

Exasperation threatened to overwhelm her so she put her hand on his arm to stop him getting in, and to steady herself.

'I think she met someone in town or at Edison Farm and found it exciting, a way to escape the stifling atmosphere in there. Think about it. The last thing Joyce said was that it would cause a scandal. Evelyn hasn't been abducted or killed; she's run away.'

◆ ◆ ◆

Less than half an hour later, but a world away from the Hartsons' mansion, Lizzie and Kember were led through to the living room of the Edison farmhouse. She took in the decor and found it warmer and a lot more welcoming. This was a home, not just a house.

'Thank you for seeing me again,' Kember said to Frances Edison. 'This is Miss Hayes, a colleague of mine helping to find Evelyn Hartson.' Lizzie exchanged greetings. 'Have either of you heard from Evelyn since the last time we spoke?'

'Of course not, Inspector,' Frances said, with a glance at her daughter. 'Otherwise we would have told you.'

'We've made enquiries along the route she should have taken to your farm, which her parents believed to be her destination,' Kember continued. 'The stationmasters at Tonbridge and Paddock Wood both confirm a sighting last Thursday, the day she left her home.'

Lizzie wondered why Kember deliberately omitted to mention the sighting at Scotney station, but said nothing.

'Do you have any idea at all whether Evelyn might have met someone last Thursday?' Kember said, softly.

Lizzie saw a momentary flash of panic in Ivy's eyes and knew she'd been right. Frances continued to stare at Kember.

Frances and Ivy both shook her heads and said, 'No.'

Kember sighed. 'Ivy told me that she doesn't know of any boys Evelyn may be sweet on, and that may in itself be true, but we've just spoken with Mrs Hartson again and I think there's a possibility she might have arranged to meet someone elsewhere.'

Lizzie watched Ivy and her mother all the time Kember was speaking and both looked to be hiding something. Ivy had her legs and arms pulled in tight and wouldn't return Lizzie's gaze but her mother stared defiantly: the typical scenario of a mother defending her child, in spite of whatever that child had done, or knew.

'Ivy, look at me,' Lizzie said, gently. In the few seconds of silence that followed, she hoped Kember and Frances wouldn't speak. Ivy looked up. 'I understand that you might not be telling us everything because you want to protect Evelyn, but she isn't in trouble with the police because she hasn't done anything wrong. I know what it feels like to meet someone nice, but for others not to understand. You want to see them, be with them, but everyone else says they're the wrong person or not good enough for you. They don't understand. How could they? They say it's an infatuation you'll get over, but it's not, is it? It's love.'

Lizzie could see Ivy struggling to decide the best thing to do. The steel in her mother's face had softened, to be replaced with concern.

'Evelyn's mother is worried sick,' Lizzie continued, and saw Ivy's eyelids flicker. 'They don't know where she is or what's happened to her.' She nodded towards Kember. 'We're worried because there's a war on and there could be very dangerous men around here. Nobody wants anything bad to happen.'

'Evie is dreadfully unhappy,' Ivy said, suddenly.

'Ivy—?' Frances started.

'Don't worry Mama. They have to know.'

'Know what?' Lizzie urged.

'Her father keeps her a virtual prisoner at home. Not because he's cruel, but he says he's worried about all the goings-on he hears about when he's at work. He wants to keep Evie safe but all he's doing is suffocating her. She met a boy in Tunbridge Wells and got to liking him. Her father wouldn't even let her go out with a chaperone, unless it was her mother. They wrote letters to each other all summer and arranged to meet. Evie told her mother she was coming to see me and I told Mrs Hartson that Evie could stay here overnight and return on the Friday. That was the arrangement I made with Evie. I thought she was being stupid but she seemed so in love. The telephone rang when Mama was outside, so I answered. Mrs Hartson asked to speak to Evie but I said she'd probably stopped off at another friend's house. I knew Evie loved this boy but I never thought she'd run away.'

'She's not run away, Ivy. She's a young woman who can do as she pleases.' Lizzie looked up at Frances. 'Mrs Edison, when did you find out?'

'After the inspector called on Saturday, I was going to telephone Joyce,' Frances said. 'Ivy told me I couldn't because we'd all get in trouble, and she told me everything. I agreed to wait a while, to see if Evelyn went home of her own accord, but . . .'

Kember sighed theatrically. 'Now that's out in the open, do either of you know who she met, or where?' The two women shook their heads. 'There is another piece of information we uncovered. A conductor on the train from Tonbridge sold her an extension for her ticket and Evelyn was spotted getting off the train and leaving the station at Scotney. Do you know of anyone she knows there?'

'She met the boy in Tunbridge Wells but she wouldn't tell me his name,' Ivy said. 'He might live in Scotney but I don't think she's ever been farther down the line than Paddock Wood.'

'Did she tell you what he looked like?' Lizzie asked.

'Only that he was tall, dark and handsome, and had a lovely smile. That's what everyone wants, isn't it?'

Lizzie's heart banged against her ribs and she forced herself not to look at Kember as he stood up from the sofa and thanked the two women for their cooperation. She followed him from the living room, out the front door and back to his car. Ivy stood in the doorway, seeing them off, her mother behind her with her chin resting on her daughter's shoulder and her arms wrapped around her protectively.

'This doesn't mean we can rule Evelyn out as another murder victim,' Kember said, as he opened his car door and got behind the wheel.

'You can never rule it out,' Lizzie agreed. 'Hopefully, this is nothing more than a case of young love.'

CHAPTER
TWENTY-FIVE

Kember's sombre mood had not improved by the time he drew up outside Scotney village Police Station and Lizzie stopped her Norton behind his Minx, the throaty rumble dying as she turned off the ignition. With two women found dead in the village in three days, Hartson's niece still missing, an exhumation on the cards and the village pantomime scheduled for tomorrow evening, Christmas Eve, he probably had no more than thirty-six hours to stop the carnage before his career was over.

Inside the station, they sat around the table in the back room, offers of tea from Wright waved away as Kember outlined the morning's progress.

'Let's go over this again,' he said. 'The methods the killer uses to subdue his victims are expedient: cutting the throat, possibly with a scalpel, or a blow to the head.'

'The Handyman has to gain control fast, before they know what he's doing, and he doesn't want them to suffer,' Lizzie said. 'After all, we know what he's really after and it's not sex or the exertion of control or power. He's committing these crimes for a specific purpose: to take the hands.'

'All right,' Kember said, grimacing at the use of the nickname and feeling pressure at his temples. 'We know how, what and when he does what he does. We think we know roughly the type of place where he does it. With your insight we could say we know a bit about why he's doing it, but it's no clearer who the killer could be. It can't be Janice Bateman, Agnes Jarvis or her nephew Dr Sam Davies, despite the killer's probable use of a scalpel, because they don't travel around the country, but until I know for certain what happened to Kenneth Jarvis, they are still under investigation relating to his disappearance. As for Kenneth, Agnes is the wife he has wronged so she has a motive to kill him. If he'd decided to go back to her, Janice would also have a motive. There's also a question mark over the deaths of her parents, Frank and June Robinson.'

He watched as Lizzie took a piece of chalk to the blackboard where the column of names remained. Next to the list of victims still on the board, she wrote *Agnes*, *Janice* and *Sam*, drew a line underneath and wrote *Frank*, *June* and *Ken*.

'That said,' Kember continued, 'we still haven't found Evelyn Hartson and the mysterious sweetheart involved in her disappearance. Until we find out who that is, I have to consider that it may be Kenneth Jarvis.'

Lizzie wrote *Ivy*, *Sweetheart* and *Ken* in a third column, drew a line underneath and wrote *Evelyn*. She moved a lock of hair from her eyes, leaving chalk dust behind, and stared at the blackboard. 'No, something's wrong here.'

'If you ask me, sir,' Wright said, 'Agnes was Ken's love of his life, and he was hers. The sisters went against their parents to marry railwaymen and you don't do that on a whim. Some men have a roving eye all their lives but he was a good husband until Janice turned his head. After all these years married to Agnes, he's taken a fancy to another woman his own age, so why would he court a girl of only twenty-one?'

'Exactly,' Lizzie said, looking at the two policemen. 'Why would he?'

Kember saw certainty in her eyes and sighed, feeling the solution getting away from him again. 'It doesn't explain why Kenneth disappeared at the same time as Evelyn. She was last seen at Scotney station but Sergeant Wright has asked around the village, and Tonbridge has police crawling all over the division but can't find any trace of her. Kenneth follows the work, but only as far north as Paddock Wood. That rules him out as the serial murderer but I still have to entertain the possibility that Kenneth and Evelyn are together.'

'I think you're looking at this the wrong way,' Lizzie said. 'If what we saw at the dockyard is repeated wherever he goes, the Handyman is collecting female hands to put on male arms. It stands to reason he'd need a male victim in every place he visits, including here. We know the ENSA schedule coincides with the known deaths so one of the troupe members must be involved. The director, Martin Onslow, makes me nervous, and he claims he stayed behind in Chatham when the others came to Scotney. Even if that's true, it doesn't mean he didn't come here without their knowledge. Turning up days later by aeroplane would supposedly give him an alibi. We can confirm Lance Atkinson as a male victim, but sadly, I really think Kenneth Jarvis is dead too and if you dig deep enough, you'll find others in Croydon and Duxford.'

Kember closed his eyes and rubbed them with his finger and thumb. Betty Fisher and the rest of the troupe were due to perform their pantomime show in the village hall the following evening but he had no idea which one of them, if any, he should be looking out for.

'Sergeant, I'm afraid we have a very busy day tomorrow. But before we call it a day and get some well-earned rest, we need to begin a house-to-house for Miss Hartson and the young gentleman who escorted her away from the railway station. That was the last time they were seen together and she hasn't been seen in the village or leaving on her own, so I think the roads nearest the station are our best bet. I pray we find her alive but we're running out of time and the Hartsons are running out of patience. Talking of praying, the exhumation order should be granted tomorrow so we can find out how Frank and June Robinson really died. And as for the serial murderer, I may end up having to ask permission to cancel the pantomime, confine the ENSA troupe to the camp, and call on the RAF Wardens and the Home Guard to enforce it. With everything else going on, I'm sure that will be a fantastic Christmas present for the chief inspector.'

Wright glanced at the wall clock. 'Now's a good time to go, sir. Most people will be back for their evening tea by now.'

'And I should be getting back to the air station,' Lizzie said. 'We're out of action but that doesn't mean I can swan around willy-nilly.'

As they gathered in the hallway near the front office, all heads turned towards the sound of a call to see Reverend Wilson approaching the open front door, wearing his winter coat and a thick scarf, his mop of fair hair ruffling as he dragged a flat cap from his head with a gloved hand.

'Reverend,' Kember said, surprised to see the vicar. 'I didn't expect another visitation from you before Christmas Eve.'

'And I didn't expect to provide one,' said Wilson. 'But I've just taken the most curious telephone call of my entire career.' He looked at Lizzie and nodded once. 'Good evening, Miss Hayes.'

Lizzie returned the greeting.

'We're just off but do come in for a moment,' Kember said, ushering everyone into the front office.

'Would you like to sit down, Reverend?' Wright offered.

'No, thank you.' Wilson shook his head. 'I have preparations to make for tomorrow night's midnight mass, but I had to come and tell you that I had a call from the Rochester Diocesan Office, relaying a message from the Bishop of Rochester, no less. I've never had any communication from the bishop, never mind a personal message, so it came as quite a shock. It seems you stirred up a hornets' nest, Inspector.'

'I'm sorry if I've caused you any problems with your employers,' Kember said.

'You haven't, but I believe the bishop thinks you may be a troublemaker. Jenny said the telephone lines have been melting with all the calls being made. Apparently, Tonbridge Police HQ submitted an exhumation order through the Tonbridge magistrates, and the bishop's office were speaking to the chief constable at Kent Police HQ in Maidstone within minutes. The chief constable called Tonbridge, Tonbridge called Jenny's office, Jenny spoke to the bishop's office and Dr Headley, and the Tonbridge magistrate had left for the day and couldn't be found.'

'That does sound like a hornets' nest,' Wright said, eyeing Kember with an expression that looked like admiration.

'I didn't think that executing my duty would cause everyone so much trouble,' Kember said. 'Did it work?' He looked enquiringly at Wilson.

'Oh, yes,' Wilson said. 'But I have to say, I'm not very happy at the prospect of having my churchyard desecrated. Those souls have been lawfully laid to rest, and even though it's been explained to me over the telephone, I still don't fully appreciate the need to disinter June Robinson. But I do understand you have your reasons and have a job to do, so I'll be on hand tomorrow morning to assist you in any way I can. Hopefully, we can get the whole operation completed with the minimum of fuss and disruption.'

'That's my hope, too,' Kember said. 'We'll need you there to ensure religious propriety is maintained, one or two men to open the grave, myself and Sergeant Wright for obvious reasons, Dr Headley to interpret any physical findings, and Miss Hayes in case an alternative view is required. Because of the rules around reburying bodies within a day, the usual practicalities of allowing as much daylight as possible to perform any examination before reburying must be considered. The accepted time for exhumations is dawn, which should be about twenty past eight. The doctor will have until sunset, about four o'clock, to do his work. Unless the cause of death is obvious, we may need to use the village hall to avoid wasting time going to and from Pembury. How shall we go about this?'

Wilson looked at the cap in his hands, frowning in thought.

'We don't hold regular services during the week but the church is open for private prayer from eight o'clock in the morning. Only one or two come to pray at that time; most prefer a quick visit in the evening after work and before their tea. I'll let our gravediggers know so they can be ready.'

'I understand the grave is on the far side of the church, away from prying eyes on the road.'

Wilson nodded.

'Let us convene at eight o'clock,' Kember said, looking around at the others. 'Hopefully, we'll have the benefit of early light, and should have a little privacy if Sergeant Wright can guard the lych-gate. I know it will be difficult, with Mrs Garner living over the road, but it's probably a good idea to not tell anyone outside this room. If the villagers get advance wind of what we're up to there could be some unrest.'

'This is Scotney village, Inspector, not London's East End,' Wilson said, with raised eyebrows.

Kember gave him a wry smile.

'You're the second person to tell me that, but the bodies still keep piling up.'

◆ ◆ ◆

As they all left the warmth and comfort of the police station, Lizzie and the reverend went their separate ways while Kember walked towards the lower end of the village with Wright.

Kember found house-to-house enquiries onerous at the best of times, and doubly so when your breath almost froze as it left your body. He longed for the team of officers he'd once been able to draw upon when policing in London. It was true that he now had as much autonomy as he'd ever wished for, but that was due to his secondment and the attitude of Chief Inspector Hartson towards him. Even Force Headquarters at Maidstone had made it clear that if they had a Scotland Yard detective at their disposal, for whatever fortuitous reason, then they were going to use him to his full capacity, but without affording him access to adequate resources.

Conscious of the noise they made, with door knockers that echoed in the still air and the sound of conversations being held on doorsteps, Kember progressed slowly along the line of dwellings, taking each house alternately with Wright. They soon completed Acorn Street and were a few doors along Meadowbank Lane when Wright stopped him at an open garden gate.

'This is Peter Yates' home,' Wright said, approaching the front door, his cloudy breath shimmering in the moonlight. 'He's the lad who came into the station.'

That had Kember's interest at full strength as Wright rapped the knocker. After a few moments, the door opened a few inches, enough for Kember to recognise the young man.

'Hello, Peter,' Wright said, through the small gap.

'Evenin', sir,' Yates replied.

'The inspector wants another word about that couple you saw last Thursday.'

The dark played tricks on the eyes but Kember was convinced he saw the briefest of flinches from Yates before he opened the door wider. Kember noted a flat cap hung from the newel post of the stair banister, and that the young man sported the same baggy trousers, loose shirt and waistcoat they'd seen him wearing on the day he'd walked into the police station.

'Can we come in?' said Wright. 'It's perishing cold out here.'

'Oh, right. Yeah.'

Kember stepped into the darkened hall with Wright, took off his fedora, and waited for the blackout curtain to be repositioned.

'I suppose the dark evenings and blackout are troublesome for farm workers like you,' Kember said, as Yates switched the light back on and led them through to a small, square-shaped living-room.

'They are a bit, sir,' Yates said. 'But it means I've no clash between old man Chapman and Captain Brown, what with me being in the Home Guard and all.'

The room was unremarkable, with drab wallpaper, a dull ceiling light and table lamp, a few pictures and ornaments, and two easy chairs set one either side of an open wood-burning fireplace. A makeshift Christmas tree stood in the corner and other home-made decorations hung from the ceiling.

'Do you mind if I have a quick look around, Peter?' Wright asked.

'What for?'

Kember saw the look of alarm on Yates' face as Wright disappeared towards the kitchen.

'We're looking in all the cottages for the young woman who went missing,' Kember said. 'Her family are worried.'

'Wh— what's that got to do with me?' he said, retreating behind one of the easy chairs.

'Probably nothing, but my chief inspector would be very upset if I told him I hadn't looked everywhere. That is all right, isn't it?' Kember held the gaze of the young man, looking for giveaway glances in the direction of where Evelyn Hartson might be hiding.

'Well . . .' His head turned as he heard the back door creak.

'Have you been working today?' Kember picked up a photograph of an older couple he supposed were Yates' parents.

'Yes, sir. I've been up at the farm helping fix some fences and suchlike. Mr Jarvis was supposed to help but he ain't been around these past few days, as I'm sure you know. And I've got to be on parade for Captain Brown this evening.'

Kember heard breathlessness in the replies that he took as a sign of anxiety. 'How's your mum? Is she in?' he said, replacing the photograph.

'Doin' well, sir, thank you, but she ain't in. She's been in Pembury Hospital since last Wednesday afternoon, having her knee seen to. Had to have an operation, see?'

'I'm sorry to hear that,' Kember said with genuine feeling.

'Don't be, sir. She's been in a lot of pain so it will help her out, no end.'

'Have you managed to visit her?'

'No, sir.' Yates shook his head, sadly. 'I did telephone from the box by the police station on Saturday morning before I went to work. The hospital said she'd had her operation and was doing well.' He looked at the living-room doorway as the back door creaked again. 'They said she couldn't come to the phone to speak to me but would pass on my message.'

'Back to the missing girl,' Kember said. 'Can you describe what you saw to me again? Leave out no detail.'

Yates looked dismayed as they heard Wright's boots stomping up the stairs.

'I – I saw a young lady link arms with a gentleman, walking briskly from the station. She was wearing her Sunday best and he was in a suit.'

'Like mine?'

'No, sir. Posh.'

Kember felt deflated, even though he wasn't actually wearing the matching items that would qualify as a suit.

'I couldn't swear as to what happened next,' Yates continued. 'But there was a car and two carriages outside and they might have taken one of them.'

Kember could see that Yates had relaxed a little. His fingers no longer showed white with the pressure of gripping the back of the chair and his breathing had deepened and lengthened.

'Can you describe them?'

'I don't know much about cars. It was a big black square-looking thing, and one of the carriages was black. The other was no more than a horse and cart, really.'

'You saw no more than that?'

'I was working so I wasn't paying much attention.' He took a couple of deep breaths before glancing to his left. 'But I think it was a proper carriage with four wheels, not two like a pony 'n' trap. And it was maroon, not black, with curved shafts and polished buckles. I could see lovely padded green-leather seats in the back because the folding head wasn't up.'

'Was anyone sitting in it or standing nearby?' Kember asked. 'A driver, perhaps?'

'I didn't see anyone, sir.'

'What about since then? Have you seen Evelyn?' Kember saw the slightest flinch at the mention of her name. 'Do you know where she is Peter?'

'No, sir. How could I?' Yates flicked a nervous glance at the door as they heard Wright's boots stomp back down.

'That's very helpful, Mr Yates.' Kember held up his hat in a farewell gesture and nodded to Wright. 'I think we have what we need for now, so we'll be on our way.'

He went to the front door with Wright and waited for the blackout precautions to be observed before they stepped back into the frosty evening.

'No one's ever called me Mr Yates before,' Yates said, eyes sparkling with forming tears. 'Thank you.'

Kember smiled and donned his hat.

He relayed his conversation with Yates as they began walking back towards the police station.

'I think he's pulling a fast one, sir, if you ask me,' Wright said.

'Why's that?' Kember said, thinking the same thing.

'Because I've never seen a carriage like that around here. There are a few, of course, but they're all black and most have two wheels with a small space at the back for goods and such. Anything else is usually a cart. The one he described is far too fancy.'

'Even for a wealthy family?'

'They've mostly got cars nowadays. I think Peter was trying to impress us and actually saw nothing.'

'I have a different suspicion,' Kember said. 'He was very vague about what the vehicles looked like at the start, but then, for someone who was working and supposedly not paying much attention, he got a bit carried away with describing the type of carriage.'

'You think he's pushing the idea of a wealthy gentleman to turn our attention away from him?' Wright asked.

'I would,' Kember said. 'What better way than to invent someone more in keeping with the kind of person Evelyn Hartson is used to meeting. It would deflect us from looking too closely at a poor farm labourer. He told us at the station that his mother had mentioned a missing girl, but just stated she went into Pembury

Hospital last Wednesday, at least a day before Miss Hartson disappeared, and he hasn't visited or spoken to her in person since.'

'So, she can't have known,' Wright said. 'What's he playing at?'

'He's flustered, and probably with good reason. Did you notice anything on your tour of the cottage?'

'I almost tripped over a battered suitcase sticking out from beneath where the coats were hung up, but otherwise everywhere was clean and tidy. Nothing out of the ordinary.'

'Except . . .' Kember said, giving Wright a sideways glance. 'I noticed a faint waft of perfume in the living room when we arrived.'

Wright stopped walking. 'Then we need to search again and bring him in for questioning.'

'Not tonight,' Kember said, quietly. He put his hand on Wright's elbow and urged him on. 'But inform Alf and Captain Brown. Let them know that we need to keep a close eye on him, I suspect Evelyn is in no immediate danger, but if my boss or Laurence Hartson finds out, Peter Yates might be.'

CHAPTER
TWENTY-SIX

Lizzie glanced at her watch as dawn broke the following morning. Twenty past eight and she was standing by the grave of Frank and June Robinson behind St Matthew's Church. It was bloody cold.

She watched from a respectable distance as two gravediggers sank their shovels for the first time into the grass around the grave, using their heavy boots and full weight to help them cut into the frozen earth. Only a simple headstone marked the site among all the others crowded into the graveyard, but the line of the trench to be dug had been marked out with rough string pegged to the ground. Reverend Wilson, wearing an overcoat, scarf and flat cap against the cold, had taken up position at the head of the grave, muttering prayers under his breath. Kember stood at her side, watching with a stony expression as the men went about their work.

Lizzie had heard all about the continuing search for Evelyn Hartson and her mind churned over the possibilities. She turned at the sound of someone struggling with a heavy load and saw Dr Headley stumbling across the uneven grass, his box of forensic instruments swinging and banging his hip every time he threatened to lose his footing.

After greeting Lizzie, Headley hissed, 'Good God, Kember,' low enough for the vicar to not hear. 'You don't do things by halves, do you?'

Kember's face remained impassive. 'I don't know what you mean, Headley.'

'I mean, you nearly had half the Home Office medico-legal pathologists from London down here, poking around. Sir Bernard and Keith Simpson were sniffing the air and it was only your chief inspector who held them at bay.'

'Would their presence have been such a bad thing?'

'Are you mad? Dr Simpson's a good chap, actually, but I've heard Sir Bernard's legendary powers are on the wane. And there's no telling what underlying motivations an outsider might bring with them.' He positioned his box on the grass and sat down, his medical bag by his side. 'The fracas you caused yesterday knew no bounds. Everyone telephoning everyone else, all wondering what on earth was going on. It's not every day that a body from over twenty years ago is dug up as part of a murder investigation. In religious parlance, all hell broke loose.'

'I'm sorry if it caused you difficulties,' Kember said.

'Difficulties? You have a knack for turning up bodies like a pig snuffling for truffles, and as if you haven't got enough of them, you upset the great and good by digging up an old one. I told you they wouldn't like it.'

Lizzie pulled the collar of her greatcoat higher to block out the icy breeze. 'The problem is, Doctor, until June Robinson's body comes out of the ground and you give us your opinion, there's no way of knowing whether we're dealing with a tragic case of a husband and wife falling to the same infectious disease, or another murder.'

'As long as you're aware of the limitations.' Headley looked at them with one eyebrow raised. 'At least dawn is at a decent time in December, even if the cold chills the bones.'

The next quarter of an hour passed with only the gravediggers' muttered complaints at the frozen earth and the sound of shovels rasping on the stony ground conveyed on the wind. Lizzie remained at the graveside with Dr Headley, who hadn't moved from his forensic-instruments box. She glanced into the trench, already three feet deep, and back at Headley, huddled in his black overcoat, scarf and homburg, eyes blinking behind the thick, round lenses of his spectacles, looking like a grieving garden gnome.

'I thought I'd done my time, sitting in cold graveyards with the wind whipping around my vitals,' Headley muttered.

'Why don't you get warm in the church until the men have finished?'

'The chain of evidence,' Headley stated. 'I have to observe the whole process to ensure the remains aren't tampered with or accidentally damaged. But you go in. As you say, it'll only be thirty minutes or so.'

Lizzie was about to refuse when she saw Sergeant Wright hurrying towards them.

'There you are, sir,' Wright said, panting and trying to catch his breath.

'What's going on?' Kember asked.

Wright took a deep breath. 'Alf tried ringing the police station but we weren't there so he sent a boy up to find us. I thought it might be important so I ran as fast as I could to the station and rang him back. He told me a young lad he recognised as Peter Yates bought two train tickets to Tonbridge this morning.'

'They've gone?' Lizzie asked, surprised that the couple had left in broad daylight.

'No, miss. He left the station without boarding a train.'

'When we called at his home last night, Sergeant, I think you'll agree that Yates was acting rather suspicious,' Kember said. 'There was the faint waft of perfume in the living room and you noticed a suitcase under where the coats were hanging.'

'That I did, sir. Nearly tripped over it.'

'Then I'm doubly certain he's with Evelyn and they're getting ready to leave.'

Lizzie nodded. 'They know you're getting close but won't risk running away until tonight when it's dark. Don't forget, the panto-mime starts at five o'clock and many villagers will be in the hall or settled at home for their tea so there'll be less chance of being seen.'

'There's a train to Tonbridge at five and another at just after half past six, if I remember correctly,' Wright said.

Lizzie looked at Kember. 'I'd take the six-thirty to make the best use of the dark and the reassurance of having fewest people around, but I'd want to make sure I had time to catch a connecting train to somewhere else. London, probably. She won't want to risk staying in Tonbridge and being recognised.'

Kember sighed. 'Legally, there's nothing I can do because they're both of age, but Chief Inspector Hartson will expect me to do something and I'm worried his brother will take matters into his own hands.'

'Kember!' Dr Headley called.

He stood looking down into the last resting place of the Robinsons. A large mound of stony earth lay piled on a nearby tarpaulin and planks of wood had been laid along each side of the open grave for safety. Lizzie looked over the rim. At the bottom lay the remains of a wooden casket, mostly rotted but with a few chunks still intact. The largest piece lay at the head end, still pro-tecting whatever lay beneath.

'I suppose you'll be wanting me to go down there?' Headley said.

'You know how my back complains in this cold,' Kember replied.

Headley grimaced and slowly descended the rungs of a ladder into the six-feet-deep cavity. The hole had been dug to reveal the length of the coffin, but twice as wide to provide an area to put one's feet. Headley's boots made no mark in the compacted earth as he stood astride the coffin.

'This will be June Robinson,' Headley said. 'She was buried last.'

'Take this, sir,' one of the diggers said, offering Headley a trowel.

Headley scraped the last of the earth from the section of lid and prised up the rotting remnant in one piece. Lizzie caught her breath and Kember muttered a curse at the sight of what lay underneath. It was only a skull and skeleton, as expected, but the sight of what used to be a human being wasn't something you experienced every day. Earth had filled in around the skull, which had become detached over the two decades, and Headley quickly but carefully flicked it away until the full shape was visible.

'Hand me my camera, will you?' Headley asked.

Kember complied and Lizzie noted the expensive Leica model he handed down to the doctor.

'Nice camera,' Lizzie said. 'German?'

'I needed a good one for my work,' Headley said, matter-of-factly. 'Can't always rely on the police photographers.'

Lizzie and Kember exchanged a look.

'All the soft tissue has long gone, of course, and some of the bones have been displaced by worms and insects,' Headley said, as he took three snaps with the Leica.

'Any sign of violence?' Kember asked.

'Hold your horses,' Headley said, irritably. He took another photograph. 'There doesn't appear to be anything unusual about the upper skeleton or front of the skull.'

Lizzie watched him use the trowel to prise beneath the skull and start to dislodge it from where the cold earth seemed reluctant to relinquish it. Headley lifted the skull and rotated it to reveal the back and top.

'Well, well,' he said, placing it on the earth and taking more photographs. 'I'd be very surprised if that is natural.'

Lizzie could see that the rear of the skull was damaged, two odd-shaped holes looking similar to a broken plant pot discarded in a garden, but she knew from her years of research that marks like that were seldom the result of an accident. She felt her chest tighten and gave the rubber band on her wrist an extra-hard ping. Kember's head turned at the sound of the snap but she ignored him and continued to stare at the skull.

'What's your opinion, Doctor?' she asked.

Headley groaned as he stood up, and held the skull so Lizzie and Kember could see.

'This is very interesting, actually,' he said, pointing to the larger hole in the back slope of the skull. 'The fracture is comminuted, smashed to bits in your parlance. Without the missing pieces still in the earth, it forms this elongated, almost inverted-teardrop shape.' He pointed to the hole on top of the skull. 'This one is also comminuted, but circular with concentric and radiating fractures.'

'Could that have happened after burial, as the coffin decayed and the earth fell in?' Kember asked.

'Improbable. The skull was face up and still protected by the coffin lid, and both wounds are indicative of having been struck with some force.'

'So, she was hit with a blunt instrument?' Kember asked.

'The different shapes of the two wounds suggest two weapons,' Headley said.

Kember frowned. 'Why would someone use two weapons when one is sufficient?'

'Would you like to swap places or shall we remain within our areas of expertise?'

Lizzie saw a cloud cross Kember's face and responded quickly. 'Could she have been attacked with a weapon and hit her head when she fell?' she suggested, trying to ease the tension between the two professionals.

'Ah, thinking like a detective,' Headley said. 'But, unlikely. If that were the case, I'd expect the wounds to be offset and the shapes to suggest a different angle of attack for each. However, one is vertically below the other, although a few inches apart.'

'Possibly two blows then,' Kember said. 'Probably in quick succession to account for the alignment.'

Headley photographed the indentations in the earth where the skull had been, and the myriad fragments of bone, almost dust by now, missing from the wounds. Then he bent low and looked closely at the arm and rib bones.

'The arms, ribs, etcetera are in situ, with no breakages or blade marks consistent with violent trauma, so I surmise that June Robinson died from a blow or blows to the back of her head. Whether she was alive, conscious or restrained when the fatal blow was struck, we can never know.' Headley put the camera back in its case. 'I have enough photographs for our purposes so I don't think there's any point in me taking the body to the village hall. And the bones have been in the ground so long they are too delicate to survive the journey back to Pembury mortuary. They'd probably be shaken to dust before we got halfway there. Better by far to fill this in and carry on with finding who killed her.'

Kember, looking calmer, helped Headley out of the grave and asked the diggers to wait until the reverend could say a prayer over the remains.

Lizzie's mind was racing as they walked over to the church. It was pretty obvious that Dr Sam Davies didn't even know he came from Scotney or had relations here until two days ago, which made it highly improbable that he'd murdered June Robinson twenty-two years ago. Agnes Jarvis, Robinson as she was then, might have killed her mother so she could marry Kenneth Jarvis, but where was Kenneth? Had he cracked from the strain of keeping Agnes's deadly secret for so long and been killed by her to keep him quiet? And was Evelyn Hartson really alive as they hoped?

Lizzie waited with Kember and Wright as Wilson remained at the graveside, and Dr Headley stumbled back, his medical bag in one hand and the forensic box banging against his opposite hip. As the sound of Wilson reciting a prayer reached them on the breeze, the two gravediggers, smoking nearby and huddled against the cold, removed their flat caps and bowed their heads respectfully.

'As exhumations go, that was one of the better ones,' Headley said in a low voice, and put his forensic box on the path. 'Always a good result if there's no need to fully disinter.'

'You're sure you have enough to make a full report?' Kember said.

'Of course.' Headley gave Kember a sideways look. 'The photographs will be ready this afternoon, and you saw the skull. Obviously, with no soft tissue remaining, I can't state categorically that the damage to the skull was the cause of death. It could have occurred ante-, peri- or post-mortem.'

'But?' Kember said, and waited.

'But,' Headley obliged, 'if she wasn't dead when the blows were struck, she would definitely have died of a massive brain haemorrhage soon after.'

'That will do.'

'Glad to hear it. A lot of blood will have come from these wounds, and injuries as severe as these would almost certainly have caused secondary bleeding from her mouth and nose. Probably some colourless cerebrospinal fluid from her nose as well.'

Kember visibly shuddered. 'We'll need to arrest Agnes Jarvis and search her cottage, then.'

As Wilson finished the short service at the graveside with the 'Lord's Prayer', Lizzie felt the surge of energy that had sustained her during the exhumation begin to dissipate. The cold began to bite harder and she was glad when the diggers had again taken their shovels to the pile of earth.

Lizzie, Kember and Wright walked with Headley towards the lychgate at the front of the church.

'I'll come with you,' Lizzie said, having no intention of returning to the air station any time soon.

'Actually,' Headley said, pulling the strap of his box high on his shoulder. 'I'll come, too.'

'That would be very helpful,' Kember said. 'You've as much experience with crime scenes as I do. This one is twenty-two years old so another pair of expert eyes would be most welcome.'

'Expert now, am I.' Headley laughed. 'And there was I thinking you were the detective. But seriously, I might have something better to offer you than my expert eye,' he said, with a mischievous smile. 'I have something with me that I've not tried in the field. In fact, I've had it no more than a few weeks and only tried it out a few times in the mortuary.'

'Intriguing. What is it?'

'All in good time.' Headley tapped the side of his nose.

Lizzie was surprised by Headley's offer, even though pathologists regularly attended the sites of recent murders to offer their medical expertise and trained eyes to unlock complex crime scenes. But for Dr Headley to expect to give his interpretation of a home that had been lived in, rearranged, cleaned and tidied for twenty-two years, was absurd.

As they reached Headley's car beyond the lychgate, the noise from an ENSA lorry drowned out their conversation as it grumbled past towards where others were parked outside the village hall. Lizzie saw the woman driver smile across at them and wave. She wondered whether she knew the woman but then saw the embarrassed half-smile on Kember's face.

'Friend of yours?' she said, ice in her voice.

'That's Paula Unwin,' Kember said. 'Sergeant Wright and I spoke to her at the camp.' He looked at Headley. 'Looks like the pantomime is going ahead. Are you going?'

Lizzie felt an unexpected surge of jealousy and a flash of irritation at the flat response but let it go. There would be a better time to ask.

'I might stick my head around the door, if there's nothing interesting on the wireless,' Headley said, peering down the road. 'Actually, while you're escorting Mrs Jarvis to the station, I need to grab something from the tea shop. I'm starving.'

'Mention Sergeant Wright. He knows the owner so if you're pleasant enough, she might give you an extra slice of toast.'

'I'm always pleasant,' Headley said, his frown returning. 'But I've a pile of work waiting for me back at Pembury, and you keep finding me more.'

CHAPTER
TWENTY-SEVEN

Kember heard the front door open and Wright's voice casting instructions to inquisitive villagers to remain outside. The door closed and a squeaky bolt slid home. Kember had gone to arrest Agnes Jarvis the moment he'd left the churchyard and she now sat opposite him in the police station's back room, looking scared but being comforted by Dr Davies. Davies had got wind of the exhumation and arrived at the station just as Kember had escorted Agnes inside. The introduction of aunt and nephew, especially under such circumstances, had been awkward at first and then tearful, with Davies giving Agnes a big hug to calm her sobbing.

Sergeant Wright came through and sat next to Kember. Lizzie had elected to sit at the end of the table to observe.

Kember cleared his throat.

'You've been informed about the exhumation of your mother, June Robinson, that took place this morning. I'm afraid Dr Headley found evidence that she may have been the victim of a murder.' Davies put his arm around Agnes as tears began flowing again. 'I know this is distressing news but I will need you to answer some more questions.'

'Whatever for?' Davies said, drawing himself up to his full height in his chair.

'Because this is now a murder inquiry, Doctor.'

'But she's been dead for twenty-two years.'

'I'm sure you'll understand, I still have a duty to try to find out who killed her, if anyone.'

Davies held Agnes to him as a wave of sobbing wracked her body, and Kember watched them with interest. Confusion and anguish lay painted clearly on the face of Davies. On the other hand, the fear so recently exhibited by Agnes had transformed into an expression of deep grief, and who could blame her? In his opinion, the chances were very high that Agnes had murdered her mother in order to marry the lover she'd been forbidden to even see. Why else would her reaction be so extreme when the mother she'd hated had been dead for over two decades?

As the sobs subsided, Agnes stared blankly ahead and Davies cast his eyes down. The wind had been taken out of their sails and they looked deflated and defeated. Kember sighed. The woman sitting in front of him, to whom he'd not long read out the standard police caution, looked nothing like the image of a killer you might have in your mind. But he knew murderers came in all shapes and sizes.

'I'm going to make this as brief as I can,' Kember began. He looked at Davies. 'I would appreciate you letting Mrs Jarvis answer in her own time. Is that understood? You'll have the opportunity to ask questions later.'

Kember hoped the doctor would recognise and respect his jurisdiction and was relieved when Davies nodded.

'Of course, Inspector.'

'Thank you.' He looked directly at Agnes. 'Mrs Jarvis, we asked for your parents' grave to be opened because we had reason to believe the cause of death was not as stated on your mother's death certificate. We checked with Dr Smith, who was here at the time and certified the death. However, his account of that morning threw up some questions. He was certain that your mother was already in a coffin by the time he was called to your home. Is that right?'

Mrs Jarvis didn't react, but Davies glanced at her in surprise, confirming to Kember that he knew nothing about that night.

'Yes,' she said, and began speaking quietly and slowly. 'Mum had been unwell for a while before she passed away in the early hours of the morning. I was in a bit of a state after I found her and didn't know what to do so I went to see Ken. He calmed me down and said the government wanted burials to be quick to avoid the spread of infection. He was good with his hands and had started making cheap coffins because so many were needed. He said he had a nice one ready round the back and he'd take it to my house while I went to fetch the doctor.'

'And is that what happened?'

Mrs Jarvis nodded. 'Dr Smith came straight away, and by the time we got home, Ken had managed to get Mum into the coffin. Looked so peaceful, she did.'

'How long had you been?'

'I don't remember. Probably no longer than fifteen minutes.'

Kember frowned, and he caught Lizzie's quizzical look out of the corner of his eye.

'That doesn't seem very long for Kenneth to take the coffin to your house, take it upstairs and lay your mother inside.'

Mrs Jarvis took a handkerchief from her pocket and dabbed her nose.

'Mum had been sleeping downstairs because she was too ill to get upstairs and Ken had managed to wrap her in a sheet and get her into the coffin. He was right: it was a simple but nice one, and I was grateful.'

Still seems a strange way to proceed, Kember thought. 'What did Dr Smith do?'

'I didn't see.' She twisted the handkerchief with her fingers. 'I stood outside while Ken went in with him. Ken said Dr Smith checked her pulse, and her mouth for signs of breathing. He felt her forehead and checked her eyes. Then he came out and pronounced her dead of the flu and pneumonia. Said he'd do the necessary paperwork straight away.'

'Did the doctor not examine her for possible other causes of death?'

'Why would he? Mum had perked up a bit that week but she'd been so ill so it wasn't unexpected.'

'Perked up?'

'She took some soup with bread soaked in it, which had put some colour back in her cheeks.' Agnes looked down at the square of cloth she was squeezing in her hands.

'When was she buried?' Kember asked.

'The following day. Spanish flu had taken Dad a few months before, while he was still in the army, and the ground above his grave had hardly had time to settle before they opened it up for Mum.'

'Were you alone in the house with your mother that night?'

'Of course, I was.'

Kember stared at her and she looked away. By confirming she'd been alone in the house with her mother, had she all but confessed? If she was telling the truth about fetching Kenneth before alerting the doctor, Kenneth couldn't have been in the house and killed her mother. But he must have known what had happened because even if she'd cleared up the blood, there was no way he could not have seen the head wounds.

As he waited for Agnes to look back at him, Kember could hear Lizzie's breathing beside him. She leant forward and put her elbows on the table, ignoring the sharp look he gave her.

'Mrs Jarvis,' Lizzie said, softly. 'I know you're upset and this has come as a shock, but can you cast your mind back to the days leading up to your mother's passing. How were things at home? Were you getting on?'

'Not really.' Agnes's gaze darted from Lizzie to Kember. 'As I said, Mum had started eating and seemed brighter. She managed to get up and . . .' She turned the cloth over and over in her hands.

'It's all right, Mrs Jarvis,' Lizzie soothed. 'Please go on.'

'She was able to potter around the house. Only downstairs, mind.'

'Were you or your mother receiving visitors at that time?'

'No.' Agnes's gaze cast back down to the twisted cloth, now barely recognisable as a handkerchief.

Kember waited for her to look up.

'Dr Headley found physical evidence that someone attacked your mother. The fact that Kenneth was so quick to put her in the coffin, before even the doctor had arrived to certify her death, suggests you killed her and Kenneth helped you cover it up.'

'No! I didn't do it.' She nearly tore the handkerchief in half.

'There can be no other explanation,' Kember insisted.

'Maybe we had a burglar,' said Agnes, her eyes wide with sudden panic.

'Who stole nothing from the house but decided to kill an ill woman on her sickbed?' Kember scoffed. 'If it was an intruder, why didn't you hear him or see any blood? If you did see blood, why did you or Kenneth clean it up and not call the police?'

'There was blood on my mother's lips but the doctor said that was probably caused by all the coughing.'

'Yes, he told us that, but admitted he'd performed only a cursory examination. He also told us that he thought your mother's mouth had been wiped with a damp cloth. The head injury Dr

310

Headley found would have caused a lot of blood, but hard-pressed Dr Smith, roused from his sleep early in the morning, seeing an old lady lying peacefully in her coffin, all clean and pristine, might well have looked no further than the obvious and certified death from influenza and pneumonia.'

Kember could see Agnes's chest rising and falling with quick, shallow breathing and knew he had her rattled.

'Mrs Jarvis,' he said. 'Did you kill your mother?'

'No!'

'Inspector, please,' Davies complained.

'Then I think we need to find your husband, Kenneth, and question him,' Kember continued. 'We'll also need to search your house.'

Mrs Jarvis looked wide-eyed at Dr Davies.

'Do you really expect to find anything so long after the fact, Inspector?' Davies said.

'It's my duty to look, Doctor.' Kember stood. 'I think that's all we can achieve for now. Mrs Jarvis, I'm afraid you'll need to stay in one of the cells downstairs for a while, until we search your house. Doctor, you're welcome to stay with your aunt but there's nothing else you can do. If you want to return to the air station, we can telephone you if there are further developments.'

'I'll stay here for a while, if I may. I'm not expected back until one o'clock and it's all far too much of a shock for me to go back at the moment, or leave my aunt on her own.'

'Very well. If you could leave your door key, Mrs Jarvis, then both please go with Sergeant Wright.'

Kember waited for them to go to the basement before he turned to Lizzie.

'What did you make of that?'

'I don't think she did it,' Lizzie said.

'Why not?' Kember's eyebrows rose in surprise. 'She could have killed her mother any time that night, anywhere in the house and cleaned up.'

'She was lying.' Lizzie stood up and faced him. 'Did you see the way she looked away or down when talking about the murder?' She took her coat from the back of the chair. 'I'd like to be there when you search the house.'

'It looked a normal little house when I visited. There won't be much to see.'

'Not for you, perhaps. But as I'm always told, I'm not quite normal.'

◆ ◆ ◆

Having left Agnes Jarvis and Dr Davies comforting each other in a cell, Lizzie walked with Kember and Wright to collect Dr Headley from the tea shop before they moved on to the cottage. Kember used a key Agnes had given him to enter her home. Lizzie, Wright and Headley followed him through the front door.

The hallway was wider than Lizzie had expected but three men crowding in made it seem cramped, forcing her to take two steps up the staircase. The casual exclusion irked her but it did enable her to see over their heads and snatch a first glimpse into the living room where June Robinson had slept, possibly died, and been put into her coffin.

'Sergeant, can you check upstairs while we take downstairs?' Kember said. 'I'm not sure what we're looking for but shout if anything looks unusual or out of place.'

'Aye, sir,' Wright acknowledged.

Lizzie waited for Kember and Headley to enter the living room before stepping down and out of Wright's way. His heavy boots clumped up the carpet runner held in place on the stairs by dull metal rods. She joined Kember and saw a living room similar to the picture she had formed in her mind. Light coming through the open curtains showed it to be neither plush nor threadbare, neither brand-new nor dilapidated. It was clean and tidy – Lizzie ran her finger along the mantelpiece – with no dust. The Christmas decorations were spartan, but that was the war for you, and a photograph of Kenneth stood alongside one of Agnes. Behind the armchair nearest the window was a blackout screen, taken down during daylight hours. *Made by Kenneth, no doubt*, she thought.

'First impressions?' Kember asked.

Headley took a deep breath and sighed loudly. 'I can't see anything untoward, but what would you expect after so long. I'm used to seeing overturned furniture, blood and guts everywhere, and dead bodies lying in unnatural positions.'

'It's such a small cottage,' Lizzie said, and saw their puzzled expressions. 'What I mean is, it must have caused Agnes great strain to have her mother ill and sleeping downstairs. Upstairs is out of sight and out of mind. For a while, at least. But here . . .' She indicated the room with her open hand. 'The only place to escape to is the kitchen or bedroom, and who wants to spend all their time in those rooms?'

'Are you suggesting Agnes killed her mother because they were living on top of each other?' Kember asked.

'No – well, yes. Partly.' Lizzie shook her head to clear it and allow her thoughts to get in order. 'I'm saying it must be difficult when you're courting and living in a small house with your parents who hate your choice of sweetheart. There's no privacy. Nowhere to talk without someone listening.' She looked at the framed photographs as if they were alive. 'You only had your mother but she hated railwaymen as much as your father. Her illness must have been a godsend, but it would have been even easier had she been upstairs, not down.'

'Easier to canoodle, d'you mean?' Headley said.

Lizzie ignored him and turned to Kember.

'Agnes said she was alone in the house with her mother and had no visitors, but the way she answered and held her body, and the gestures she made told me different. I'm no removals expert but I think there's just enough room to manoeuvre a coffin through the front door and hallway into here without the need for taking the doors off their hinges or removing the banister. But it's a job for two people and she said Kenneth had already got the coffin into the living room and put her mother inside on his own by the time she got back with the doctor.'

'When you put it like that, it doesn't sound very feasible,' Headley said. 'I mentioned before how difficult it is to cart around a deadweight.'

'All right,' Kember said. 'The two of them killed her here, she cleaned up while he went to get the coffin, and they both put her in before she ran to fetch the doctor.'

'Not in here,' Lizzie said. 'I mean, look at it. All these nooks and crannies, rugs, lampshades and fabric furniture.' They looked perplexed. 'The amount of blood from June Robinson's head wound would have saturated the floor, chairs and everywhere. It would have taken days to clean up but the doctor couldn't have seen any blood because he would have been suspicious and found the real cause of death.'

'Then where?'

'I think Kenneth took advantage of Mrs Robinson being ill to visit Agnes regularly. But you can probably hear everything going on upstairs from in here so they won't have used the bedrooms.' She shook her head. 'I think he called on Agnes and they went to the kitchen. It's the obvious place because the solid walls would muffle any sounds. I bet they thought she would be in her bed in the living room as usual, unable to move. But they didn't know she'd recovered sufficiently to be up and about that night. Her mother must have heard him come in and gone to confront them. An argument took place and . . .'

'Agnes lashed out, hit her mother on the head and killed her,' Kember finished.

Wright stomped back down the stairs and came into the living room.

'All clear upstairs, sir. Just two pokey bedrooms.'

'I agree with Miss Hayes,' Headley said. 'Let's have a look at this kitchen, shall we?'

Kember led the way and Lizzie brought up the rear. Excluded again.

'I agree, this is the more likely place, if she was murdered indoors at all,' Kember said. 'It's certainly big enough to swing a weapon with the force needed to crack open a skull.'

'You're the doctor now, are you?' Headley said, giving Kember a withering look.

'Easier to clean up in here,' Lizzie said, looking at the walls, cooking range, small table. 'Which is as it should be when you're preparing food. After all the years of regular cleaning, it looks spotless.'

'To the naked eye, perhaps, but . . .' Headley put his forensic-instruments box on the small kitchen table, opened it and began selecting items. 'A German chap you won't have heard of took a substance that was discovered in the latter part of the last century and found that if mixed with hydrogen peroxide, some other substances enhanced the chemiluminescence, making it glow blue. Most notably, blood. A few years later, this compound was given the name Luminol. Shut all the doors please.'

Wright and Lizzie obliged as Headley lined up a small glass beaker, small glass jars containing liquid, a tiny spray can of the kind Kember had only seen used for tending delicate plants, a metal funnel, and an earthenware jar with unseen contents.

'Two more Germans found it was the iron contained in the haemoglobin part of blood that caused the glow. Switch the light on and put the blackout screen up at the window, if you would.'

Wright secured the screen and Kember flicked the light switch as Headley poured some of the contents of the jars into the beaker, measuring carefully, and followed this with some of the pale-yellow crystalline contents from the earthenware jar.

'Yet another clever German used it on blood at crime scenes and achieved startling results. Would you set up my camera on that tripod, please.'

Kember extended the legs of the tripod and eventually got the camera attached. Meanwhile, Headley stirred the contents of the beaker with a wooden tongue-depressor, placed the funnel in the spray can and poured the mixture in.

'Last year, two equally clever men, as all pathologists are, this time in San Francisco, discovered that dried and old blood gives an even stronger and longer-lasting effect than freshly spilt blood.' He pressurised the can with a few strokes of its pump. 'All of which means, if Miss Hayes is right, that we might be lucky enough to see something of what went on in here.'

'What is it you think you're going to find with a fly spray?' Kember said, as Headley fiddled with the settings on his camera.

'It's not a fly spray.' Headley scowled. 'I still have friends who work in the Metropolitan Police Forensic Science Laboratory in Hendon.' He bent to look through the camera's viewfinder. 'They kindly sent me a sample of the Luminol crystals for me to play around with.'

'It's a toy?'

'Figure of speech, Kember. It's far from being a toy.' Headley held out his arms for the others to stand as far back as possible. 'I tested it in the mortuary and although it has its limitations, I was astonished, and I think you will be too.'

'What are we looking for, Doctor?' Lizzie said, her curiosity supplanting the feeling of dread and panic that had begun to tighten her chest.

'Blood,' Headley said, matter-of-factly. 'But not animal blood from preparing the Sunday dinner or a finger cut on a carving knife. If we assume June Robinson was killed and this is the most likely room for the incident to have taken place, we should see the spattered, splashed, pooled blood that gushed from two holes punched into a human skull.'

'I can't see anything,' Kember said.

Headley sighed. 'Give a man a chance, why don't you?' He indicated the hollow rubber bulb attached to the camera's shutter-release button. 'Hold that carefully and press it once when I say so.' Kember took the bulb. 'Miss Hayes, you're on the light switch this time, if you will.' Lizzie took up position. 'On my say so . . .'

Lizzie could feel the tension making her hand tremble as Headley gave the can one more pump and pointed the nozzle to the left side of the cooking range. The can hissed as he sprayed the liquid from side to side.

'Light.'

Lizzie flicked the switch.

'Bulb.'

Lizzie heard a click from the camera and another a few seconds later. The pitch-darkness remained. She heard Headley sigh loudly.

'Light.'

Lizzie switched the light on and blinked away the glare. Wright's stony expression was the epitome of scepticism, and Headley had his lips pursed in frustration.

'Say nothing, Kember,' Headley said, already adjusting the position of the camera.

'The thought never crossed my mind,' Kember said with a thin smile.

'Waste of time, if you ask me,' Wright muttered, not quite inaudibly.

'Again, please,' Headley said in a clipped voice.

Wright raised his eyebrows at Lizzie as she reached for the light switch, Kember held the bulb, and Headley gave the can two more pumps. The spray can hissed again.

'Light.'

Lizzie flicked the switch.

'Bloody Nora!' Wright cried.

'Bulb,' Headley snapped.

The camera clicked and Lizzie gasped.

Kember swore under his breath.

A bright-blue glow from spots and streaks extended from the range to a cupboard in the corner. In cracks and crevices where a mop and cloth could not easily reach, the glow was at its brightest. Right in the corner, the glow formed a smooth-edged shape, no doubt the result of repeated attempts at cleaning over the decades.

'What on God's green earth is that?' Wright asked.

'The Luminol is reacting with the iron in the blood as I told you it would,' said Headley, his voice coming from the dark. 'I'd say we've found where June Robinson was killed.'

The camera clicked again.

The glow began to dissipate after half a minute or so, and Lizzie switched the light back on. Wright's face was pale with shock while Kember's reflected obvious amazement. Headley had a smug smile of satisfaction at having pleased his audience and been proved right.

'Well, Headley,' Kember said. 'I must say I was not expecting that. Was that all blood?'

'Yes, indeed,' Headley confirmed. 'If you leave me with Sergeant Wright for another half hour or so, I'll take some more photographs and let you have copies as soon as I can get them processed.'

'You can do that again?' Lizzie asked.

'Absolutely. I don't believe it's infinite but it will certainly work a few more times. Based on where the residue is, I'd say Mrs Robinson came through that door, possibly went for Agnes or Kenneth and was distracted by one of them while the other struck her once from behind.'

'Once?' Lizzie said. 'I thought you said twice?'

'I've changed my opinion about that. A second blow struck after the first should have produced much more blood, and research has shown that splatter goes far and wide. Even allowing for years of cleaning, there's not enough spread. I believe she was hit once, possibly falling against the wall and to the floor down there.' He pointed to the corner by the cupboard.

Lizzie's mind was racing again. She could see Mrs Robinson bursting in, weak with recent illness, seeing the young and powerful Kenneth Jarvis with her youngest daughter. She saw her shouting at Agnes, scolding her for letting him in and pleading with her to listen. Then she was bleeding to death on the ground, a fire-poker in Kenneth's hand.

'Lizzie?'

Her eyes refocused and she saw Kember looking at her with concern.

'You should spray that on possible weapons, like pokers,' she said. 'Check the attic and any garden shed or air-raid shelter too.'

'Good idea,' Headley said. 'Give me some elbow room for a while.'

'Sergeant,' Kember said. 'You stay with the doctor. Lizzie and I will have a look outside.'

'Aye, sir,' said Wright.

Lizzie followed Kember to the back garden, which was nothing more than a well-kept patch of grass with a few twiggy shrubs around the border. A wooden tool-shed and smaller hut at the far end flanked a half-buried Anderson shelter. She opened the hut's door, recoiling at the smell from the outside toilet, while Kember checked the shelter and declared it empty of anything resembling a murder weapon.

'Would you keep the weapon, even if it was a poker?' Kember said.

'I might,' Lizzie said. 'If someone you know well calls on you and the poker is missing, you have to make up an excuse and lie. Better to clean it and leave it in plain sight doing its job than risk it becoming of interest.'

Kember nodded and opened the shed door.

'The usual spade, fork, rake,' he said, moving the handles. 'A hoe, shears, watering can.' He ducked and swiped at cobwebs above his head. 'Jesus Christ,' he swore. 'Thank God it's not spider season.'

Lizzie smiled without letting him see. Creepy-crawlies didn't bother her much but it amused her to think this tall detective wasn't keen.

Beyond his shoulder, she could see the usual equipment of a gardener but also of a man used to working with his hands. A grindstone with turning handle for sharpening blades was clamped to the workbench next to a wood plane; hammers, chisels, a metal file and pliers hung on strings tied to nails, and an axe, hammer, mallet, and four kinds of saw were fixed along one wall. Beneath the bench were wooden crates, boxes, seed trays and stacks of terracotta plant pots. The odd thing about the shed was the railway paraphernalia displayed around the interior. Kenneth Jarvis had been a railwayman for many years before his injury and had obviously enjoyed keeping the odd item as a memento. She knew nothing about railways but the small wheels, gears, metal information plates and bric-a-brac looked brand-new.

'Looks like he was a collector of railway equipment,' Lizzie said. 'And not all of it from the rubbish heap.'

'I noticed that,' Kember said, donning rubber gloves. 'Obviously purloined from the branch-line stores.'

Lizzie moved away as he stepped back, bringing out a handful of tools and a sack of something that clanked as it moved. He laid the hammer, axe and mallet, that had been hanging on the wall, on the grass and opened the sack. She saw three metal items that looked like they were part of a bigger machine, an assortment of handles and levers, and a host of smaller bits and pieces.

'I'll get Headley to spray the tools with that stuff,' he said, inspecting the contents of the sack.

She watched him sort through the clanking metal and discard each item.

'Doesn't seem much likely here,' he said. 'It's all smooth, too long to swing in that small kitchen, or the wrong shape. Seems like more railway components.'

'What about that one?' she said, bending down to move a thick metal rod aside to reveal another about two feet long with a spring-loaded squeeze-handle at one end. 'It looks like a lever of some kind.'

As he removed it from the sack, Lizzie gasped as an image of the murder flashed into her mind. She saw the lever swing down only once, not twice, and the strength almost went from her legs as if it were she who had been struck.

'What's the matter?' she heard him say, hearing concern in his voice.

She took a deep breath to clear her head and waved him away. 'I'm all right,' she said, her strength returning although her heart still thumped in her chest and blood throbbed at her temples. 'I imagined the murder in my head when I saw the shape of that thing.'

Kember held the lever up and turned it around in his hands for them to see. At the end of the lever, on the opposite side to the squeeze-handle, was a cylindrical projection.

'One blow,' Lizzie said. 'That's all it would have taken. The main bar would have knocked a hole in the back of June Robinson's skull and that protuberance would have punched a round hole in the top.'

'I've no idea what it is,' Kember said, 'but it must be part of Kenneth's collection. Let's get it inside to Dr Headley.'

Lizzie pinged the rubber band on her left wrist as a precaution and followed Kember back to the kitchen, where Dr Headley was repositioning his camera on its tripod. The poker from the living room lay on the floor and Wright came in with another.

'This is the only other poker I could find upstairs, Doctor,' Wright said, and he laid it next to the other.

'I've sprayed the other walls and the table,' Headley said. 'I've even tried the most likely patch of ceiling, where one might find blood droplets cast off from a swinging weapon.'

'And?' Kember raised his eyebrows.

Headley shook his head.

'You might want to try these,' Kember said, putting the tools and lever with the pokers. 'We found them in the shed.'

Headley did a double take and pointed at the lever. 'Never thought I'd see one of those again. I attended an accidental death at Victoria Station a couple of years ago when the driver of a shunting engine miscalculated and gave a goods train a proper jolt. The fireman in the other locomotive was knocked off his feet and fell on the reversing lever with such force that it punctured his abdomen.' Headley shook his head, sadly. 'Bled to death before I got there.'

Lizzie fought to keep the image out of her mind, focusing instead on the death of June Robinson.

The four of them went through the same procedure as before and the Luminol worked its magic. The tools and pokers stayed almost invisible in the darkened kitchen, but the top of the lever, parts of the squeeze-handle, and the join of the jutting bar glowed with bright-blue speckles.

'It's been well cleaned,' said Headley's voice. 'But there's no mistaking that reaction.'

Headley took two more photographs before Wright switched the light back on at Kember's command and removed the blackout screen from the window, allowing light to flood in again.

'That's fair shaken me up,' Wright said, retrieving the pokers. 'Making blood glow that you can't even see with your naked eye. Who'd've thought it?'

Kember took the lever and held it for Headley to place a clear cellophane bag over the end, securing it in place with Sellotape.

'We might be able to get a fingerprint or two from this as well,' Kember said. 'It's a good job you've got this new technique, Doctor. Without it, all we'd have is a broken skull and circumstantial evidence.'

'Maybe so,' Headley said, as he packed his camera away. 'I don't know what a judge and jury will make of it, though. One usually has little tolerance of science: the other, very little understanding.'

'Nevertheless.' Kember nodded at Wright and looked at Lizzie. 'Time to have another talk with Agnes Jarvis.'

CHAPTER TWENTY-EIGHT

Back at the police station, Kember sat next to Sergeant Wright at the table, on which lay the reversing lever with the cellophane bag protecting the top. Dr Davies sat opposite with Agnes Jarvis, who stared blankly at the lever. Lizzie had elected to sit out of the way in the corner to observe.

Kember took a deep breath and sighed. Here was a woman, bullied by her mother and denied happiness, who had become a victim of circumstance and now found herself subject to expressions of pity from everyone in the room.

'Mrs Jarvis,' Kember said, indicating the lever. 'We found this in your garden shed. Can you tell me what it is?'

'I've no idea,' Agnes said.

'Actually, we know it is a reversing lever, used for changing the direction of a steam locomotive, and I believe it's part of the collection your husband made before his injury stopped him working on the railways.'

Agnes shook her head slowly. 'I don't think I ever went in the shed.'

'Did you use this lever to kill your mother twenty-two years ago?'

He watched Agnes deflate a little more, as if punched in the stomach.

'Unfortunately, Dr Headley needed to get back to Pembury Hospital, but we three' – he indicated Lizzie and Wright – 'witnessed the use of a remarkable new scientific technique this morning. By spraying a special solution on the walls of your kitchen and this lever, Dr Headley revealed the presence of old blood residue.'

Davies looked as shocked as his aunt, a similar look of anguish slowly settling across their features.

'Is that legal?' Davies asked.

'It's been used on the Continent and in America with great success. I'm assured it is both robust and legal.'

Davies looked at Agnes. 'Aunty?'

She looked away from him and started to cry silent tears. Davies seemed confused, as if unsure whether he should comfort the aunt he'd only recently learned he had or shy away from someone who looked increasingly like a murderer.

'Mrs Jarvis,' Kember said. 'I know it's difficult but I must hear from you the truth of what happened all those years ago. We know this lever was used to kill your mother in your kitchen.'

'You're the detective,' she snapped, glaring at him. 'You seem to have all the answers. You tell me what happened.'

'I'd rather not speculate, Mrs Jarvis,' Kember said, a little taken aback by the sudden flare of anger. 'I need you to remember because I want to understand.' He waited, knowing she would fill the silence.

Agnes raised her head slowly and dabbed her eyes with her handkerchief before taking a long look at the lever.

'Ken called on me, like he had most days when Mum was ill, and we went into the kitchen. Those were the few times we could talk alone, because she was bedridden in the living room. Or we thought she was.'

'Why did you hit your mother?' Kember asked.

Agnes looked at the lever again. 'Ken always loved the railways and collected all sorts of bits and pieces he found doing his job. I thought it was rubbish but said he could keep it all in the shed after we were married. That night, he came round to see me and had another bag of bits with that sticking out the top.' She nodded at the lever. 'Later, when Mum burst in unexpectedly and started shouting, having a go at Ken, I grabbed it from the bag. I took a swipe at her and she fell, hitting her head on the table. I knew she was dead because of all the blood in the middle of the floor.'

'What did Kenneth do?'

'We couldn't call the police because I would hang for murder and we would never be together, but we had an idea.'

'The coffin?'

Agnes nodded.

'People knew she'd been seriously ill with flu and wouldn't be surprised if they heard she'd died. I couldn't even look at Mum so Ken moved her and cleaned her up while I started cleaning the kitchen. He left and I'd just finished when he came back with the coffin. I helped him get it into the living room and we put it on the floor. Mum was heavy but we got her inside and Ken made her look . . . presentable. Ken wanted to fetch the doctor but I said we should wait for early morning. That way we could say she died in her sleep. I've lived with what we did that night for twenty-two years and the only comfort I've had is Ken. We did a bad thing but she was a bad mother, a miserable woman, and I deserved happiness. I know I'll be punished, but you need to find Ken. I'm beside myself with worry that something dreadful has happened to him.'

Kember sighed and waited for Wright to finish writing in his notebook.

'We are looking for Kenneth and will continue to do so,' Kember said. 'We'll let you know if we hear anything. In the meantime, Sergeant Wright will write out your statement and get you to sign it. You'll be transferred to Maidstone Prison as soon as we can arrange it, to await trial for murder.'

Agnes burst into tears and Davies put his arm around her. Both looked distraught. Kember wondered how many other strict parents had died at the hands of their children because of affairs of the heart.

He felt a tickle by his ear.

'Can I talk to you in private?' Lizzie whispered.

He turned to look at her and she raised her eyebrows questioningly. Wondering what she'd seen that he hadn't, he followed her to the front office.

◆ ◆ ◆

'What is it?' Kember asked, when the door had closed.

'She's not a very good liar,' Lizzie said, flapping her hand in the direction of the back room and trying not to let the speed of her thoughts jumble her words. 'Oh, she started well enough before we searched her home, sticking close to the truth but keeping some of it vague. When confronted with the lever, she then had a go at you, which was a good smokescreen. Put you off your guard. But she made a mistake and answered a question you didn't ask.'

'I don't recall that,' Kember said.

He stepped back as she stepped towards him.

'You asked her why she hit her mother, not how.'

'But I wanted to know how, too.'

'Yes, but that wasn't the question. She was volunteering information you hadn't asked for.' Lizzie turned away and began to pace. 'She had the version she wanted to tell you already in her head and got that in first. In doing so, she overdid it by giving you too much detail.' She looked at Kember. 'We know the blood was by the wall, not in the middle of the floor, and Dr Headley's magic spray showed up nothing anywhere on the table.'

'Perhaps the table had been too well cleaned after all,' Kember said. 'And it's been a long time, her memory will have faded after all these years.'

'Maybe.' Lizzie conceded he might have a point about the table, but this wasn't general memory they were talking about, it was a specific moment of traumatic experience, and that wasn't easily forgotten. 'But the closer you stick to the truth, the more likely you are to get away with the lie.' She looked at Kember. 'If you'd killed your mother in the kitchen with something as unusual as a railway lever, splashing scarlet on the wall, putting her in a coffin as if you were the undertaker, lying to the doctor, the police and the vicar, every detail would be etched into your memory forever, wouldn't it?'

'If it didn't happen the way she said, what do you think happened?' Kember said.

'Oh, I think it happened mostly as she described,' Lizzie said. 'But Kenneth killed June Robinson, not Agnes.'

Kember thought for a moment.

'I agree,' he said.

'I beg your pardon?' Lizzie said, taken aback.

'I agree with you. *We* couldn't call the police,' he said. '*We* would never be together. *We* had to wait until morning to tell the doctor. *I* would hang for murder. Those aren't her words, they're Kenneth's, to convince her that she was just as responsible for the murder he had just committed. She's confessed to protect him.'

'Exactly,' Lizzie said, turning away. She made her thoughts Kenneth's and turned back. 'I'm Kenneth Jarvis and Agnes has been smitten with me for a long time but the only person standing in our way is her mother. I called in one evening, and far from being at death's door as I'd hoped, she was recovering. She was like an animal, snarling and shouting at me, and went for Agnes. I saw red and hit her with the first thing I could lay my hands on, the lever from my bag, just to shut her up. She fell to the floor and I saw the blood. Agnes was in shock, but she always does as I tell her and she did that now, going to her room while I cleaned up. I told her what to do, when to do it and what to say. It was the only way I could be safe.'

Lizzie stopped and waited. Kember was nodding his head slowly, eyebrows knitted into a frown as if life had become one long period of exasperation.

'Whatever we think, the only way we're going to get to the truth is if we find her husband,' Kember said. 'If Agnes refuses to change her story, they'll both be hanged.'

'You're forgetting the Handyman,' Lizzie said, seeing Kember grimace at the name. 'I think Kenneth Jarvis is already dead.'

Despite his belief that Agnes had been no more than an unwilling accomplice, the evidence as it stood leant heavily towards her and Kember had no option but to keep her locked in the cells beneath Scotney Police Station. Kember doubted any fingerprints would have survived on the lever after being wiped clean of June Robinson's blood. Lizzie had wanted to continue the interview and Dr Davies had been reluctant to leave his aunt, but both were required to report back to RAF Scotney, and Wright had his daily duties to attend to.

Kember felt a rumble in his stomach and remembered he'd missed breakfast because of the dawn start. A glance at the wall clock told him it was past his lunchtime and he wished he'd been able to grab some toast with Headley. He took his overcoat and fedora and stood outside, weighing up the pros and cons of the pub versus the tea shop, hoping Wright would soon return from his rounds. An ENSA lorry stopped nearby, obscuring his view of the High Street, and a woman's voice called through the open passenger window of the cab.

'Hello, Inspector. Do you need a lift?'

Kember recognised Paula Unwin, the woman who had been unloading sacks at the encampment, the same one who had waved at him that morning and riled Lizzie.

'No, thank you,' he said. 'I'm waiting for my sergeant.'

'Each to his own,' she said with a smile. 'I'll be around most of the day if you need me.'

He felt himself blush as the lorry pulled away and she waggled her fingers at him. The telephone jangled him out of his embarrassment and he returned inside, snatching at the handset.

'DI Kember,' he said, not appreciating another interruption in an already full day.

'Why haven't you found my niece yet?'

Kember's hackles rose at the sound of Hartson's voice. 'I assure you that we have a strong lead, sir, and should have more news this evening.'

'Well, you'd better have. Because of your dilly-dallying, my brother has already questioned the effectiveness of the Kent County Constabulary. I need a quick resolution for the sake of me, my brother and the chief constable.'

Kember smiled thinly, noting the order in which Hartson had listed the priorities.

'The exhumation went well, thank you for asking,' he said, with as much sarcasm as he thought he could get away with.

'Don't be flippant,' Hartson snapped. 'Do any good, did it, digging up a dead body when you should be out searching for Evelyn?'

Kember bit his tongue. 'Yes, sir. It's a confirmed murder and we have a suspect in custody. The other suspect we want to question is the man reported missing a few days ago.' Kember took a breath. 'There was one other thing, sir. I want your permission to cancel an ENSA pantomime scheduled for tonight in the Scotney village hall. For safety reasons. Given my previous encounter with Group Captain Dallington, and having met the director of the ENSA troupe and his team, I feel it would be beneficial to have your support.'

'You know I can't be seen interfering in military matters, Kember. Even ENSA.'

'But sir, I believe the serial murderer—'

'That bloody term again,' Hartson spat. 'If I hear one more word about your so-called Handyman or hear you're still cavorting with that charlatan psychic—'

'I'm sorry, sir. The connection is bad. I'll call on a better line when I have news. Merry Christmas.'

'Merry bloody—?'

Kember put the receiver back with more force than he'd intended before Hartson could explode. Running two murder inquiries, a missing-person case and a possible kidnapping was difficult enough without senior police officers and government officials breathing down his neck, and offering not a shred of help.

He rang the air station and asked to be put through to Group Captain Dallington, holding little hope of gaining any support from him either, and so it proved. Dallington hung up and Kember grabbed his coat and hat again. 'Will nobody take some responsibility,' he muttered, as he left the station.

Elias Brown, in full Home Guard uniform, arrived on his pushbike as Kember crossed the road to meet Sergeant Wright. The bike's brakes squealed as Brown swung his right leg over the saddle while standing on the left pedal, and he brought it to a well-practised halt.

'Ah, Captain. While you're here. I have a request to make of you.'

'Oh, yes?'

'If any of your men aren't going to the pantomime tonight, could you spare them to guard the village hall and watch for signs of suspicious activity?'

Brown's eyebrows rose in surprise. 'You want my men to look out for the Handyman? Are there no police available?'

Kember pressed his lips into a thin line and shook his head. 'Unfortunately, like everywhere, we're overstretched. Group Captain Dallington is allowing Flight Lieutenant Vickers to bring some of his men to watch the High Street. I don't want a repeat of the assault that occurred at the last performance.'

'Cancel it.'

'I asked.'

Brown sighed. 'Very well. I'll see you tonight. If you'll excuse me, Inspector.'

Kember noticed Brown's odd cuff button that Jim Corcoran had mentioned as Brown saluted and wheeled away.

'Pompous arse,' Wright muttered.

Kember couldn't disagree.

'The pantomime starts in' – he looked at his watch – 'three hours, and I don't want anyone to get hurt this time. Hartson may not think so but lives are at stake tonight, including that of his niece. We need to keep an eye on Martin Onslow and the rest of the cast.'

'You told me Onslow is a middle-aged man with grey hair and no moustache,' Wright said, with a frown. 'And he smokes cigars.'

'He's a performer. He could easily wear a wig and a glued-on moustache, and smoke the occasional cigarette. After all, I'm as unconvinced as Lizzie, by his explanation of why he doesn't travel with the rest of the troupe when they move to their next engagement.'

'Perhaps he shies away from getting his hands dirty, sir,' Wright said. 'In my experience, the higher up they are, the more they rely on others to do the donkey work.' He gave Kember a sideways glance.

Kember ignored the sly dig. 'It also gives him plenty of time to look over a new place on his own. Perhaps he makes little forays into a new area, scouts for likely victims, and decides the when, where and how before turning up officially with everything mapped out in his head.'

'Is that likely, sir, with a war on and movement difficult?'

'I suspect it might be easier to get around than anyone thinks, or is willing to admit. Talking of which, Evelyn's lingering perfume suggested she'd been in Peter's cottage just before we arrived but she might be hiding elsewhere. We know Peter bought two train tickets but their plan might be to meet at the station.'

'Not a good idea with a killer on the loose,' Wright said.

'Precisely, but I doubt they'll be thinking about that,' Kember said. 'Make sure Captain Brown puts a man beyond Peter's cottage in Meadowbank Lane tonight; two, if possible. They can detain whoever comes out and we'll be there to intercept if either of them reaches the station.'

'What will you do with them, sir, if no crime's been committed?'

Kember sighed and pinched the bridge of his nose with a thumb and forefinger. 'With any luck, they'll turn up early so I can give them a good talking-to. If I can convince them they're making a mistake, I might still conclude these investigations with my warrant card and career intact.'

As they walked past a parked Bedford back to the station, Kember glanced at the lorry and recognised the familiar face of

Paula Unwin. She was standing by the open door, wearing a thin grey raincoat buckled at the waist, smoking a cigarette, staring blankly into the distance. As she trod on the stub of her cigarette and reached up to pull herself into the cab, she caught him looking and smiled. A picture of Lizzie inexplicably flooded his mind as he returned a hesitant smile.

'You all right, sir?' Wright asked. When Kember didn't reply, he shrugged. 'Maybe Bert Garner's car was unavailable. Can't get petrol in the village, now that Andy Wingate's garage stands idle.'

Kember wasn't really listening. His thoughts were of Onslow, Jarvis and Yates. The killer had already shown the desire to take another victim before the troupe left Scotney, and Onslow had the perfect cover and opportunity. Agnes had confessed to the murder of her mother, although he didn't believe her, and she shared culpability for the cover-up. Peter Yates was trickier. If he and Evelyn really were runaway sweethearts, there was little he could do except persuade the both of them that a future away from the support of their families did not offer good prospects.

He opened the door of the police station.

Within a few short hours, he should be able to conclude three tricky investigations. But only if luck was on his side.

◆ ◆ ◆

As Lizzie entered the officers' lounge from the hall, Geraldine rose from the table where she had been speaking to Vickers and walked towards her.

'Ah, Lizzie,' Geraldine said. 'I've not long experienced another tirade from the group captain. Apparently, he just refused to support a request from DI Kember to cancel the pantomime, not that Dallington has any authority over ENSA. It set him off, of course, and your name cropped up again.'

'That wasn't my doing, ma'am,' Lizzie said, fearing that was no defence.

'Even so, you, more than most, should realise that the group captain and wing commander have never warmed to us being on this air station, and it's hard enough for me to keep them off our backs as it is, without you playing at detectives again with DI Kember. I'm told the airfield repairs will be finished by Boxing Day, so I trust your business with him will be concluded soon?'

'I hope so, ma'am,' Lizzie said.

'See that it is.' Geraldine gave her a curt nod and left her standing on her own.

Lizzie went over to Vickers, who was still reading documents in the chair near the windows. She'd been mulling over conversations had with Martin Onslow and Agnes Jarvis, and her concern that Kember was barking up wrong trees had deepened.

'Have you seen Onslow?' she asked, as he looked up.

'Not since breakfast,' Vickers replied. 'Aren't all the performers down at the village hall, getting ready for tonight?'

Lizzie sat. 'They should be, but I don't trust him.' She glanced over her shoulder as if he might catch them talking about him. 'He strikes me as a slippery character.'

'He's a comedian.' Vickers gave a half-smile. 'You've got to have a lot of front to stand before an audience and tell jokes. I couldn't do it.'

Lizzie shook her head. 'There's a difference between confidence and arrogance, and he tips into the latter. He still hasn't given a good explanation for why he never travels with the troupe, and that time gives him ample opportunity to look for new victims. Travelling later gives him an alibi because if bodies are discovered, the times of death would show it couldn't possibly have been him because he wasn't around.' She saw scepticism in the look Vickers gave her, conceding to herself that it did sound unconvincing. 'I'm not saying: if it can't be him, it must be him. I'm saying: I bet no one's bothered to check what he really gets up to when or if he stays behind.'

'Look here.' Vickers leant forward and placed what Lizzie supposed he thought was a reassuring hand on her arm. 'Dallington wouldn't do anything to stop the pantomime going ahead but he did give permission for me to take some men to the village. "On your own head be it" was the phrase he used. That means I'll be on the village streets tonight with my men, and the Home Guard: a show of strength. If anything happens, someone will raise merry hell. If the killer tries again tonight, we *will* catch him.' He tapped her on the arm and leant back.

Lizzie understood Geraldine's position, and knew Vickers had meant to be comforting, but she couldn't help feeling something was wrong. Onslow hadn't been seen for a while, which meant he was probably preparing for the show. But what if he was also preparing to attack another woman?

'I've decided to go to the pantomime tonight,' Lizzie said.

'What for?' Vickers asked, pausing in the opening of his cigarette packet. 'You've seen it.' He offered her one; Lizzie declined.

'To keep an eye on Onslow, if I can.'

Vickers' eyes narrowed. 'Kember won't like that. I don't like that.'

Lizzie stood up and straightened her tunic as Vickers lit a cigarette. He looked up at her through a swirl of smoke.

'I could stop you going; have you confined to the air station.'

She gave him a hard stare and he sighed. 'At least take someone with you. And stick with them this time.'

'I heard Dr Headley's going,' Lizzie said. 'I'll accompany him.'

CHAPTER
TWENTY-NINE

Alf Lewis, long-time stationmaster of Scotney Railway Station, unlocked the ticket office and pushed open the door.

'Thank you, Alf,' Wright said, as Kember stepped inside.

Logs that crackled and glowed in a tiny fireplace kept the small room warm, while a simple mesh guard protected the wooden floor from the dangers of stray sparks and errant hot coals. A rack holding a poker, brush, ash pan and coal tongs stood on one side of the fireplace; a coal scuttle on the other. A wooden rack secured to the back wall contained forms and leaflets, and a tray of tickets ready for purchase lay on the counter by the ticket window. A black telephone, rubber stamps on ink pads, and an array of pencils and fountain pens were positioned on another desk near a window currently obscured by a blackout screen. Miscellaneous administrative paraphernalia necessary for the smooth running of a railway station filled every other shelf and tabletop.

'We're grateful for your help, Mr Lewis,' Kember said. 'I know it's an imposition.'

'It's no trouble at all,' Lewis replied. 'Always happy to help Den out. What do you want me to do?'

Kember nodded towards the ticket gate. 'If you can stand over there so as not to draw attention to us in here, that would be a great help. If you think you see Peter Yates approaching, touch the peak of your cap. We won't show ourselves until Yates and Miss Hartson are on the platform or in the waiting room.'

Lewis consulted a silver pocket-watch before slipping it back into his waistcoat. 'The five o'clock to Paddock Wood is due in twenty minutes.'

'We'd better get ready then.' Kember glanced at the ticket-hall clock for confirmation. 'We think they're more likely to catch the half past six, but they could arrive at any time.'

'You want me to stand out here for over an hour?'

Kember tried to look apologetic. 'I'm hoping they'll turn up before then.'

Judging by his grimace and sagging shoulders, Lewis had clearly miscalculated his potential role in the operation. He adjusted his peaked cap and stepped away from the office to take up a position by the ticket gate, muttering to himself and giving the policemen a sideways glare. Kember had some sympathy. Despite the blackout screens fixed to the windows, only one dim light was on in the ticket hall, casting barely as much illumination as a candle, and even with the door closed against the night frost, the stationmaster's breath bloomed in a ghostly white cloud.

In the confines of the office, a desk lamp with a low-wattage bulb cast an eerie, pale-yellow glow that competed with the flickering orange from the fireplace. Wright closed the door and stood with his back to the wall while Kember took off his hat and positioned himself on the far side of the ticket window. They were both out of sight of customers but Kember kept Lewis just in view. He felt his Webley revolver dig into his hip and adjusted his position. They were waiting for a timid pair of runaway sweethearts but, with a vicious killer on the loose, Wright had insisted they break out the police-issue guns.

◆ ◆ ◆

In the weak moonlight, Lizzie could see the black shapes of four ENSA lorries lined up along one side of the High Street. She'd parked her own motorbike outside the police station before walking up to the village hall, where she now stood enjoying a warming cigarette. Bobbing glows from other numerous cigarettes and masked torches, and the excited chattering of children, identified villagers making their way across to the pantomime. She looked up and hoped the Luftwaffe would stay away tonight. It was Christmas Eve, after all.

Brian Greenway approached, removed his ARP helmet and ran his hand back across his head.

'I'm all for having a good time but it wasn't that long ago that London was getting a right pasting,' he said. 'Jerry's unpredictable and could come back at any time.'

'I was thinking the same thing,' Lizzie said. 'But we have more to worry about tonight.'

'Ah, your prey?' Greenway put his helmet on. 'I don't think he'll make a move tonight. Too many people, police and military about.'

'Let's hope so.'

That didn't help last time, she thought. She took a final drag and crushed her cigarette into the ground with her heel. 'Will you be joining us inside?'

Greenway made a face. 'Not my cup of tea.' He adjusted his chin strap. 'Anyway, I'll be out here with the RAF chaps and Home Guard, looking out for your man.'

'You be careful,' Lizzie said. 'There's no telling how dangerous he could be if he thinks he's cornered.' She saw Greenway grin.

'Don't you worry, miss. I've got a whistle and a pair of lungs. The lads with guns will come running. You look out for yourself, mind.' He gave her a loose salute. 'Have a good evening.'

As Lizzie watched him walking slowly towards the church end of the village on another of his ARP patrols, she saw a brief flare of light towards the rear of the village hall. The match illuminated two faces for a few seconds as it lit a cigarette and a cigar, and her heart jumped.

Martin Onslow and Betty Fisher had sneaked out the back way for a private smoke before the performance. Lizzie didn't begrudge them that pleasure, but if he was the Handyman, Betty was in serious danger. Lizzie frowned, suddenly aware of how close they were standing to each other and she wondered whether they had more in common than just smoking. A shudder rippled through her and she realised how cold the night had become, so perhaps all they were doing was huddling together for warmth. Or maybe Onslow had Betty Fisher in his sights as another conquest. Or victim. He had certainly proved to be a smarmy, middle-aged man with an eye for younger women, but did that really make him a killer?

Another match flare much further up the village caught Lizzie's attention. It was too dark to see properly but she thought it must have come from one of Captain Brown's men, the one she'd noticed standing under the canopy of the lychgate, yawning as she'd passed on her Norton.

A car drew up near the hall and disgorged Dr Headley, looking harassed and slightly dishevelled. He saw Lizzie and hurried towards her.

'I must apologise for my tardiness, Miss Hayes.'

'Lizzie, please,' she said. 'Thank you for agreeing to escort me at such short notice. And don't worry, it hasn't started yet.'

'In that case, call me Michael.' He offered his arm. 'Shall we?'

She felt perfectly able to walk in without aid but smiled and accepted the gallant gesture for what it was. Having doors opened for you or chairs pulled out were not life-threatening or soul-destroying acts. As long as the man expected nothing untoward in return, she and many others appreciated such old-fashioned gestures of respect.

She glanced towards where Onslow and Fisher had been standing, but only in time to see the rear door closing.

Inside, the spacious hall seemed unusually small and cramped. Several men stood along the sides and back while their womenfolk and fidgeting children sat in tightly packed rows. A haze of smoke from many cigarettes had already found its way to the ceiling, all of the windows having been closed and locked behind their blackout screens. A small band of musicians seated at the side of the hall near the stage struck up a gentle tune as Headley and Lizzie took their seats, and the buzz of anticipation increased.

◆　◆　◆

Kember raised his eyebrows questioningly at the sounds of metallic clicks and squeaking hinges, and Wright mouthed 'Level-crossing gates'. Soon, the toot and hiss of an approaching steam train filtered through into the office, and the train came to a halt amid louder squeals of metal on metal. Kember heard voices and the slamming of a door. The sharp peep of Lewis's whistle signalled for the train driver to depart and a few deep chuffs told Kember the engine was pulling away from the platform. The chuffs became less laboured and more distant, and the rattle and clanks of the carriages faded as the ticket gate opened and one passenger passed through. Lewis followed and waited for the front door to shut before he sauntered casually over to the ticket window.

'That was the five o'clock,' he said. 'One arrival.' Lewis leant an elbow on the small shelf on his side of the window. 'If you say your suspects are running away, I wouldn't expect to see them before quarter past six. They won't want to hang around here for too long.'

'That's true,' Kember agreed. 'We've got a bit of a wait, then.'

'Aye. You can stay in there, if you like, but I've got to get on. The Hawkhurst train comes through at five-fifty but I've got to see to the coal fire in the waiting room, and make sure the postbag and goods crates are ready before then.'

'You get on, Mr Lewis. As long as you're at the ticket gate by six o'clock.'

Lewis nodded and grunted before his shape disappeared into the gloom and through the ticket gate.

'Do you think they'll show, sir?' Wright said, leaning over to stretch his back. 'If I were them, I'd have bought the tickets as a ploy and got off straight away by other means.'

Kember sat heavily on the only chair in the office, his back aching from standing still in one position for so long. 'I still think they'll take a chance on the train.' At least, he hoped so. If Evelyn did get away from Scotney undetected with Peter Yates, Laurence Hartson would explode with anger and his brother, Kember's superior officer, would hold him personally responsible. It would be another nail in the coffin of his career.

◆ ◆ ◆

The curtains across the front of the stage moved as if in a breeze and a head appeared through an open gap, probably to check whether the hall was full. Laughter rippled through the audience and the head disappeared. The band immediately changed tune and tempo, and the lights went down. A few gasps of wonder escaped from the audience as the curtains opened to reveal the colourful scenery.

Several children squealed as Onslow stomped onstage, dressed as the Fairy Godmother but wearing army boots and puffing on a large cigar. He waved a silver wand and recited his opening lines.

'I am the Fairy Godmother so you have no need to worry,

Dear Scotney folk, pin back your ears and listen to my story.

Once upon a while ago, Baron Hardup and his wife,

Had a baby daughter who brought joy into their life.

They thought they'd struck it lucky but their luckiness did plummet,

When the Baroness got ill and sadly kicked the bucket.

Hardup married once again but all they do is row,

She soon turned out quite nasty, a rather wicked—'

'Hello mums and dads, boys and girls!' George Wilkes bounded onstage in a scarlet uniform with shiny buttons, cutting off Onslow's risqué rhyme. 'My name's Buttons. Are you here to have a good time?'

Many adults were still chuckling at Onslow but Ethel Garner's gossip circle tutted.

'Blimey, has Hitler invaded already? Let's try that again. Hello mums and dads, boys and girls. Are you here to have a good time?'

The shouting and waving audience satisfied Wilkes this time and he shooed Onslow offstage before launching enthusiastically into his first scene. Lizzie could see the audience getting sucked into the performance, laughing at Onslow, who appeared onstage frequently. The kids cheered and shouted 'It's behind you' at the right moments, egged on by Buttons, and most of the adults roared with laughter at Onslow's double entendres, even Reverend Wilson.

But something niggled at the back of Lizzie's mind the more Prince Charming's aide and confidant, Dandini, as played by Betty Fisher, appeared onstage. Lizzie's gaze became more distant as she relaxed her eyes, looking through the performance taking place, and thought about the profile she had written in Kember's pocket book.

Lizzie's eyes refocused as Dandini strode onstage again, and her mouth opened as realisation hit like a blow to the head. Here, in front of her eyes, was a woman dressed as a man, using costumes and make-up to change her appearance. Betty Fisher had access to all the disguises she wanted, including her own mask of Frankenstein's monster used to try to frame the carpenter. It would have been easy for her to steal the hatchet, too.

Lizzie looked at Headley beside her, who was wrapped up in the antics onstage, grinning along with everyone else in the hall. She looked back at the stage and the scene had changed: Prince Charming and Dandini had disappeared. She glanced at her watch: quarter past six. Fifteen minutes to the interval. Lizzie mouthed to Headley that she needed some fresh air, and touched his arm for him to stay when he began to rise from his seat. She smiled reassuringly and left through the two sets of double doors, deftly negotiating their blackout curtains.

The cold hit, her breath forming clouds in front of her face, and she buttoned her greatcoat up to the neck. It took a couple of minutes before her eyes adjusted to the blackout but she could no longer distinguish any other presence than that of the Home

Guard private who stood looking bored by the sandbags to one side of the entrance.

The Handyman killer could be anywhere out here. What if she was wrong about who and what he – or she – was? She'd been convinced it was a man and now she thought it was a woman. She needed a smoke and reached for her cigarettes but froze when she heard the rasp of a shoe on a stone step. She moved to the corner of the hall and gently leant forward until she could see along the whole length of the building. There, barely visible in the darkness at the far end, stood Onslow and Fisher again, but this time they weren't smoking.

Lizzie moved away silently and frowned with puzzlement. Onslow and Fisher were kissing. Passionately. Suddenly, a piece of the jigsaw she thought had been in the right place moved into another and Onslow's dalliances made a different kind of sense. She'd thought he delayed his departures and arrivals to provide him with an alibi of being in a different place while actually he scouted ahead to seek out further victims in a new hunting ground. Now she realised it was to allow him, an older man, and Betty Fisher, a much younger married woman, to carry on a clandestine affair. The splitting up of the so-called poster group made sense too. McNee played the part of the faithful lookout while Wilkes and Fisher pretended to be lovers cheating on their spouses. From what Kember had said, Wilkes did seem to have genuine affection for Fisher. Maybe he'd been assisting with her subterfuge to keep her close and in her good books, in the hope that her affair would fizzle out and he'd get his own chance. It was a simple thing for them to say Fisher, who had travelled ahead with the troupe, had been with them to give her an alibi while she was off meeting Onslow. The secret affair was none of her business and she didn't begrudge either of them a little fun. She might think Onslow was lecherous, what people called *a ladies' man*, and the unfaithful Fisher rather

345

foolish, but in these times, you found love, comfort and solace wherever you could.

What did worry her though was the hole left by moving the jigsaw piece. If neither Onslow nor Fisher was the Handyman, who was?

Kember peered through the ticket window into the gloom beyond. Lewis was back in position by the ticket gate rubbing his hands together and stomping his feet for warmth, the five-fifty to Hawkhurst long gone, preparations for the six-thirty to Paddock Wood completed.

'They're cutting it fine, sir,' Wright said.

Kember glanced at the office clock. Twenty past six. It would only take a minute to rush through the ticket gate to the platform and board the train, but even he'd thought the couple would have arrived by now. Could they – *he* – be wrong? What if buying the tickets had been a ruse all along? He was supposed to be a detective, a Scotland Yard detective. Surely his knowledge, experience and intuition counted for something?

'Not long now, Sergeant,' Kember said, more as reassurance to himself than to Wright. 'Not long now.'

CHAPTER THIRTY

Lizzie strolled towards the police station, her mind churning over what she'd just witnessed, and had just reached her parked Norton when the door of the telephone box squeaked open. She jumped but the RAF warder positioned inside seemed to not notice.

'Miss,' he hissed.

She looked over, enquiringly.

'Best stay inside, miss.'

'Have you seen anyone tonight?' she whispered back, her heart still thumping.

'Only one of the ENSA girls, but best be safe than sorry.'

Lizzie's ears pricked up. 'ENSA girl? Was she wearing men's clothes? Did you speak to her?'

'She wore an overcoat and an ENSA cap, if that's what you mean, miss. I warned her to go back but she showed me her papers and said she needed to check the oil in the lorry she drove.'

Pain stabbed at her temples: she'd been wrong all along. It wasn't Onslow or Betty Fisher after all. It was Paula Unwin, the woman driver who'd made eyes at Kember.

'Are you all right, miss?'

'Did she say where her lorry was parked?'

'Down by the crossroads.'

'Jesus Christ,' she hissed. 'Come with me.' She opened the door wider.

'I can't leave my post,' he complained.

'If you don't, someone else may be murdered and the killer you're looking for will get away.'

The RAF warder looked pained, but nodded and stepped from the box.

'This way,' Lizzie commanded.

She hurried towards where the Bedford lorry was parked on the garage forecourt by the crossroads. A quick check proved it to be empty. Acorn Street appeared deserted but what looked like two pieces of luggage and a bundle were lying on the ground about fifty yards to the left, along Meadowbank Lane. Lizzie approached cautiously, the soldier by her shoulder with his .303 Lee-Enfield rifle at the ready, her shoes and his boots echoing in the still of the night. Her worst fears were realised when the soldier prodded the bundle with his rifle and it groaned. Lizzie bent down and turned Yates' head gently to look at his face. He groaned louder and her hand came away black and sticky with blood.

'Where's Evelyn?' Lizzie said, forcibly.

'Not a man,' Yates slurred. 'Took Evie. This.'

Lizzie could barely make out his words, and Yates groaned again as he tried to get up. Then she noticed he was offering her what looked like oily rags. She took them and realised with a jolt that it was the dark hair of a man's wig. The driver must have put it on after leaving the soldier and Peter must have torn it off her head in the struggle.

Lizzie looked up at the soldier.

'Have you got a whistle?'

'Yes, miss.'

'Blow it loud, then fetch DI Kember from the railway station and Dr Headley from the hall. And give me your torch.'

The soldier handed over his torch and ran back to the cross-roads blowing his whistle.

'Lie still for a while,' she said to Yates. 'Help is on its way.'

Something clattered further down the lane and the hairs of her neck stood up. Lizzie left Yates lying in the middle of the lane, hoping help would come soon, and walked slowly towards where she'd heard the noise. After a few yards, she noticed what looked like a boot sticking out from behind a bush. Moving closer, she recognised the shape of another bundle as being a man in Home Guard uniform. Captain Brown must have stationed him close by to watch for Peter and Evelyn, but a dark, shiny line across his neck told her how he'd died.

She moved on as quietly as possible, at a crouch, although she didn't know why she should in the dark. She had nothing with which to defend herself, but if the clatter had been the driver escaping with Evelyn, she had no choice but to follow.

The distant whistle-blowing stopped and so did Lizzie. In front of her was a gate leading into the fields. Every sound she made might now be heard and every movement might be seen, putting her own life and that of Evelyn in greater danger. Lizzie knew nothing about the countryside beyond the gate. Yes, she knew there were meadows, fields, trees and the River Glassen, but not enough to know where to tread and where to look. And it was too dark. The blood pumping in her ears sounded louder than the breathing she was trying to control, but now was not the time for her body to take over. She focused on letting her mind do the unique thing that others thought made her *not quite normal*, allowing her to imagine what she would do if she was the killer.

I can't kill the girl because she is too heavy to carry very far. I could cut her hands off here and now but I can't stop in case my pursuers catch up. All I can do is threaten her with the consequences of struggling or making a noise, and make it back to my place of safety.

My place of safety.

Lizzie's own thoughts resurfaced. Where would be a place of safety? She thought back to the curate seated in the dockyard storeroom like a king in his throne room. And it hit her. Somewhere nearby must be a barn or building. Disused, maybe. Somewhere sheltered where a man could be kept. By looking for the killer in the places she'd left the dead bodies of the women, they'd forgotten to look for the places she might keep a man, alive.

An image flashed into her consciousness and she knew.

Arriving at a run, back to where Yates was now sitting at the side of the road being tended by Dr Headley, she almost vomited when she realised that two rifles and a revolver were aimed at her chest.

'I'm Lizzie Hayes,' she managed to gasp, trying to catch her breath.

'Lizzie?' Vickers stepped forward.

'Where's Kember?' she panted.

'He's being fetched as we speak.' He holstered his revolver.

'Paula Unwin, the ENSA driver, has taken Evelyn Hartson.' She pointed towards the end of the lane. 'She's just gone through there and I think she's heading in the direction of the camp.'

Vickers barked orders for his men to begin pursuit and the two of them set off at a trot in the direction Lizzie had indicated, rifles at the ready.

'I've given him morphine and we've called an ambulance,' Headley said. 'He'll live but he'll have a cracking headache in the morning, like a hangover from hell.'

'I'm afraid you've a Home Guard man over there with his throat cut,' Lizzie said. 'Sorry,' she added, turning away. 'I've got to get to the old shepherd's hut in case your men miss Unwin.'

'Where?' Vickers asked.

'Kember will know where I mean,' she called back. 'Follow me as soon as he gets here.' She starting running towards the cross-roads, knowing Unwin had a head start and there was little time to lose.

Lizzie turned right at the garage and ran to her Norton, her lungs on fire. She heard Vickers close behind, shouting for her to wait, but she swung a leg over and kick-started the engine, the roar echoing off nearby buildings. The rear wheel skidded with a squeal of rubber as she opened the throttle but she kept control, heading for a cloud of bobbing torchlights, scattering the men who were crossing from the village hall to the pub for a quick pint in the interval.

Her destination only half a mile away, Lizzie still took the bends in the lane as quick as she dared, passing the burnt-out barn, until she reached the field where Maisie Chapman had died. Turning off the engine, she let the Norton coast to a stop by the five-bar gate. She pulled the Norton onto its stand and reached for the motorbike toolkit she kept in a pouch behind the saddle.

The only thing in there worthy of being called a weapon was a screwdriver.

It would have to do.

She opened the gate just enough to squeeze through and stepped onto the grass, crispy and white with frost. She heard it crunch underfoot as she crept along the side of the field, next to the drainage ditch where Maisie had lain. She continued to follow the hedgerow along the next side until a stile crossed into the adjacent field. This was the route the birdwatchers had taken back to the lane before they had discovered her body. It was in this direction she remembered seeing the roof of the shepherd's hut Wright had mentioned. The one sometimes occupied by summer workers but no longer fit for winter living.

The perfect place to keep a man out of sight, ready to receive the hands of women.

Lizzie crossed another stile into the field where the old Victorian shepherd's hut sat by a fence in front of a line of bushes and a thin screen of trees. This led along the left side of the field to another fence at the start of Glassen Wood.

The hut's small iron wheels, often used in its heyday to move it around the manorial estate, had sunk a few inches into the earth, forever tethered there by the undergrowth that sought to claim it for its own. Paint flaked off the rusted corrugated-iron cladding and frost glistened on the curved roof with its stubby chimney. The glass in its window was grubby and broken, and the wooden steps looked rotten, but they bore her weight as she moved up to the door.

She stopped, cold air searing her lungs.

No sound came from inside or out, except the blood whooshing in her ears.

She hoped she was right and Unwin would bring Evelyn here. It would be difficult to drag a reluctant victim across the fields and meadows all the way from the village in the dark so she believed she'd arrived in good time. She nestled a closed padlock in the palm of her hand and remembered Wright saying the police from Tonbridge had checked the hut and found it locked. Irritation made her frown. She knew locks could be picked but had she made a mistake? Was she in the wrong place? She gave the padlock a sharp tug of frustration and almost cried out in surprise when it came away in her hand, still attached to the hasp and complete with rusty screws. The wood of the door and frame hadn't rotted to that degree so she could only suppose that Unwin had levered it off, and pushed it back in place to look untouched.

Holding the screwdriver like a knife, Lizzie opened the door one inch and listened. No sound came from inside but her nose detected the faint odour of death underneath the strong smell of rotting wood and damp, and she supposed this cold snap had been as effective as a refrigerator for preserving a dead body. She paused for a moment, listening and hoping to squeeze a little bit more night vision from her eyes.

She opened her eyes wide and pulled the door fully open, screwdriver brandished in the way many of the criminals she'd interviewed in Oxford Prison had described when relating their own street fights. She peered inside the hut.

Silence.

Confident she was alone, she made sure she left the lock outside in a position she hoped could be mistaken for it having dropped off of its own accord, stepped inside and shut the door.

She switched on the soldier's torch, gasped and stepped back.

A man, eyes frozen open in death, was sitting on a wooden chair, propped up against the far stone wall, his legs stretched out before him. Lizzie immediately recognised Kenneth Jarvis from the photograph in the house he shared with his wife, Agnes. Lizzie had been right. Kenneth hadn't run away with Evelyn; he'd been a victim all along. A pair of ghostly-white feminine hands lay in his lap, positioned at the ends of his arms where his own hands used to be, to give the illusion of one body. She'd been right about this, too. He, or she as Lizzie now knew, had been collecting the hands of women to fix to the body of a man. She didn't yet fully understand why, but it wouldn't be long before Unwin arrived with Evelyn.

Lizzie moved cautiously around the room, trying to find a suitable position to lie in wait, and almost screamed when she stepped on something squishy that gave way under her weight. She shone the masked torch down, expecting to see a dead animal, and recoiled at the sight of two pairs of hands discarded like chicken bones at a medieval banquet. One pair had the thick wedding band of a man. *Kenneth's*, she thought. The other was feminine. *Respectful of the dead, but not the hands if they don't fit.*

Maisie Chapman, Dorothy Ingram, Kenneth Jarvis: their hands were all here.

Lizzie felt the usual telltale signs of her empathic trinity – an oncoming anxiety attack, a sense of foreboding and sadness – beginning to build and moved away from the decaying flesh. Passing behind a chair, she noticed a dog-eared photograph lying face down on a table set against the wood-lined wall. She picked it up and looked at the monochrome image, creased across the middle where the owner had folded it. If she didn't know better, she might mistake it for Kenneth Jarvis. The likeness was striking but not perfect. She remembered the photograph of Kenneth she'd seen in his house, a man with strong workman's hands. There was something very different about the man in this image, and at first she couldn't pinpoint it. And then, suddenly, there it was. The man she was looking at had, in marked contrast to Jarvis, unusually delicate, almost feminine hands. She turned the photograph over and read the inscription she'd noticed written in pencil on the back:

Dr Jeremy Unwin FRCS. 1878-1940

Now she understood what had driven Paula Unwin to pursue young women.

It had all been about love: never hate.

She knew death affected people in many ways and some were unable to cope with the loss of those closest to them, especially a beloved parent. She had lost count of the number of cases she'd heard about where a child left behind, however old, had turned to crime, ended up in a mental asylum or had committed suicide. The grief from bereavement could be all consuming, but those who turned to serial murder for any reason were as rare as hen's teeth, thank God.

Paula Unwin had become one of the less fortunate, but grief had only been the finger to flick the switch in her mind.

Lizzie turned the photograph over again. *A handsome man*, she thought. If the eyes really were windows to the soul, Dr Unwin had been a good man. It was easy to imagine that Paula's mind, unable to deal with the trauma of her father's death, had convinced her he couldn't really have died. It was all a lie and he was still out there somewhere. As the days passed and her father never returned, her descent into madness would have begun. Lizzie remembered the ENSA headpiece. Seeing Betty Fisher playing Frankenstein's monster may have sown the seed and convinced her that she could recreate him, resurrect him, if only she could find a strong man on which to place delicate hands.

Lizzie's heart jumped as the hut's steps creaked, and she turned as the door was pulled open. Framed in the opening was a young woman she knew must be Evelyn, eyes wide with fear, being held by Paula Unwin. Lizzie saw the glint of moonlight on the revolver Unwin held against Evelyn's temple.

'Drop that and turn around.'

Lizzie had no option but to comply, and heard shuffling as Unwin manoeuvred Evelyn into the hut.

Lizzie started to turn her head. 'I—'

The pain that exploded across the back of her neck was as unexpected as it was short, as consciousness left her and she fell to the floor.

CHAPTER
THIRTY-ONE

With barely five minutes to go until the arrival of the six-thirty to Paddock Wood, the silence of the ticket hall ruptured when its doors burst open. Wright was already opening the ticket-office door for Kember as he leapt from his chair. They both ran into the hall, expecting Yates and Evelyn to be making their escape. Kember stopped suddenly, causing Wright to bump into him, and stared at the figure of an RAF warder brandishing a rifle. Lewis stood stiff and wide-eyed with shock, and the warder's gaze darted between all three of them.

'DI Kember?' the warder snapped.

'That's me,' Kember said, stepping forward.

'Urgent message from Flight Lieutenant Vickers, sir. The boy has been attacked and the girl taken.'

'Taken?' The news felt like a physical blow.

'Two of our men are chasing them across the fields, and Miss Hayes says to meet her at the old shepherd's hut. The doctor is with the boy.'

'Shepherd's hut?' Kember couldn't help keep echoing the warder's words. 'Did she say why?'

'No, sir.'

'What the bloody hell was she doing in the village tonight?' Kember turned to Wright. 'Do you know which hut she means?'

'I can think of one, sir,' Wright said. 'Near where Maisie Chapman was found.'

'Of course.' Kember remembered seeing the dilapidated roof of a small building beyond a hedgerow in a distant field. 'Didn't we search it?'

'It was padlocked and not considered necessary. Anyway, it's too old, broken and bitterly cold to live in at this time of year.'

'But perhaps the kind of place to take bodies – or bits of them.' He made for the exit, opened a door and stopped. 'Can you come with us?' he said to the warder. 'We may need your help.'

'Yes, sir. The flight lieutenant put me at your disposal.'

Wasting no more time on talk, Kember yanked the ticket-hall doors open and ran to his Minx, parked out of sight around the side of the building. He had already switched on the ignition by the time the warder had clambered in the back, and started the engine as Wright returned the back of the passenger seat to its upright position. Wright plonked down heavily and Kember had the Minx rolling before he'd slammed the passenger door.

'Careful, sir,' Wright cautioned. 'Steady, The Buffs!'

Kember ignored the warning and accelerated through the gateposts into the lane, icy wind whipping in through the missing side window. He saw Wright out of the corner of his eye, wedging himself into his seat with hands braced against the dashboard. The narrow slits of light from the masked headlights were more of a warning to other road users than effective illumination of the road ahead. Quickly reaching the crossroads by Wingate's garage, Kember stamped on the brake at the sight of a masked torch being waved, and skidded the Minx to a halt. Vickers ran across and opened his mouth to speak but Kember was already out and had his seat tipped forward.

'Get in,' Kember snapped, and waited impatiently as Vickers complied without argument.

Kember got back in and pulled the Minx away sharply, tyres squealing, flinging Vickers onto the warder.

'Any chance of winding the window up?' Vickers asked, heaving himself upright again.

'I would if I had one,' Kember said. 'I've not had a chance to get it replaced since it was shot out.'

The horn sounded louder at night, scattering a few stragglers still crossing the road for a drink. Kember concentrated on not hitting anyone but was loath to slow down. Fortunately, men and machine stayed apart and Kember accelerated along High Street and into Manor Lane, leading to the air station.

'Do you know where the hut is?' Vickers asked.

'Near where Maisie Chapman was found,' Kember answered. 'Did your men or the Home Guard see anything?' he asked, furious that the killer had struck unhindered.

'The Home Guard posted a sentry as you asked,' Vickers said. 'I'm afraid he's dead. The Handyman slit his throat.'

Kember fought hard not to swear. 'Who found him and Yates?'

'Beg your pardon, sir,' the warder said. 'It was me and Miss Hayes. I was watching from inside the telephone box when Miss Hayes walked up. She got worried when I said I'd seen another woman walk in the same direction earlier on, so we went to look.'

'What woman?' Kember snapped, not daring to look at the man in his rear-view mirror as black hedgerows flashed by the car.

'One of the drivers from ENSA. Said she was going to check the oil in her lorry.'

'Paula Unwin,' Kember said to himself, thinking that made some kind of sense. It explained the travelling and access to

costumes, including the Frankenstein headpiece and men's clothing. He thought back to his first sight of Unwin, when she'd been
unloading sacks from a lorry. A physically strong women very capable of carrying the deadweight of a body. The thought of *deadweight*
brought a feeling of dread down around his shoulders.

He powered the Minx into a four-wheel drift around an open
left bend, spinning the steering wheel and flinging the car back
as the icy road took a sharp right corner. The rear flicked out and
caught the grass verge, lifting the driver's side wheels momentarily
and threatening to tip the car on its roof, but Kember spun the
steering wheel again and the car slammed back on the tarmac.

'Oh, my,' Wright said.

The language from the back seat was coarser.

The moon obliged with some wintery light as they approached
the familiar field and Kember switched off the headlights, gliding
the Minx to the gap in the hedgerow. Within seconds, they all
stood on the frost-hard ground by the five-bar gate.

'It's open,' Vickers noted.

'And here's Miss Hayes' motorbike,' Wright whispered.

Kember clenched his jaw to prevent himself calling Lizzie's
name. That would alert Paula Unwin and put her in danger.
Instead, he motioned for the others to follow and they began to
creep along the same route that Lizzie had obviously followed earlier. When they stopped at the final stile and looked at the hut
beyond, Kember tapped his pocket, comforted by the weight of
his revolver. Unwin might consider it a refuge, but sitting back
against the fence and bushes, squat and black in the moonlight
like some mythical creature in hiding, the hut looked forbidding
and dangerous.

His heart leapt when he heard a click, and he strained his eyes
for the killer and Evelyn. But the next click had his head snapping
in the direction of the warder. The stupid bastard had chosen the

wrong time to cock his rifle and had probably given away their presence.

◆ ◆ ◆

Lizzie's thoughts began to string together as she regained consciousness. Her head throbbed painfully, a reminder of where she was and what had happened. Her arms, tied together at the wrists, felt like lead weights but she managed to lift them slowly. Turning her head to feel the back of her neck caused a flash of white light and searing pain. Being hit on the head twice in a few days was no good for anyone and she wasn't surprised when she felt the sticky warmth of blood. *It'll be a swine to get that stain out of my collar*, she thought. She was slumped on the frame of a wooden bed in the far-left corner of the room. No mattress. As her eyes began to focus, she found the flickering, yellow glow from a single candle quite adequate to see everything in the hut.

Paula Unwin was leaning over the dead form of Kenneth Jarvis, adjusting his position; the door was closed and sackcloth covered the window; the photograph of Dr Unwin had been bent slightly along its crease and stood upright on the table next to a revolver; and something or someone was on the bed with her. Moving her head again brought another stab of pain to her neck already stiff with bruising, but Lizzie managed to see Evelyn Hartson sitting wide-eyed but unmoving, gag in her mouth and hands tied in front. She looked petrified.

'Ah, you're awake,' Unwin said, plucking the dead hands from Jarvis's lap and discarding them on the floor with the others.

Unwin was dressed in the grey raincoat Lizzie guessed she'd needed after leaving her own blood-soaked greatcoat on the body of Dorothy Ingram. A fake moustache askew on her top lip and her dishevelled hair might have looked comical in other circumstances.

Knowing she'd had the disguise of a man's wig ripped off in the process of killing a soldier and battering Peter Yates over the head, and having bound and carried Evelyn Hartson for half a mile, put a different slant on things.

'You've been quite a nuisance,' Unwin said, turning towards Lizzie. 'Do you know that?'

'I really hope so,' Lizzie said, with her tongue feeling twice its usual size. She took a deep breath and focused her concentration on Unwin to stave off a drift back to unconsciousness.

'But it's fortunate you're here at last. Your hands are exquisite.'

Lizzie automatically pulled her hands tight to her body. Not that it would do any good if Unwin came for them. 'If you cut them off, they'll be dead but still mine. The same as the body of Kenneth Jarvis is still his.' Unwin ignored her and carried on tidying the body of Jarvis. 'I saw the photograph of your father. He was a handsome man, but you can't bring him back.'

This time, Unwin paused and looked over to her.

'I can try.'

Good, Lizzie thought. Unwin was prepared to respond, to talk about her father. It was a way in, however small.

'However hard you try, whatever you think you're making, it will never be your father.'

'What do you know?' Unwin snapped, ripping off her false moustache and flinging it onto the table.

'I know the creations you put together will only ever be pieces stolen from other people, never your father,' Lizzie said, her voice as steady and calm as she could manage. 'And the police know about the others, here in Scotney, Chatham, Croydon, and my friend, Catherine Summers, in Duxford.'

Unwin, revolver held loosely in her right hand, retreated to the chair by the table. On the floor beneath lay what looked like another blood-soaked bundle of cloth, probably the overcoat she had worn when she killed Maisie Chapman.

'Mary Shelley knew what she was writing about,' Unwin said, a sparkle in her eyes like a child who has discovered Santa Claus is real. 'I realised from the start that I wouldn't get it right first time. All I need is someone with his likeness, and the right pair of hands.'

'You'll never find what you're looking for this way, Paula,' Lizzie said, in the soothing voice she'd used when interviewing so many prisoners at Oxford Prison. She hoped using Paula's first name would draw her in further and help her to see Lizzie as a confidante. 'You know in your heart that the pieces you put together will never be as perfect as he was. I know it's hard and I know it hurts, but until you let your father go, trust me, you'll never be free of this pain.'

'That's what I'm trying to do,' Unwin said, the elation suddenly gone. She put the revolver on the table and wiped her eyes.

'How did he die?' Lizzie asked.

'Bowel cancer.' Unwin blew her nose. 'All those people he'd saved and helped over the years and his colleagues couldn't save him. It wasn't fair. He'd done so much good; he'd earned a longer life.'

Lizzie nodded. 'You thought that by doing this, God would take pity and resurrect him.'

'Do you think I'm stupid?' Unwin snapped, eyes blazing. 'I loved him, but I know I can't bring him back forever.'

The sudden mood swings worried Lizzie as she studied Unwin looking at the photograph again. She'd been wrong about there being a measure of hate in her actions. They'd been about love all the time. But something in the way she'd said she loved her father seemed odd. Almost too forceful.

'Most children love their parents,' Lizzie said softly. 'Why did you love him so much?'

Unwin wiped another tear. 'Mum died when I was very young and he took care of me. Every day. I don't mean just dressed me and fed me when I was little. He was always . . . affectionate and attentive.' She gave Lizzie a sharp glance. 'Nothing inappropriate. He gave me the love of two parents, and was always a gentleman and by my side when I needed him, but I couldn't be with him when he died.'

It seemed to Lizzie that the way she spoke about her father said more about her own love for him than the other way around.

Unwin sniffed and sighed. 'All I wanted to do is see him for a few more seconds, a minute, to kiss him goodbye.'

Lizzie tried to remember the work of Sigmund Freud. He had described a female version of his male Oedipus complex theory. Yes, that was it, something Carl Jung had later renamed the Electra complex. His theory suggested that a daughter needed to go through a stage of competing with her mother for her father's affections. Girls flirted with their fathers and practised sexual behaviours, but with no sexual contact.

Lizzie frowned.

According to the theory, all that should have worked itself out by the time Unwin was about six years old, but if her mother had died that early . . . the Electra complex might never have been resolved. Unwin could still be experiencing possessive love for her father. Nothing sexual, but if her feelings were strong enough, that might be the reason she couldn't let him go and could explain why his untimely death had caused her to try to see him one last time, in some way that made sense to her.

'I can see that Kenneth looked like your father,' Lizzie said. 'Why wasn't that enough? Why did you need the hands?'

Unwin looked tired now.

'Dad used to stroke my hair and tell me everything would be all right because we had each other,' she said. 'He was a Fellow of the Royal College of Surgeons so his hands were as important to him as they were to me. I often sat in the students' gallery, watching him as he taught surgery. We were mesmerised by him as he performed miracles in front of us, using his scalpel with such skill like a conductor uses his baton.'

And the last jigsaw piece slotted into place.

That was where Unwin had gained her knowledge and why she used a scalpel. With such a deep-rooted but skewed connection to her father and his memory, that was why the curate, Kenneth Jarvis and the women could never be enough.

Suddenly, Unwin grabbed the revolver and leapt to her feet. Lizzie hauled herself off the bed, fighting momentary dizziness, and gave Evelyn a sharp look as she began to whimper. Sounds carried at night and they'd all heard the noise, the cocking of a rifle. She was torn between hoping it was Kember and hoping it wasn't, praying he'd stay safe. Then she felt guilty that it might be Wright or Vickers about to be shot. As grateful as Lizzie was for the arrival of help, it had put them in serious danger. She had almost broken through to the woman inside the serial murderer but now they were worse off than back to square one.

They all jumped as the body of Jarvis slid sideways and fell off the chair.

Unwin scowled and tied a length of cloth across Lizzie's mouth to gag her. She then crossed to the bed. 'Grab the headboard and help move this to the front door,' she hissed at Lizzie. 'That detective has taken a fancy to you so keep quiet.' She yanked Evelyn to her feet. 'If you don't, I'll kill the girl first, then you.'

Lizzie complied but froze, ready for a bullet, when one of the bed's legs scraped the floor. Unwin gave her a sharp look but didn't shoot, instead motioning her to a thick tarpaulin sheet hanging on the wall where the bed had been.

'Pull it,' Unwin snapped.

Lizzie ripped away the sheet and her heart sank to her stomach at the sight of a warped square of plywood barely covering a large, irregular-shaped hole the size of half a door. The protective, corrugated-iron panel must have been missing for decades, leaving the wood exposed and rotting away. Unwin took hold of Evelyn and ordered Lizzie to remove the plywood. Certain that Unwin would kill them both without compunction, she moved the wood aside and felt bitter-cold air whip through the opening.

She turned her head and watched Unwin take a dusty old rag, tear the rotten material into three, and hold them over the candle flame. When they were alight, she threw one against the door, one across the table and chair, and one onto the bed's wooden frame. Finally, she placed the candle by the body of Jarvis, ensuring his clothing caught in the flame.

As the fire took hold against the dry rot, Lizzie turned away, sickened, and gasped at the jab of the gun in her back, painful even through the thickness of her greatcoat. She took the hint and manoeuvred herself into a sitting position at the edge of the hole. The wood here had become spongy with wet rot and pieces broke away as she tried to grab hold. After another jab from the gun, she stepped into the dark night.

CHAPTER
THIRTY-TWO

Kember and the others froze at a sound from inside the hut. Someone was definitely inside but there was no way of knowing who or how many. Lizzie's motorbike confirmed she had made it here and suggested she might be inside. They'd given Paula Unwin a head start, and she must have made it back with Evelyn Hartson by now. That meant all three could be inside. It was a corrugated-iron, single-storey hut on wheels, with one window and one door. How on earth could they get everyone out safely?

Frozen grass crunched.

Kember spun to his right, gun raised. The others copied, waiting for the next sound. Two figures with rifles stumbled from the shadows and became recognisable as RAF warders. Vickers held up his hand to signal 'halt' and pressed a finger to his lips for silence. His men obeyed and Kember lowered his revolver.

Wright leant towards Kember and whispered in his ear. 'If we heard them, Unwin must have heard us. What do we do now?'

Good question, Kember thought. Unwin couldn't escape without being seen and they couldn't go in with all guns blazing in case they hit Lizzie or Evelyn. If they weren't already dead, Unwin might have tied them up and be ready to shoot them. He glanced at Vickers, who was watching him. Clearly, the RAF policeman had never faced a situation like this. Even Kember had limited experience of sieges and the taking of hostages. Some had gone well; some had not.

Kember looked back to the hut. Here he was, standing in the corner of a frozen field, in the dark, with the chief inspector's niece and someone he had great affection for trapped inside a rundown hut with a serial murderer, someone intent on building effigies from living people. A blast of icy wind cut through his overcoat and he realised his back was aching. For one moment he thought he heard the sound of running water but shook his head to clear it. They were all waiting for him, and he'd made his decision. He beckoned to Vickers and whispered in his ear.

'There's nothing we can do while they're inside. We need to get her talking and persuade her to show herself.'

'Is that wise?' Vickers whispered back.

'I don't think she's finished her search for hands just yet and won't want to surrender, or die, so I'm going to talk to her. Maybe she'll make some demands.'

'Such as?'

'I'd put money on her telling you to drop your guns and step away,' Kember said. 'She can't stay in there forever, so I think she'll take a chance on using Lizzie and Evelyn as hostages to get away.' Kember suddenly remembered seeing Unwin at the ENSA camp with a gun and swore at himself for not querying why a civilian, even one wearing khaki, was armed. 'I'm sure she has a gun; probably a .455 Webley revolver.'

'How the hell do you know that?' Vickers asked.

'I saw her with a gun and I'm convinced it was she who shot out my car window near Glassen Farm.'

'Jesus.'

367

Kember gave him a wry smile. 'He's not going to help us now, Ben.'

'Should we shoot her?' Vickers asked.

'She'll have no qualms about killing us, especially if she realises that we're not going to let her leave.' Kember became aware of the weight of the .38 Webley still in his hand. 'Maybe she'll see sense, but if there's any doubt about her intentions . . .'

Vickers nodded his understanding.

'Sergeant Wright and I will stay by the stile,' Kember continued. 'You and your men should space out along this hedgerow, keeping to the shadows.'

Kember wasn't sure people like Paula Unwin could see sense in the way others did. She had a warped idea of what needed to be done and how to do it, and he suspected any rational request would be met with suspicion and hostility. He saw Vickers give his men the orders and watched as they melted back into the shadows.

'Paula Unwin,' Kember shouted. 'This is DI Kember of the Kent Police. Give yourself up and let the others go.'

Kember waited but expected no response to this first attempt. None came.

'Let Miss Hartson and Miss Hayes go,' he tried again. 'They've done nothing to deserve this.'

Kember thought he heard running water again, louder this time, but they were nowhere near a stream.

'Come on, Paula,' he urged. 'If you talk to me, I'm sure we can work something out.'

Using her name to gain rapport and trust was an old ploy and he found it odd that Unwin wasn't responding at all. Hostage takers usually said something, even if it was to make demands, threaten or hurl abuse. Silence was highly unusual.

'Can you promise me that Miss Hartson and Miss Hayes are all right?'

Making a few simple requests was a good way to wheedle his way in. But there it was again. He listened hard and realised it wasn't water.

'Christ! It's on fire!' he shouted. 'We have to get in there.'

Caution was thrown to the wind as he stepped from safety and moved to the window. Vickers ran forward and flattened himself against the iron wall on one side of the door, a warder taking the other side. The sound of crackling timbers became louder and smoke began to drift through the gap around the door.

'We'll have to kick it in,' Kember said.

Vickers beckoned to his other men, who came forward at a run, but they stopped short as part of the roof sagged and flames shot skyward.

◆　◆　◆

Lizzie heard someone shouting but was already through the hole and tumbling onto the thick grass behind the hut. Evelyn came next followed very quickly by Unwin. Broken fence rails provided a gap through which they were bundled into the next field on the far side of the line of trees. Lizzie and Evelyn stumbled along in front of Unwin, feet crunching on the ground but disguised by the crackle of burning as flames took hold. She thought she could smell burning flesh but the wind was in the opposite direction and she chided herself for being stupid. Evelyn cried out through her gag each time she stumbled, Lizzie at her elbow for support, but Unwin kept driving them towards the woods beyond.

The cold had really started to get to Lizzie. It had been bearable in the hut but the wind had got up and it plucked at her with icy fingers. She saw light playing on the trees, not so far in front of them now, and heard glass breaking.

She risked a glance back.

Flames escaping through the roof sent showers of sparks swirling in the wind. The firelight gave the plume of smoke an eerie tinge of orange, as if Hell had opened and let the demons loose. Tightness constricted her chest and her breathing became laboured as she thought, for a few terrifying seconds, that Kember might have rushed in to rescue them and been trapped beneath the collapsing roof.

A shove from Unwin made Lizzie stumble forward again and they continued the final few yards to the last stile before the path disappeared into the wood. Unwin seemed in two minds, and Lizzie guessed she was worried about being shown up by the light of the blazing hut and spotted by Kember, but the pause was short. Lizzie helped Evelyn over the stile, watched and then followed by Unwin, and they were soon swallowed among the trees.

◆　◆　◆

Vickers' men yanked open the door, momentarily driven back as a ball of hot smoke and flame escaped and tumbled skyward. Kember smashed the window with the grip of his Webley and snatched the burning sackcloth from its nails. For a moment, all he could see was smoke and flames, but it cleared enough for him to see a burning body against the far wall. In a corner of the hut, a gaping hole showed an escape route and he clenched his teeth in frustration. He stumbled to the rear of the hut, brambles catching and trying to trip him, and saw the gap in the fence. As he rushed through, his first thought was that Unwin was heading for the lane, but his heart thumped when he saw two figures rise above the far hedgerow and disappear in the opposite direction, followed by another.

Kember ran back to the hut where Wright bent down as the two men emerged from the hut, dragging the charred body. 'Ken,' he announced.

Kember signalled to Vickers with a wave of his gun and beckoned to Wright before disappearing through a cloud of hot, swirling smoke. He could hear the others following and set off on a stumbling run until he reached the last stile, the one recently crossed by the women. He could see a path leading into Glassen Wood but nothing that moved. He climbed over and waited.

'You know these woods,' he said to Wright, when he and the others arrived. 'Where are they going?'

'This is all Glassen's land,' Wright said. 'The path goes through the woods, across the river and eventually past the trees into fields the other side. This isn't the only path, though. They criss-cross through the woods, lead south towards the village, north towards the air station, or south-east towards the farm itself.'

Kember swore.

'Is there anywhere someone could hide?' he asked.

'I knew loads of places when I used to play here as a kid. If I was Unwin, I'd stick to the main path, the one I could see, and try to make it through to the other side of the bridge and out of the woods. I'd leave the others behind, make for Cranbrook and try to get an early bus to Maidstone. To be honest, she could go anywhere from there.'

Kember clenched his fists in frustration. He knew *leave the others behind* meant kill them.

'Follow me,' he said. 'We have to stop her shooting Lizzie and Evelyn at all costs and we can't let her get away or she'll start again.'

He didn't wait for an acknowledgement but made straight for the gap in the trees where the path disappeared into the shadows. He thought about using the small bicycle torch he often carried in his overcoat pocket but decided it would destroy his returning night vision and give away their position. Instead, he walked as quickly as he could, trying to avoiding tree roots, brambles and ferns without making too much noise. He hoped Unwin would be too preoccupied and making enough noise herself to be listening out too intently.

A squeal brought him to a sudden halt, and he heard Wright stop a split second after. Sound carried at night but they were in a thick wood so he guessed the sound had come from no more than fifty yards away. He heard the sound of a woman's voice, angry and commanding.

He started forward again, placing his feet more carefully now, until he saw a clearing in the trees. Three figures stood by parallel railings, which he guessed were on the bridge Wright had spoken about. He could hear running water and the faint sound of sobbing. *Evelyn*, he thought. Despite Lizzie's condition, Kember couldn't imagine her breaking down in tears. She had been through too much already to let Unwin get the better of her and wouldn't give the woman the satisfaction of knowing she was scared.

He heard the sharp sound of Unwin's voice and froze. She couldn't know how close he was and would think Lizzie and Evelyn were slowing her down, their usefulness as hostages at an end.

He crept forward along the path and saw Unwin standing at the far end of the bridge, looking agitated. Evelyn was sitting on the step up to the bridge, rubbing her ankle, her hands tied at the wrists and a gag in her mouth. Lizzie was bending over her, a gag in her mouth too.

Unwin suddenly turned and strode back along the bridge, waving her gun at Evelyn.

Time was running out.

Kember realised he was too far away to use his revolver and cursed himself for not asking Vickers for a rifle. Moonlight washed into the clearing through a gap in the tree canopy, fortuitously illuminating the three women on the bridge like performers on a theatre stage, but it would also allow Unwin to see his approach.

He had no choice.

He had to get closer.

Lizzie could feel her anxiety rising in line with Unwin's agitation and knew the woman would become more unpredictable as time wore on. She had stumbled along with Evelyn as best she could, trying to keep up a decent pace so they wouldn't antagonise Unwin into killing one or both of them before help came. Lizzie could neither reach nor employ any of her usual countermeasures, a fact that made the constriction in her throat and chest even worse. Suppressing her own fear while trying to cajole Evelyn into carrying on, especially as the frightened girl had tripped over the step onto the bridge, was no easy task.

'Right, that's it,' Unwin hissed, striding towards them from the far end of the bridge.

Lizzie saw the gun waving and hauled Evelyn to her feet. She was damned if she was going to let this naive young girl get her killed because of a sore ankle.

She tugged the gag from her mouth and said, 'We're coming.'

Unwin pointed her gun at Lizzie's stomach. 'Why don't I just kill you here and now?'

Lizzie's breath caught in her throat when she saw the familiar dead look in Unwin's eyes, and the words refused to come.

Just then, Evelyn swayed as if about to faint. Lizzie would have put her arm around her waist but her own wrists were still tightly bound. Evelyn leant against one of the railings for support and squealed as the old wood moved and cracked under her weight. Lizzie grabbed Evelyn's hands to steady her as Unwin raised her Webley in an instant and pointed it at Evelyn's head.

'I wouldn't do that if I were you,' a voice said from the dark.

Their three heads swivelled towards the direction of the voice, eyes wide with shock, searching for the source. Lizzie gasped as Kember stepped out of the shadows and into the moonlight,

Wright to his left, revolvers in their hands, arms outstretched, pointed at Unwin.

Unwin grabbed Lizzie around the waist with one hand and pressed the gun to her head. 'Careful, I have your sweetheart here.'

Lizzie's thoughts tumbled over themselves as she sought a solution but there was nothing she could do. She had her area of expertise.

This was Kember's.

The seconds seemed to drag on forever as Lizzie waited for the bullet to come. She knew it would be close, but knowing she might be shot instead had a strange effect. Instead of panicking as her anxiety skyrocketed, she became calm and still, as if her mind and body had accepted their possible fate. Out of the corner of her eye, she saw Evelyn slump down and sit on the step, crying again. At least she was out of the firing line.

Lizzie looked Kember in the eyes and said, 'Shoot.'

◆ ◆ ◆

Having stepped away from the safety of the trees and shadows, Kember continued to creep forward until Unwin pressed her Webley against Lizzie's neck. He stopped, keeping his eyes on her. With only her head and one shoulder visible behind Lizzie, fifteen feet wasn't close enough for the accurate shot he needed. He'd missed before. His heart thumping its way out of his chest wasn't helping either. The rushing of blood in his ears, merging with the disorientating hiss and gurgle of running water, wasn't creating the ideal conditions for a clean kill. If his first shot missed, he might kill Lizzie and be shot by Unwin in return.

'What was all that with the hatchet and the Frankenstein mask?' Kember asked, more to himself to snap out of it than to question Unwin.

'I attacked your sweetheart and used them to throw you off the scent. Had you looking at the carpenter and poor old Betty Fisher,' Unwin sneered. 'And the first time I ever saw that mask, I realised Dr Frankenstein had the right idea. All I want is to bring my father back for a few moments. Not much to ask for.'

Kember felt his outstretched gun arm getting tired and adjusted his stance, standing square on and grabbing his wrist with his other hand.

'Steady, Inspector,' Unwin said, sternly. 'Your sweetheart has no value now Kenneth Jarvis is gone.'

Kember felt the piercing stare from Unwin slice right through him.

'Turn back and let me go and I'll leave the pair of them here.' The corners of her eyes wrinkled and she chuckled. 'I meant the girls, not that one's hands.' She indicated Evelyn with a tilt of her head.

He almost shuddered at the constant changes in her voice, as if more than one Unwin stood before him. He could hear scuffles in the distance behind him and knew Vickers and his men would arrive in seconds.

He had to make a decision.

Shoot, or not shoot.

Wright stood with his gun raised. Evelyn had almost crumpled into a ball on the cold step.

'You're not going to let me go, are you, Inspector?' Unwin said, pushing the barrel of the Webley into the soft flesh of Lizzie's neck. 'So say goodbye.'

Lizzie suddenly threw her head back into Unwin's face and screamed, 'Shoot her!' Blood erupted from Unwin's nose and she roared in pain. Despite her tied hands, Lizzie twisted away to her left and jabbed her elbow into Unwin's ribs.

Unwin shouted.

Three shots.

Two bloody flowers, looking black in the monochrome moonlight, bloomed on the front of her overcoat as she pirouetted into the railing, grabbing Lizzie by the collar of her greatcoat. Kember rushed forward but the rotten wood, weakened by Evelyn a few moments earlier, cracked loudly and broke. Lizzie had her arms stretched towards him, but they were already falling backwards into the river.

Kember shed his overcoat, threw himself down the steep bank next to the bridge and landed in five feet of icy water that knocked the air from his lungs and set him panting. He grabbed at a body and turned it towards him: Unwin, mouth open and eyes shut. He let her go as Lizzie surfaced next to him, coughing and gasping for air. He caught her around the waist, dragging her to the bank against the weight of rushing water pulling at their coats.

'Here,' he heard Vickers call and looked up to see his friend's outstretched hand. In turn, two of his men stopped him from sliding down the bank.

'Take his hand,' Kember shouted at Lizzie, who had started to shiver and shake with the shock of the cold.

Lizzie reached up with her tied hands and Vickers pulled her unceremoniously up the bank. Kember managed to haul himself partially clear of the water but was grateful when Vickers' hand reappeared to drag him up to where Lizzie was sitting. He pulled off his dripping jacket and dumped it next to Lizzie's ATA greatcoat that lay in a sodden heap on the ground. She was now enveloped in an RAF greatcoat, her hands untied, and Kember was grateful when his was thrown around his shoulders.

'You two all right?' Vickers asked, peering at them like children who'd suffered nothing more than falling over in the playground.

'I'm fine,' Lizzie said, her teeth chattering. 'What about Evelyn?'

'A sprained ankle is my bet,' said Vickers. 'Otherwise, she's cold and shaken but unharmed.'

'Sir.' One of the RAF warders approached. 'Found this on the bridge.'

Vickers took the gun offered to him. 'A .455 Webley. The gun that shot at you?'

'More than likely,' Kember said, shivering.

He'd heard three shots, fired only one, and seen two hits on Unwin. He felt bile rising. Had he missed? It wouldn't have been the first time, and he doubted the warders would have been slack with their rifles at that range.

He looked enquiringly at Vickers. 'Where's Unwin?'

Vickers shouted to the opposite bank where two masked torches bobbed and weaved as his men searched the water for signs of life.

'Can't see anyone, sir,' one shouted back.

Sergeant Wright appeared at Vickers' shoulder and handed Kember the hat and the gun he'd dropped before going into the water.

'I've checked this bank, too,' he said. 'She's gone.'

CHAPTER
THIRTY-THREE

An hour later, Lizzie sat in the back room of the police station, wearing an old dress and a cardigan borrowed from Alice Brannan. She nursed a mug of insipid tea in her hands, made by one of the RAF warders. The smell of wet cloth pervaded the room as her uniform and greatcoat hung from the backs of chairs in front of the fire to dry. Her hair was flattened and still damp, and the minimal make-up she wore had long since disappeared, but she didn't care what she looked like. All she kept seeing were the three muzzle flashes before she tumbled into the river. It had all been so loud and sudden, she thought she'd been shot. Then she'd feared she'd drown. Kember hadn't exactly risked his life in the six feet of water, however freezing cold, but the gesture meant more to her than the circumstances around it. He'd jumped in when no one else had, not knowing the depth.

She looked up at him, standing by the blackboard with a mug of tea having returned briefly to his room at the pub and come back in dry clothes. He looked preoccupied. Concerned, even. He'd reported the incident to Chief Inspector Hartson and telephoned Laurence Hartson about the safe return of his daughter. Neither conversation seemed to have gone well, almost as if all this had been Kember's fault. He'd rescued Evelyn and found two killers; what more could the Hartsons want from him?

Lizzie looked at Evelyn, sitting on a chair sipping her own mug of tea. Outwardly, the young woman seemed unaffected by the ordeal, but Lizzie could see the signs. Evelyn's hands trembled ever so slightly as she raised the mug to her lips, she picked at the skin around her fingernails, and she chewed the inside of her mouth. Lizzie resisted the urge to do the same.

'I want to see Peter,' Evelyn said.

'Peter's been taken to Pembury Hospital,' Kember explained. 'Dr Headley says he got a nasty crack on the head and lost some blood but he'll be all right. He's being kept in for a couple of days as a precaution.'

Beyond the effects of her ordeal, Lizzie could see being separated from her sweetheart was badly affecting Evelyn. She was understandably worried, especially as the last time she'd seen him he'd been lying in the street, bleeding from a head wound. Lizzie's thoughts turned to Evelyn's parents. Laurence Hartson set great store by status, reputation and saving face, and his wife Joyce had appeared unwilling, or unable, to say anything contrary to his views. Just another well-to-do husband grinding his wife into submission. But the world was changing fast and it seemed increasingly unlikely that the old order would return after the war. Women were back in the factories and fields, just like they had been during the Great War, and Lizzie saw no reason why they should give it all up once the fighting finished. No woman, or man for that matter, regardless of class, background, or circumstance, should be castigated for who they fell in love with, or chose to spend the rest of their life with. She sighed, knowing it was not a popular view.

A new leaflet pinned to the noticeboard caught her eye and set her thinking.

'I'd like to offer you some advice,' she said to Evelyn, standing up and moving to the board.

'I don't want advice,' Evelyn said, sullenly.

'Not if it means seeing Peter?'

Kember almost choked on his tea and Lizzie ignored the warning look he shot her.

Evelyn looked at her. 'How?'

Lizzie glanced at the doorway to ensure they were not being overheard and unpinned the leaflet. 'Sign up for the Women's Land Army.'

'Land Army?' Evelyn scoffed. 'What good will that do?'

'Exactly,' Kember said. 'What good will it do?'

Lizzie ignored him and looked Evelyn straight in the eye. 'Your father doesn't know about Peter, does he?' Evelyn hesitated and finally shook her head. 'The inspector will have to make a full report so I'm afraid you'll have to tell him, not least because you got your friend Ivy to lie for you. But my advice would be to join the Land Army.' Lizzie flicked a glance at Kember. 'Volunteer to work at Glassen Farm, that's where he works, isn't it?' Evelyn nodded. 'It's a big old place so I'm sure it needs a few more workers over there. That way, you still get to see each other and you can work on buttering up your father and mother.'

'My father would never agree.'

'You don't have to tell him until you've joined. He works for the Ministry of Information so he's unlikely to stop you doing your patriotic duty. It would reflect badly on him.'

'I don't think—'

Kember's response was cut short as Vickers suddenly entered the back room, wafting in cold air and the smell of the night.

'They've got Unwin,' he said. 'She's dead.'

Relief flooded across Kember's face and he barely glanced at Lizzie as he hurried from the room.

Lizzie desperately wanted to follow, to make sure the woman who'd nearly killed her really was dead, but she held back and offered Evelyn the leaflet. Evelyn hesitated before taking the paper, then hesitated again, but Lizzie saw something change in her demeanour. The young woman's chin rose and she sat a little straighter before folding the leaflet into a small square and putting it in her pocket.

They exchanged a look, and Lizzie nodded before following Kember.

She found him outside the police station with Vickers and Wright, crowded around the open rear doors of a Morris van, with lettering on the side identifying it as belonging to Glassen Farm. Derek Chapman was standing by the driver's open door, clouds of smoke emanating from the bowl of his pipe.

Lizzie pressed forward and saw Dr Headley examining a body laid in the back of the van, illuminated by their masked torches.

'She got washed downstream and caught by the hawthorn and brambles in the eddy by the oxbow,' Wright said. 'Me and one of the flight lieutenant's chaps pulled her out not half an hour ago.'

'I'll have to open her up back at the mortuary to see if she tried to breathe underwater,' said Dr Headley. 'My guess is, the two bullet entry wounds in her chest gives the game away.' He rolled Unwin's body onto its side. 'Judging by the exit wounds in her back, and the weapons you lot have, I'd say they're probably from a Lee-Enfield rifle.'

Lizzie felt unexpectedly numb. She'd seen dead bodies before but the woman who'd inhabited this one until so recently had killed her friend and so many others, all because the loss of her father had tipped her over the edge. She tried to feel empathy, even sympathy, but all she dredged up was contempt and repugnance.

Kember drew back from the van and took a deep breath. Rifle bullets. So, he'd missed again. It wasn't exactly a habit but how many times would he be faced with a gunfight, only to put people in danger because he couldn't shoot someone? And this time it had been Lizzie. He felt nauseous and wanted to go back inside, but Lizzie was standing next to him. How long had she been there? Had she noticed his horror at Headley's conclusion?

He turned to her as she squeezed his arm and gave him a smile.

He returned the smile and felt a surge of longing and the need to kiss her. As he leant forward, masked headlights swung their way and a car drew up in front of the van. The door flung open almost before it had stopped and Chief Inspector Hartson launched himself out.

'Where's my niece?' he bellowed.

'Inside, sir,' Kember said, feeling Lizzie remove her hand as she took a step backwards. 'Miss Hartson is shaken but unharmed, apart from a minor sprain to her ankle. Dr Headley bandaged it for her.'

'Who had her? Have you got him? I'll kill him.'

'Not a he; she,' Kember said. 'And she was shot tonight by the RAF Police while trying to escape.' He gestured towards the rear of the van. 'Dr Headley has just pronounced her dead. Miss Hartson was held captive by Paula Unwin, one of the ENSA lorry drivers. She was the so-called Handyman, and we have reason to believe she's killed many more men and women, for their hands, including a curate at Chatham Dockyard.'

'Why in God's name wasn't this picked up before it got this far?' Hartson's face, flushed and frowning, came close to Kember's own and he could smell the sweet aroma of port wine on his breath. 'You're supposed to be a Scotland Yard detective, God damn you.'

Kember took a step sideways, ostensibly to show Hartson the body of Paula Unwin but actually to restore breathing distance.

'That's one for the superintendent to take up with the chief constable and Scotland Yard, sir,' Kember said, trying for a wry smile but achieving a sneer. 'ENSA only arrived here a week ago and I seem to remember mentioning the hands, and asking *you* for more men.'

The two men held each other's gaze until Hartson broke away.

'And what of the young scruff with whom my niece was supposedly running away?' Hartson looked over Kember's shoulder towards where the audience was pouring through the open doors of the village hall at the end of the pantomime, as if the young man might be hiding among them. 'What did you say his name was?'

'Peter Yates,' Kember replied, watching Lizzie tying her wet things to her motorbike, and remembering what she had said to Evelyn. 'Miss Hartson met him on a number of occasions in Tonbridge and Tunbridge Wells and they struck up a firm friendship. She wasn't running away, merely staying with him for a few days, but she knew you'd disapprove.'

'Disapprove? Of course, I disapprove. She's a child!'

'She is of age, sir,' Kember said firmly. 'No crime has been committed nor any impropriety.' He paused, seeing Hartson about to explode with rage. 'In actual fact, he fought with Unwin when she attacked them and took your niece, even though Unwin had a gun and Yates was unarmed. Got a nasty crack on the head and lost a lot of blood for his bravery.' He had his fingers crossed so tightly as protection against the lie that he thought they'd break.

'Bravery, eh?' Hartson said, momentarily confused by Kember speaking his language.

'He's a fine young man, sir. A credit to his family and member of the local Home Guard.'

Kember's face fell when he heard a motorbike chug into life. Hartson saw Kember's expression and looked back over his shoulder to where Lizzie sat astride her Norton, putting on her helmet.

'Was she in on this, too?' he growled, glaring at her. 'After everything I said?'

'Only on the periphery, sir. She was held captive by Unwin, too, but managed to keep your niece safe and her spirits up, by all accounts.'

'Uncle!'

Evelyn appeared at the police station doorway and threw herself at the chief inspector, burying her head in his shoulder. Kember was surprised to see Hartson's expression soften. It was a look, almost paternal, that he'd never seen on his superior officer's face before. Words tumbled from Evelyn in a stream, explaining how wonderful and kind and brave Peter was. Kember wanted to take the opportunity to speak to Lizzie alone but her black shape, and that of the Norton with the white slit of its masked headlamp, sped past in a roar of acceleration.

Kember's attention snapped back as the doors of Hartson's car and Glassen's van slammed shut.

'Mr Chapman's kindly agreed to take the body to Pembury,' Headley said, as Hartson's car pulled out and swung around, heading away from the village towards the Lamberhurst Road. 'I'll give you all the bits and bobs tomorrow but I suggest you get some rest. You look like death warmed up.'

'He's right, sir,' Sergeant Wright agreed as Dr Headley walked away to his own car. 'Flight Lieutenant Vickers and I can deal with anything else for the moment. You get some hot toast and jam inside you and have an early night.'

'Quite right,' Vickers said, grinning at him. 'If you will insist on going for a swim in the dead of winter, you'd better get the hot water bottle out.'

Despite feeling like he was being ganged up on, his back had started aching again after his unexpected swim and he appreciated their concern.

'Will you gentlemen be joining us for midnight mass later tonight?' came Wilson's voice, jaunty and hopeful. 'To celebrate the light of the Lord coming into our lives, and the glory and love of God?'

Among all the activity, Kember hadn't seen Reverend Wilson approach and he found he really wasn't in the right frame of mind to sing hymns and carols, tonight of all nights.

'I'm afraid not.' Kember shook his head and put his hands in his overcoat pockets. 'I think He can do without me for one night.' He gave them a short nod. 'Gentlemen.'

He could feel their eyes on him as he turned his back and walked diagonally across the road towards his lodgings at the Castle, but didn't care what they thought. This was the second Christmas of the war and people were killing their own countrymen, even as Hitler pressed his jackboot on the throat of Europe and sent the Luftwaffe to bomb British cities every night. Where was the light and love in that?

The ENSA troupe were busy loading equipment back into their lorries but the pantomime audience had already dissipated, finding it too cold and dark to remain chatting in the street. He thought of Lizzie, returning to the air station to resume her duties in the Air Transport Auxiliary. He had no right to expect her help in the future, but he hoped . . .

He reached the pub and opened the door to the saloon bar, where the low hum of conversation, warm fug of beer and log fire, and the promise of a festive cup of eggnog welcomed him in.

AUTHOR'S NOTE

In the late-nineteenth and early-twentieth centuries, many treatments used on those with mental illness were also tried on sufferers of extreme anxiety, panic attacks and OCD (called Obsessive Compulsive Neurosis during the period of my story). Hydrotherapy, injecting insulin or Metrazol, and electroshocks were used to try shocking the body and brain back to 'normality'. However, many thousands of other people experienced, and continue to endure, milder forms of these conditions, such as those I have given my character of Lizzie Hayes, allowing them to live reasonably normal lives, albeit with certain interventions.

'Thought stopping', first suggested by psychologist James Alexander in his 1928 book, *Thought-control in Everyday Life*, is one of the oldest cognitive behaviour techniques still used. It can help disrupt the irrational thoughts and negative thinking patterns that make it difficult to focus on anything else. While attending a World War Two 'living history' event, I heard one elderly lady speak of cowering in the corner of the family's Anderson shelter as a young girl, snapping a rubber band on her wrist to distract herself from whatever might be happening overhead. My brother, also a sufferer, has tried a wide variety of techniques and found snapping rubber bands against the skin, counting up and down, and inhaling

Vicks to be the most effective. These devices are also portable and discreet, allowing him to employ them and carry on without others noticing anything is wrong. I am grateful to him for sharing his experiences with me.

With the use of these early techniques, and the support and discretion of her friends, Lizzie is able to continue flying for as long as her conditions remain hidden from those in authority. In reality, the mental capacity of women to handle a machine as complex as an aeroplane was openly questioned at the time, and this despite a number of women having been experienced pilots long before war was declared. It was easier for the men, for whom it seemed very little could prevent from flying. At the start of World War Two, many male civilian pilots had been unable to join the RAF because of age or disability. Instead, they joined the Air Transport Auxiliary, and there are documented instances of men with short sight, one eye, one leg, and even one arm being allowed to join the ATA and ferry warplanes. Not for no reason was the ATA first nicknamed *Ancient and Tattered Airmen*!

ACKNOWLEDGEMENTS

Firstly, my thanks must go to my wife, Jane, our daughters, Laura and Holly, and G'ma Mavis. My life would have had less colour, cake and chocolate in it without them.

Thanks also to my brother Steven, whose personal experience of anxiety, panic attacks and OCD informs much about how my character, Lizzie Hayes, feels about these same afflictions and copes with them on a daily basis. In addition, I'm grateful that he continues to attend more living history events, air shows and museums with me than is probably good for either of us.

A special mention goes to Victoria Mulford and her colleagues at the Chatham Historic Dockyard Trust for providing speedy answers to my questions, despite the challenges of the Covid-19 pandemic.

Thank you to Leodora Darlington, Victoria Haslam, Bill Massey, Nicole Wagner, Dolly Emmerson, Sadie Mayne, Swati Gamble, Caroline McArthur and everyone at Thomas & Mercer and Amazon Publishing for taking the rough edges off my work and presenting it so beautifully.

Finally, thank you to my fantastic agent, Nelle Andrew, and Rachel Mills, Alexandra Cliff and Charlotte Bowerman of RML. Nelle was deservedly awarded the accolade of *Literary Agent of the*

Year at the *2021 British Book Awards* because she has the talent to recognise the value in emerging authors and their works, and toils tenaciously on their behalf.

Agents are seen as the gatekeepers to the inner sanctum, that vital link between being traditionally published or not. And it is true – in many ways they are – but they are also the dreamcatchers. They hold their hands under the flood, trying to sieve through the deluge, always hoping something worthy, something of note catches in their fingers. They are like bears fishing for salmon or prospectors panning for gold, searching for the giant nugget but often seeing the tiny sparkling flecks that will one day shine. In my case, she saw my dream, took it and polished it until others could see its shine – and for that I shall be forever grateful.

ABOUT THE AUTHOR

Born in Croydon, Surrey, in 1959, Neil Daws has been a decent waiter, an average baker and a pretty good printer, but most notably a diligent civil servant, retiring in 2015 after thirty years, twenty spent in security and counter-terrorism. Enthralled by tales of adventure and exploration, he became a hiker, skier, lover of travel, history and maps, and is a long-standing Fellow of the Royal Geographical Society. Following the death of his father and uncle from heart disease, he became a volunteer fundraiser and was awarded an MBE for charitable services in 2006. An alumnus of the Curtis Brown Creative writing school, he achieved Highly Commended in the Blue Pencil Agency's First Novel Award, 2019, where he met his agent, Nelle Andrew of Rachel Mills Literary. He is finally making use of his Open University psychology degree and interest in history, especially World War Two, to write historical crime fiction. Most importantly, he has a wife and two daughters and lives in his adopted county of Kent.